Praise for J.T. Ellison

"Carefully orchestrated plot twists and engrossing characters... The story moves at breakneck speed... Flawed yet identifiable characters and genuinely terrifying villains populate this impressive and arresting thriller."
—*Publishers Weekly* on *Judas Kiss*
[starred review]

"Crime fiction has a new name to watch."
—John Connolly

"Combines *The Silence of the Lambs* with *The Wire*."
—*January Magazine* on *The Cold Room*

"Darkly compelling and thoroughly chilling... everything a great crime thriller should be."
—Allison Brennan on *All the Pretty Girls*

"A twisty, creepy and wonderful book... Ellison is relentless and grabs the reader from the first page and refuses to let go until the soul tearing climax."
—*Crimespree* on *14*

"[A] tight and powerful story. *Judas Kiss* moves at a rapid-fire rate...rushing like adrenaline through the bloodstream."
—*The Strand Magazine*

"Flawlessly plotted, with well-defined characters and conflict...quite simply a gem."
—*RT Book Reviews* [Top Pick]
on *The Cold Room*

"A terrific lead character, terrific suspense, terrific twists...a completely convincing debut."
—Lee Child on *All the Pretty Girls*

Also by J.T. Ellison

THE COLD ROOM
JUDAS KISS
14
ALL THE PRETTY GIRLS

Look for J.T. Ellison's next novel

SO CLOSE THE HAND OF DEATH

available March 2011

J.T. ELLISON

the immortals

MIRA®

MIRA®

Recycling programs for this product may not exist in your area.

ISBN-13: 978-0-7783-2763-9

THE IMMORTALS

Copyright © 2010 by J.T. Ellison.

For questions and comments about the quality of this book please contact us at Customer_eCare@Harlequin.ca.

www.MIRABooks.com

Printed in U.S.A.

For Jill Thompson (*ti amo molto!*)
and my darling Randy.

These eight words the Rede fulfill:
"An ye harm none, do what ye will."
　　　　　—Doreen Valiente
　　　　　　The Wiccan Rede

Because I could not stop for Death,
He kindly stopped for me;
The carriage held but just ourselves
And Immortality.
　　　　　—Emily Dickinson
　　　　　　Because I Could Not Stop
　　　　　　for Death

Third Quarter Moon
Samhain (Halloween)

One

Nashville, Tennessee
October 31
3:30 p.m.

Taylor Jackson stood at attention, arms behind her back, her dress blues itching her wrists. She was feeling more than a bit embarrassed. She'd asked for this to be done without ceremony, just a simple here you go, you're back in our good graces, but the chief was having nothing of it. He'd insisted she not only receive her lieutenant's badge again, but be decorated as well, in a very public ceremony. Her union rep was thrilled, and at her direction, had dropped the lawsuit she'd been forced to file against the department when they demoted her without cause. Taylor was pleased, as well. She'd been fighting to get reinstated, and she had to admit it was nice to put all of this behind her. But the pomp and circumstance was a bit much.

It had been a long afternoon. Taylor felt like a show pony, was flushed with the overly exuberant praise of her career, her involvement in catching the Conductor, a serial killer who'd killed two women back-to-back, kidnapped a third and fled Nashville with Taylor hot on his heels. She'd arrested him in Italy, and the story had immediately caught

international headlines, because at the same time, she'd
been party to the capture of one of Italy's most notorious
serial killers, Il Macellaio. In the world of sound bites and
news at your fingertips, taking two serial killers into custody
had garnered so much attention that the chief had been
forced into action.

Not only was she being reinstated; Taylor had command
of the murder squad again, and her team was being reassem-
bled. Detectives Lincoln Ross and Marcus Wade were
shipped back up from the South Sector, and after a long discussion with the chief, she'd even talked him into allowing
Renn McKenzie to become part of the permanent team. She
had her boys back.

Most of them.

Pete Fitzgerald had fallen off the face of the earth. Taylor
had last talked to him when he was in Barbados, anchored
and waiting for a new part for his boat's engine. He'd called
to let her know he thought he'd seen their old nemesis, and
she hadn't heard from him since. She was sick with worry,
convinced that Fitz had been taken by the Pretender, a killer
so obscene, so cruel that he invaded her dreams and con-
sumed her waking moments. A killer Taylor hadn't caught;
the one who'd quite literally gotten away.

Her concerns had been compounded just last week, when
the Coast Guard had picked up a distress signal off the coast
of North Carolina. The GPS beacon matched the registered
number for Fitz's boat. Despite countless days of searching,
nothing had been found. The Coast Guard had been forced
to call off the search, and the police in North Carolina
couldn't get involved because there was no crime to be investigated. She had a call in to the North Carolina State
Bureau of Investigations, in the hope they would see things
differently, but she hadn't heard anything yet.

Taylor tried to shake off the thought of Fitz, of his body
broken and battered, of what the Pretender was doing to
him, or had done. The guilt spilled through her blood,
making it chilly. She'd issued a challenge to the Pretender,

told him to come and get her. Instead, she was positive he'd taken her friend, the man closest to her, aside from Baldwin. Her father figure. She had probably gotten Fitz killed, and she found that knowledge desperately hard to stomach.

She looked into the crowd, the sea of blue seated in compact rows before her. John Baldwin, her fiancé, sat in the front, grinning. His hair was too long again, the black waves falling over his forehead and ears in a tumble. She resisted the urge to roll her eyes; that was sure to get on the evening news, and she didn't want any more attention than she already had. She touched her engagement ring instead, twisting the channel-set diamonds around her finger.

Her team sat beside him: Lincoln Ross, hair grown out just enough to slip in some tiny dreadlocks; Marcus Wade, brown-eyed and sweetly happy. He was getting serious with his girlfriend, and Taylor had never seen him so content. The new member of the team, Renn McKenzie, was at Marcus's left. Taylor saw McKenzie's partner, Hugh Bangor, a few rows back. They'd been very discreet—only Taylor and Baldwin knew they were an item.

Even her old boss Mitchell Price was there, smiling benevolently at her. He'd been a casualty of the events that led to Taylor losing her badge in the first place, but had moved on. He was running a personal protection service catering to country music stars, and had made it clear that anytime Taylor wanted to bail on Nashville Metro, she was welcome to join him.

Fitz was the only one missing. She forced the lump in her throat away.

The chief was pinning something to her uniform now. He stood back with a wide smile and started clapping. The audience followed suit, and Taylor wished she could disappear. This was not what she wanted, this open, public enthusiasm on her behalf.

The chief gestured to the microphone. Taylor took a deep breath and stepped to the podium.

"Thank you all for being here today. I appreciate it more

than you know. But we really should be honoring the entire team who participated. I couldn't have done any of this without the help of Detective Renn McKenzie, Supervisory Special Agent John Baldwin, Detective James Highsmythe of the London Metropolitan Police, and all the officers of the Metro Police who participated, in small ways and in large, on the case. The city of Nashville owes these men and women a debt of gratitude. Now, enough of the hoopla. Let's go back to work."

Laughter rippled through the crowd, and they clapped again. Lincoln whistled, two fingers stuck in his mouth, and this time she did roll her eyes. Baldwin winked at her, his clear green gaze full of pride. With her back ramrod straight and her ears burning, she thanked the chief and the other dignitaries, nodded at her new boss, Commander Joan Huston, and made her way off the dais. People began milling about; the language of the force rang in her ears like a mother's lullaby. She was back, and it felt damn good.

Baldwin met her, took her hand. "So how's the Investigator of the Year?"

She took a deep breath and blew it out noisily. "Don't start," she said. "This is mortifying enough as it is."

He laughed and kissed her palm. A promise for later.

Lincoln and Marcus both hugged her, and McKenzie shook her hand.

"Congratulations, LT!" Lincoln's gap-toothed smile felt like coming home, and she clapped him on the back. Price joined their group, shaking her hand gravely, his red handlebar mustache neatly trimmed and waxed for the occasion.

"What's your first act as a newly restored lieutenant, Loot?" Marcus asked.

"Buying y'all a beer. It is Halloween, after all. Let's get out of here. How about we head down to Mulligan's and grab a Guinness?"

"You're on," Marcus said.

She gestured to her stiffly starched uniform. "I just need to change."

"Us, too. Race you to the locker rooms."

Ten minutes later, once again in civilian clothes—jeans, cowboy boots, a black cashmere turtleneck and gray corduroy blazer, left open—Taylor felt much more comfortable. She snapped her holster onto her belt, then risked a glance at her shield. Her phantom limb. Losing it had just about cost her everything. She lovingly caressed the gold for the briefest of moments, then attached it to her belt in front of her holster. Complete. Again. She slammed her locker shut and met the boys in the hall. She saw Baldwin's eyes stray to her waist and pretended she didn't see his satisfied smile.

As they left the Criminal Justice Center, Taylor's spirits lifted. The joshing, joking group of men behind her, Baldwin in step at her side, all served to remind her how lucky she was. Now, if she could only find Fitz and do away with the Pretender, life would be grand indeed.

They'd just passed Hooters when Taylor's cell rang. She looked at the screen, saw it was dispatch. She held up a hand and stopped on the sidewalk to answer.

"Jackson," she said.

"Lieutenant, we need your response at a 10-64J, possible homicide, 3800 Estes Road. Repeat, 10-64J."

The *J* designator made a shiver go up her spine. *J* meant the victim was a juvenile. She hated working crimes with kids involved.

"Roger that, Dispatch. I'm on my way." She slapped the phone shut. "Hey, guys, I'm sorry. I've got to go to this scene." She pulled her wallet out of her jacket's interior pocket and handed Lincoln two twenties. He shook his head.

"Hell, no, LT. You're back on the job, so are we."

"But you're not on today. Go on ahead."

"No way," Marcus said. They lined up shoulder to shoulder, a wall of testosterone and insistence. She knew better than to fight. They were all just as happy as she was to be back together.

"I'll drive," McKenzie offered.

She smiled at them, then turned to Baldwin. "Well, aren't you coming, too?"

"What, the Nashville police want the help of a profiler?" he teased, his green eyes flashing.

"Of course we do. Come on then, let's go. We'll have to take two cars."

They drove up West End, McKenzie in the lead, Taylor and Baldwin following. Getting to Green Hills at this time of day was difficult at best, the traffic stop-and-start, so McKenzie was leading them through the back roads. Up West End, then left on Bowling, through the gloriously wooded neighborhoods, wide green lawns, large homes set far back from the main streets.

Many of the houses were decorated for Halloween, some professionally, with complete horror tableaus on their front yards: Black-and-orange twinkling lights and tombstones and full-size mummies—some crafted with the obvious hand of a child—fake spider webs and friendly ghosts. On the corner of Bowling and Woodmont there was a large inflatable headless horseman. It was starting to get dark, and there had been rain earlier in the day. Fog rose in wispy streams from the lawns. A few jack-o'-lanterns had been lit, their insides glowing with sinister comfort.

Once they turned left onto Estes, it only took a moment to reach the address. The first responders—firefighters and EMTs—had already left. Patrol cars littered the street, crime-scene tape was strung across the road. Blue-and-white lights flashed in the evening sky, reflecting off the brick houses. Farther down the street, moving away from the commotion, small groups had started floating from door to door; the youngest trick-or-treaters escorted by their parents before full dark set in. Even if it hadn't been Halloween, it would have been an eerie scene.

Paula Simari was there, standing by her patrol car. Her canine partner, Max, was in the backseat, grinning a doggie smile at the activity. His services had not been needed tonight, it seemed.

The five of them approached and Paula held up her hands. "Whoa. No need to bring out all the big guns. Just one body up there." She gestured over her shoulder at the second story of an expansive Georgian red brick house. "How's it being back in charge, Lieutenant?"

"Very nice, Officer." Taylor liked Simari. She was good people, always ready with a quip, but knew when to be serious. "Why don't you brief us, then we'll take a cruise through the scene." She signed in to the crime-scene call sheet, then handed the pen to Baldwin. By the book, that was her new middle name.

"Sure. Body is that of a seventeen-year-old male Caucasian, name Jerrold King. His sister, Letha, came home from shopping with friends—they both go to Hillsboro but they had a half day today. It's a teachers' in-service afternoon. Said she went into his room to borrow a CD and found him naked on the bed. She called 911 and they responded, but he was deceased when they arrived."

"Suicide?" Taylor asked.

"Not exactly," Simari replied grimly. "Not unless he was into pain."

"Pain?" Baldwin said, eyebrow raised.

Simari bit her lip. "I think you should see this for yourself. That's why I had dispatch call you directly."

Taylor looked at her for a long moment, then shrugged. "Okay. Let's go. Baldwin, you're with me. Marcus, Lincoln, could you start chatting with the crowd?" She pointed to the driveway of the house next door, which was accumulating people, some dressed in costumes, some obviously just home from a day at the office. The suits outnumbered the costumes three to one. "See if anyone saw anything. McKenzie? Make sure the medical examiner is on the way. We need a death investigator and crime-scene techs."

"Will do."

She followed Simari up the elaborate steps of the house,

through white Doric columns onto a wide brick porch. A trio of witches nestled in between two spider-webbed rocking chairs; dual arrays of orange chrysanthemums in black wrought-iron planters were parked on either side of the door, their blossoms bright and new.

Taylor took a second to wind her hair into a bun and secure it, slipped her hands into purple nitrile gloves. Baldwin followed suit—their hands suddenly all professional, no more the recipients of holy palmers' kiss. They couldn't afford to confuse the crime-scene techs with their own DNA, nor allow their personal relationship to affect the case. It had been difficult for Taylor at first, pretending she and Baldwin weren't emotionally entwined. It was easier now. She was learning his detachment skills.

Simari was already gloved up, and let them in.

A teenager with rough skin and a jet-black bob sat at the foot of the stairs, white and shaking. She had black circles under her eyes and the faintest trace of dark lipstick in one corner of her mouth. Her lips were jammed together in a thin line; it seemed she knew if she opened her mouth the world would collapse.

"Lieutenant Jackson, this is Letha King. She found the body."

Taylor bent at the waist to get to the girl's level. "Letha. I'm so sorry for your loss. Are your parents on their way home?"

The girl didn't meet her eye, just shook her head. Simari stepped in. "They're out of town. We're tracking them down now."

Letha wrapped her arms around her waist, trying to hold herself together. Her nails were painted black, the polish wearing away. Taylor was tempted to reach out and touch her, to give a bit of warmth, of comfort, but refrained. She needed to see the body first, then she could worry about the living.

She stepped back onto the porch and whistled at McKenzie. He was on his cell phone, raised his eyebrows in question. She gestured for him to come to her. He nodded, said something briefly into the cell, then slapped it shut and bounded up the stairs. Taylor spoke quietly.

"I've got the victim's sister in the house. Kid's completely shattered. She needs to have someone with her. Would you mind?"

"Not at all. Everyone's on their way."

"Great, thanks. Come with me."

They reentered the house, and Taylor led McKenzie to Letha.

"Letha, this is Detective McKenzie. He's going to talk to you for a few minutes while we check on your brother. We're going to go upstairs now. If you need anything, anything at all, you just ask Detective McKenzie, okay?"

The girl nodded, silent as the grave. She gave Taylor an odd feeling, a premonition that worse things were to come, though she couldn't pinpoint why.

"How about we go into the kitchen, Letha?" McKenzie held out a hand. The girl took it and rose, unsteady on her feet, eyes blank. She allowed herself to be towed away. Shock. Poor, creepy little thing.

The staircase was mahogany, sweeping, twin rises that met together in a catwalk loft on the second floor. They took the left set of steps, Taylor unconsciously counting as they went up. Thirty-three stairs. The view down to the grand foyer was only slightly obscured by a brilliant chandelier strung with fake cobwebs, creating a gauzy veil on the downstairs. The hallway floor was wide-planked oak topped with elegant throw rugs and capriciously placed tables covered in ethnic crystal and wood tchotchkes. Tribal masks lined the corridor. The parents were either travelers or collectors.

Four doors bled off the center hall. One was open.

Taylor glanced back over her shoulder at Baldwin. His face was calm, placid, ready for anything. His eyes met hers briefly, questioning. She hadn't realized she'd stopped in her tracks until Simari cleared her throat.

"Everything okay?"

Was it? Taylor had the strangest sense, almost like a strong hand was pushing at her chest, pushing her away from the bedroom door. She couldn't detect any of the usual smells that accompanied a violent crime scene—blood, fear, human waste. It smelled…like flowers. Once she realized that the scent was coming from the open bedroom, she placed it. Jasmine. The murder scene smelled like jasmine. Once her nose got used to that idea, she did catch just the tiniest hint of copper, tangy underneath the cloying sweetness.

The odd sensation left her. She smiled at Simari.

"Sorry. I'm fine. Just…smelling."

"I know," Simari said. "It's weird. I don't usually expect boys to wear perfume, but what do I know? In this world, anything is possible. He's in there." She pointed toward the open door, let Taylor take the lead.

"Probably the sister's. Though I didn't catch it downstairs," Baldwin said.

Sometimes at a crime scene Taylor had the overwhelming feeling that she was on camera, that some unseen videographer tracked her every move. She was fodder for the silver screen, walking down a darkened hallway while the audience knew something horrible lay just beyond her grasp. Look out behind you, don't go into that dark space alone, better run out of the safety of the house into the forest when the killer is coming after you with a knife. Goose bumps paraded up and down her arms. God, she hated horror movies.

She shook it off. Halloween always got to her. A crime scene on Halloween was just designed to play into her overactive imagination.

Steeled, she stepped into Jerrold King's bedroom.

She struggled to take in the whole scene and not make judgments. Her job as lead investigator was to make sure her detectives didn't jump to conclusions, didn't make snap decisions about the case. She emphasized considered opinions, reasoning, a belief in the evidence.

But Jerrold King's body made her want to discard all she'd been taught.

She edged closer. He was naked, lying on his back, arms spread to the sides. His mouth was open, slack, with small edges of spittle gathered in the corners. His lips were blue; eyes unfocused and slitted. There were no ligature marks, no strangulation bruises. Granted, that could show up later—contusions took time to develop. But for now, his naked skin was free of visible hematomas. In their place were bloody channels, carved into his flesh. The red-on-white effect was startling, gapes in the tender skin. A sharp knife, no doubt. But these weren't stab wounds. There was a distinct pattern to the slashes.

She was a foot away from the bed now, and carefully bent to get a closer look. Baldwin was on the other side of the bed. She looked up from the wounds into his worried eyes.

"No," she said. "It can't be."

"It most certainly can," he said.

"Urban legend," Simari said.

Taylor stepped back a few feet to see if she could make sense of the wounds. Yes, from a distance, she could see it plainly.

Five slashes, connected at the points, outlined in a ragged circle.

A pentacle, carved into the dead boy's chest.

Two

The scream startled Taylor, and she jerked back from the body.

Simari's shoulder radio crackled and Taylor's cell rang almost simultaneously. She looked at the caller ID. It was Lincoln.

"Yes?" she answered.

"You need to get down here now. We've got a serious problem."

"What?"

"There's another one."

"Another victim?"

Simari was already hightailing it out of Jerrold King's bedroom. Taylor slapped her phone shut. She and Baldwin followed Simari down the staircase and onto the porch. The screaming was coming from the other side of the street, three houses down.

"Help! Please help me!"

A woman stood in the driveway, waving her arms. Lincoln was standing by her, unsuccessfully trying to calm her down.

The street was nearly as bright as day—all the houses' front lights were on, headlights from the influx of patrol cars cut through the murk, multitudes of Maglites were trained on the faces of people standing frozen in their driveways.

As they ran up the street, Taylor felt all eyes turn to them. Her boots clanged against the asphalt, ringing out louder than Baldwin's steps. She had an odd thought; terror wasn't a familiar feeling in this neighborhood.

They reached Lincoln, and Taylor skidded to a stop, some loose gravel nearly causing her to turn an ankle. She caught her breath.

"Ma'am, I'm Taylor Jackson, Metro Homicide. What's the problem?"

"My daughter. My daughter is—" Her voice caught, the sobs breaking free from her chest. "She's dead in her room."

"Show us," Taylor said.

"I can't. I can't go back in there."

Imploring Lincoln with her eyes, Taylor nodded at Baldwin and Simari. They hurried into the house, strangely similar to the King home, and up a sweeping staircase. The scent of jasmine lingered in the air. Taylor's chest felt tight.

The scene was easy to find. There were towels scattered on the floor, the mother must have been bringing up some laundry. A plaque on the girl's door had the name Ashley in pink bubble letters. Below it was a stop sign that screamed, Ashley's Environs. KEEP OUT!

The door was ajar. Taylor stepped over the wad of towels into the girl's room.

She was faceup on the bed, arms stretched out over her head. Her brown hair was pulled into a ponytail and a green mask had dried on her skin. There was an open bottle of nail polish on the bedside table, the scent acrid. Giving herself a home spa treatment, a facial, a manicure. Typical afternoon in a teenage girl's life, her innocent ablutions cruelly interrupted by death.

She'd been stripped like the previous victim. The skin of her breasts and her groin was nearly translucent compared to the tan skin around it. She'd either been lying out in the sun or using a tanning bed recently; the brown skin only slightly dulled the knife slashes in her stomach. Familiar cuts, five points connected by a circle of rent flesh.

"Some sort of overdose, I'd expect," Baldwin said, gesturing to the girl's blue lips.

"Same as Jerrold King. What in the hell happened here this afternoon?"

A frantic movement caught Taylor's eye, her peripheral vision picking up hurried motions outside, lights swinging crazily in the semidarkness. Maglites, their blue-white beams bobbing and weaving up the street, away from her location. She abandoned the body, went to the window. People were running back and forth, screaming, crying, cursing. The sharp wail of a siren split the nubilous air. Patrol cars were edging their way through the crowds, driving farther up Estes, toward Abbott Martin Drive. One kept going, disappeared over the edge of the hill.

When her cell phone rang, she almost didn't answer. Running away was sounding like an excellent option. Though if she were honest with herself, the adrenaline was building in her gut. Intrigue. A new case. She opened her phone.

"What in the hell is going on?" Taylor snapped.

"I need you now!" Lincoln yelled into the phone.

"I'm on my way." She turned to Baldwin. "We need to go."

"What in the world is happening?" he asked.

"I don't know. But I think we better find out."

They rushed down the stairs and into the night. The street had turned into utter chaos in the five minutes Taylor and Baldwin had been in Ashley's room. It looked like a bomb had gone off—no bloody limbs or smoking ruins of cars, but people rushing aimlessly up and down the street. Many years earlier, Taylor had seen a man walk out of a burning building—eyes vacant, clothes on fire—and try to walk up the street, away from help. Shell shock. She could identify with that.

The riot of people surged up and down the street, neighbors mixed with patrol officers and emergency workers.

Taylor didn't see Lincoln right away, but caught the eye of Marcus Wade, gestured him over.

"What happened? We were upstairs at the second victim's house and all hell broke loose."

"There are more, Taylor. I've already got reports of another three, and dispatch has been receiving 911 calls for the last ten minutes."

"More," Taylor said, quite uncomprehending. "Three more bodies?"

Marcus swiped his hair out of his eyes, and Taylor saw the beads of sweat building on his forehead in the reflection of the nearest patrol car's headlights. "Yes. All teenagers. All in this neighborhood."

She saw Lincoln then, running past them. He turned into a house two doors up. The wailing of sirens was overwhelming, so noisy and loud Taylor thought her eardrums might burst.

Her cell phone trilled again. Headquarters. She took a deep breath, calmed herself, then answered. It was her new commander, Joan Huston.

"What's happening out there, Jackson? I just got word from the 911 call center that they've been overloaded with emergencies."

"Yes, ma'am. Multiple victims, multiple crime scenes. I have no sure count on the dead at this point, minimum of five casualties. We need a full tactical response on Estes Road in Green Hills. Send every available officer. I'll need Dan Franklin and everyone the medical examiner can spare. I need to go manage the scene. I'll call you back when I know more."

"Biological threat? Do we need Hazmat? I can put the Emergency Operations Plan into action."

"I don't think that's necessary. It looks like several homicides, but it's going to take a while to sort through. We don't even know how many scenes we have." She stopped, looked at the street. The swelling mass of people seemed to grow with every minute. "The parents are coming home from work to find their children dead. I can't tell you much more than that." No sense sharing the information about the pentacles until she had a clear view of what was happening. That wasn't the leak she needed for the local news—Satanists Rampaging Through Green Hills.

She turned away from the chaos, spoke quietly into the phone. "Whoever did this wanted our attention, and now they have it. We've already blocked off part of Estes Road. I'm going to push those roadblocks to Hobbs and Woodmont, move the perimeters back on all of these houses, start trying to sort this out. You'll need to get out ahead of it. The media is going to have a field day."

She heard finger snapping in the background—Huston getting some unwary soul's attention. "Thank you, Lieutenant. Go to it."

She closed the phone. Baldwin put a hand on her shoulder. Her team was already responding, people being gathered into manageable knots, patrol cars stationed at the corners of Estes and Woodmont, blocking access to the street. She could hear more sirens coming closer, the response almost immediate. She looked at Baldwin. His eyes were dark in the gloom.

"Satanists murdering people is something for urban legends, not Nashville," she said.

"I agree. I find it hard to believe, but it is Halloween."

"Meaning?"

"What better time to try and spook people with occult images?"

Taylor shook her head. "Someone wanted to send a message. This was a coordinated plan of attack. It takes a level of sophistication to pull off multiple murders. Let's just see what we can find out."

Three

Controlling the bedlam only took half an hour, which was incredible, considering. Taylor had set up a temporary headquarters on the street in front of the King house. She'd assigned each of her team a role managing a group of patrols on their specific tasks. She had officers interviewing every person who tried to enter the area, getting addresses and finding out if they had children. Those who did were passed into a secondary control—do you know where your children are? If the child couldn't be reached by phone, the address was marked and a team sent out. A fourth group of patrol officers were responding to the 911 calls and reporting in their findings.

The body count was up to seven, in five separate houses. She could only pray that they'd discovered all the victims.

Four females and three males, all between the ages of fourteen and eighteen, were dead. It quickly became apparent that all of the victims attended Hillsboro High School—so far no students from any of the multiple private schools or the robust homeschool network in the area had been reported missing or deceased.

Two crime scenes held multiple victims—a couple involved in a sexual interlude, a condom still on the tip of the boy's penis, and two girls hanging out for the afternoon, their physics books on the floor, the scene scattered with *US*

Magazine, People and *Cosmopolitan.* Half studying, half gossiping.

The neighborhood wasn't pleased with her identification system, but she couldn't figure out a more efficient way to determine the breadth and depth of the situation. She had to show a calm face, a force, a presence. She needed to be composed and reasonable. She'd been trained to handle major emergencies, and she was exercising her training to the fullest. They had the situation under control.

A little voice in the back of her head kept screaming— you might be missing him, you might be letting the killer get away with more—but second-guessing herself wasn't going to make things better. Once they'd determined that the primary event was over, they could start putting the pieces together.

The first victim found, Jerrold King, had been dead for at least a couple of hours. Taylor was working on the premise that the murders had taken place sometime between 12:30 p.m. and 3:00 p.m. School had let out at noon, the first body was found at 3:00 p.m. Assuming the victims had attended the half day of school this morning, she had an initial framework to follow.

She shuddered, thinking about the methodical staging, and wished she could fast-forward a day so she had an idea of what killed them. Drugs of some kind—the cyanosis and pinpoint pupils pointed to an overdose—something they had all ingested or injected. She was having dark thoughts about mass suicides. But that couldn't explain the pentacles, could it? Could seven teenagers all coordinate a mass suicide and carve pentacles into their flesh as they were dying?

No. These crimes were committed by an outside hand. One who'd struck quickly, mercilessly and efficiently.

Taylor saw McKenzie putting Letha King into a patrol car. It pulled away, the child's blank stare fixed forward. McKenzie stood next to Taylor, watching her go.

"What's up?" Taylor asked. "She give you anything?"

"She hasn't said much of anything. I thought it best to hold on to her until her aunt comes to get her, out of the house, at least. She called a few minutes ago, she's on her way."

"Good. We'll want to talk to her again, once things settle down."

They walked back to the Kings' house. Despite the crowd, the kitchen was strangely quiet.

Baldwin handed her a stack of photos. "Are you ready? Simari gave me her extra Polaroids so we can start recreating the scenes. Though I'll be able to pull this from memory for a while."

"No kidding. Have all the victims been identified?"

Lincoln nodded. "For the most part, yes. There's going to be formal IDs done for a few of them tomorrow, once next of kin are notified. Two of the families are traveling."

"We can't release names to the media until we have all the notifications done. I think it would be best to wait, make all the names public at once."

"We can try, but you know some of the names will leak. Nature of the beast."

"I know. Do your best, okay? Run me through the scenes, give me some names to put with the faces. After Jerrold King and Ashley Norton, who was found next?"

She laid the pictures on the granite countertop. Lincoln shuffled them around until he had them in order.

"We have Jerrold, then Ashley Norton. The two doubles after that, Xander Norwood and Amanda Vanderwood, then Chelsea Mott and Rachel Welch. Then we go back to a single we just found, Brandon Scott." He tapped the last photograph. The picture showed the rictus-gripped face of a young man who'd not seen enough sunrises. Beautiful features ruined by death. Taylor wondered what they looked like alive, then pushed that thought away. No sense in it—she'd be haunted by their death masks forever.

"Are you hearing of any links between the victims? Any enemies?"

"No. No one knows a damn thing."

"Where was the first couple found?"

"At the Vanderwood girl's house."

"Then let's go there."

The trek didn't take them long—the Vanderwoods' house was only a quarter mile up Estes. It was less showy than the previous two homes, smaller, with whitewashed clapboard and a red front door. All the lights were on, and crime-scene techs darted in and out. A small group of neighbors watched silently from the lawn, sadness etched on their faces.

The stairs seemed endless, the now-familiar scent of jasmine clinging to the air in the hallway. Amanda's room was the first at the top of the stairs. A death investigator took pictures, the shutter's snap rang in Taylor's ears. It was one of the most common sounds she heard at a crime scene, but it felt invasive and new tonight.

Xander Norwood was on the floor, on his back, naked. Amanda Vanderwood was also nude, her body faceup and partially on the bed, arms trailing onto the floor. Taylor noticed that Amanda's forefinger was touching Xander's palm. It looked like she'd managed to use the last of her strength to partially shift her body off the bed, and Xander had reached out to her, struggling to get their flesh together in the waning moments of their young lives. Love everlasting.

For the first time in many years of crime scenes, Taylor felt sick to her stomach.

Wouldn't Baldwin's caress be the last she'd ever want to feel? Wouldn't his face be the last image she'd want to see, his lips the last to touch hers, his words to fill her ears? To die with the one you loved at hand, that was grace.

Taylor forced the romanticism away, became clinical and cool. Rigor was setting in. Their lips were tinged with blue, the bodies carved with the same pentacles as the others. Xander was partially wearing a condom, the wrapper was on the floor next to the night table. Were they in the act, getting ready to have sex or finishing when the killer struck? She supposed it didn't matter, there were no defensive wounds, no real disturbance in the room. It was like they'd simply gone to sleep in permanently awkward positions, with a large, glowing star cut into their flesh.

Baldwin circled the bodies, then stepped to the girl's messy desk.

"Have you photographed all of this?" he asked. The 'gator nodded. Baldwin poked through the girl's gym bag, then moved to her purse. He withdrew a plastic bag from the inside pocket of the Coach hobo, four small pills riding in the bottom.

"Taylor," he said.

"Yeah?"

"Look at this."

The pills were blue, tiny as baby aspirin, with a heart stamped on one side.

"X," Taylor said.

"Yep." He handed them to the death investigator who was attending the body.

"Don't lose these," Baldwin admonished.

"Like that would happen," the kid replied. He was new— Taylor didn't recognize him. She felt like she'd seen him somewhere before, but couldn't place him. Not surprising—with Metro's influx of new people, there were plenty of faces she couldn't put to names. His ID card was strung on a yellow-and-black lanyard around his neck, she saw his picture and the name B. Iles. He took the Baggie from Baldwin reverently, photographed it and labeled it into evidence.

"They were found like this?" Taylor asked the young man.

"Yes, ma'am. Nothing's been moved. We're waiting for the medical examiner to declare."

"Can't you do it?" She was surprised. Death investigators, fondly referred to as 'gators, had the power to run a scene without the presence of a medical examiner.

"I can, but word came down that each scene had to be cleared by one of the ME's."

"Who gave that word?"

"Commander Huston."

Ah. Her new boss was by the book, too. Taylor had no problem with that, though she knew Sam would be frustrated as hell. They'd have to roust the entire staff of Forensic Medical, all six of the medical examiners, to handle this mess.

"That's good enough for me. Anything else you saw that I should know about?"

"No, ma'am. I've documented everything, stills and video. Crime Scene's been looking for the weapon, the knife that was used, but as far as I know, none have been found at any of the scenes. We've lifted fibers galore, trace, fingerprints. If the killer left anything of himself behind, we'll find it."

"Why do you say 'himself'?" Taylor asked.

Iles blushed. "Well, I shouldn't jump to conclusions, but we found a couple of black hairs that obviously didn't belong to either of these two. One was lying right on top of the male decedent's chest. It was short, I just assumed it was male."

"That's interesting. Does it have a tag?" They'd be able to get DNA off the hair if a follicle was attached.

"No. It was broken off."

"Too bad. Keep looking, there might be more. If you see something that matches what he used to carve them up, let me know immediately. We need to make sure that every kid's effects are accounted for, that their gym bags, backpacks and purses are all searched. Find their cell phones and planners, too. Okay? Pass that down the line to your other investigators for me, tell the crime-scene techs, too. And ask them to keep an eye out for more drugs."

"I'll take care of it right now."

"Thank you. Hey, what's your first name?"

"Barclay. Barclay Iles."

"Okay, Barclay. I'm Taylor Jackson. This is Supervisory Special Agent John Baldwin."

"I know," he said, his voice tinged with the kind of awe that made her cringe. Ah, well. Better awe than derision.

"Get on it," she said. The 'gator scooted from the room. Taylor heard him breathing deeply in the hall. This was bound to be rough on all of them, heck, half the investigative staff were fresh out of college themselves.

She stared into the room one more time, at the touching, the carving, the silent agony Xander and Amanda had experienced. She wished she could rewind their day and prevent this. It was a fruitless wish.

"What do you think happened here, Baldwin? Is there something I'm missing?"

He was stalking around the room carefully, taking everything in. She knew that look—he was there, but completely abstracted, thinking about the incidents that would have led to the murders.

"I'm just wondering about the timing."

"Halloween?"

"No, the time of death. All of the victims died around the same time. If the killer was in every house…"

"We have to wait for Sam to determine time and cause of death, but I think you're right. Too many dead for just one person—is that where you're going?"

He looked at her with a smile of appreciation. "I am."

"How many killers, do you think?"

"I don't know." He turned away from her, ran his gloved finger along the spine of a book. Taylor saw it was one of her favorites, *Wuthering Heights,* and felt a pang. Amanda Vanderwood would never read again.

She heard a commotion from downstairs, voices raised.

"Now what?" she asked, resisting the urge to pull her hair down and run her fingers through it to help her think. The gesture was so compulsive, so ingrained that she had to stick her hands in her pockets, the nitrile catching on the edge of her jeans. Baldwin leaned his head toward the open door, where the voices were growing louder.

"We better go find out what's going on."

"I know." Taylor sighed. Please, God, not more bodies.

They made their way downstairs to see Lincoln arguing with an older couple. Taylor was surprised, she thought the Vanderwoods were out of town. When Lincoln made the introductions, she understood and immediately went on guard.

"Lieutenant, this is Laura and Aaron Norwood, Xander's parents."

Taylor took off her gloves and shook hands with them. The Norwoods were an older couple, the husband still dressed for work in a blue suit and light blue tie, his wife in a brown velour jogging suit that stretched tight across her ample chest. She'd been weeping and her eyes were swollen and red, but dry of tears at the moment.

"I'm so sorry for your loss," Taylor said automatically, knowing the words were hardly a comfort.

Mr. Norwood nodded brusquely. "We came when we heard. We wanted to be close. We want to see our son. Who did this?"

"We're trying to figure that out, sir. Can you excuse us for a moment?"

She stepped into the hallway with Lincoln and Baldwin, speaking to Lincoln in a low undertone.

"We need Father Victor and some more chaplains. Can you get him over here?" The department chaplain was required to be a part of notifications to family members, and Taylor was so used to having a member of the clergy along that she was uncomfortable speaking to the Norwoods without him.

Lincoln whispered, "He's at another scene. We've asked for backup, and we'll get it for tomorrow, but right now, we're it. Just FYI, Norwood's being awfully pushy. I had to restrain him when he first got here. He's calm now, but I'm not sure how long that's going to last."

Taylor indulged at last, took her hair down, rubbed her fingers across her scalp, then put her hair back in its bun. It wasn't like she could go back to the Norwoods and say, sorry, I can't talk, my favorite priest isn't here to shelter me from your distress.

Baldwin's cell phone started to ring. He put up an apologetic hand, murmured, "I need to get this," and disappeared outside.

Taylor watched him go. "Can't blame him. I hate this part, too. All right. Let's do this."

She reentered the living room with Lincoln, met the pain in their eyes full on. They'd retreated into that helpless state, unbelieving, unresisting, the reality of their son's death still trying to seep into their souls. She didn't have much time— they'd either slip away entirely into a grief so profound nothing would rouse them, or fly off the handle, become belligerent and difficult. Better to keep them focused on the here and now, if at all possible.

"Mr. and Mrs. Norwood, can you tell me more about Xander and Amanda?"

Mr. Norwood shook his head, reiterated his request. "We want to see Xander. It's only right. We deserve a chance to say goodbye to our son."

Just in case they decided to ignore her, Taylor crossed her arms on her chest and leaned against the doorjamb, effectively blocking their access to the stairs.

"I'm sorry, but I can't let you do that. We have to work on the scene, and I'll be completely honest with you, it's not pretty. You don't want this vision of Xander as the last you'll ever have. You're going to have to trust me. I give you my word that I'll take good care of him."

Mr. Norwood stared into her eyes for a long moment. She took his gaze, unflinching. *I will treat him with respect. I will see his killer punished.* After a long minute, he dropped his eyes to the floor and nodded. She seized the opportunity to try again.

"It would be a big help if you could answer some questions for me. Can you talk about Xander for a few minutes? Tell me about him? About Amanda?"

Laura Norwood breathed out a ragged sigh, a small smile of remembrance playing on her lips.

"What do you want to know? They were inseparable. Been going together for two years, were probably going to be together forever. You know how there's always that couple, the ones who met early and that was it? That's Xander and Amanda. The big joke was they were going to change their name to Woods, since our last names are so similar. That's what their friends called them, the Woods. Amanda's nickname was Woodie before she met Xander, so her friend's teased her, called her Woodie Woodpecker. Xander and Amanda loved it. She was on the cheerleading squad, and it was just announced that she'd be captain next year. My God, I can't believe this is happening." Her hands started to shake and her husband took them, held them hard between his palms.

"Now, Laura, that's not the kind of thing the police want to know. They need to know about enemies, and last moves, what kind of drugs and alcohol they were into. They only want to know the bad things. I've seen it all on TV. Just the bad things…." He broke off with a sob.

Taylor put her hand on his arm, spoke gently.

"No, sir. We want to know it all. Everything you tell us is relevant. Everything matters, the good and the bad. The more information we can gather today, the quicker we can catch the person who hurt your son. But if he did have any enemies or problems, we need to know."

As she said it, she realized she was going to have this conversation with seven families, and the thought nearly made her legs buckle. Who could do such a thing? Who could annihilate seven children? *Focus, Taylor.*

She looked around the room. "You know what, why don't we sit down? We'll be more comfortable. And you tell me anything that comes to mind about your son. It sounds like he had a lot of friends. Was that the case?"

They settled on opposite sides of a walnut coffee table, on facing barn-red twill couches, the perfect conversational grouping in the living room. The Vanderwoods obviously entertained—the whole house was set with various nooks and spots for small gatherings to linger.

Mrs. Norwood wiped her eyes with a ragged tissue. "Of course. Xander was very popular. Captain of the wrestling team, letterman, honor society. Smart, that was our boy. He was accepted early to Vanderbilt, that way he could stay at home his first year until Amanda graduated and joined him. Amanda is…oh, God, was, such a lovely girl. We were proud to have her as a part of our family. Even Xander's sister seemed to like Amanda, and she's not usually fond of her big brother's friends." As she spoke, her eyes started to shine, the recollection pulling her from her misery. Just as quickly, she collapsed back into tears. Mr. Norwood tried to take over, but his voice was shaking, too.

"Xander was a good boy. Reckless, sometimes, like any boy his age. Had a slew of speeding tickets. He was probably going to lose his license if he didn't buckle down and go through that class you have to take. He loved to drive."

"Does he have his own car?"

"Yes, a Volvo. We took one look at his driving skills and got him the safest car we could find. Amanda had a Jeep, and I was always worried about him driving it and tipping over."

The Norwoods shared a private laugh. Taylor was struck by their composure. It was rare for parents to pull themselves together so quickly. The shell had tightened; the cool, calm, rational people were poking through. It was strange— some parents became hysterical and unable to talk, some would sit you down and relay every detail. She never knew what to expect, was happy the Norwoods fell into the latter category. She needed this information, needed to build a victimology on their son.

"Is that his Volvo parked in the driveway?"

"Yes, it is."

She nodded at Lincoln, silently indicating that he needed to get Crime Scene on the car. He nodded back. Oh, it was good to have her team together again.

Taylor tried to figure out how to put the next question delicately. "Was it…typical for Xander and Amanda to have private time alone?"

Mrs. Norwood blew her nose, then said, "Are you asking if we knew they were having sex, Lieutenant?"

"Yes, ma'am."

She sighed heavily. "Surely you remember what it was like being a teenager in love. We discouraged them, of course, but they were hell-bent. We talked to Xander extensively—he promised that they were being careful. I believe Amanda was taking birth control pills, but you'll have to ask her mother about that. We've called her parents, but they're overseas. It's going to take them a day to get back home. Just terrible for them. At least we're here, can be with Xander's sister through this."

"Where is your daughter?"

"Susan? She's at home with our housekeeper. Aaron, we really should start getting back there for her." They started the small shiftings that told Taylor their interview was at an end.

"Before you go, can you tell me anything else about Amanda?"

"Oh, Mandy was…sunny. Beautiful. Smart. She was in honor society too, debate, student council, you name it. Her parents are from a very old Nashville family who wanted her to be as proletariat as possible. They were pushing her toward a life in public service. They could have sent her anywhere, but they both went to public school and wanted her to, as well. That's how many of us feel around here. Really, she and Xander were the perfect couple."

A perfect couple who'd been targeted by a madman. There was something wicked this way, Taylor was sure of it. No child is perfect, and if Taylor's background could be any sort of guide, it was the ones who seemed rosy on the surface that hid the biggest secrets.

"Was there any drug or alcohol use that you know of?"

"Here we go," Mr. Norwood muttered.

"I'm sorry, sir. I have to ask."

"Nothing that was out of the ordinary. Xander was an eighteen-year-old boy. But he's a straight arrow, had to be for the wrestling."

Mrs. Norwood shook her head. "He's been caught with beer a few times, but nothing more than that. We always grounded him. There were repercussions. But you know how it is. Sometimes it's easier to let them do what they're going to do in a place where you can keep your eye on them."

That was the trick. Serve your child the liquor at home so you could monitor them. Taylor's family had always allowed alcohol at the table, but if she drank out with friends and got caught, she was grounded. Nothing out of the ordinary there, outside of a few laws or fifty broken.

Taylor nodded. This wasn't her battle right now. "Okay. So school let out at noon today. Did you talk to Xander this afternoon?"

Mrs. Norwood's face fell. "No, I'm afraid we didn't. The last I saw him, he was walking out the door this morning, happy as a lark because it was Halloween. They had a party to go to tonight."

That got Taylor's attention. "Where was the party supposed to be?"

"At his friend Theo Howell's. Evelyn and Harold are friends of ours. They're actually traveling with Amanda's parents now. But we know them well. We've always trusted Xander to be at their place without supervision."

Taylor made a note. With any luck, the party was still going on, or at least had a gathering of kids who might have a better handle on the victims. She couldn't push the thought from her mind that they might be a target too. She couldn't take that chance, but she didn't want to alarm the Norwoods.

"Do you have the address? I'd like to talk to Theo, if I could."

"Certainly. I have Theo's numbers too, home and cell. I'll get them. They're in my purse." Mrs. Norwood straightened out of her chair and disappeared, returning a moment later with a handwritten note and more tissues. When she sat, Taylor noticed the woman looked gray. It was time to wrap it up for now. This family needed a chance to grieve, and Taylor was itching to get someone to the party, to get more information from the living. To protect them, if need be. She stood and shook their hands.

"Ma'am, sir, I'm going to leave you now. I need to get back to another scene. If you think of anything that might be relevant, please don't hesitate to call."

They seemed smaller, less consequential than when she had first walked in. It was always that way—reality set in and sapped their strength, their air, their very being.

Mr. Norwood looked at his wife, pale as a ghost, and said, "Are you sure we can't see him?"

Taylor touched him on the shoulder, light and reassuring.

"I'm sure. It's for the best, believe me. I think you and Mrs. Norwood need to go home to Susan now."

Defeated, they struggled to their feet, arms wrapped around each other. Holding themselves together. "We'll be at the house if you need anything."

Taylor was terribly relieved. Sometimes families fought her harder on this, insisted on sticking at the crime scene, even going so far as to sneak into the scene for a last peek. It was never a good idea. At least at the medical examiner's office, the visual identifications were done on a closed loop feed, so parents and loved ones wouldn't be face-to-face with their dead. The little bit of distance sometimes helped.

Sometimes.

Lincoln escorted the Norwoods out the front door. The moment they were out of earshot, she called McKenzie, ordered him over to the Howells' house with four patrols to stand guard. Protection for their case, and the innocent lives, all in one swoop.

She just hoped she wasn't too late.

Four

Samhain
Moonrise

They were four—the points of a compass, the corners of the earth. North, South, East and West. The elements of their worship: Earth, Air, Fire and Water. Wraiths dressed in black, scurrying through the graveyard one by one so they weren't seen from the road.

This was a desolate place, far from the safety lights that peppered the modern landscape, astride a pitted country lane. A family cemetery: the husband and wife were buried at the head of the path. The road cut through their progeny, one side of the path for the man's family, the other side for the woman's. It had started as a cow path, centuries before, wormed its way into the earth gradually, until it was a clear demarcation. The people who took the earth felt it was prophetic, a way to walk amongst their dead without trampling on their spirits. They were considerate thinkers, these hardy men and women. The intent to travel, to wander, was stamped on all who sprang from the loins of this family, permanently marked by the meandering path through their consecrated land that allowed travelers to disturb their eternal rest.

Balance was necessary. That's why he'd chosen this cemetery in the first place. He'd spent hours combing the countryside, looking for his sacred place. Once he found it, he claimed it as his own, drew an invisible circle, grounded his body and cast his spell, making a sacrifice to the land— three drops of his blood mixed into the earth beneath the tall, stately oak that bounded the west border of the graveyard. The oak had responded in kind, accepting his offering and allowing a limb to drop at his feet. It was exactly the length of his arm from his elbow to the point of his middle finger, already smooth of bark and leaves, tapered slightly at the end, which created a perfect place for his hand to grasp.

The branch became his wand, and he used his athamé, a two-sided blade with a hilt of the blackest obsidian, to carve his name into the oak in sigil letters—the witches' alphabet—each corresponding to a point on the numerological chart, giving the wand incalculable powers at his hand. The athamé had cost him a year's allowance, the wand cost him blood, but it was well worth it. They were the tools of his religion.

He worshipped alone at the base of the oak, calling on the Goddess to bless him, the God to give him strength. He danced in the moonlight, cast harmless spells against his enemies carefully, followed close to the Wiccan's Rede— First, do no harm. He knew that whatever he cast forth would return to him threefold, so he didn't seek to maim, just annoy. He worshipped with joy, with despair, with love in his heart, with pain in his limbs.

When he felt the space was so completely attuned to his nature that it greeted him when he returned, the oak dropping leaves or bending to the whispering breeze, he brought his friends.

They were four—the corners, the watchers. North, South, East and West. Two boys, two girls. Balance.

The older of the two girls belonged to him, six feet of creamy, milky skin so pale she almost didn't need to use makeup to make herself disappear, with tumbling black locks that reached nearly to her waist. She was green-eyed, thin as a whippet but with womanly curves in all the right places, and if it weren't against all his beliefs he would worship her as the Goddess. But she was flesh and blood. His flesh and his blood. They shared everything, every fluid, every waking moment. He felt incomplete when she wasn't near, and as such kept her close always.

The boy was his closest friend and his occasional lover. He was handsome, with tousled blond hair and brown eyes, short and stocky and incredibly strong. Their youngest member had dark hair too, uncontrollably curly. She was a good physical match for her mate, small and solid, with thick calves and a cleft chin.

He trusted them with his life.

The four shared blood; through sacrifice, through a common vision, through the Great Act. Sex was their most powerful union, the blessing on their worship. They had been handfast, in the tradition of the Old Ways, declaring themselves for one another. They were looking for a Wiccan high priest who would do the official ceremony, legalizing their marriages in the eyes of the Goddess. They would go as couples, then as a quadrant.

While his magick was powerful, with his corners he could shift the very earth. His corners were his friends and lovers. His coven. They would follow him anywhere, and he would sacrifice himself for them in turn.

So when he told them the nonbelievers must die, they believed. They were The Immortals, and the night was theirs.

They had come tonight, the first night of the new moon, to cast a spell to Azræl, the Angel of Death. The last new moon, they had congregated, taken earth from the grave-yard, said their spells and magickally charged it to allow the earth time to open, to allow a rift in the universe to form. Tonight they sought Azræl's blessing; a celebration of their wondrous evening.

Samhain, what the Christians and Jews called Halloween, was a sacred night, when the veil between the two worlds was at its thinnest and spirits walked openly between the afterlife and the living. Samhain marked the Wiccan New Year, a sober celebration, a time for reflection. Messages were sent, ancestors honored, blessings bestowed. He had chosen Samhain as the night of the cleansing, the night when they would rid the world of their enemies. If they received the proper blessings tonight, he could put the rest of his plan into action.

It was nearly time. They had a great deal of work to do. He led the four to the oak.

"Who comes to call Azræl?" he cried.

They stepped forward in turn, beginning with the tall girl.

"It is I, Fane. Blessed be."

"I am Thorn. So mote it be."

"It is Ember, the bright spark. Blessed be."

He stood with them, head thrown back to the sky, speaking slowly and carefully. Their names conjured great power—he could already feel the ripples of energy coursing through the air.

"I am Raven, leader of this coven. In the name of the God and the Goddess, so mote it be."

He struck a match and touched the flame to a stick of jasmine incense, then lit twelve black candles, three for each of them. The clearing began to glow. They'd already set out the stones: a violet amethyst, melanite, dark tiger's eye and a piece of jet. The elestial stone, their record-keeper—a jagged piece of milky quartz—sat on top of the pile. It would be buried near the site after the ceremony, a permanent archaic tie to the earth.

Contact with the netherworld was meant as a silent meditation, but Raven had written a beautiful oral spell in his Book of Shadows, had copied it out neatly three times for his coven. They'd memorized it silently on the way over, each poring through the letters until they'd committed the words to heart.

They shed their clothes, kicked the dark stacks of cloth

well out of the way of the candles so there was no chance
of fire. They worshipped skyclad, naked in the cool night
air, never feeling a moment's embarrassment. Their bodies
were astral temples, and beautiful despite any superficial
cultural flaw.

They drew cords from their bags, each nine feet in length,
and took up their athamés and wands. They shuffled a bit,
from foot to foot, shaking away any last bits of energy that
would disrupt their ritual. Focusing.

Raven glanced at his watch, looked to the moon-blank
sky. It was time.

They lined up in their corners, facing one another in a
circle, silent and serious. The dark was broken only by the
shimmering candles that reflected the glow of their pale
flesh.

Raven began the ceremony. "We come together in perfect
love and perfect trust. So mote it be."

"Perfect love and perfect trust. So mote it be," they
repeated after him, speaking in practiced unison. He used
his athamé to draw a wide, invisible circle at their feet,
chanting, "Cast the circle, draw it right, bring the corners to
us tonight." He walked in a wide arc, sprinkling salt water
to create the borders of the circle. Fane followed behind him
with the lit incense, sanctifying their footsteps. The circle
was where they practiced their magick—inside the consecrated space, their prayers could be heard.

Once the circle was cast, Raven stepped inside, bade his
coven to follow suit. When they were secure, he called the
corners, using his athamé to trace specific angled pentacles
in the air, each slightly different, depending on the corner
he was calling.

"All hail to the element of air, Watchtower of the East.
May you stand in strength and bless our prayers. Powers of
the air, we summon you to join our circle." He turned to his
right and drew in the air again, forceful slashes, purposeful.
Practiced.

"All hail the element of fire, Watchtower of the South.

May you stand in strength and bless our prayers. Powers of fire, we summon you to protect our circle."

He turned again, and again. "All hail to the element of water, Watchtower of the West. May you stand in strength and bless our prayers. Power of water, we summon you to guard our circle.

"All hail to the element of earth, Watchtower of the North. May you stand in strength and bless our prayers. Powers of earth, we summon you to provide us guidance and success in our ministrations."

The calls complete, Raven reached into the bag next to him and sprinkled the magickally charged earth they'd taken at the last new moon around the circle in a slow dribble. This would open the portal between the two worlds while keeping them safely grounded in the now.

"May the Goddess and the God look upon us in favor. All hail the Goddess. All hail the God."

The group spoke in turn. "All hail the Goddess. All hail the God."

He kissed the blade of his athamé, the others followed suit. Then they took up their cords, intertwining them, feeding them through each other's hands until they were bound together. Raven caught each eye, nodding slightly. It was time to call Azræl. Time for their reward.

They pushed their personal energy into the earth, grounding, then reversed, bringing the earth's power into their bodies. The force of it made them shiver. With their hands facing into the circle, they directed their power to the center and created an invisible cone, then walked widdershins, counter-clockwise, three times, pushing that energy down, toward their goal, ending back in their original spots. There was great danger in casting a widdershins circle, but Raven had assured them that the best, most direct route to Azræl was through a negative portal, downward, not upward to the light. Besides, they were guarded by the four Watchtowers and the God and Goddess. He was confident they were safe.

He reached behind him and withdrew a small finger bone

from his bag. Death liked bones—it was the soul's truest form. Death understood that he was a part of all natural life.

The four of them turned to face the west, and Raven carefully, gently laid the finger bone in the dirt beside their stones. They breathed slowly, modulating their breath to match their partner, calming and balancing their energy. Deeper breaths now, with pauses in between to help them overoxygenate their blood and raise their consciousness. Raven could tell when they were all perfectly attuned, and he began to chant. The others followed a fraction of a second later. Their voices carried through the graveyard.

Azræl Azræl Az-rah-el.
Azræl Azræl Az-rah-el.
Azræl Azræl Azzzz-raaaah-elllll.
Angel of darkness, come bless us.
Angel of darkness, come bend us.
Angel of darkness, bring our true natures to the fore.
Bring us your power, and a sign of your blessing. We call to you, O ancient one, who dwells beyond the realms.
You who once reigned in the time before time. Come, hear our call.
Assist us to open the way, give us the power!

They repeated the poem three times, building into a tuneless chant.

Then Raven spoke, his arms spread wide, his head thrown back. "Bless us for finding the strength to rid the world of those who hurt us, who deceived and tortured. Fight our oppressors—punish those who are cruel to us. Allow us to know your divinity, to understand your ways, to find a painless path to keep us from shame. Show us the way, oh, Azræl. Night and need give life to your helping fire. Rectify our darkness, spread your wings of shadow through our souls. Watch over our houses, deflect their ire."

At the end, they repeated their nocturnal God's name

over and over and over, turning in circles, winding themselves around each other, sinuous as snakes, then at the moment they felt the energy peak, consecrated their prayers with the Great Act. Raven and Thorn were so attuned to each other that they were able to climax at the same time. Their energy, like their seed, spilled into the earth, sanctifying their pact. The girls kissed, and the boys. They smeared the fluids along each other's bodies, intricate glowing trails of symbols, then switched partners. The men writhed together while the women brought each other to a wild, breathless climax. They were all so good together, so right. The strongest magick was cast during the Great Act at the moment of shared orgasm.

Panting in the dust, they allowed their minds to come back. They stood, shakily, and unbound their cords. Raven thanked the corners, bid them hail and farewell. He closed the circle, careful to walk deosil, clockwise, to close their downward portal.

There was still energy in the air, crisp and crackling, so Raven told his coven to ground again so it wouldn't drain their essences. Raven shut his eyes and envisioned a long, glowing root leaving his body and securing itself in the land, then let all his extra energy pour down the root. He felt better when he finished, smiled at Fane. They busied themselves with ending their prayers, burying the stone and the finger, blowing out the candles, dressing silently.

A breeze started, getting stronger until their hair was whipping around their faces. Thunder rumbled in the distance, then again, and lightning flashed, suddenly close. The sharp scent of ozone invaded Raven's nose. He smiled.

"I didn't think it was going to rain tonight," Fane whispered.

"It wasn't. Azræl has blessed our prayers," Raven said. "We have been blessed. Nothing can stop us now."

Five

Baldwin circled the Vanderwoods' house until he found a quiet spot in the backyard.

"Sorry about that, Garrett. Needed to get clear of a situation. What's up?"

"Well, I don't have good news. The crypto boys sent a report in about some things they found on Charlotte Douglas's computer."

Baldwin stood straighter. Charlotte Douglas was a profiler he'd worked with years ago, and again just a few months back, on the Snow White case. She'd ended up embarrassing the Bureau before her untimely demise at the hands of a killer she'd recruited into her life—the same killer who stalked Taylor now. The Pretender was Charlotte's creation, first an apprentice of the Snow White, then a self-named terror who'd invaded all of their lives.

Charlotte had brought death to their doors, and now it sounded like the Bureau was resurrecting the past. He held out hope that Charlotte's records would help identify who the Pretender really was. But when she died, and the Bureau tried accessing her files, they self-destructed using a sophisticated encryption. Their best people had been working for months to resuscitate her work.

Charlotte was just as dangerous dead as she had been alive.

"And?"

"It seems she has some files pertaining to you. To a...relationship the two of you were having. She was rather graphic. And she's made some other allegations against you."

"Son of a bitch."

"Yes. Well, we knew parts of this might come back to bite us. Don't worry, okay?"

"Garrett, you know that Charlotte—"

"Baldwin, I know. Trust me, I know. I'm sorry, but this is out of my hands. I've been instructed to recall you to Quantico immediately so you can go before the disciplinary board first thing tomorrow morning for a little chat. I caught a shitload of heat when I told them you were in Nashville. So get yourself back up here. I've sent the plane for you. It should be ready to collect you shortly."

"Is this serious, Garrett?"

His boss was silent for a few moments. "Yes, I think it is. They haven't disclosed everything to me. I've arranged for Reginald Beauchamp to represent your interests at the hearing, just in case."

"Whoa, I need counsel? I thought you said this was just a chat."

"Baldwin, I'm not willing to take any chances. I've already defended you, told them any charges against you by that woman were ludicrous. But they're very insistent."

"Making an example out of me," Baldwin grumbled.

"It's possible. They have her files now. The focus isn't on you and Charlotte—it's gone deeper. They're especially interested in the Harold Arlen incident. The past is catching up with us."

This time Baldwin groaned aloud. "Damn it, that case has been closed for years. I was cleared of all wrongdoing. Why are they bringing it up again?"

"You know why."

Baldwin breathed deeply through his nose, surprised that all he could smell was burned leaves tinged with fresh blood. He'd spent years trying to forget, to move on. To erase the dank scent of basement rot, the vision of shattered lives. The self-fulfilling prophecy that was Charlotte Douglas. God, Taylor couldn't know. He needed to make sure of that.

Garrett was speaking again.

"I need to warn you. Apparently, Charlotte's files had some extras that weren't in your original reports. They want…clarification."

"Clarifications that include lawyers and hearings. Are you talking about what I think you're talking about?"

"Yes. Obviously, the phone…"

Baldwin felt himself shutting down, the rigid professionalism that got him through the most heinous of crime scenes filtering into his system. His detachment was his gift, and he readily employed it now. To think, to speculate about what might be waiting for him in Quantico would surely derail him before they asked the first question. He'd need all his powers of stability to face this issue all over again. The last time it had nearly cost him his life. He had much more to lose now.

"I'll be there. Thanks for trying, Garrett. You've been carrying this load for a long time. We're just going to have to take our chances and see how things shake out."

Baldwin hung up his cell phone and slumped back against the deck. The woods behind the house were dark and foreboding, alive with crickets and the rustlings of small rodents. He thought he heard thunder roiling in the distance. This was not good news. Two thousand-four had been a horrible year, and reliving it, as he was sure to have to do, wasn't going to be a good experience. He'd fought hard to clear his name back then, and he'd do it again now. Surely Charlotte's notes were exaggerations of the truth. That was her forte.

He could only hope that it didn't go any deeper.

Six

Taylor shut the door on the Norwoods and leaned back against the frame. She needed to see the last two crime scenes—the second double especially—but she needed a break. She wondered where Baldwin had gone.

She had just flipped open her cell phone to call him when he rounded the corner of the house, hands in his hair. The ends were sticking up in the back. She stepped off the porch and met him in the yard. He was white, obviously furious.

"What's wrong?" she asked.

He look startled for a moment, then shook his head. "Nothing. I've just got to go back up to Quantico. Garrett needs me on a case."

There was something in his voice, a note of doubt that she immediately seized on. He wasn't telling her the whole truth. She reached out and touched his chin, turning his face to hers.

"A case?"

He gave her a halfhearted grin. "An old case. They need some testimony about it. I'm so sorry to have to run out on you."

"We'll be fine. Are you leaving in the morning?"

"Now, actually. Garrett sent the plane. I'll have to review my notes and the hearing starts at 7:00."

She could feel his distraction, decided not to force it. One thing she'd learned about Baldwin, he would eventually tell her what was going on. Pushing him when he was still working things out wouldn't get her anywhere. And she had enough on her hands here.

"Do you need a ride? I can get a patrol to take you to the airport."

He nodded. "That would be great. Thank you."

He kissed her, letting his hand linger for a moment around the back of her neck. He felt so…sad. It was coming off him in waves. She wished she could help, knew he'd come to her when he was ready for actual consolation.

"Honey, can I help?" she asked softly.

His answering smile was grim. "I wish you could, Taylor. But I have to handle this myself."

Taylor watched the patrol car drive away, wondering again what in the world could drag Baldwin to Quantico at this hour. She didn't have time to worry about it; she had too much work to do. The chill was setting in, the air crisp with cold. She shivered, started to go back inside the Vanderwoods' when her cell rang.

It was Marcus, distraught and short.

"We have another body," he said. "Female teen, four streets over from Estes, Warfield Lane. Completely off the original path."

Jesus. She thought they were in the clear. There'd been no new reports for over an hour. The house-to-house canvass had calmed, people were off the streets and barricaded in their homes. The media was frustrated, being kept away from the crime scenes. Too bad. They'd be able to dine out on this news for weeks anyway.

"I'll be right there," she said.

Taylor bolted out the front door, ran directly into Sam.

She grabbed Sam's arm for balance, narrowly avoided falling down the front steps.

"Good grief, cookie, who lit your hair on fire?"

"Sorry about that, Sam. I've got another. Want to hit it with me?"

"Another? Good God. That makes, what?"

"Eight. Can we go now? Marcus just called and he's obviously crushed."

"Yeah. I'll come back and declare this one afterward. Where's Baldwin?"

"He got called back to Quantico, some sort of emergency."

"Like this isn't one."

"No kidding."

They wound their way under the crime-scene tape strung across the road and drove down a few streets to Warfield Lane. This house wasn't as fancy as those on Estes—just a single-story cottage, but still spacious with a lovely, well-groomed yard. A pumpkin sat on the steps, not yet carved.

Marcus met them at the door, face pale.

"She's in the back room. And just so you know, that's not the only part of the pattern that's broken. She's not a Hillsboro student, she goes to St. Cecilia's."

Taylor took that in. "Hmm. She wasn't in her bedroom, either?"

"No, a den. Looks like she was doing her homework. She's on the floor behind the desk. Her mom said she likes to work in the window seat. The dog is lying next to her. He won't leave her side."

His voice was thick with sorrow. Taylor empathized. They were all going to be taking turns with the department shrink after this was over. Now they were up to eight. Eight teenagers in a single day. The only way it could get worse was if it had happened at school, with more children witnessing the deaths of their classmates.

A narrow hallway, voices from the kitchen. She caught a glimpse of color—a red blouse, the mother sobbing at the kitchen table—then they were at the entrance to the den. The room was paneled in walnut, small and cozy, with bookshelves lining the walls and a big bay window. Taylor and Sam stepped behind the desk.

A chocolate lab growled at them, the whites of his eyes showing. He dropped his head on his paws and whined, the hackles raised on the back of his neck.

"Down, boy. It's okay." She turned to Marcus. "What's his name?"

"Ranger."

"Okay, Ranger. It's okay." She inched closer. The dog seemed to sense the inevitable. He bared his teeth and snapped at her, then slowly, as if his bones ached, got to his feet. His back legs hitched as he moved. Hip dysplasia, Taylor noted absently. Poor thing was old.

"You've done your job, Ranger. She'll be safe with us." As Taylor spoke, she gently eased her hand around the dog's neck and got ahold of his collar. She could feel him shaking. "He's exhausted. Okay, sweet boy. Time to go."

The dog sighed, then allowed himself to be led away. Taylor scratched him behind the ears as she handed him off to Marcus, then turned back to the body.

The girl was petite, blond hair in a disheveled ponytail, strands sneaking out and falling in tendrils around her face. Her lips were blue. She was naked from the waist up, her budding breasts smeared with blood, the top button of her jeans undone. The pentacle carved in the long curves on her flat stomach was oozing blood. Her small body started to shake.

"Wait a minute," Sam said. "Son of a bitch. She's convulsing." Taylor saw a small bubble of blood form on the girl's lip. She stared in dull horror for a moment, then both women leaped to the girl's side. Taylor pushed her fingers into the girl's neck, felt a tiny, thready pulsing.

"Get the EMTs! She's alive."

The ambulance screamed away into the night, EMTs pumping hard on the girl's chest, her mother crying, holding her free hand. Taylor stood in the doorway to Brittany Carson's house. Ranger was cuddled against her legs.

Sam was behind her. She ripped off her gloves, snapped, "It's been within the last hour. And it's definitely drugs— her pupils were fixed and pinpoint. Whatever they've taken, it's some kind of narcotic."

Taylor turned back to her best friend. "Do you think that's why the dog wouldn't leave her side? Because he knew she was alive?"

Sam tucked a swoop of bang behind her right ear, then rubbed her hand across her eyes. She suddenly looked older, more harassed. She sighed, then said, "I don't know. Maybe. It's probably a moot point. She's lost a lot of blood, and she was cyanotic. All the other bodies were carved up post-mortem. Their hearts weren't pumping blood. Hers was a steady, slow loss. Depending on what she took…regardless, it's definitely more recent than the others."

Taylor watched her sharply. "Are you okay?"

"Yeah. I'm just really tired. Can't seem to catch up on my sleep these days." Sam stepped away, started loading her gear back into her scene kit.

"Sam?"

"What?"

"You know the last time you looked tired like this?"

"No, when?"

Taylor smiled, crossed her arms. "I don't know, think back. Maybe…twenty, twenty-one months ago?"

Sam stopped, still and frozen in time. Her eyes met Taylor's. "No."

"I think that's the wrong answer, Mommy."

Sam sank into a chair, groaning. "No, no, no! I can't be. Not yet, not now. I refuse. The twins just had their first birthday. Oh, shit. Simon is going to murder me."

Taylor laughed at her best friend. "I think he might be thrilled. How far along do you think you are?"

"Hold on, I'm trying to count." She grew silent for a moment, then said, "I can't…oh, yeah." She exhaled a laugh and blushed, then looked at Taylor. "I can't be more than six weeks. Simon had that forensics conference in Denver, and I went with him. We got a suite and a sitter and had ourselves a little night out. I've been so freakin' busy I didn't even realize I missed my period."

Taylor kneeled by the chair, swept her into a hug. "Honey, this is the most wonderful news. I'm thrilled for you."

Sam hugged her back briefly. "Don't tell anyone, for God's sake. I need to warn Simon, and get to the OB. Shit, shit, shit." But she was smiling, and the dark circles under her eyes looked a little less threatening.

Taylor gestured toward the den door. "When you warn him, let him know I may need his services. I seriously doubt you're going to be able to handle tox and trace for all these crime scenes, and the TBI is backed up for months. We could probably ask Baldwin to send some of the samples to his lab at Quantico, but I'd rather do this quickly and quietly. I'll arrange for some extra funding to get Simon's lab to help you out."

Sam's husband, Dr. Simon Loughley, ran a firm called Private Match, one of the leading forensic specialty labs in the country. DNA matches for paternity were their bread and butter, which allowed Simon to take on outside work that fascinated him. He was always there in a pinch when Metro needed an immediate turnaround; the Tennessee Bureau of Investigation lab was so far behind on rape and murder samples that sometimes it was necessary to take their labs to independent, private vendors. It would cost, but Taylor didn't anticipate that would be a problem. My God, six crime scenes in one day's event? Even their notoriously tightfisted chief would agree with the necessity.

She couldn't wait for their new crime lab to open. The funding was in place, a site selected. Everything was moving forward. No more relying on the kindness of others to get their pressing forensic evidence processed.

The dog whined at the door, jerking Taylor from her reverie.

"Okay. On that happy note, we need to get back to work." She looked at the blood that had soaked into the carpet where Brittany Carson had lain bleeding to death. "Wish we'd gotten here sooner. She might've had a better chance."

"How were you supposed to know? Are you telepathic now?"

"No, but—"

Sam shook her head. "No buts about it. You're not a mind reader. You've got a killer who's obviously thought this through very, very carefully. I'm praying this is the last call we get tonight."

A horrible thought dawned in Taylor's mind. "Do you think he could have been watching, waiting for us to arrive, before he came down here and finished up with Brittany?"

"Watching? Sure. You know how these kooks love to watch. He could have been at one of the houses at the far end of the neighborhood while we were in one of the other residences."

"Jesus. The media is going to have my head."

Sam was back to being all professional. She and Sam hadn't hung out in a few weeks, and Taylor missed her. "Taylor, you've done the best you can. Let's get back, I still have two bodies to declare."

"Okay. Let me tell Marcus, I'll need to come back here later."

She found him in the kitchen, staring hard out the back window into nothingness. His shoulders were slumped in defeat. She knew exactly what was going through his mind. Blame, guilt. Taylor decided to give him the same pep talk Sam had just given her.

"Hey," she said softly. "It's okay. It wasn't your fault."

He met her eyes, bleak with despair. "She didn't have a pulse earlier, Taylor. I swear it. The EMT who came couldn't find one, either. Jesus, she's been lying here dying while I chatted up her mom and figured a way to get the dog to leave her side."

Ranger sat heavily on Marcus's feet. He reached down and petted the dog absently.

"Did the mom have any idea what went down this afternoon?"

"No. She's a single mother, a nurse. Name's Elissa. She worked late, came home and found Brittany in the den. Brittany's a scholarship student, I did find that out. Strait-laced, shy. Her mom says there's no way she was doing drugs voluntarily."

"There's no sign of forced entry. Whoever tried to kill her, she let him in."

"She's younger than the others, too. I've got a patrol canvassing, but this house is set back so far that no one has come forward yet to say they saw anything out of the ordinary."

"Then we need to start looking for the ordinary. A killer who can disappear into this neighborhood for hours unnoticed."

"Caucasian, then. Dressed professionally, or in a Halloween costume. It could be anyone."

"Could be a kid."

"You think another kid did this?"

"I don't know. But we need to take that into consideration."

"If we'd just gotten to her earlier," he repeated, voice hollow.

She got in his face, forced him to make eye contact.

"Marcus, let's just focus on the now. Get me a report from the hospital, and let's take it from there. If the girl lives, post a guard on her room. She's the only witness we have to this afternoon's events. I need to get back to Estes—there are still two bodies that Sam hasn't declared. Take it easy on yourself. Get the patrols to secure this house and we'll come back to it. This one goes in the win column. Okay?"

"Okay," he mumbled, misery etched on his handsome

features. He wasn't fooling her. She'd need to talk him off the ledge some more, but right now she needed to attend to the rest of the dead.

"Here, I've got something that will distract you. I think our killer may be watching us, waiting to see our reactions. We need to talk to everyone within one hundred yards of these crime scenes that might have a video camera trained our way. Check with the media first. They know to get some crowd shots in the B-roll, and Keri McGee will, too. I've noticed some of these homes have a little extra security—they may have cameras that aren't readily visible. Get through to the security firms in the area, see if any of them service houses near the crime scenes. Can you handle that for me?"

"Of course." He nodded, putting away the upset, becoming all business again. His eyes shuttered and he snapped open his cell phone, started giving instructions. Taylor squeezed his shoulder and went to join Sam.

She closed the front door and stepped onto the small porch. She stopped for a moment, took a deep breath and blew it out. What a night. Eight kids. Eight.

She started down the steps and caught a flash out of the corner of her eye. She whipped to the side, flat up against the railing, her hand on her Glock. She heard a snap, then the rushing of feet through dry leaves. A mounted spotlight turned on in the backyard.

"Sam, get down," she stage-whispered, then took off around the corner of the house, yelling, "Police, stop!" The house's lights were on a motion detector, and the heavily wooded lot was lit up like a Christmas tree. Taylor stopped for a moment, let her eyes adjust to the light, listened to the steps running away from her, stumbling into the darkness.

"Marcus," she yelled, but he was already next to her, gun drawn.

"I saw the lights go on. What's up?"

"Someone was on the side of the house, took off running.

They're headed west, deeper into these trees. What's on the other side?"

"Hobbs Road. There's nothing between us and there."

"Okay, slow and steady. Watch out for yourself. You take the left perimeter, I'll take the right. Let's see if we can't circle around and catch him before he hits the road."

"You get a look at him?"

"No. Heavy footsteps though." Taylor wasn't an idiot—she wasn't about to set off without backup. She grabbed her radio. "All units, this is Lieutenant Jackson, in pursuit of an unknown subject running west toward Hobbs Road. We're at 2135 Warfield Lane. I need a K-9 unit on the scene, repeat, get Simari and Max out here ASAP."

There were affirmatives, and she stowed the radio. They jogged off at slight right angles into the woods. The fog was heavier here, the leaves on the trees turned so their undersides were showing, aglow in the feeble moonlight. The mist enveloped them—Taylor could hardly see Marcus, though he was running relatively parallel to her, within fifteen feet.

It got darker as they moved away from the Carsons' backyard, and they slowed. This was no good. This was definitely no good. A small rain started up, spattering against her face. The loamy scent of rotting leaves grew stronger. She could still hear their suspect thrashing in the dark, probably fifty yards ahead of them. The thick haze and lack of light meant he'd slowed, too. That helped. She started off again, at a walk, weapon at her side.

A hard crack made her draw up short and dive behind the nearest tree. Her Glock was tight in her palm, her forefinger alongside the trigger. Her heart hammered in her throat—what was that? She listened, felt her chest rise and fall frantically, inhaling deeply through her nose so she could catch her breath. Another sharp snap went off, then another, a whole string of cherry bombs. A firecracker, definitely not a gun. Son of a bitch.

Something about the fact that the calendar denoted a

holiday meant the fine people of Nashville felt it their duty
to celebrate, and firecrackers, illegal in Davidson County,
were their favorite pastime.

Her heart went back to a manageable pace and she
whistled to Marcus, slow and quiet. He answered, a decent
imitation of a whip-poor-will, trilling at the end, and they
set off again, more cautiously this time.

She could see maybe five to ten feet in front of her. She
held up again, heard the whoosh of tires on wet pavement.
They were getting close to the road. Throaty, staccato barks
bled in from the south. Simari had arrived, and Max, her
canine companion, was on the hunt. It wouldn't be long now.
Max was nimble and quick, could take down a suspect in a
fraction of the time of a human officer during a chase. It was
amazing to watch, and Taylor was sorry the visibility was
so bad.

It took about a minute before she heard cries to her left.
She turned and saw a thin path, jogged up it into a small
clearing. Max had done his job and landed the suspect, had
his strong jaw clamped around the man's leg. Officers con-
verged from all sides, Maglites focused on their suspect,
weapons drawn. Simari called Max off with a command in
German. He whined, but released the suspect's jeans from
his mouth, trotted back to his master with a satisfied air.
Simari always fed Max a bloody, raw steak when he had a
successful takedown; the German shepherd would be
rewarded fully tonight.

Their suspect was moaning, holding his leg like it had
been amputated high across his thigh. Taylor approached
him carefully, but quickly saw that he was, indeed, down for
the count. Blood pooled beneath his torn jeans. Max had
taken a decent chunk of flesh out of the man's leg.

No, it wasn't a man. The flashlights showed a smooth,
round face. This was a boy, Caucasian, no more than thirteen
or fourteen. Short for his age, it seemed.

The adrenaline was leaking away; everyone was giddy,
joking and laughing. People began to disappear off into the

night, back to their cars, back to the multiple crime scenes they'd been pulled away from.

"Hope that was worth it," she heard one officer grumble.

No kidding. Taylor let out the breath she hadn't realized she was holding as Marcus snapped cuffs on the boy.

Taylor Mirandized him, mentally cursing the new laws that forced her to do so immediately in order to question anyone suspect in the commission of a crime, then asked, "What's your name?"

He just shook his head, looked down at his leg.

"I need a doctor," he said in a surprisingly deep voice.

"What's your name first?"

He shook his head.

"Okay, anonymous. We'll call an ambulance and have you transferred, but without a name, there isn't a hospital in the city that will treat you. They don't give it away for free, you know. They'll need to call your parents to get payment. Sure would be a shame to lose a leg just because you want to play hardball with me."

The boy went whiter than the Maglite's beam. He thought about it for a moment, then shrugged. "My last name is Edvin. My first name is Juri."

"Like a jury of your peers?"

"No," he said.

"Spell it."

"*J-U-R-I*. It's Finnish."

"Where do you live?"

He squinted at her, she didn't know if it was from pain or the Maglites pointed at him. "On Granny White Pike, near Lipscomb University," he said at last.

"We need to inform your parents."

The whites of his eyes flashed and he started to struggle again. Taylor pressed her arm across his chest, applied enough pressure that he couldn't move without a real fight.

"Stop that. Give me your telephone number so I can contact them, right now."

He narrowed his eyes at her, then mumbled seven

numbers. Taylor memorized them, then let up the pressure. She signaled for the EMTs to come in. They worked quickly, cutting away the torn jeans to show an impressive row of deep punctures, placing a compression pad against the seeping wound, efficiently tying the boy to the stretcher.

"Did you struggle when the dog bit you?" one of the EMTs asked.

"Yeah," Edvin mumbled. "I tried to get away. Did I hurt the dog? I punched it in the mouth when it bit me."

Taylor hid a smile. Max was tough, and in the throes of a kill probably hadn't noticed an ineffectual punch thrown by a scared kid.

"He'll be fine," she said. "Why did you run from us?"

The boy was chatty now that his big scare had passed.

"You're cops. What else would I do?"

"Stop when I said stop, for starters. What were you doing at the Carson house?"

"Whose house?" But his eyes slid away, down and to the left, and Taylor knew he was lying.

"Let's try that again. You were at the Carson house. What can you tell us about what happened there this afternoon?"

"Don't know anyone named Carson. I was walking home. Been trick-or-treating."

"Without a costume? All the way to Granny White? That's going to take you a while."

"I'm too old to play dress-up. And I like to walk. You scared me, I ran. Simple as dat."

In a fraction of a second, the boy had gone from scared and hurt to snarly and mature, talking gangster to her. She'd hit a nerve, no question about it.

One of the paramedics made a twirly motion with his finger. She looked at him and stepped a few feet away. He joined her and whispered, "We need to transport him now. He's bleeding pretty heavily. Dog might've nicked an artery."

She glanced back at the kid, who did look to be fading. "Okay. I'll send Marcus with you guys. The kid's full of crap, and I want to make sure any excited utterances are transcribed exactly. Keep an eye on him, and if he says anything, you write it down, okay?"

"Will do, boss."

She motioned to Marcus, repeated the same thing and asked him to call Juri Edvin's parents. She recited the number, waited while he wrote it in his notebook. He promised to check on Brittany Carson for her. She watched him follow the stretcher to the ambulance, the metal legs wobbly on the uneven ground. They nearly pitched the kid headfirst off the thing once.

Shaking her head, she called Lincoln and retasked him to the crime-scene videos, then touched base with McKenzie. He was at the party, had the place on lockdown. Good God, this was a logistical nightmare. She had officers and detectives spread over half of Davidson County.

It took less than five minutes to trek her way out of the woods and back to her car. Sam had left a note on the windshield. *Needed to go. Call when you're done.*

Taylor flipped open her cell phone. Sam answered on the first ring.

"You catch him?" she asked.

"Yeah. Just a kid, but he lied to me about being near the house. I'm going to drag a crime-scene tech up here and have them comb the perimeter. Something was fishy there."

"I'm at the fifth crime scene. I found some interesting stuff. You should come over here."

"Which one?"

Sam gave her the address, and Taylor hung up. She climbed in her unmarked and drove the few streets over to 5567 Foxhall Close, the home of victim number five, Brandon Scott.

It was all becoming numbingly familiar: the beautifully appointed home, the incongruity of yellow crime-scene tape and people milling about, roaming in and out of the house in a coordinated plan. It looked like moving day, with forensics and blood-spatter experts.

She made her way inside. The focus of attention was again on the second floor. She took the stairs two at a time and went to the beehive.

Sam was standing against the wall, making notes, leaving a clear view of the body. Taylor sucked in her breath, edged closer.

The body presented like the others, on his back, arms down by his side this time, but the carving in the boy's chest was much more intense. There was pure fury in the slashes. They penetrated much deeper than the other bodies, so far that bone was visible. The sheets were caked with blood, the odd scent of jasmine and viscera combining in a gorge-rising miasma.

He was partially dressed, gray sweatpants with a tie at the waist that had been disturbed—one side hung down over his right buttock. The edge of his pants was black with blood.

Taylor swallowed, hard. "He's been flayed," she said. "Our killer really didn't like Mr. Scott here."

Sam kicked off from the wall, stowed her notebook in her pocket, walked over to Taylor.

"That's an understatement. Roll him," she instructed the death investigator who had joined them.

The boy's back was covered in strips of bloody channels, long and unevenly spaced.

"What caused this?" Taylor asked.

"Honestly?" Sam pursed her lips, a piece of her too-long bangs caught in her lip gloss. She brushed her hair away impatiently. "I think he was whipped."

"Whipped?"

"Yeah. Remember Todd Wolff's basement? He had all that sex paraphernalia down there?"

Did she remember? That wasn't a case she'd soon forget. She nodded, eyes veiled.

"There's an S&M tool called a cat-o'-nine-tails. Most are made of leather and not intended to inflict more than pain, but some have sharp, barbed tips on the ends of the separate whips. I've seen this before, in another case several years ago. Guy in East Nashville took one to his boyfriend. Got carried away, the guy ended up on my table. He was covered head to toe in slashes like this."

"Jesus."

The 'gator laid Scott back, gently. Taylor took in the fury, the anger, the sheer rage. She could *feel* the intense hatred.

"He's got defensive wounds, Sam. Look at his hands. They're all scratched up. That's different from our other victims too, isn't it?"

"Yes. The other bodies look like the carvings were done postmortem, and they were stripped completely. Two of them I assume were already naked—the couple. But the rest were probably undressed after they died, before the cutting began."

"Were there signs of sexual assault on any of the victims?"

Sam shook her head. "Nothing that jumped out and bit me, but I won't know for sure until I take swabs."

"It's not the easiest thing to get the clothes off a dead body. If there wasn't a sexual assault, why do you think the killer removed the victims' clothes? Maybe they were already naked."

"Faulty logic. Think about it, Taylor. How many kids do you know sit around naked in their rooms? Other than the couple, who were obviously interrupted. Plus, if you're pressed for time and you need your victim to ingest something against their will, are you going to make them take off their clothes first?"

"If you want to humiliate them, yes. I don't think we can rule it out just yet."

"But was there time for humiliation? These killings were sandwiched into a pretty tight window. I'm betting the killer removed their clothing after they were dead. But this is different." She waved her hand toward the victim. "These wounds were infected while the victim was alive, still dressed, and he fought hard. See the bruise on his right shoulder?"

Taylor looked closer. There was the slightest discoloration from the boy's collarbone to the top of his shoulder, an elongated oval mark.

"A knee?"

"I'd say so. He was held down."

"Would it take someone very big to leave that kind of mark? He looks like he's in pretty good shape."

"Not necessarily. There was a violent struggle, but anyone can be overcome under the right circumstances. There are also marks around his neck—maybe an attempt at strangulation."

"Hopefully our killer left something of himself behind. Your new 'gator, Barclay Iles, collected a few black hairs off the body of Xander Norwood. Maybe there's more to be had here."

"Maybe. You know I'll look carefully."

"Thanks, Sam. I know you will. What I'd like to know is why this one wasn't drugged, since all the others were. Especially if he needed to be subdued."

"I won't be able to answer that until I do the post. He's a big boy, bigger than all the rest. There may be something interesting in his tox screen, I just don't know. Speaking of which, I need to get back to Gass Street, supervise all of these bodies coming in." Sam was retreating into medical examiner mode, the cool facade closing in again.

Taylor let her. She needed some distance herself.

Seven

Taylor drove back to the command post on Estes in silence. She tried Baldwin on his cell, he answered on the first ring.

"I just landed. What's happening there?"

"We found one alive, kid named Brittany Carson. She was pretty far gone. I'll be surprised if she makes it. Then we got in a foot chase with another kid who was lurking outside her house. Simari had to unleash Max on him. Anything more from Garrett?"

"No. Just this emergency thing in the morning."

"Well, get it over with and get back down here. I think we're going to need your expertise. We're starting to have breaks in the original pattern. One crime scene was different from the others—the victim was flayed, probably with some kind of whip. I'm telling you, Baldwin, I thought this was done. I'm afraid there may still be more. I need to get my hands on whoever did this."

"What does Sam think?"

"She feels they ingested a narcotic of some kind, though this last one I attended, Brandon Scott? No signs of cyanosis. It looks like he was either strangled or exsanguinated. We're about to do a walk-through of each crime scene."

Her call-waiting beeped. She looked and saw it was Lincoln. "Hey, I've got to go. Call me in the morning, okay? Love you."

"Love you, too. Luck."

She clicked over. "Hey, Linc. What's up?"

"We have the entire neighborhood frozen, and we've got some very upset parents. They've got the pitchforks and stakes out."

"That's to be understood. But we need those scenes stationary for now. Tell them we'll release the bodies and get them back in their homes as soon as we can."

She hoped she was telling the truth.

Quantico

Garrett had sent a car for him. Baldwin climbed into the backseat and gave the yawning driver his address. He had a small apartment near the grounds of Quantico that he used when he was in town working.

He was tired, but getting to sleep was going to be near to impossible. He needed to be sharp and alert in the morning. Artificial means, then. He checked his watch and calculated, decided against half an Ambien, settled on a Benadryl. It would knock him out for at least six hours. That would have to be good enough. He dry-swallowed the capsule and stared out into the dark of the night.

It was always darkest just before the dawn. He could only hope that the light of day would bring good news.

Eight

The rain was letting up, the evening now bittered into teeth-chattering cold. Taylor ran the gauntlet down Estes, driving through a phalanx of Metro blue-and-whites and medical examiner's vans. A patrol officer waved her through and she parked the Lumina in front of the Kings' driveway.

Dan Franklin, the department's spokesman, met her car. Dan was a big guy, light brown hair and blue eyes with a relatively nondescript, almost homely face, but six foot two and an easy two-thirty. He spent a lot of time in the gym, and the hard work showed. Physically, he was threatening at best, emotionally, he was the rock the department depended on. He was their first line of defense against the media. It was a precarious position to maintain—Metro needed the media and the media needed Metro, but sometimes they didn't like to play nice. Franklin assured everyone on both sides that the road to the news would be as smooth as could be.

He opened her door and she climbed out. "What's up?"

"I need to talk to you."

Taylor stopped. "Shoot."

"I think it would be a good idea to have you give the presser." He tapped his hand on the hood of her car as he spoke, and the emphasis felt contrived. She was immediately suspicious.

"Oh, come on. The press conference is your job."

"I know it is, and I'll be up there with you." He quit tapping, leaned against the car. He crossed his bulky arms and said, "We've been friends for a long time, right?"

"Going on ten years."

"You trust me, right?"

"Yes."

"Then do the presser. I promise it's the right thing to do."

"But—"

He cut her off. "Taylor, the city of Nashville wants to see you lead again. You've been fodder for the press for a couple of months now, and practically the moment you're reinstated, a huge string of murders happens on your watch. They know about Fitz going missing, they know about the Snow White Killer's apprentice. You need to regain their confidence. You need to let them know that you're in control, that the old Taylor Jackson is back in business. Your close rate is still head and shoulders above any cop in the city— hell, most of the country. This is the perfect opportunity for you to get them back in your court." He took a breath, then quickly said, "And we can put a camera behind you, film forward, see what the crowd shows us."

"Ah, so that's the plan. Bribery by B-roll. You're just appealing to my need to find the creeps who did this." But she smiled, and he smiled back.

"I honestly think it will do you some good. Quell the scuttlebutt."

She blew out a breath and thought for a few minutes. Dan was right, she did need to get the city's confidence back. Badges and honors were all well and good, but in the long run, the only thing that mattered was the close. Though the people of Nashville were a forgiving bunch, the escapades over the past year had tarnished her spotless reputation, and in turn the reputation of Metro. They needed to know that she was back, one hundred percent back, solid and able to solve this case. Because eight teenagers in one night was going to rock Nashville unlike any case it had previously faced.

Too bad Baldwin had to leave town. She'd worked with his team on other cases and knew that, despite their differences in the past, the chief of police liked having the FBI involved in major crimes. He felt it engendered confidence from the masses. No matter what, when people heard those magic letters, *F-B-I,* they felt safer. Well, most people.

She heard her mother's voice in her head. *Beggars can't be choosers.* No kidding, Mother.

She ran it through her head for a minute. They could use the extra footage of the scene. She had a feeling that their killer was watching, reveling.

"Okay, I'll do it. When?"

"We're live in fifteen minutes."

She put her hand on his arm to stop him. "Hey, Dan? Thanks."

He just nodded and left her.

She scooted inside and found Lincoln making notes on his netbook.

"Hey," she said.

"Hey back," Lincoln replied. "Just talked to McKenzie. He's got the party frozen. Says there's some parents frothing at the mouth to get their kids home under their own roofs. When you're done here he's ready for you to go over there and chat with the kids."

"You have the video covered?"

"Yes. I'm going to head back to the CJC, upload everything we have and start searching for squirrels."

"Good. Dan wants me to do the presser, so wait for that footage. Did you two cook this little plan up?"

"Nope. It was his idea. But he did ask if you'd shoot him on the spot if he suggested it. I told him you weren't quite that trigger-happy."

She narrowed her eyes at him, and he gave her a small smile.

"I need to get prepped. Do we have next-of-kin notifications on all the victims?"

"All but one. Here's your information." Lincoln handed her a sheaf of papers. It was hard to believe that only four hours had passed since they'd arrived at the first scene. It felt like days.

"Got pics from the rest of the scenes?"

He handed her some Polaroids and his notebook, where he'd accurately sketched the layout of each tableau.

"This is perfect, thanks. Oh, a little something to tuck into the back of your mind—the crime scene I just came from, Brandon Scott? You'll see the level of violence was ten times the rest of the victims. I think he may have been the target, and the rest of the victims were just to cover the killer's tracks. You need to get as much information on this kid as humanly possible, and fast. He may be the best link we have to our killer."

"Really? Then maybe the suspect is still close by."

"I get that feeling, don't you? This is all so damn... showy."

"Yes, it is. And coordinated. Not a single person we've interviewed saw anything out of the ordinary. No bogeymen creeping in the backyards, nothing. The killer fits into the neighborhood."

Taylor flipped the page on Lincoln's notes. He was so thorough, she felt like she'd just relived the last few hours.

"On our suspect? I'm going to hazard a guess that we're looking for a Caucasian male between fifteen and twenty-five."

"Fifteen...you think a kid could be responsible for this level of destruction?"

"Anything's possible. The victimology is the first clue—you know that. But I wouldn't recommend saying that out loud. I think we need to roust some of the school administrators and see if anyone has been making threats first."

"I'll keep all options on the table."

"Okay, then." She took Lincoln's notes and stepped into the Kings' kitchen to gather her thoughts. Her mind was abuzz with possibilities.

Was Brandon Scott the intended victim and the rest of the murders collateral damage? That was a horrid thought, but something that she certainly needed to be aware of. It was entirely possible that this wasn't the work of an adult. She knew they had a monster on their hands, but if that monster turned out to be a kid himself, they had bigger problems.

Nine

Taylor stood in front of the whirring cameras, Dan Franklin next to her. She was speaking into forced light, and couldn't see much, just the outlines of bodies, a journalistic nightmare of the living dead. She'd been hoping that she'd be able to look into the crowd, recognize the killer and end this charade, but that wasn't going to happen.

She held up a hand to silence them and began.

"I'm sorry to see you under these circumstances. Tonight we've been struck by a tragedy, the magnitude of which we're only just beginning to understand. We've lost seven of our children. An eighth is fighting for her life at Vanderbilt Children's Hospital. We have the very best men and women at Metro, and they are working around the clock to assure two things—one, that we catch the suspect who committed these crimes, and two, that you and your children are safe.

"I won't be releasing the names of the victims at this moment because not all next of kin have been notified. We're doing all we can to make that happen, and as soon as we do Dan Franklin will have the list for you. I'd anticipate that happening overnight. I can confirm that three males and five females were targeted in this attack.

"We are confident we will be able to bring this suspect to justice very soon. We ask that anyone who has information about these crimes come forward. A tip line is available at 888-555-9880 and will be manned twenty-four hours a day. You can remain anonymous if you wish. We do ask that you call the tip line instead of Crime Stoppers so we can keep all information relevant to these cases in one place."

She steeled herself, then said, "I'll take questions now."

There was a cacophony of voices. She picked one she recognized, Cindy Carter from FOX, and focused on it. Cindy asked, "Are there any leads?"

The crowd quieted down.

"The question was, do we have any leads. Rest assured that we are doing everything possible to capture the suspect, and are working these crimes as a single event. We believe the same person is responsible for all of the murders this afternoon. But, as I'm sure you're aware, I'm not in a position to discuss anything that relates to the ongoing investigation."

There were groans, then the typical repositioning of questions, all of which Taylor was forced to deflect. That was how the game was played—feed a little bit of information to the reporters, let them ask their questions with the knowledge that they wouldn't be getting an answer on the air. Off camera, each would sidle up to Taylor, or Dan, or any of the other officers and get the inside scoop. Most of Nashville's reporters had a great tradition of being told the truth, because the police trusted that they wouldn't put that truth directly onto the air and ruin their cases.

"If you'll excuse me, I need to get back to work. I'm going to turn this over to Dan Franklin now. He'll do his level best to answer as many of your questions as he can. Thank you for your time, and for being patient with us." She paused for a moment, looked right into the cameras. "You have my word. We are doing everything in our power to solve these heinous crimes."

She stepped away from the makeshift podium, and Dan caught her eye, nodded imperceptibly. He took her place, faced the group and was immediately barraged with questions. She avoided smirking and backed away until she was out of camera range. Lincoln came up beside her.

"I was watching the crowd. I can't tell who's a part of the neighborhood and who isn't. Feels like half of Nashville is out here watching the show. We've got a long-ass night ahead of us."

"You're telling me. Okay, I'm heading to the party. You start on these tapes. Lincoln? Find me something."

"Will do."

"Okay. I'm outta here."

Taylor opened her cell and called Marcus. He answered with a morose, "Hey."

"Hey yourself. Any word on the vic?"

"She's in a coma. They've loaded her full of Narcan. They think it was some kind of drug overdose. But they don't know if she's going to make it—you know how quickly Narcan works. She didn't come to, just slipped into the coma."

"A drug overdose makes sense. That's what Sam thought, too. The presentation screams drugs—I instructed the 'gators and crime-scene techs to look for anything that might be the culprit. I need you to join us at this address—8900 Sneed Terrace. It's the home of Theo Howell, best friend of victim number three, Xander Norwood. He's supposed to be having a Halloween party. I sent McKenzie over there a while ago to get everyone corralled, and apparently some of the kids' parents have shown up there, as well. I'm going to need your help taking all of the statements. I'm sure word has spread, and a few kids may have scattered by now, but McKenzie's got at least thirty people waiting around.

"The victims are being described as the perfect kids, and

I want to find out what the real story is. Sam's gone to Gass Street, and Lincoln's doing the video footage. So that leaves us. You up for it?" She wanted to get him away from Brittany Carson, away from the guilt, get him preoccupied with something else. Interviewing thirty teenagers should do the trick.

"Yeah, I'll be there. Give me fifteen. Want me to wrangle up a couple of lattes? I'm across the street from Starbucks."

Her stomach growled in a Pavlovian response. "That would be heavenly. I'll see you there."

"Will do, Taylor."

"Thanks, Marcus. Hang in there, okay? I know you've had a bitch of an afternoon."

"I'll be okay."

"Good man. See you in a few."

Ten

Raven lay on his narrow bed, watching Fane apply her makeup. Next to feeling his body inside hers, her warmth enveloping him, it was possibly the most sensual experience they shared.

She was an expert, her hand sure. First the layer of foundation, two shades lighter than her skin, which gave her a pearly glow. Then a dusting of powder, also two shades lighter, to set the makeup. She used a sponge to feather the color into her neck so there was no line of demarcation. She put just a hint of blush on her cheeks, from the apples right into her hairline, then started on her eyes.

Raven had filmed her doing her makeup once. He overlaid it with music, a pulsing track from The Crüxshadows called—appropriately enough—"Immortal." He'd known it was their song the first time he heard it, the lyrics crying out to him, "With hearts immortal, we stand before our lives." It was perfect for the video—fast, wicked hot and theirs.

He'd sped the tape up to five times speed and posted it to YouTube as a Goth makeup tutorial. It had garnered more

than five hundred thousand views so far. It gave him an un-
believable rush to think about all those baby bats out there
using his woman as a guide.

They'd have even more to admire him for now.

Raven sat up and put his chin in his hand, watched Fane
create the mystical black cloud that made the green of her
eyes look like fifteen-carat emeralds. The long swoops of
black liquid eyeliner, the deep black M-A-C eye shadow,
more liner, five coats of mascara, then the intricate swirls
dripping off the edges of her eyes like she was a bedouin
princess decorated for her wedding night. A dark princess.
The ruler of his heart.

She finished, screwed the top on her liner, then outlined
her lips with a burgundy pencil. She dug into her makeup
tray and pulled out a deep, deep cherry-black lipstick. He
appreciated the symbolism. Fane sometimes had difficulty
talking to others, and the black lipstick reminded her that
she was the one with the power. He knew she'd imbued it
with strength—they'd done the spell together.

She bent over and ratted her hair so it stood out from her
head, allowing it to fall in glorious waves nearly to her ass,
then finished with a liberal dose of Aqua Net.

When she flipped up and smiled at him, he could barely
contain himself. His love. His perfect, perfect love.

"Your turn," she said, shrugging into her corset. The
stays made her waist about the span of his hand.

Raven tried to distract himself from his woman's faultless form and glossed his face with makeup, disappearing
behind the foundation. He never felt so strong as when he
was in full Goth mode. He had to temper it down at school
a bit—the administration had strict rules about boys wearing
makeup. Capitalist bastards. They had no idea how strong
he was.

But tonight, in celebration, they were headed to a club.
They would feed on the energy of the crowd, be themselves.
There was nothing like a good night of clubbing. Subver-
sion had a five-dollar cover in honor of Samhain, and there

was a guest DJ in from Los Angeles, a guy called The Baron. Raven had heard some amazing things about his playlist— he always seemed to have the newest bands at his disposal. He supposed that was the whole Hollywood thing—the Nashville Goth scene rocked, but it was still Nashville. Full-on industrial wasteland. He'd been to a couple of clubs in Washington, D.C., that were out of this world. But beggars couldn't be choosers—traditional Goth was all Nashville could offer tonight. One day soon he and Fane would head out to Los Angeles, would ride the wave of the Goth scene, rising to the top, glorified in their power. Their art would be watched by millions, and they would never be parted. That day was coming. He'd already purchased their tickets— they'd be gone on Monday. Just a few things left to accomplish before then.

In the meantime, they had to make do with what they had. First Subversion, then they'd hit Salvation to cap off the night and meet up with Thorn and Ember. Ember was going to have to sneak out tonight, especially after—

"Raven, love, you need to get moving. I want to get downtown."

Fane had her hands on her hips, stamping her foot in frustration. The platform industrial boots with buckles up to her knee made her six-foot-four and ethereally spectacular. He smiled at her in the mirror, baring his fangs, running his tongue lovingly along the sharp edges. They'd cost him a pretty penny, but they were so worth it. Fane loved hers just as much—it made biting one another so much easier. Better teeth than the athamé any day. It was so much more real.

He took one last swipe of black shadow under his eyes and turned off the makeup mirror's light. He grabbed Fane by the hand, danced in a circle in the center of his room.

"Let's go."

Blue lights were revolving one street over, but theirs was quiet. Raven felt a rush of excitement, squeezed Fane's hand. The commotion was for him. *Him.*

They folded themselves into his beat-up Elantra, Ratty-thing, the Rat, and drove away from the turmoil.

The Rat was feeling feisty tonight, so he let it have its head. Besides, all the Nashville cops were hung up in Green Hills. They took the shortcut through the west side of town to Twenty-first Avenue, then got on Broadway. The streets were hopping tonight, everyone dressed up. It was the one night of the year that he and Fane could walk among the masses and fit in.

And he found that pedestrian. He didn't want to fit in. He wanted to stand apart, to be different. Different was arresting, exciting. These poseurs, thinking they were being so avant-garde, their individuality cloaked in Halloween getups, were nothing compared to Raven. His ability to be unique was legendary among their brethren.

He turned left on Second Avenue, then scooted the Rat into the parking garage above SATCO, the San Antonio Taco Company. The garage was packed tonight—they had to drive all the way up to the sixth level to find a spot. They bundled out of the car and into the elevator, Fane getting more and more exasperated when they stopped at every floor to let revelers on board. They gawked at her, and she didn't like it. Raven finally bared his fangs at one idiot dressed as a pirate, and he flipped Raven off and turned around.

They ran across the street, not bothering to go to the intersection, and narrowly missed a car barreling up Second. Choking with laughter at the man's shocked face, they ran into the club, cloaks flowing behind them. They handed their money to Tony, Subversion's gargantuan bouncer, climbed the darkened stairway, feeling the *bam, bam, bam* of the bass line thrumming through the walls.

When they entered the strobe-lit room, Zombie Girl's "Creepy Crawler" was on the turntable and the energy nearly knocked them off their feet. Raven grabbed Fane's hand and pulled her through the masses into the center of the dance floor. He dug into his pocket and extracted two little blue pills, ones he'd carefully dipped and kept separate from the rest of the stash. He fed one to Fane, slipped the other under his own tongue. The Ecstasy started working quickly, sending golden warmth through his body.

Then the trip began in earnest. They kissed, feeling the energy rushing between them, coursing through their veins. They swayed and jumped, threw their arms in the air. Raven felt a scream building deep in his chest and went with it, riding the energy, building and building until he let loose with a war cry so intense he realized he had an erection and was inches from coming.

This was what it was all about. This was his place, his life, his world.

He stopped, stood still in the middle of the dance floor, his head thrown back, the music building in his very soul, feeding. As the music peaked, his orgasm built to a crescendo, and he howled. He was a God now.

She watched from the corner of the darkened space. Word had spread like wildfire through her community that a series of murders had been committed, and she knew in her soul that whoever did it was in this room, right now. A few minutes before she'd felt the air change, felt the energies shift. A very powerful spell had been cast, and she began to drain. Someone was feeding, close by. Damn vampires. She snapped back and shielded herself deeper, stronger, felt her strength return. She kept her eyes sharp on the crowd.

He was here. She could feel him.

What he'd done was wrong. It broke all their laws. He would have to be punished.

She sighed. Tonight was supposed to be a sober, somber evening, one of great reflection and inwardness, a night to make contact with the departed and assure them that memories of their lives were still precious. A night to look forward with great anticipation at the dying of the God and the rebirth of the Goddess. She'd conducted her spells earlier, at sunset. Set her altar with a white candle and a black, her athamé, her wand, a small skull, real and very powerful, that she'd purchased at the Pagan Festival at Montgomery Bell State Park a few years back, plus black, red and white ribbons.

She'd snapped sprigs of rosemary off her windowsill during the last new moon, let it dry for full potency, then made a posy with it, braiding the ribbons and winding them around the rosemary thrice, chanting, "Rosemary is for remembrance, tonight I remember those who have passed. Those who have crossed through the veil, I will remember." She'd meditated about those she'd lost, communed with their spirits. She'd left the ceremony feeling peaceful. The posy would stay on her altar until Yule. She always felt such an affinity with Samhain—celebrating the circle of death and life was how she'd begun in Wicca.

Though her phone was off, she had begun to receive calls before her ceremony was over. By the time she had finished and checked her voice mail, she had eight messages. When she heard the news, she knew her evening's peace was over. It was her responsibility to find who had broken their laws. She needed to look through the veil again, so she lit a fire, set her altar and did a scrying ritual. The flames told her she needed to be among the masses tonight, so she'd hurriedly dressed and come to the gathering.

She recognized many of the faces in the crowd, though not as many could place her. She'd done a strong shielding spell with a cloaking element so she could walk among her kind relatively unseen. It wasn't like she was invisible, ghostly—far from it. The spell just worked to entice people to look away. She didn't need the attention.

There was the usual buzzing in the crowd, but it had spiked a fever tonight. Word was spreading about the multiple murders, that there was a satanic component. Everyone in the room knew that was a joke—Satan was a Christian deity, and none of them were practicing Christians. Wiccans, pagans, Goths, vampires—all coexisted in the harmony of the club. Satan was for those who didn't understand.

But when crimes like this happened, they all got a bad name. What small foothold they enjoyed in the community was immediately severed, and they had to hide again.

She secreted herself in the corner that afforded the best view and watched. The club was crawling with poseurs tonight, civilians who wanted to walk on the dark side for an evening. They were easy to spot, with their inexpertly applied makeup and ridiculous, darting eyes. They'd come in, dance for a song or two, shove each other around in embarrassment, then leave. The true followers would sigh in relief and go back to being themselves.

There.

At the center of the dance floor, two swayed in time to the music. A male and a female, young, but powerful. The moment she saw them her heart constricted. Divination was an elegant art, one best practiced by those with a true understanding of path work. She had the gift of understanding, was able to see into their minds. She felt the evil lurking there, and knew.

She stood, ready to approach, but halted when a small girl strode through the crowd, went directly to the male, pulled at his shoulder until he faced her, then slapped him, hard. His head snapped to the side and tears formed in his kohl-lined eyes. They started to argue, so she hung back to see what would happen. The boy looked startled for a moment, then shrugged. The interloper took off, tears running down her face. The tall girl put her hand on the boy's shoulder and they conversed, then followed the girl. As they left, the air in the club lightened. The music became louder, and the room felt happier.

What kind of baby bats were these three? Dominants, that was certain, possessing a darkness and authority unusual in ones so young.

She followed, building energy, cloak swinging out behind her. She'd need all of her extensive power to deal with them.

Eleven

Theo Howell's house was obviously the place to be.

It seemed like most of Hillsboro High School's senior class was in attendance, congregating at the Howell home. The street was lined with vehicles, Jettas and BMWs and Mercedes and Volvos and Jeeps parading up and down the skinny road with wheels half in the ditch and half on the scree. McKenzie's unmarked was parked across the street.

There was no loud music or yelling, though, just a somber grayness. The rain had started in earnest again and the lights of the Howells' house did little to illuminate their driveway. A dog began barking incessantly next door. Taylor felt each yap in the back of her skull.

Time to enter the land of text messaging. The door was red, with a bold brass lion-face knocker. Taylor grasped its protruding tongue and banged on the plate three times.

A handsome teenager opened the door, brown hair cut long over his forehead, wearing a Ralph Lauren button-down oxford cloth shirt and khaki trousers. His eyes were puffy, the trace of tears past shed. He gave her a sad smile, looking much older than his age.

"I'm Theo Howell. Please." He shook her hand and gestured for her to come in. Once she was in the foyer, he threw the dead bolt on the door.

A hush fell over the group of kids. Taylor was faced with a bevy of scared teenagers, all looking her over, and a few parents—she counted seven in all—drinking coffee in the living room. They stood when they saw her, faces bleak and scared.

She could hear the murmurs. *What's happened? Are there more?*

McKenzie extricated himself from the group of teenage girls that surrounded him in the kitchen, trying to comfort one another, and came into the foyer to greet them.

"Oh, good. You're here. You've met Theo, I see."

"Yes," Taylor said, turning back to the boy. "Thanks for keeping everyone here for us."

"You're welcome, ma'am. To be honest, I think everyone realized we could be safe if we had strength in numbers. It would be hard to get in here and take anyone down. A few kids' parents insisted they come home, and the rest just came on over. We were most appreciative that you sent Detective McKenzie to keep an eye out for us. Do you have any ideas who might have done this? Who killed our friends?"

The locked door. The air loaded with fright. The poor kids had been sitting here all night, friends dying a few streets away, worrying that they were being targeted, too. And the parents didn't know why, or how, or who had threatened their children's lives. Not that she blamed them. She'd been worried about them being targeted herself, but seeing their abject fear gave her a whole new perspective on this tragedy.

She faced the group and answered the unasked questions. "We're doing everything we can. Nothing has changed. We don't have a suspect or a motive just yet. You're doing the right thing, sticking together. We'll keep you posted."

The murmurs began again, this time tinged with relief. She stepped back into the foyer to get out of their line of sight, and turned to Theo.

"We're hoping you can shed some light on what's been happening. I know you were close friends with Xander Norwood. I'd like to talk to you about him, about everyone who was killed today. Is there someplace private we can go?"

"Yes, ma'am. My father's office is just through here. No one is allowed in there when we, I mean Daisy and I, have guests over."

"Who's Daisy?"

"My sister." He pointed to a neat blond girl sitting on a stool at the kitchen counter. "She's in there with some of her friends. She's a junior. They all knew Amanda, and Chelsea and Rachel."

There was a knock behind her and Theo started. Poor kid.

"That's going to be Detective Wade. McKenzie, do you have everyone's statements?"

"Nearly. A few more to go."

"Okay. Don't let me keep you. Marcus and I will talk with Theo."

"Gotcha, boss. I'll let him in."

"Detective, sir? Please lock the door behind you," Theo asked softly. McKenzie nodded at him. She was happy to see that McKenzie had established some rapport with these kids—it would help. In her experience, teenagers were a secretive lot.

Marcus joined her, and she introduced him to Theo. He shook Marcus's hand, then led them to a set of closed double doors. He fetched a key out of his front pocket, turned the lock and swung the right-hand door open. He allowed her to enter first, twisted his arm around the door frame to pull the chain on a floor lamp. The warm wooden space glowed in the soft light. The walls were lined with bookshelves, and a ladder on rails leaned against the far wall. It smelled pleasantly of paper and leather, without a hint of must.

Theo turned on a few more lights, then stood calmly by a large rosewood desk with a leather top. He saw Taylor looking at the books, waved nonchalantly toward the shelves.

"My father is a collector. He owns the Classics Bookstore in Franklin. He does some work with the public, but his passion, his occupation, is with serious collectors overseas. He's at a conference in Geneva right now. My mom's with him. They had their eyes on a first-edition Hemingway. They're supposed to be bidding on it at auction tonight. Dad thinks he can get it for a steal. He's got a client in Toronto willing to pay through the nose for it." He broke off. "I'm sorry, I must be boring you. I forget that not everyone is a bibliophile. I'm hoping to take the store over for him one day."

"Actually, that's not boring at all. I love books. And I'd love to hear more about what your dad does. I'm familiar with his store, actually. But that will have to wait for another time. Can we sit?"

There were two large leather chairs facing a cognac-colored sofa in the center of the room. Theo nodded, took a seat on the sofa. He hardly seemed like an eighteen-year-old whose best friend had just died. His presence was comforting her.

Marcus went to the bookcase, trailing his fingers along the spines, and Taylor arranged herself in one of the chairs with her notebook.

"So, Theo. Xander was your best friend. How many of the victims do you know personally?"

"From what I've heard about who was killed, all of them."

"Who have you heard about?"

"Jerry King, Ashley Norton, Mandy and Xander. Chelsea Mott and Rachel Welch were together too, and Brandon. I also heard a rumor that another girl was taken to the hospital."

"News travels fast. It's not a rumor. Do you know Brittany Carson?"

"Is that her name? No, I don't. Never heard of her."

"She attends St. Cecilia's. I was hoping she had some ties to your friends at Hillsboro."

"Well, you know how it is. The kids who live on either side of us go to private school, Montgomery Bell and Ensworth, but we don't hang out. It's the neighborhood dynamic, I guess."

"So how did you hear about the murders?"

He held up his cell. "Everyone's been talking. I've gotten nearly two hundred texts this afternoon. I'm way over my limit—my parents are going to kill me." He winced as soon as the words were out.

"Would you be willing to let me see your texts?" she asked.

He paused for the barest of moments. "They'll look like gibberish to you. I know my father absolutely hates it when I abbreviate, the language we use. He thinks it represents the decline of modern society. But the smart keyboard makes it so much easier to talk quickly."

"I can't say I disagree with your father there. My computer expert is pretty handy with all things technical. He should be able to translate for us. Tell me how you heard about Xander."

Theo squirmed in his seat. He'd paled when she mentioned Lincoln's expertise, and she knew he was hiding something.

"Theo?"

His eyes filled with tears. "I think I talked to him right before he died."

"You do? Why is that?"

Theo went from a prepossessed young man to a child in an instant, face screwed up in an attempt not to start weeping. She gave him a few breaths to get back under control.

"It's okay, Theo. We're just talking. You're not in trouble, not unless you had something to do with the murders."

"God, no. Of course I didn't. You can't actually think that."

"Then relax. I just want to know what happened this afternoon."

"Are you going to tell my parents what I say?"

"Are you eighteen?" He nodded. "Then so long as you haven't broken any laws, I see no need to divulge the information. Just tell me the truth, okay? We'll get along much better if you tell me the truth."

Theo looked miserable for a moment. "Ah, jeez. Okay, I'll tell you. But you have to swear not to tell anyone I did. Promise?"

"I'll do my best," she said.

"Okay. Xander…he and Mandy were partying this afternoon. So were Jerry and the girls. Of course, Chelsea and Rachel weren't exactly known for their restraint," he spit out.

"Partying?" Marcus asked.

"Drugs. Getting geared up for tonight, for the party."

"What kind of drugs?"

Theo stood and went to his father's desk. He flicked back the leather blotter and drew out another key. Taylor watched him, tense. She didn't like people going into locked drawers in her presence. But Marcus sidled behind Theo, and she relaxed a fraction.

Theo slid open the top drawer, pulled out a Ziploc baggie. It was full of pastel-blue and yellow pills the size of aspirin. There had to be a hundred, maybe a hundred fifty pills in the bag. He handed it to her gingerly.

"Holy mother…what is all this?" She saw the stamps, hearts, on some of the outward facing pills. Just like the ones they'd seen in Amanda Vanderwood's room. "Ecstasy?"

"Yeah." Theo sat on the sofa again, his head in his hands.

"Were you dealing it? Is that why you have so much?"

"No. God, no. I'm no dealer. That's everyone's."

"What do you mean, everyone's?"

Taylor sank back into the chair opposite Theo. He looked at her, gave her a half smile.

"Jeez, I'm gonna get creamed for this."

"Start talking, Mr. Howell."

Now that he'd made up his mind to cooperate, the words flowed easily. "It's all from Vi-Fri. Vicodin Fridays. Every Friday the kids who party get their drugs, usually on the bus on the way home or in our lockers after sixth period. We never know what it's going to be, it's kinda like a lottery. The first time it was Vicodin—that's where the name came from. But it can be anything—mushrooms, X, oxy, Valium, meth, coke, even. Whatever he's got to sell. You can't tell our parents. They'll never understand."

Taylor couldn't believe she was hearing this. Not that there was a bunch of high school idiots doing drugs— cocaine had been the drug of choice when she was in high school. With affluent parents and heavy allowances, it was always readily available. But the fact that a group was taking whatever they could get their hands on, that's what surprised her.

"Who is the dealer?"

"This punk-ass underclassman. I don't know his real name. He calls himself something stupid, like out of a comic book. Starts with a T. Thor, I think. He started at Hillsboro this year—word got out he was dealing his second week. He's got good shit, clean and cheap. Everyone buys from him."

"Who might know his real name?"

"Honestly? I have no idea. Some of the younger kids might. But they're not here. We were just supposed to be juniors and seniors tonight, maybe the odd sophomore. This kid is a freshman, and I've tried to keep myself away from it. I'm not a big fan of Vi-Fri."

Taylor shook the plastic bag. "Would you be able to identify him if we showed you pictures? Or would he be in the yearbook?"

"He wouldn't be in it yet. I'm on the yearbook staff, and we haven't gotten the class pictures yet. I won't have any way to know if his was in it or not until next semester when the company that does the portraits sends us the proofs. Besides, half the people don't show for their pictures. Yearbook is considered passé."

"What's he look like?"

"Short. Blond hair. He hangs with the Goth kids."

"So let me get this straight. Did you take this bag off the dealer?"

"No. See, I was talking to Xander. He said he and Mandy were going to do a couple of hits early, fool around before the party. They'd be over after so we could all get ready. We got off the phone and I started getting things set up. Then my sister, Daisy, got a text from Letha King. Jerry's sister."

"We met her at the Kings' house this afternoon."

"Well, Letha said she'd come home and Jerry was passed out in his room, was blue. He had some sort of wound in his stomach. She didn't know what to do. So we went over there—"

Marcus leaned forward in his chair, jumped in. "You were at the Kings' house this afternoon?"

"Just for a few minutes."

"Oh, Lord," Taylor groaned. "Who else was there? And what did you touch?"

"Nothing. It was just me and Daisy and Letha, I swear. Letha was totally freaking out. I looked at Jerry, I didn't touch him. He had that crazy star carved in his stomach, he looked totally dead. It looked like he'd OD'd. I told her to call 911 and we hightailed it out of there. I started calling around to everyone, told them not to take their X."

"What time was this?" Taylor asked.

"Probably around three. Let me look, I can tell you exactly when she sent the text." He fiddled with his phone. "Two-fifty. I called Xander, but he didn't answer. Letha let Daisy know the cops had shown up, and everyone started filing in over here. They brought their stash, and I put it all together."

"You showed quite a clear head, Theo."

"Yeah, well. I don't know what the fuck—pardon, ma'am—what the hell happened. That carving in Jerry's stomach freaked me out."

Marcus took the Ziploc bag, turned it over and over in his hands. The pills inside clinked together softly. Still playing with the bag, he raised his eyebrow and spoke.

"Theo, there's more, isn't there? You can tell us. You've told us almost everything anyway. We understand what you were doing, and I have to tell you, man, I'm damn impressed. You showed a great deal of maturity and bravery here today. But there's something you aren't sharing with us."

He shook his head, eyes miserable. "I don't know what you mean. I've told you everything I know."

"No, you haven't. You automatically assumed the Ecstasy was the culprit, that the kids who were murdered had taken it. You said you thought Jerry had OD'd. Why would you draw that conclusion?"

Theo scuffed his foot into the deep burgundy Aubusson rug. He was wearing Doc Marten boots, which didn't quite fit with his preppy exterior. They let him have a moment. There were answers to be found here.

Theo cleared his throat, but the words came out in a whisper.

"We might have heard that someone was planning to screw with us."

"Screw with who?"

Theo rounded his hand in a circle. "Us. The jocks. The cool kids. The popular ones. Whatever ridiculous cliché you want to call us. We were the target, and whoever did this got us good."

"Who made the threats?"

"I don't know. But look around you. Whoever it was managed to take out two cheerleaders, the captain of the wrestling team and four members of the student council. I don't know who this last chick was, but she probably had an in with us somewhere. If Daisy and I hadn't gotten the word out, who knows how many more of us would have died?"

"You're sure this wasn't some sort of prearranged event?"

"You mean like Jonestown? Or Heaven's Gate? I hardly imagine revolutionary suicide has found its way into Hillsboro." At her incredulous look, he explained. "I did a paper on cults for history last year. My dad's interested in that kind of stuff."

"Okay. Yes, that's exactly what I'm wondering about."

"I can't see it. No one from this crowd was into anything more than the occasional good time, if you know what I mean."

"Do you think someone you went to school with would be capable of killing?" Marcus asked.

"I don't know. Honestly, I don't know."

"Could it have been this dealer you're talking about?"

The kid was getting frustrated now—small lines appeared in his forehead. "I swear to you, I don't know who was behind it. It was one of those vague rumors that floats around. I don't know where he gets his drugs, but he's always got a ready supply. Whoever he buys from could be involved, too."

"So why the pentacles carved into their stomachs? Do you know anything about that?"

He looked up, startled. "It was more than just Jerry?"

Taylor nodded. "Yes. All the victims had been cut perimortem. That means at the time of death."

"I *know.* I watch *Forensic Files,*" he said with such disdain she nearly laughed aloud. The DNA generation. Taylor saw it more and more lately, people who watched *CSI* and *Law & Order* and thought they were experts on crime. It was damned inconvenient—the prosecutors had the worst of it. Every jury seemed to think that DNA was the magic bullet, the only way to acquit or convict and still sleep at night.

"Sorry," Theo said. "I'm just a little stressed. I assume you're going to arrest me now?"

"Because of the drugs?"

"Yes," he said, squaring his shoulders. He stood up straight and put his hands together in front of him so she could cuff him.

Taylor looked him deep in the eye, and he bravely took her gaze. She could see his lower lip trembling just the tiniest bit.

"Right now, Theo, you're more of a help than a threat. Would you be willing to come down and make a formal statement? Maybe look at some pictures, see if you can pick the dealer out for us?"

"You're not going to arrest me?"

"Not at the moment, no."

"Oh, thank God." He dropped his hands to his side. "Yes, of course. I'll do anything you need."

"Okay, then. I can't promise that you won't have some sort of charges filed against you eventually, but I'll do everything I can to make sure there are mitigating circumstances. What I really need is for you to get some information on who might have threatened your clique. Think you could do that for me?"

The proud man inside him finally deflated completely, and he looked young, vulnerable. She could see the child peeking out behind the face of the man he'd become today.

"Yes, ma'am. I'll do whatever you need me to. Thank you, ma'am."

Taylor sent Theo back out to the crowd, shut the door behind him. She sat back in the chair and sighed deeply.

"Do you believe him?" she asked Marcus.

"I want to say yes, but I'd have to talk with him some more. He's scared, scared enough that he's willing to face charges to get to the bottom of this. Of course, he also placed the blame squarely on an unidentified person, someone we can't touch. We have to get the drugs tested—he might have saved a number of lives today."

"Or he's our dealer and he's covering his ass. A prepossessed young man, Mr. Howell." She took the plastic bag from Marcus. "I need to get these taken into evidence and to the lab. Tim Davis can do a workup for us pretty quickly, see if there's anything in these pills that might have caused an OD in those kids. But who went behind and carved the pentacles in their stomachs? What the hell was that about?"

"That's one question. But there's another, I think. How would the killer know which kids had taken the drugs and which hadn't?"

She stood up. "That's what I was wondering. I'm getting more and more convinced that our suspect knows these kids very well. Let's get these pills to Tim, then see where we stand."

They found McKenzie and stepped out onto the front porch to compare notes.

"What did you hear from the kids? Anything that will help?" Taylor asked.

McKenzie nodded. "The girls, Chelsea and Rachel? Supposedly they were feuding—the general consensus was complete surprise that they'd been found together."

"Teenage girls," Taylor said, shaking her head. "They fight and make up, fight and make up. That's why I always preferred being friends with boys. You always knew where you stood."

McKenzie's eyes twinkled at her. "Yeah, I know what you mean. Anyway, that's what I'm hearing. They were best friends, did most everything together when they weren't fighting. Other than the most recent spat, they were a close-knit group—Rachel, Chelsea and Ashley Norton. Tight as ticks. They all know Brandon Scott and Jerry King. Xander Norwood seems to have been the de facto leader of the cool kids, the one everyone wanted to be friends with. You can tell who was close to him and who wanted to be, but everyone loved him. I doubt our suspect felt the same, of course."

"Theo Howell mentioned a threat against the group. Did anyone else mention that?" Taylor asked.

"Just Daisy Howell," McKenzie answered. "She's too upset to make much sense—she was friends with all the girls, as well. She said there'd been a rumor floating around that something was coming, just underground rumblings. No one really took it seriously. It's high school. There's always some sort of drama going on. If it doesn't affect them directly, they ignore it."

"Good work, guys. We need to finish interviewing the victims' families, see if we can piece together a timeline for these kids once they left school at noon today. See who they came into contact with, either on their way home or once they arrived. Crime Scene's been taking evidence from all the scenes, and there's plenty to keep us busy. Let's get to it."

Twelve

Raven chased after Ember. She darted out the club doors onto Second Avenue, moving nimbly through the crowds. Fane rushed alongside him, cursing under her breath.

"Ember, wait. Wait, damn it. Quit being so damn wangsty!"

Ember glanced back over her shoulder, pure fury on her face, lips moving rapidly. Raven felt the spell she cast hit him like a wall of bricks. Damn, that girl was getting good at shielding. But he was better. He tuned out all the other surrounding noise, thoughts, emotions, fears and read her. Even on the go like this, he could drowse, listen to her thoughts. His extensive practice was paying off. After working and loving together for so long, they were attuned, like a stereophonic radio station. He could dial into her mind with ease now.

He felt her as they moved away from the crowds, down by the river. She was furious, he could sense that. And scared.

Riverfront Park was dark tonight, people milling about, the homeless reveling in the crowds. A row of mounted patrol, their horses' flanks weary with inactivity, were on duty at the bridge to the Titans' stadium, keeping people somewhat under control.

Ember scooted down to the log fort astride the Cumberland River—the first structure in Nashville, built back when the city was still called Nashboro and the insurgent Cherokee fought the newly arrived settlers for their land. The original structure dated to 1779; a perfect replica had been painstakingly built in 1962. It was supposed to be locked after hours, but Raven had found a way in, and assumed Ember was heading there. They'd practiced down here last month, when they needed the full moon's glow off the river for a spell's efficacy.

Ember slipped through the loose boards on the edge of the fort. Raven and Fane followed her in.

Though light shimmered above them, the inside of the structure was dark, cool. Raven felt Fane shiver next to him, drew her close for a moment to warm her. The minute he let his mind move toward Fane, the connection with Ember was broken. He heard movement in the black, then the world exploded into a million colors. He fell to the ground, hands on his crotch.

He heard a low moaning, didn't realize it was coming from his own throat. Pressure at his back now, Fane hissing like a furious cat.

"Christ, Ember. Did you really need to knee him in the balls? Grow up, why don't you? Hurting Raven isn't going to fix the situation. You've been all Gothier-than-thou the past couple of weeks anyway. What's your fucking problem?"

She knelt next to Raven, pulled his head into her lap. Ember appeared in the edge of his peripheral vision, swimming in and out of focus. She'd dropped her shield, was sending off powerful negativity, sharp as knives.

Fane brushed a lock of black hair off Raven's forehead. "It wasn't Raven's fault. Your stupid brother couldn't keep his hands off perfect little Mandy. Xander went over there to fuck her. How were we supposed to know she'd share her stash with him? I thought you said he didn't do X."

Ember came right to Fane's face, words biting through her gritted teeth. "He doesn't. And that's not what happened—you know it isn't. He was there when you arrived, and you forced him. You killed him. And then you cut him up like all the rest. How could you? How could you? He's my brother! And you two are out celebrating. I can't believe you'd do this to me. To us!"

Raven was still nonsensical. Damn, that hurt. Fane shifted him to the right, and some of the pressure started to leak away.

"Ember, you have to get a grip. Right now. Where's Thorn?"

The smaller girl shuffled her feet uncertainly. "I have no idea."

"What do you mean, you have no idea?"

"He was supposed to sneak into my house. My parents took off and went to Mandy's when they heard. I called him and he never answered."

Raven was finally starting to feel better. At least, he didn't think he was going to throw up anymore. He struggled into a sitting position, leaning on Fane for support. His voice was laced with pain, but the authority was there.

"Ember. How did you get downtown if Thorn didn't bring you?"

"I took the bus. There were plenty of people headed down—I blended right in."

"Where are your parents now?"

"I don't know. I split when they did."

"We need to get you home. They're going to notice you're gone and get worried. You weren't supposed to leave until they went to sleep."

"In case you forgot, you murdered my brother tonight, you stupid prick. I doubt they're going to be doing much sleeping. I fixed my bed, my room. They won't look. They never do."

"You need to go home."

"Fuck that, Raven. I don't have to do everything you command. I want to know why you included Xander in your plan."

Raven's fury started to build in turn. He forgot the soreness in his groin, stood so he towered over Ember. He grabbed her by the upper shoulders and gave her a powerful shake, the anger boiling in his gut. "I told you. I had no control over that. He's the one that was there. He's the one who interjected himself into the plan. Get off my back, now, or there *will* be consequences. Do you understand?"

She didn't respond.

"Do you understand?" he roared.

Ember was silent for a moment, pulled away from his grasp. He let her go. She turned her back. He could see her breathing deeply, felt a calm steal over them. Good. He had her back. Losing control of his coven could be disastrous, especially now.

He turned to Fane, seeking her eyes in the gloom. She glowed in the darkness, and he saw her teeth flash in a smile. He answered with his own, reset his center and turned back to Ember.

"Ember, I'm sorry. I didn't know you would be this upset. It was unavoidable. And we need to go now, before someone hears us fighting."

Ember's shoulders began to shake. She whirled back around and snarled at Raven, sharp little teeth bared.

"I don't believe you. I think you murdered Xander because you wanted to, not by accident. Do you hear me, you freak? I think you did it on purpose. And I won't let you get away with it, Raven. I break with you and Fane. I break with you. I break with you."

She darted out into the night, her sobs trailing behind her.

Waning Crescent Moon
Twenty-five Percent of Full
Hallowmas
(All Saints' Day)

Thirteen

"Hey, Reever, it's Baldwin. Again. I'm here waiting for you. Where are you, buddy? Don't really want to go into this hearing without you. Call me, okay?"

Baldwin hung up and stashed his phone in his pocket. He should have just defended himself. He was licensed to practice in Virginia, had passed the bar there years ago. He'd gotten his J.D. at George Washington. Of course, that's what led him directly to the FBI, and Garrett Woods. Maybe if he hadn't wanted to be a medical ethicist, he wouldn't be in this situation now.

He could call Taylor. She'd certainly be sympathetic, take his mind off the situation. But she was knee-deep in her own murder investigation. He decided not to bother her. Too many bad memories were going to get dredged up— just having Taylor in his head would sully her.

How did it all end up here? All the years he spent working so hard to protect the innocent, to help his fellow law enforcement officers, to make a name in the FBI, to recover from his own personal trauma…was it all going to be for naught? Would he be summarily thrown out of his position at the FBI? It would be ironic, considering how reluctant he'd been to return to the unit full-time.

Baldwin began to pace, wondering where in the hell his lawyer was. He looked at his watch. The hearing was supposed to start in less than five minutes, and Reever still hadn't shown. He flipped open his phone to call, again, but heard a flurry in the hallway. Reginald Harold Beauchamp, known as Reever to his friends and clients, came bustling around the corner.

"Sorry, sorry, sorry. The third kid barfed on me as I was kissing her goodbye. I had to change, then I got stuck behind a tractor, and then I got waylaid by a train. This has not been my morning. Sorry."

He skidded to a halt and stuck out his hand.

"How ya doing, Baldwin?"

"Better, now that you're finally here. I thought I was going to have to dust off my license."

"Ha-ha. Like that would ever happen. I wouldn't desert you in your hour of need." Reever tugged his arm, pulled him away from the wall. They walked a few steps together, heads bent conspiratorially. Baldwin smelled a variety of odors coming off of his lawyer, baby shit mingled with a subtle splash of cologne, sweat and an underlying note of sour milk. Great. That was going to be fun to sit next to all day.

"I've seen the charges, and it's gonna be fine."

"So says you. I'm screwed, aren't I?" Baldwin asked.

Reever's brown eyes were full of concern. "Listen, Doc, I promise you, this is all just a formality. There's no real danger to your career. They're going to make you squirm, and make you admit how sorry you are. Probably throw a suspension at you, something temporary. Then we'll all go back to work happy. Okay? In and out, lickety-split." He snapped his fingers.

"Yeah. Got it," Baldwin said, not believing a word.

Reever was infamous for his pep talks, but the FBI didn't convene disciplinary hearings for their good health.

Baldwin heard shuffling inside the corridor, and a door opened. A man he didn't recognize said, "We're ready for you, Dr. Baldwin."

Reever clapped him on the back. "Let's do it."

He hid an overwhelming sigh, straightened his back and, eyes ahead, marched into the room. His heart was pounding harder than it should. *Stop it, Baldwin. You knew this would come up sooner or later. There's nothing to hide. You didn't do anything wrong. Not completely wrong, at least.*

The room they entered was empty, devoid of personality, decorated only with FBI and American flags on golden stands, the oversize FBI seal framing the back wall, and a large picture of the president next to a photograph of the director himself. There was a wooden dais—similar to a small-scale Senate hearing room, all American oak-and-brass fixtures. Three men were waiting for them, their faces stern and forbidding, facing a table with two microphones. A clerk sat to one side, fingers poised over a stenotype machine. Just a subtle reminder that this hearing was on the record—the transcripts would be in his personnel jacket for life.

He got settled at the table, Reever at his side, pulling out pads of paper for them both, pens, basically making a show of it. Baldwin didn't know whether to laugh or scream. Reever was one of the best counsels in the FBI, and a good friend. Baldwin was very happy to have him on his side, helping him through this hearing. The fumbling around was a ploy, something to disarm the men sitting in judgment upon them. They all knew the farce for what it was. After an interminable few minutes, Reever nodded toward the dais.

"We're ready," he said, his dirty-blond hair falling into his eyes. He shoved it back and grinned.

"At last." The man at the center of the dais, Supervisory

Special Agent Perry Tucker, motioned to the clerk, who began typing.

"Dr. Baldwin, please raise your right hand. Do you swear that your forthcoming testimony will be the truth, the whole truth and nothing but the truth?"

"Yes, I do." Baldwin didn't shift, kept his eyes focused straight ahead. The disciplinary procedures at the FBI had been recently scrutinized and revamped to make sure the higher-level executives and the lower-level workers all got a fair shake. Which meant your peers decided your fate, and the executives and SES-level agents were taking it on the nose in an attempt to show how impartial everything was.

All employees of the FBI, agents at every level, were required to serve their time on the disciplinary committee in six-month shifts. Baldwin had sat on the board just last year, and he knew this was far beyond a fact-finding mission. The committee had the power to chastise, censure and otherwise make an agent's life miserable, but it took seriously egregious actions to be stripped. He hadn't done anything that warranted losing his status as an agent, not yet. Not that they knew about, at least.

Regardless, the pallor of suspicion hung expectantly in the room. It was going to be a rough couple of days.

Tucker's chair squeaked in protest as he leaned back and rocked, staring Baldwin down. After a few moments of silence, he leaned forward, steepled his fingers against his chin and looked over his tortoiseshell reading glasses like a principal disappointed with the school quarterback.

"As you are aware, we are here to determine the truth in the matter of *U.S. versus Harold Arlen.* As a result of new information that has come to our attention, there have been allegations of wrongdoing specific to your involvement in this case. The charges filed include falsifying evidence, neglect, and involuntary manslaughter, conduct unbecoming an agent with the Federal Bureau of Investigation and fraternization with a subordinate. The charges have been leveled by former Special Agent Charlotte Douglas, who is sadly not with us to lay claim to her indictment. Her computer, as you know, has been the source of a great deal of information on the Arlen case. The accusations of misconduct were included in her copious notes.

"The main focus of our hearing today is to determine your culpability in the deaths of Agents Caleb Geroux, Jessamine Sparrow and Olen Butler. According to the files, Agent Douglas made it clear that their deaths were the direct result of your actions during the Arlen case. The panel takes these charges very seriously."

Baldwin was about to say something, anything, to defend himself, but Reever came to life. "We take these accusations very seriously, as well. We all know what kind of agent Charlotte Douglas was, sir. She was a liar on her best days, and made a mockery of this entire department. We can't trust that anything she claims has any validity. And may I say, for the record, that any charges of wrongdoing against my client are ridiculous. Dr. Baldwin is one of the most decorated agents in the Bureau. His character is above reproach, and we have a multitude of witnesses willing to testify on his behalf."

Tucker harrumphed, and the other two judges shifted in their chairs. Everyone knew that this was highly unusual. Charlotte Douglas wasn't exactly a trustworthy source. Baldwin felt some semblance of calm steal into him; while Tucker looked hell-bent on his destruction, the other two were obviously uncomfortable. A dead agent didn't make a very good witness, especially when her record was as sullied as Special Agent Douglas's.

"Be that as it may, we have to look at the entire case. Charges of this magnitude cannot go without scrutiny." He shuffled his papers. "Dr. Baldwin. Since this matter is one of the highest delicacy, I think it would be best for you to start at the beginning, and walk us through the details of the case. Let me caution you—spare nothing. We will know if you're obfuscating. If you'd please start by answering this question. What exactly was your relationship with Dr. Douglas?"

Baldwin couldn't help himself, his jaw clenched and his fists tightened. Just the mention of Charlotte could do that to him. Lying, conniving bitch that she was, this last echo from the grave was the ultimate slap in the face.

He cleared his throat, and glanced at his notes. Not for the first time, he was glad of his attentiveness to detail.

"We were…close."

There weren't many shocked faces on the panel—this wasn't the first time two agents had gotten together.

The inquisitor raised an eyebrow, made a note on the sheet in front of him and continued.

"'Close.' Could you expand on that, please?"

Reever nodded at Baldwin, his head moving almost imperceptibly.

Expand on that. Sure he could. He could give them gritty details all day long, but he wouldn't. Instead, he referred to his notes, straightened his shoulders and cleared his throat.

"It started on June 14, 2004. The day the fifth body was found."

Fourteen

Dawn had passed and Taylor's stomach was growling viciously before she'd finished taking statements from all the victims' families. She was exhausted, and most of her questions remained unanswered. The facts were straightforward—someone had slipped into the home of each victim and marked their flesh. Each victim had ingested some sort of poison.

The one exception was Brandon Scott.

She and McKenzie were loading up on coffee at the Starbucks on West End. There was no sense in sleeping. Taylor knew Sam was going to be at it bright and early—she had seven autopsies today, and her team had worked through the night. So far the last victim, Brittany Carson, had been holding her own, though she was in a deep coma.

Tim Davis had stayed up all night running tests on the Ecstasy tablets Theo Howell had provided them. Theo's theory was wrong—the drugs he had collected weren't laced. Which meant the victims weren't random, proving Taylor's initial theory.

Preliminary toxicology reports showed a mishmash of chemical components: Ecstasy combined with high doses of PMA, codeine, Ritalin and Valium. Apart, none of the drugs were immediately fatal. Together, the combination was overwhelmingly deadly. There were many more tests to be run, and the results combined with autopsy would help define exactly what effect the drugs had on the children's systems.

Lincoln had been running through video feeds, looking for familiar or repeat faces. He had one, and he was waiting at the CJC for Taylor to look it over.

Marcus and McKenzie had taken statements from every kid at the party, all of whom had been honest and open about the events of the afternoon. They'd had the fear of God put into them, without a doubt. They weren't aware that the pills they had turned over to Theo Howell weren't deadly. As far as they knew, if they hadn't checked their text messages, had turned off their phones, gone to a movie, anything—any little tiny thing—might have sent them to their deaths. Mortality weighed heavily on the young—the entire school was deep in mourning. Worry, relief and extreme pain had caused all of them to come together. Taylor could only hope they'd had their fill of messing around with drugs.

Hillsboro High School was expecting them at 10:00 a.m. to discuss possible suspects among the students. Taylor had talked to the principal at three in the morning—she had grief counselors ready to be unleashed on the school. There was talk of canceling classes on Monday, but Taylor had advised against it. Normalcy was best. Plus, she would be able to walk the halls, talk to some other people, see if they could find out who this kid dealer might be, assuming he really was a Hillsboro student. No one at the party last night knew his real name.

Taylor needed a few minutes to regroup. She drank deeply from her triple-shot latte, hoping for strength from the meager caffeine the espresso beans provided. She probably should have gone with black coffee, but her stomach wouldn't stand for that. She nibbled on a piece of lemon pound cake, realized she hadn't eaten the evening before. She was suddenly ravenously hungry and ate the rest of the cake in three bites.

McKenzie joined her, crashing in the chair next to hers. He had dark circles under his eyes, his sandy hair in total disarray. She could only imagine what she looked like.

"We've made serious progress, you know that," McKenzie said.

"I do. Still, we need a quick solve on this. Tell me what else you're thinking about this mysterious drug dealer before we jump back into the fray."

"Well, I hardly think a fourteen-year-old is running a drug cartel through Nashville. You should put the word out through the Specialized Investigative Unit, see who's selling to him. He's being run by someone on the outside."

"Three steps ahead of you. I've already called my friend there. Lincoln said the same guy was on video at four of the crime scenes, and at the press conference, lingering in the background. He's trying to match it to people in the databases, sex offenders and the like."

"I think the sex offender route is a solid one. Whoever's behind the drugs is an adult. Who else would be able to get that quantity and quality of drugs into the school? And we all know how much our friendly neighborhood pedophiles like to peddle drugs to their innocent prey."

"That expands our suspect pool exponentially, you know that."

"Yes, I do. Are you ready? Why don't we go take a look at those tapes."

They gathered up their cups and coats. They'd just reached the parking lot when Taylor's phone rang. The caller ID read Tennessean. A reporter, no doubt. She let it go to voice mail. They got into her Lumina—she'd never made it back to headquarters to retrieve her 4Runner the night before.

She turned right on West End, past the stunning foliage

of Vanderbilt's campus. Fall had come late this year, the colors not reaching their peak until the last week of October. There were still plenty of leaves on the trees, but the reds and golds were starting to be muddled by dead, brown chunks. Soon it would be time to hire one of the neighborhood boys to collect and bag leaves, get their lawn ready for winter. My God, had she really just had that thought? Eight victims, all kids, and she was worried about the grass. Something was wrong with her.

Her phone rang again. This time it was Commander Huston.

"Morning, ma'am," Taylor answered.

"Lieutenant, David Greenleaf is trying to reach you."

Crap. So that was the phone call. She played dumb.

"The editor of *The Tennessean?* Why?"

"You need to go over there right now. I'm sending Tim Davis along, as well. They have a possible piece of evidence that pertains to your cases."

"You're kidding. What is it?"

"A letter about the murders, apparently. You know they're good at sussing out the real from the fake. Greenleaf called me directly, said he'd tried you but you didn't answer. He didn't tell me what it said, just that they were in possession of a letter that seemed credible, and they thought an evidence technician would be a good idea."

"That's interesting. Yes, I just got the call. I figured it was just another reporter. My apologies."

"No matter, I wouldn't have answered it myself."

Taylor smiled. One of the things she especially liked about Joan Huston was her inability to mince words.

"I'll head over there right now. Thanks for letting me know."

"Check in with me when you get in the building."

"Yes, ma'am." She clicked off, looked over at McKenzie.

"*The Tennessean* has a letter that pertains to the case. We need to go there first."

She was just crossing the interstate; *The Tennessean*

building was on her left. She turned left into the parking lot and took the last space, sandwiching the Lumina into one of the too-small spots. The paper's parking left a lot to be desired.

She and McKenzie walked in, gave their names to the security desk and waited. The lobby had changed dramatically since the last time she'd been forced to make a visit, to tell then Managing Editor David Greenleaf his good friend Frank Richardson had been murdered.

Greenleaf himself came through the locked door off the lobby. They shook hands awkwardly, and Taylor introduced McKenzie. *The Tennessean* had dined out for weeks on her fall from grace, and she still smarted from the drubbing. But they'd been trying to make amends, had done a positive piece on her ascension back to the head of Homicide just a few days earlier. She couldn't blame them too much—they were in the business of news, and unfortunately she had been the lead story.

Greenleaf waved them into the hallway. He talked as they walked.

"How are you, Lieutenant?"

"Good, David. What's been going on here?"

"Oh, you know. Buyouts and layoffs. This building can be like a ghost town sometimes. Whoops, here we are."

He led them into a conference room, where two people were standing with their backs to the door, staring at a single sheet of paper lying on the table.

"Lieutenant, you remember Daphne Beauchamp? She's our head archivist now, runs the morgue. And this is George Rodríguez, our head of security."

Taylor did remember Daphne, with her funky glasses and her quiet strength. She'd been an intern in the archives when they'd first met, peripheral to a case. Her roommate had been kidnapped and held by the Snow White Killer, had barely escaped with her life. She was also quietly dating Marcus Wade, but Taylor knew they were keeping the seriousness of their relationship under wraps from both their employers.

"Daphne, good to see you again. Have you heard from Jane Macias recently?"

"You don't read the *New York Times,* do you, Lieutenant? Jane's making a name for herself as an investigative journalist. She's halfway to a Pulitzer by now. Detective McKenzie." She shook his hand gravely. "I found the letter this morning when I came in. It was on the floor near the back door, the Porter Street entrance."

Daphne had grown up a bit, the last vestiges of college coed replaced by a calm assurance. Close contact with violent crime did that to a person.

Taylor turned to the head of security, a short, stocky Hispanic man with eyes as black as jet. "Mr. Rodríguez. I'm Lieutenant Jackson. This is Detective Renn McKenzie. Perhaps you could pull the security tapes from the back lobby for us, see if we can identify who might have dropped the letter off."

"Call me George. I've already got them queued, but I can't see anything amiss. There's the usual mishmash of people coming in and out of that back entrance. The camera faces the street, and I didn't see anyone out of place. It's entirely possible someone ducked under the camera and slipped it through the door."

"Isn't there security at that entrance?"

"There's a security booth, yes. But it was unmanned. Cutbacks, you know."

"We'll look at it more closely. Thanks for getting things set for us." Taylor pulled a set of nitrile gloves out of her jacket pocket, snapped them on. "This is the letter?"

Greenleaf nodded. "Yes. I knew you needed to see it. I trust you'll let us print this. I have a right to tell this story."

She ignored the last question. "Who all's touched it?"

"Security, Daphne, my assistant, too. It was addressed to me, so Daphne dropped it after she came in. My assistant opened it, saw what it was and set it on her desk. After that, no one. We used another sheet of paper to bring it in here for you."

"Okay. I've got a crime-scene tech on his way over. He'll need to take fingerprints for exclusion. Thanks for being so cautious—that helps." She only had one more glove in her pocket—it was time to stock up. She handed it to McKenzie, then stepped closer.

The letter was typed, on regular white paper. What she read took her breath away.

October 31, 2010

The Tennessean
David Greenleaf, Editor
1100 Broadway
Nashville, Tennessee 37203

Dear Mr. Greenleaf,

You can't possibly begin to understand the impetus of this letter, so we would advise against trying. We're sure that you will feel that our actions, while difficult, were purely motivated and absolutely justified.

We are responsible for the murders. We are not sorry, they were horrible people who needed to be cleansed from this earth. We need to tell you why we came to this decision. Why we felt compelled to end their suffering. We have found the one true path. We had to show them the way. They hurt us. Over and over and over, they hurt us, and humiliated us.

We sought only to release them from their dreary existence, to lead them unknowing out of their cave and school them in the bright, harsh light of the world's realities, showing the underlying truth to their very existence. We are goodness and light, temperance and justice, sophists, skeptics, purveyors of platonic love. Ideal beauty and absolute goodness. We are truth. We are their deliverance. We are the sun, essential to the creation and sustaining life of their world. We guide the archangel into their corporeal bodies, fight to pilot their souls to the radiance, where together, as one, we can achieve the ultimate bliss.

But words are not enough to satisfy our meaning. The best way to explain ourselves is through the medium of film. We have included a Web site address which has a movie of yesterday's events. We would greatly appreciate you sharing this with your staff and helping us place it in the hands of a producer who can bring it to the big screen.

The Immortals

Φ ✪ ▽ ☾ ✶ ◯ ✚ ℅

Blood is intensity; it is all I can give you.
http://www.youtube.wearetheimmortals.com

The row of symbols was smeared, the edges ragged, the ink suspiciously crackly and imperfect, ranging from dark pink to deepest burgundy.

"Son of a bitch. Is that blood?" Taylor asked.

McKenzie stooped over the letter, looking closely. "Looks like it. Tim will have to do a presumptive test."

"What's the black underneath?"

"There are words handwritten under the symbols." "Can you make it out?"

"I think so." He picked up the letter, moving it back and forth in the light. "It looks like it reads, 'Blood is intensity, it is all I can give you.'"

"What the hell does that mean?"

He met her eyes. "I have no idea."

She turned to Greenleaf. "We need a computer. I want to see this 'movie' they're talking about. Have you watched it?"

"Just the beginning. I…I couldn't go any further."

Greenleaf blanched, and she felt the dread building in her stomach.

It only took Greenleaf a few minutes to get them ready—he'd been anticipating their desire to see the Web site immediately. Daphne had a laptop already tied into the high-definition screen that was used for presentations. She dimmed the lights a bit, apologizing—the screen showed up better in the dark.

Taylor shook her head. What now?

She could see that the video lasted twenty minutes, and didn't want to imagine what might be contained in that time period.

The film began in darkness, a pinpoint of light in the center growing larger and larger until they could clearly see it was a full moon. A deep voice narrated, one that sounded familiar, but Taylor couldn't place it. The words were a jumble, overwrought with purple prose, but their message was clear. The vampires were recreating their race from the nonbelievers. It reminded Taylor of any number of ads for horror films she'd seen over the years—films she would never, ever watch. She lived horror every day, had her own nightmares. She certainly didn't need someone else's twisted imagination inside her own head.

The narration ceased, silence crowding through the speakers. The distinct sounds of footsteps grew louder as the shot came into focus. She recognized the scene—it was filmed from the front lawn of the Kings' house.

"Fast-forward," she said.

"It will take a minute. The upload isn't done yet." Daphne fiddled with the controls, tried sliding the play bar forward, but it wouldn't move. "We just have to wait for it to load all the way."

It didn't take long. The next scene flashed up, and Taylor leaned forward in her chair. It was a long shot of the hall leading to Jerrold King's bedroom. Taylor sucked in her breath as a hand appeared in the frame, pushing open the boy's bedroom door. King's body was spread-eagled on the bed, naked. The camera never panned to his face, just showed the long shot, then his torso. He appeared dead.

The disembodied hand disappeared, then came back into the frame with a long, wicked, gleaming knife. Taylor forced herself to watch as the knife got closer to Jerrold's body, and the tip pierced the boy's flesh, loving, gentle, then whipped into slashes and circles, the pentacle appearing in a blur of motion. The wound oozed, but didn't bleed freely—Jerrold was newly dead, but dead for all that.

The scene cut to an open mouth. A high-pitched laugh, disembodied and androgynous, filled the frame. The camera pulled back slightly, enough to allow a vision to appear, a specter in black, unidentifiable but with black hair. The camera zoomed onto its chin, then did a close-up on the mouth, black-stained lips drawn back in a grin, as sharp, pointed fangs drew closer to Jerrold's stomach. A pointed tongue flicked out of the mouth into the fresh wound, lapped up a bit of Jerrold's blood. The lips tainted red, and were licked suggestively. Taylor noted absently that they looked chapped.

"Jesus," McKenzie muttered.

"Stop it there," Taylor said. Daphne clicked the pause button.

Taylor stood, hoping that movement would settle her stomach. She flipped open her cell phone, called Forensic Medical. Kris, the receptionist, answered. Taylor asked to speak with Sam.

A few moments later, the phone clicked and Sam came on the line.

"I'm glad I caught you. Have you started the post on Jerrold King?"

"I'm about to. Stuart's working the prelims now."

"Catch him, quick. We might have the killer's DNA on King's body."

Fifteen

They watched the rest of the film in horrified silence. The tableau was repeated three more times—the vampire arriving at the scene, carving open the flesh of the dead. The dancing figure in black, fangs and lips growing bloody again and again. The only reason she recognized the bodies was because she'd been at each scene. The killer had been very careful not to show the victims' faces outright.

They scrutinized the repetition, looking for anything that might reveal the killer's identity. The editing was superb, cutaway shots of deepest black inserted at the perfect time to obscure the identity of the film's star. There was never more of the murderer shown than the leering mouth, and that hand draped in black clutching the knife.

Taylor had Daphne rewind and forward the film several times—it seemed like the act of licking the wounds was the same every time. She didn't know what that meant. Had the killer only licked the wound of Jerrold King, or all the victims'? She filed the thought away.

It wasn't until Brandon Scott's scene that it all changed. Brandon was caught by surprise, obviously changing to go for a run. He turned to face the camera, shouted "No" several times, then was attacked with a fury. The cat-o'-nine-tails bit into his flesh again and again, his hoarse cries became begging screams.

The shot faded into a haze, and it was over, Brandon Scott's shrieks of agony settling into a silence that echoed through the conference room. Brittany Carson's attack had not been documented.

They were all dulled for a moment, absorbing. Taylor was the first to regain herself.

"That's it. We have to get this video down from the site now," Taylor said. Lincoln would be able to handle that. "How many people have seen this?"

Daphne pointed to the counter. "It's going viral. It's only been up since late last night, and we're already at five hundred thousand views."

McKenzie glanced at the page. "Can you tell who posted it?"

"I was looking at that before you came. There's no real way—the user name is generic, letters and numbers, nothing personal. This is the first video posted using that name, there are no identifying details. Obviously, the company will have more information."

"Lieutenant?"

Greenleaf was still sitting, his face pale.

"Yes?"

"Was that, I mean, could that?" He breathed out in a great gust. "Was that *real?*"

Taylor was suddenly very conscious of where she was. They were sitting in the conference room of the statewide newspaper, owned by a national media conglomerate, Gannett, and this would be mind-blowing, startling news that would capture the headlines for days. A scoop like this could sustain them for weeks.

"I'm not sure," she said carefully. "It seems this video has some elements of reality to it. But David, don't run it. Please." *The Tennessean* had a robust online community with breaking news updates sent to computers, phones and PDAs all over the city. A rallying cry like this would force the video even further into circulation. Then again, maybe it would crash the server and they'd have half their work done for them.

Greenleaf didn't look her in the eye, but nodded. She hoped that meant he'd sit on it, at least until they could get the video taken down.

"Thank you. Daphne. David." Taylor shook hands with Greenleaf, who was actively sweating. She couldn't blame him—that would have horrified anyone. She was feeling rather sick herself. There was no doubt about it—the video most certainly was real.

Taylor and McKenzie took the security films with them, headed to the CJC. Tim Davis had the letter in evidence and was bringing them a copy with his results. Taylor had phoned ahead to Lincoln, warning him about the video upload. He said he'd get right on it.

Taylor was still a little shaky. She slid behind the wheel and turned to McKenzie, watched him placidly click his seat belt home.

"I can't believe this. I can't remember a murder case that had an accompanying video. Have you ever seen anything like this?" she asked.

He nodded. "Once, unfortunately. This guy in Orlando was making snuff films in his basement. He killed three girls before the Orange County Sheriff's Office got to him. But those were getting sold on the black market, through the fetish sex clubs, not being broadcast to anyone who wanted to look. And I didn't see the victim at the scene where it took place, either. It's not without precedent—we're living in our very own brave new world."

McKenzie had jotted down the symbols from the letter and was staring at them with an intensity that she thought might burn a hole in his notebook.

"What do they mean?" she asked.

"I don't know. I think they're meant to be pagan, or at least symbolize the occult—that much I can tell you."

"Really? So they match with the pentacles?"

"Yes, to an extent. Here's the irony. The pentacle is a symbol of protection. It's a sign of unending life, the cycles of the year, the interconnectedness of the universe. It doesn't represent evil, and it's not meant to invoke fear. It's a very misinterpreted symbol."

Taylor glanced over at him. "McKenzie, how do you know that?"

He was quiet for a moment, then sighed loudly. "Listen, this is going to sound ridiculous, okay?"

"Okay."

"I was kind of into this stuff when I was in junior high. And high school."

"You were a Goth?"

"Well, yeah, sort of. I got into it to avoid dealing with my sexuality. It was a great release, and there were a lot of other kids who were *confused,* as well. We did a bunch of experimenting, and I ended up with…quite an education."

"Renn, you never cease to amaze me. So you can be our resident expert in all things occult?"

"I guess. But do we have to tell everyone? I feel sort of dumb about it."

"We'll see how dumb you feel when you've helped close seven murders in one fell swoop, okay? Tell me more about the video. You said the pentacle was for protection. The victims certainly weren't protected, so maybe they were meant for the killer's security?"

"It's much more than that. The fangs were real. Whoever starred in the film had them created, filed, lengthened with bonding agents to look that way. There are dentists that will do that kind of work. We should take a still shot around to some of the local cosmetic dentists and see if any of them recognize their handiwork. We're dealing with someone who believes they are a vampire. Most are content to role-play—there are very few genuine sanguine vampires out there. Combine that with the symbols—this is someone who is trying out several different religions, trying to find their place."

"Sanguine?"

"Blood drinking."

"Right. So this was a religious killing done by a blood-drinking vampire?" she asked, her sarcastic incredulity ringing though the car. Hell, she didn't believe in vampires. Or witches, for that matter.

"No. It doesn't feel like we have a true believer on our hands, someone who is against the pagan world and trying to make a point. This feels more like seeking to me. Someone searching for answers, for their place in the world. The symbols from the letter are old markings. A couple of them are obvious—the pentacle again, the moon and sun represent the seasonal cycles of the earth, the cross and the thunderbolt. The inverted triangles and the circle with the cross inside, they may mean something else. It could be a bunch of drawings meant to look like pagan symbols, too. They may mean nothing to the killer, outside of looking interesting. You never know."

"So if the symbols aren't meant to portend evil, what the hell is this self-described vampire doing sending letters with them? And why does it say 'we'?"

"More than one, probably. A coven. If you could drop me at the library, I bet I could find their meanings quicker."

She turned the ignition over, edged out onto Broadway. "Sure, but why not look online?"

"Well, I could, but I've got a hunch about these. Have you ever heard of the Strega?"

"No."

"Stregheria, or Italian witchcraft. It's an earth-based religion, pagan to its core, probably the oldest of the pagan religions that's still practiced today. Nature is life, and magick, spelled *M-A-G-I-C-K,* is knowing how to control the interconnectedness of all the natural forces of life. Strega look for ways to manipulate the earth through their worship. It's a positive journey. They aren't worshiping the devil or anything like that. No animal sacrifices to dark angels. Not anymore, or at least not publicly."

She glanced over at him, saw he was trying to tease. It didn't work, they were both too rattled. McKenzie continued, looking out the window.

"Some of these look suspiciously like Strega symbols. We're talking mythology worship here, the polytheistic society. Earth, moon and stars, all represented by the different Gods and Goddesses."

"Let me guess. You speak witch, too?"

He shot her a look, saw she was teasing him back. "You're funny. Didn't you study the classics in college?"

"I took a class in mythology to satisfy one of the liberal arts credits I had to take, but that's it. All I remember is Zeus and his lightning bolt and something about the Tower of Babel."

"Poor you. It's very cool stuff. All of the pagan religions are based in polytheistic pantheon worship. The Christians had to work within the confines of the pagan structure when they converted the masses. That's why Catholicism has so many pagan rituals. The incense, the candles, the feast days, the saints. Mary correlates to the Goddess, Christ to the God. The saints are also a direct corollary to the pantheon of Gods and goddesses. They represent the same things, protection for specific parts of life—crops, welfare, war. It's fascinating, actually."

"Honey, we're in the belt buckle of the Bible Belt. They didn't teach us about that. It is interesting, but what does it have to do with this case? You think we're dealing with pagans? I thought you said sanguine vampires."

He sighed. "I'm thinking that there's more to all of this than meets the eye, and I'm trying to keep an open mind."

"Well, I think we're dealing with crazy people, people who took it upon themselves to kill seven children. I can get all romantic about the old ways too, but that's not going to solve this case. I have to produce a suspect, and fast. Which means regular old police work instead of a history lesson."

"Let me go do some research. The killer might be in an altered state, especially if he's under the influence of drugs.

We can't forget that someone shot the video, and that shakiness means handheld camera. We're certainly dealing with more than one person."

"Great. Just what we need." She thought for a moment. "Maybe the killer in the video is the person Lincoln saw in the videotapes we took from the scenes last night. God. We have seven dead, one clinging to life, a letter from someone claiming to have killed them and a film of the whole event. Vampires and witches running amok in Nashville. This will definitely make the national news," she muttered, turning onto Eighth Avenue, then onto Church.

She stopped in front of the Nashville Public Library. The soaring three-story stone edifice with its Roman columns seemed overwhelmingly prescient. Great, she was going to be seeing symbols in everything now.

A homeless man wandered near the car and glared at her, then turned back to his meandering shuffle, across to the park to join his cronies. The irony wasn't lost on her—the library and its traditional representation of enlightenment and education being watched over by the forgotten people.

"Do you still want to go with me to Hillsboro? I can pick you up on the way."

"Yeah. That sounds good. I'll call you in a bit. This shouldn't take me long."

He climbed out of the car, already lost in his world. He disappeared through the ornate doors and she sighed. She didn't know why, but seeing him walk away reminded her of Memphis. James "Memphis" Highsmythe, the Viscount Dulsie, special liaison to the terrorism Behavioral Analysis Unit in Quantico for the Metropolitan Police at New Scotland Yard, to be precise.

Baldwin had seen Memphis in Quantico last week, moving into his new office. She hadn't told Baldwin that Memphis had also been in touch with her.

Memphis had been good for the past few weeks. After their interlude in Florence, a kiss that stayed with her for days after, she'd received a few discreet texts and e-mails, nothing that couldn't be shown to Baldwin if the question arose. But yesterday, before she'd been publicly reinstated, a bouquet of white roses had appeared on her desk. The card simply read, *Love, M.*

She'd gone through all of the appropriate emotions, and the not so appropriate ones, as well. *Love, M,* indeed. It would have been fine—nothing—really, if Baldwin hadn't seen it. He hadn't said anything, but clenched his jaw so tightly that the muscle jumped deep in the flesh. She hated Memphis for upsetting Baldwin, hated him for being so arrogant as to send her roses with a card that read, *Love.* But she was happy at the same time, and didn't understand what that meant.

She got mad thinking about it again, slammed the car into gear and pushed the accelerator harder than necessary, making the wheels squeal under her as she shot away from the curb. Distracted, she barely watched the lanes in front of her, crowded with tourists intent on crossing the streets against the lights to enjoy a few hours of entertainment on Lower Broad. She finally got fed up, cut across to Union Street and flew up Fifth, wrestling all thoughts of Memphis back into their appropriate place. She couldn't keep doing this, but she didn't know how to make it stop. She didn't want him. That should be all that mattered. Yet thoughts of him kept crowding in at the most inopportune moments.

She wanted to talk to Sam about it, but Sam was already upset and attuned to the breach in Taylor's mental protocol. They'd assiduously avoided the topic after Sam bitched her out for flirting with Memphis at an autopsy. Taylor's face burned at the thought of their fight—she hadn't been consciously flirting and was hurt that Sam had implied otherwise. But now, after Memphis told her so starkly what he was feeling, now that they'd had some physical contact, regardless of how minute it was, she didn't know how to put her emotions into words for her best friend.

And since Sam was pregnant again, she'd be drawing in, focusing on herself and her family. Taylor's silliness wouldn't be of importance. She suddenly felt isolated, alone, for the first time in several years. Truth be told, she didn't have that many friends who she felt she could talk to, not about matters of the heart.

Nothing to be done for it, then. Shrugging to herself, she chalked it up to being lucky to be found attractive by two men, and left it at that. Baldwin was the better of the two, the one she wanted to be with forever, and she certainly didn't plan on endangering their relationship because another man had a little crush on her.

Thinking about other men invariably led her to Fitz, and she reminded herself to call the North Carolina State Bureau of Investigation again. Surely she'd find someone there who could listen to her side of the story, who would be willing to put pressure on the Coast Guard, or search the ports, something, anything, to help her find him. She felt her blood pressure rise thinking about her theory—that the Pretender had taken Fitz—and felt better. Fired up. Worrying about Fitz was much more important than worrying about Memphis.

She passed the offices of Channel Five, wondered what they were cooking up today. The Green Hills Massacre, they'd called it this morning, with shots of Taylor speaking at the press conference. She honestly didn't think she'd ever felt more pressure to move forward on a case than she did at this moment.

Sixteen

The alarm rang insistently.

God, morning already? There was a dull ache in his head. He kept his eyes closed against the glare. He'd forgotten the blinds last night, and sun was leaking in through the wooden slats. His mouth was completely dry—it took a few tries to work up enough lubrication to swallow. When he did, the taste of bourbon rose on his tongue. That's right. He'd been drinking last night. They all had. The sight of that little body just off the trail in Great Falls Park, broken and pale, her legs shattered, her blond hair slashing across her face like a golden blindfold, was enough to set them all off.

He shifted his head, and pain shot through his temples. Wonderful. A hangover to help with the autopsy of little Susan Travers.

He cracked an eye and saw the clock—7:45 a.m. The beeping seemed to be getting louder. He reached out to stifle the god-awful racket and realized his arm was pinned. He tugged experimentally and felt the pressure, wasn't cogent enough to realize why. He swiveled his head to the left slowly and saw a spill of dark red hair, like blood, across his pillow.

He fought the urge to pull his arm back as if bitten by a snake. Oh, shit. What had he done?

The owner of the red hair shifted slightly, allowing him to retrieve his arm. It was fully asleep, and he gasped slightly as blood rushed back into the deadened nerves.

"Aren't you going to turn that off?" a sleepy, throaty voice asked.

Charlotte.

Jesus, he must have had more to drink than he thought. He didn't remember…oh, now it was coming back. He'd walked her to her car. She'd been crying. He, ever the gallant savior, had brushed a tear away with his knuckle, and then she'd been closer, touching him in a way they both knew wasn't a good idea. His head had dipped and the feeling of her soft lips overwhelmed him. It had been too long since he'd been with a woman, and his body ached with the need to feel inside her.

He'd felt inside her, all right. He could feel the stickiness in his groin, and the flesh there tightened in memory.

He reached over and silenced the alarm. He glanced to his left, saw the wide amber eyes staring at him. An awkward quiet settled upon them, then Charlotte smiled. He felt a delicate hand straying up his thigh. He couldn't help himself—he reacted quickly. With one part of his mind screaming, *What in the hell are you doing?* he shifted his hips a bit so her hand landed directly on him. She stroked him, softly, expertly, her free hand roaming across his chest, and when he could stand it no longer he rolled on top of her, parting her legs with his knee, catching her lips in a kiss. He drove himself deep between her thighs, not caring if he hurt her. From what he remembered of last night, Charlotte liked it a bit rough.

He heard her breath catch as he entered her, felt her teeth on his lower lip. She raked her nails along the already tender flesh of his back—Jesus, she'd scratched him open. He had a moment's urge to bite her in payback. Instead, he reached his arms around her back and used his hands to cup her buttocks and lift her slightly, allowing him to go deeper and deeper. She was fighting him now, matching each thrust with one of her own, her legs thrown around his waist, her eyes focused inward. He remembered that look from last night, and smiled. The exquisite building began, the age-old rhythm going faster and faster, and he lost himself, not hearing her triumphant cries.

Thirty minutes later, freshly showered and holding a cup of steaming coffee, he stood in the kitchen of his apartment, watching Charlotte move around his home with a practiced eye.

She picked up the new John Connolly he was reading, *Bad Men*. Baldwin almost laughed when he saw the book in her hand; the title took on a whole new meaning for him this morning.

Charlotte smiled at him, a predatory housecat on the prowl. "You have good taste."

"He's always been one of my favorites. Coffee?"

She looked across the room at him, the mask dropped, her body angled in sly invitation. She arched her back and said, "Mmm, yes, please."

"Coming right up." He moved to the coffeepot and poured her a cup, pretending he didn't hear her next statement.

"I could get used to this," she said, and he shuddered inside. The last thing he needed was an involvement with one of his team. He'd already stepped over the line.

He splashed another swallow of coffee in his mug, then turned to her, keeping his face as neutral as possible. He didn't want to encourage this. It was a mistake. He handed her the cup.

"When you're done, let me drop you at your car. We can't go into the office together. I don't need any more scrutiny than I already have."

Her face dropped for the briefest of seconds, then she

recovered, raising a delicate eyebrow. "Like that, is it? You'd rather pretend that last night and this morning never happened?"

She sidled into the kitchen, sinuous and graceful, slipping her arms around his waist. He had to admit, she was incredibly appealing. The scent of musk and roses filled his nostrils, and he breathed in deeply, aware that he was hard again. Good grief. He'd unleashed the genie in the bottle.

"It's not a good idea, Charlotte. You're a beautiful, intelligent woman, but—"

Charlotte was rubbing against him again, grinding her hips into his with precision. She set her coffee down, then took the mug from his hand and transferred the warmed flesh to her now-exposed breast. How did she manage to get out of her shirt so quickly? He lowered his head and flicked his tongue across her nipple. She accepted the invitation and eased down his zipper. He glanced over her head at the clock on the stove and decided, what the hell. He'd been under enough pressure lately. Maybe he'd been wrong to fight this. Maybe being with Charlotte was exactly what he needed.

Charlotte was small, only around five foot five, and easily lifted. She was wearing a tight black skirt, the same one that had been bothering him the night before. He quickly discovered she'd neglected to put on any underwear. He settled her on the counter, bent her backward, running his palm down the length of her body, and sheathed himself again. She giggled, and he felt a laugh build in his own chest. Here they were, going at it like a couple of teenagers, not even bothering to undress. It felt good. Better than he could have ever expected.

Charlotte

Baldwin dropped her at the car in a strangled silence. Embarrassed? Regretful? She didn't know his looks well enough to be able to tell what he was thinking. Not yet.

She respected his discomfiture, slipped out of the car without saying anything. She had a fresh change of clothes in her trunk—she always had a go bag packed for the times they needed to attend to a crime scene in person. She drove to work, slung the bag over her shoulder and slipped inside. Only the guards at the desk saw her, and who were they to comment? It wasn't the first time an agent had done the walk of shame into work.

After she changed, Charlotte took an extralong time in the bathroom. She hadn't been able to do her hair properly— instead of fine, red silk, the ends were waving and a bit frizzy. She used a special boar-bristle brush to get them tamed down, then reapplied some makeup.

There, that was better. Would they be able to tell? She stared in the mirror, taking in every detail. Yes, her lips were a bit puffy and red around the edges. His beard, all bristly, had scraped the tender skin nearly raw. She thought about the other parts that were raw and was pleased to see a fine flush make its way up the bone-china skin of her neck into her cheeks. Oh, that was pretty. She looked ripe, a perfect grape plucked from the vine.

No wonder he couldn't resist. She'd make sure he never would again. She knew how to press his buttons now.

She grabbed her bag and went to her desk. The rest of the team was already assembled. Butler and Geroux didn't give her much of a second glance, but Sparrow looked at her, eyes narrowing. Charlotte mustered up the most angelic, innocent smile she could, then raised her eyebrow in a sultry hello. Sparrow openly thawed.

She'd need to be careful there. It was going to be tricky navigating two relationships, especially if Sparrow wanted to start getting possessive. Sparrow was a pretty girl, prettier than she knew, trim and athletic, with an adorable crossbite. Charlotte had seduced her three weeks ago, after a long evening celebrating the close of their first case as a team. They'd done the girl thing, slipped off to the bathroom together, and Charlotte had locked the door behind them and let Sparrow go down on her while she sat on the counter with her legs spread wide.

Goodness, she was starting to feel quite warm. Mmm, maybe Baldwin and Sparrow? No, probably not. Baldwin seemed a bit too parochial for all that. But it made for a nice fantasy. This was the way she preferred to live her life, with one partner of each sex on the hook. Hard and soft, dark and light. She smiled to herself, then opened her computer, just barely pushing the image of the three of them intertwined on Baldwin's office floor from her mind. She needed to focus. This case, this stupidly named case, was driving her mad.

She didn't understand men who committed crimes against children. Adult-on-adult violence, yes, she could fathom that. It was one of the things that made her a good profiler—she had a certain empathy with the killers. For her dissertation she'd interviewed more than forty serial offenders, and almost all of them had given new information in their cases. One had even coughed up the location of a body—shocking, considering he'd been using it as leverage to keep his privileges.

Yes, she was good with killers. She'd excelled in her classes, gotten her Ph.D. in record time, had been snapped up by the Bureau right out of school. She'd worked her way into the BAU with a combination of intelligence and sheer guts. But working cases involving children was not her forte.

Sparrow came into her office with a stack of files.

"More sex offenders to interview today." She barely brushed her arm against Charlotte's shoulder as she placed the folders on the desk.

Charlotte scooted her chair back a little and swiveled so she could see Sparrow face on. She raised an eyebrow and waited in silence. She knew what was coming.

"I tried calling you last night. I thought we were supposed to meet up."

"You called?" Charlotte feigned innocence—God, she

should win an Oscar for that tone. "I must have slept right through it. Yesterday was so awful, and I had a lot to drink last night. I'm sorry, honey."

Sparrow blushed at the endearment. "Well, maybe tonight? We could get Indian. I know how much you love it. Drink some wine, unwind a little?"

"Maybe tonight, sugar. We'll have to see what the day brings though, right? Lord knows there's a creep out there just waiting to be caught. Let's go get him, yeah?"

She ran her fingernail up Sparrow's leg, then flipped her chair back into the proper position and pulled the first file off the stack. Sparrow, firmly dismissed, hesitated a moment, then left her in peace.

Yes, this was going to be very, very complicated.

Seventeen

The CJC sat baking in the late fall sun, heat shimmering off the building's bricks. Taylor hadn't realized just how warm it was today—after the previous night's chill, it felt almost like summer. Crazy weather for the first of November.

People flowed in and out of the building, officers in uniform and plainclothes detectives, random strangers looking for the courts, black and white and yellow and brown, all mingling into one stew of justice. The diversity of Nashville was never better represented than in this one spot—the Criminal Justice Center in the morning.

She parked the Lumina in the back lot and headed inside, up the stairs to the landing that held a new industrial ashtray, dark gray and heavy plastic, with a slot at the top for the spent cigarettes to disappear into. Though she'd quit more than a year before, she still had cravings now and then. She had to admit it was nice not seeing used butts sticking up like matchstick men arrayed for battle from the depths of the reusable kitty litter that used to serve as sand.

She swiped her card and entered, wondering just how

many times she'd followed this exact route in the past. Hundreds, thousands of times. Always hurrying into the office to work on the most pressing cases. She rather envied her old boss Mitchell Price his new late-night office hours.

The place was buzzing with activity, the hallways full of people moving between appointments. Nodding to faces she recognized, she stopped at the soda machine—she desperately needed a Diet Coke this morning. Cold can in hand, she entered the homicide offices.

Commander Huston was standing by Marcus Wade's desk, flipping through a manila file folder.

"Morning, ma'am," Taylor said.

Huston turned and nodded to her. The woman was no-nonsense, five foot six, a runner with muscled calves and a compact body, veins protruding in her forearms. She wore no makeup. Her hair was short and hand-styled over her ears, a light brown streaked with blond from excessive time in the sun. She'd been training for a marathon, and Taylor knew she ran fifteen miles after work every evening. She admired the dedication Huston put into her life—work and running took all of her focus and she was good at both.

And she let Taylor manage things in Homicide, which was even better.

Huston turned and gestured to Taylor's office. The two women went inside and shut the door. Huston took the chair opposite the desk.

"Fill me in, Lieutenant. What's happening?"

"We have some crazies, that's what's going on. The letter sent to the paper was marked at the end in blood with a grouping of symbols that look to be pagan. McKenzie is at the library right now, trying to make sense of them. There was a phrase under the bloody marks, 'Blood is intensity, it is all I can give you.' Tim Davis is running through everything now, getting what he can from it."

"Prints? Delivery method?"

"I don't know about the prints yet, and the letter was

found on the floor in the ground-floor hallway—that's the back entrance near the printing presses. Those doors are locked—only *Tennessean* employees can get inside that way. Their security guy figures someone shoved the letter through the doors, but he didn't see it happen on film. We've got the tapes. I'll have Lincoln look through them and see if he can spot anyone. What I'm worried about is the film."

As she spoke, she tapped in the address of the video. She swiveled her monitor toward Huston, made sure the volume wasn't overly loud. When the screaming started, she didn't want the entire building to come running.

Huston watched for a few minutes, pale under her tan, then met Taylor's gaze with worried brown eyes.

"What can we do?" she asked.

Taylor clicked the stop button. The screen froze, the wide-fanged mouth mocking her. "I've already asked Lincoln to get in touch with the company and get it pulled from the site. I can't imagine they'll fight us on this. I need to check in with him, see where we stand."

"You're meeting with the administration at Hillsboro this morning?"

"Yes, ma'am. Ten."

"It's nearly nine now, I'd best let you get to work. Keep me informed, especially about this movie. I've heard from the hospital. Young Brittany Carson is not doing well. She isn't expected to make it, it's just a matter of time. She never regained consciousness. Too much damage done by the drugs, I suppose. I'm sorry, I know you worked to save her."

Taylor sighed deeply. "I work to save them all, ma'am. It seems to be a losing battle somedays."

"Yes, it does, Lieutenant. Yes, it does. Make sure your detectives talk to the department psychiatrist by the end of business today. I'm sensing this case will be bothering everyone for quite some time. That goes for you, too."

"I'll pass the word along. Ma'am, I have a request. Forensic Medical is going to be overloaded on this case, and the multiple toxicology screens and DNA runs are going to take weeks if we send them to TBI."

"Yes, they will. What do you propose?"

"In the past, we've used a company called Private Match to do time-sensitive work. I'd like to get permission to have the samples sent there for testing."

Huston cocked her head to the side. "I think that's a good idea. I'm already getting pressure from on high to get this case solved as quickly as possible. If you think that Private Match can help us attain that goal, then I'm all for it. I'll make the necessary arrangements."

"Thank you. That's going to be a help."

"Get some sleep, Lieutenant. That's an order."

Huston shook Taylor's hand, then opened the door and disappeared. Taylor took her hair out of its ponytail and ran her fingers through it, combing it out. Huston was easy to work with, though much more formal than she was used to. Regardless, she was a woman who knew how to get things done, and that's exactly what Taylor needed right now.

One problem solved. She didn't have time to get meditative about Brittany Carson. She had to admit, she'd been hoping the girl would pull through. And she really didn't feel like sitting down with the department shrink.

Marcus came to her door, knocked softly on the doorjamb.

"Yeah," she said.

"We've got a name on the man who appeared in the crime-scene footage. We've sent a patrol to pick him up. With any luck we'll have him here by 11:00 or so."

"Why so long?"

"He lives north of town—it's transport time."

"What's his name?"

"Keith Barent Johnson."

"Okay. What's so special about Mr. Johnson that we were able to identify him so quickly?"

"You don't recognize the name?"

"No. Should I?"

Marcus smiled. "He was in the system, so I checked him out. He was arrested last year after making threats against the president. Ended up getting busted for tax evasion."

"Oh, yeah. I remember him. He's a kook."

"Yep. A kook who's all over the Internet calling himself the king of the vampires."

That got her attention. "You're kidding."

"I kid you not. Lincoln needs to see you, if you have a minute."

"I have just a minute. I need to get to Hillsboro. Will you look over the security tapes from *The Tennessean* for me, see if you can see anyone slipping a letter through the back doors?"

"The letter from the killer?"

"Yeah. Keep it quiet. I want to hold as much of it back as possible." She briefed him, then said, "McKenzie's researching all the symbols right now. Hey, listen. What happened to our kid from last night, the one Simari's dog took a chunk out of?"

"He's still in the hospital. The bite hit into the muscle in his leg. He's going to have surgery this afternoon, then some recovery time."

"Good. I want to talk to him again."

Lincoln joined them, dreads standing on end. He looked rough. They all did—no one had gotten any sleep last night. They were all wearing yesterday's clothes, running off of caffeine and adrenaline.

"The video company is working with us, but it doesn't seem to matter," he said simply, sinking into the chair closest to the door. He ran a weary hand across his dreadlocks, getting them into a bit of order.

"What do you mean? They won't take the video down?"

"No, they complied immediately. It breaks their community guidelines. YouTube took the video down after it got flagged by several viewers as obscene. But it's gone viral. People have downloaded it to their own computers and are uploading it to other video-sharing sites. They all have a version running—Vimeo, Vuze, MSN, Yahoo!—and everyone's trying to work with us, but it's growing too quickly. At last count ten video sharing sites on the Internet have it. Some have cut the end, where Brandon Scott is murdered, some have it intact. We can't keep up, though I've been doing my best. Word on the street is this is the work of an underground film crew. Some of the Hollywood wannabes apparently do high-quality independent work, especially in the horror genre. The message board and comments are lit up like Christmas trees, debating whether it's real or just incredibly excellent editing. And people are e-mailing it around, too."

"Son of a bitch. It's like a bloody hydra. Get on the horn to Judge Botelli, and call A.D.A. Julia Page. See if there's anything legal that can be done. And make sure YouTube releases the information about how and where the original upload is from. That's evidence, and I'll be damned if I let their free speech issues get in the way of an eventual conviction."

"Not going to be a problem, they're working on it. Whoever posted it was pretty sophisticated, was able to reroute through several servers to cover his tracks. They'll get back to me as soon as they nail it down."

"Has the news picked it up?"

"Yes."

"Fuck!" she said, slamming her palm onto her desk.

Eyes blurred with fatigue, Lincoln managed a grimace. "That's pretty much my sentiment, too."

Taylor texted McKenzie as she left the CJC to let him know she could pick him up at the entrance to the library in five minutes. As she exited the building, Sam called.

"We swabbed the wounds of all the victims. I'm certain the cause of death was a drug overdose, so I'm sending the blood work in for more comprehensive toxicology. I talked to Vanderbilt. Brittany Carson's blood showed high concentrations of methylphenidate, methylmorphine, paramethoxyamphetamine, methylenedioxymethamphetamine and diazepam. Lethal levels. I assume that's what we're dealing with here, too."

"English, Sam?"

"Sorry. Just what the early tox screens indicated— Ritalin, codeine, PMA and MDMA, that's the stuff in Ecstasy and Valium."

"From the laced Ecstasy? Jesus. Someone took a great deal of time to get the right chemical compound together and disguise it in the tabs of X. When will the posts be done?"

"Not until this afternoon. I just wanted you to know that we're on the possible DNA. It's going to take time, though."

"Reroute everything to Private Match. I've already gotten permission for them to run the extra toxicology screens and the DNA. Tell them to put a rush on it, okay?"

"Will do. Everything okay over there? I heard that there's a video of the murders floating around."

Taylor got in the car and snapped on her safety belt. "There is, though the Internet companies are working to get it taken down. It's gone viral, and it's everywhere. Thankfully, some people think it's a horror movie, but the truth will be out soon enough."

"I'll keep working on everything. You hang in there."

There was a note of kindness in Sam's tone that had been missing for the past few weeks, and Taylor felt tears prick at the edges of her eyes. She missed Sam badly.

"I'll do my best. Thanks for handling the posts so quickly. Is there anything else I need to know?" she asked.

"No. But if I get something new, I'll call."

"Good. Talk to you later." She slid the phone into her front pocket and picked McKenzie up at the library steps. He got in the car with a wide grin on his face.

"Hey, before I forget, you need to see the shrink today at some point. Huston's orders."

"Oh, Victoria? I mean, Dr. Willig."

"You know her?"

"Sure. She's great. I've talked to her from time to time, about…things. You know."

Taylor did know. McKenzie had lost his fiancée to suicide, and bore the weight of it on his shoulders. He would always feel responsible, because his sexual preference dictated that he had to break their engagement and the girl couldn't handle the news. He'd come from Orlando to Nashville last year to get away from the trauma of it all. Taylor knew she was one of two people who knew the whole story—the other being McKenzie's partner, Hugh Bangor. They'd met on a case and were quite close.

Make that three people. Dr. Victoria Willig was on the in with McKenzie too, it seemed. That was good. The more comfortable McKenzie became with his sexuality, the less it would matter at work. She had a tolerant bunch of cops around her—they'd have no problem with him being gay. But the department as a whole was a different matter. Metro Police was like the military and professional sports—don't ask, don't tell.

"We're going to be late," he said.

"I know that." She pulled away from the curb, turned left on Sixth and headed across Broadway to Twenty-first. "You obviously found something."

"I did. The symbols I didn't recognize, the triangles and the circles with crosses in them? They represent the Watchers. They're the guardian angels, invoked during circle spells for protection." He shoved a sketch under her nose. She glanced down to see what looked like stick figures.

| North | East | South | West |

She looked back at the road. "The Watchers represent the points on the compass?"

"More than that. They correspond to the elements, the seasons, the stars, the planets. North, South, East, West—Earth, Air, Fire, Water. The Watchers are vital to just about every aspect of witchcraft. But most importantly, they're called upon for protection. The symbols on the letter represent the protective elements. The killer, the letter writer, was looking to keep himself blessed, that's for sure. Like a talisman. A good luck charm."

Taylor glanced over at him. "I never knew it was good luck to write in blood."

"Power comes from blood. That's what it's all about."

"So what's with the stick figures?"

"Those are the positions the Wiccan holds when calling to the Watchtowers. When you go back over the crime-scene photos, you'll notice that the bodies of the victims were in these positions as well—either arms to their sides or outstretched, like the North, East and South Watchers."

"Ah. Of course."

McKenzie caught the note of sarcasm in her voice. "Some people take this very seriously, LT. They live in this world. They believe. It's not so different from going to church, you know. Everyone needs something to believe in. Pagans just look to things that are a bit more tangible than what you and I are aware of."

Taylor yawned widely, her ears cracking with the effort. The sun came out from behind a cloud, glinting off the metal of the cars around her. She slipped on her sunglasses.

"I'll tell you this. Belief or not, I want to catch whoever did this and punish them. I subscribe to the higher power of handcuffs, you know?"

Eighteen

"So you admit that you were having an affair with Dr. Douglas?"

Tucker leered at him, and Baldwin wondered what exactly was going through his mind. Had Tucker been on the receiving end of Charlotte's favors? He looked the man up and down—the bald pate, the pouchy stomach, the gray skin. Possible. Charlotte never looked at the package, only worried about what was in the box. She had a tendency to find contents that could be shifted to appease her every desire. He'd have to walk even more carefully now.

"I never denied that. We were colleagues in a pressure-cooker situation. We were working a gruesome case. You know how it gets, sir. It wasn't the first time two teammates turned to each other for solace." Baldwin refused to look away, met Tucker's eyes squarely. *Come on, you wanker. You've been boning your executive assistant for years, and we all know it. What are you really looking for?*

Tucker had the good grace to blush. "I think we can fast-forward through the gory details now, Dr. Baldwin. Let's begin again, with Susan Travers. She was the fourth alleged victim of Harold Arlen, correct?"

"No, she was the fifth."

Northern Virginia
June 15, 2004
Baldwin

The smell made him nauseous. No matter how many autopsies he participated in, which thankfully were few and far between, he could never get his stomach to cooperate properly. The drive up from Quantico, coupled with the wicked hangover and a slightly dirty feel from screwing around with Charlotte, had made him even more queasy than usual.

He let his mind drift away from the little body being examined on the autopsy table. Susan Travers was the fifth victim in as many weeks. Baldwin had been brought in after the third victim, eight-year-old Ellen Hughes, had disappeared on her way home from school. She'd been found dead three days later—legs broken, stabbed once in the chest—tied to a tree in Great Falls Park.

His team was still relatively new. Two months ago, they'd been fresh-faced agents recently acquired into the behavioral science unit. They still thought it was cool to be working there, hadn't seen enough of the horrors the work held in store for them. They were normally only tasked for crimes against adults, but they'd been pulled in on this case to help out when the lead profiler for BAU One had suffered a heart attack.

This Great Falls case had tempered their enthusiasm pretty damn quick.

Baldwin had handpicked the team: Caleb Geroux was from New Orleans, a homicide detective with a nose for wheedling confessions out of suspects; Jessamine Sparrow, as fine-boned as her name foretold, his new computer genius and a former hacker; and Olen Butler, his forensics expert.

Butler was an especially significant find—in the months before Baldwin brought him on the team, he'd developed a brand-new DNA program for their CODIS systems. The combined DNA index system was working hard to match DNA samples from crimes across the country, and Butler's intuitive program utilized an aspect of ViCAP, the Violent Criminal Apprehension Program, to make the CODIS matches quicker and deeper than ever before.

The team was a load of talent wrapped into one small entity, the Behavioral Analysis Unit Two. Baldwin's unit.

Charlotte Douglas was the most experienced profiler on his team, with a doctorate in criminal psychology from Georgetown and a gift for self-preservation. Unlike the others, she'd been assigned to the team two months earlier. His boss, Garrett Woods, had "done a favor" for another bureau chief and brought her on board.

Baldwin only knew the basics about Charlotte; the parts of her jacket he was allowed to see were straightforward: education, commendations, experience. She wasn't one for chatter about her past, and he wondered for a moment why that was. She'd made mention of boarding schools once, of being raised away from her family, but that was all he knew.

Did he want to know more?

You know a lot more about her now than you did yesterday. That she was a real redhead, for starters. That she was fearless in bed. That she cried out in her sleep like a kitten having a nightmare.

See, dumbass? This is what happens when you fuck a teammate. Great job.

He mentally berated himself for a few minutes, then dragged his focus back to the autopsy. They were finishing up now, conclusions being drawn. The wound tracts were identical, the signature too specific. Susan Travers had been killed by the same man who murdered four other little girls in the case the media was calling the Clockwork Killer. To Baldwin, he was simply the unsub, the unnamed subject.

The medical examiner was relatively certain that Travers

had been dead for four days, which meant time was running out. Their unsub was operating on a weekly schedule; it was possible that another little girl would go missing today, be murdered tonight, and turn up three days from now. Unless Baldwin got his head in the game and stopped him.

Nineteen

Hillsboro High School had none of the charm of the many private schools in town. It looked like an industrial plant from the sixties, all cramped windows and metal rebar. The gymnasium was close to the road, dirty white brick with green accents; the school itself set farther back, crouching on the surrounding land.

Sadness permeated the air, everything felt empty. Even for a Saturday, things were simply vacant.

They entered the building and Taylor was immediately struck by how small everything seemed. Granted, it had been a while since she'd last been here, during an escapade with a decidedly nonprivate-school boy who attended Hillsboro. She'd attended some dance with him—a requisite papier-mâché, roses and hand-lettered banners in the gym affair—and found herself so incredibly bored by the whole evening that she stopped returning his calls. Hell, all she could remember of him was his first name, Edward, and that he drove a motorcycle, which was the reason she'd agreed to a date with him in the first place.

Nothing of the school looked the same to her. She

shrugged; it had been nearly twenty years since she'd last been inside.

A small bundle of gray-haired energy appeared before them, stuck out her wizened hand to shake.

"Lieutenant Jackson? I'm Cornelia Landsberg. Thank you for coming."

"Ah, you're the principal. Excellent. It's nice to meet you, ma'am. This is Detective Renn McKenzie. He's going to join me in our interviews today."

Landsberg was already ushering them toward the office. Taylor couldn't help but feel like she'd done something wrong, saw McKenzie shoot her a glance, reading her body language—*when were you last in the principal's office?* She coughed, hiding her smile behind her palm.

Landsberg led them into the quiet of the main office, which looked like a thousand other school front offices she'd been in. It didn't smell right, though. Taylor still associated the school's main office with the inky perfume of mimeograph machines, even though by the time she was an upperclassman at Father Ryan it had all gone to computers.

Posters of mascots hung on the walls, cheering on the student council and basketball team. A young brunette, most likely a teacher's aide, puttered behind the desk. Landsberg ignored her, led them back through a swinging solid-wood gate into the bowels of teenage authority.

"Gwen Woodall and Ralph Poston are meeting us— they're our guidance counselors. They've pulled all the files for our problem students." She stopped and turned, looked up at Taylor with beady, black-bird's eyes rimmed in red. Taylor was struck by the woman's resemblance to a small pigeon.

"We keep a close eye on our kids, Lieutenant. After Columbine, all the schools are more in tune with the troubled children. I'm sad to say we have a grief plan in place to handle just such a situation. We've had students come in today for comforting. They're in the gym now, talking to grief counselors brought in specially to help. It's good for them to be together, to share their emotions. It doesn't lessen it, of course, but it's helpful to know others are suffering from the same sensations. Do you think a student might be responsible for this?"

"I wish we could say definitely, ma'am. We're just trying to get some information right now. We do have one student in particular that we need to talk about—a boy in the underclass called Thor."

"Thor? I can't say that I've heard that name. Do you have a surname?"

"No, just the fact that he's dealing drugs to the students."

"Drugs?" She shook her head. "They always find a way in, don't they? In my day it was grass, and the teachers smoked it with the students. Now we have a zero-tolerance policy toward anything of the sort, but one hears rumors. It seems we can't keep them safe anymore, can't keep them insulated. They all have their MySpace pages and Facebook, Twitter and text messages—goodness, they have their own language. Our English department had a meeting just last week to discuss whether to accept some of the linguistic vernacular shortcuts into the curriculum, since they can't seem to get them to stop using it. We voted against that, of course, but we're willing to do what it takes to reach the students. I have a Twitter account myself, and all the students have my phone number. They're encouraged to text me anytime they need. But drugs…I don't hold with that behavior. It's instant expulsion if we catch them at it. Oh, here we go."

She opened the door to the teacher's lounge. There was the faintest scent of cigarettes—Landsberg being the tiniest bit of a hippy, Taylor imagined she wouldn't be too fussed if one of her teachers used this room for a smoke break. Better to hide it than send the offending teacher outside, where they might be seen by the students. She was sure there was some sort of regulation prohibiting tobacco on school grounds, but so long as the state representatives could sneak a smoke in the state house, she was pretty sure the odd teacher here or there could get away with it.

Do as I say, not as I do. The lesson she'd received from every adult in her life, her father most of all. She choked back the anger that rose at the thought of Win Jackson, in a federal penitentiary in West Virginia, and the current, marked absence of her mother, Kitty, still in Europe nearly a year later with some man Taylor had never met. They'd only spoken once in that time, when Taylor called to tell her that she'd arrested Win. Her mother had been in turn livid, then resigned.

It's just so embarrassing, Taylor. What will my friends think about your behavior?

Taylor had responded hotly, *What will they think about yours, Mother, gallivanting with some moneyed playboy you have no real ties to?* Kitty had hung up on her, and that was that.

Landsberg was making the introductions. Taylor dragged her attention back to the room.

"Gwen Woodall, Ralph Poston, this is Lieutenant Taylor Jackson and Detective Renn McKenzie. I'm going to leave you for a bit—I want to check on the students in the gym. Call if you need anything." She tapped her cell phone, in a plastic holder attached to her belt, then slipped out, shutting the door behind her.

"Please, have a seat," Poston said, gesturing to the chairs opposite them. "We've spent the morning looking through the files and talking. This is just…it's just…" He choked up, and his compatriot came to his rescue, laying a hand on his arm.

"It's okay, Ralph. Let your feelings out."

He began to sob and Woodall gave Taylor an apologetic smile. "It's taken all of us hard, as you can imagine. Sit. Sit. We've got a list of names of some of the boys we've had trouble with recently."

Taylor and McKenzie settled themselves at the table, and Taylor opened her notebook.

"Please, fill us in."

"Okay." Woodall handed Poston a tissue. "There, there, Ralph. It's going to be okay."

He took it and blew his nose, a great honking sound, like a strangled goose. Taylor bit her lip to stop herself from laughing.

Woodall looked like she was having trouble not giggling, too. Taylor liked her. She had a wide brow and ready smile, blunt brown hair cut just below her chin, and freckles scattered across her nose. She looked more like a student than a psychologist. She passed a sheaf of papers over the table to them.

"We've been looking through the files, pulling all our students who've been identified with narcissistic and psychopathic personality traits. Unfortunately, as these are teenagers we're talking about, that pile is quite large. I did some cross-referencing to see which of the students were in trouble for drugs and came up with about fifteen names. They're on the second page."

Taylor glanced through the files. Wide, furious eyes crowded her mind, faces cast in belligerence, fear or disdain. Many were black; only a few were white, and there was one Asian boy, possibly Vietnamese. They all looked lost. She handed the pages to McKenzie.

"What about threats to the school, or to other students? We've heard that a threat may have been made in recent weeks against the students who were killed."

Woodall glanced down at her hands. "You know how it is, Lieutenant. We have metal detectors at the doors, a safety officer on patrol in the halls. There's a constant flow of bullying and intimidation among the students, almost too much to keep up with. Our student population is diverse, all races, ranging from wealthy to poor, from happy homes to foster children. Rivalries flare up, create animosity, schisms in the cliques. We've been having some gang-related issues lately, and I'm sure you've heard the rumors that the recent home invasions were by a gang from Hillsboro. But we're doing our best."

Taylor had heard about the ruffians—within the past month, three different families had been held hostage by a group of young black men, robbed and then forced to drive to area ATMs, withdrawing money at each stop. So far it hadn't dropped into her purview—no assaults, and, thank goodness, no murders. Robbery was having a field day trying to track down the suspects in those cases.

Poston removed himself from his tissue. "We don't think that it's any of our students, but of course we always like to think the best of them."

"Of course," McKenzie said. "I think the person we're looking for would be extremely shy, wouldn't be getting into open tiffs with other students. He would be quiet, silently angry. He'd get good grades, but wouldn't speak up a lot in class. He wouldn't have a lot of friends, maybe one or two people that he would spend time with, girls and boys like him. He may be religious, or actively keep himself isolated from the rest of the students. Watchers. We're looking for the watchers."

Taylor raised an eyebrow at him. That made sense.

Poston shook his head. Taylor was reminded of one of Christopher Robin's friends, Eeyore. "You've just described half the student body. The other half are the jocks, into sports and girls," he said.

"What about the Goths?" Woodall asked. "I heard that there was a pentagram at each crime scene. That might fit."

"A pentacle," McKenzie corrected. "Pentagrams are a geometrical symbol, just a simple star. Pentacles are stars within a circle. Do you have any students who seem to be into the occult?"

"Well, sure. The Goths celebrate their differences, cover their notebooks in strange drawings, write bleak poetry. They're hassled from time to time, but they manage to keep to themselves. We've got a strict policy against the makeup—we don't want to encourage them to be that different from their peers. But they do congregate together, take some of the same classes."

"Who's in the Goth clique?" Taylor asked. "And do any of them show up in these files you pulled for us today?"

Woodall flipped through the pages, as if refreshing her memory, though Taylor got the sense she knew them backward and forward. "Strangely enough, none of them. They're all so sad, but not what we deem threatening. We try to get them to open up, but they hang back, don't want to be a part of things."

"What about a boy who may be dealing drugs to the upperclassmen, specifically to the popular crowd. He's been described as short with blond hair, possibly named after a comic book character, like Thor."

"Thor?" Woodall looked puzzled for a minute. "Could you mean Thorn? I've heard that name. But I can't remember from where. Ralph, do you know?"

"I thought it was a code word for getting out of class. Like a thorn in my side."

Woodall openly rolled her eyes this time. "No, I distinctly remember a conversation I heard last week about a boy named Thorn. It was two of the seniors…well, my goodness, it was Jerrold King and Brandon Scott. They were having a fight, actually. I stepped in before the fists began to fly. But for the life of me I couldn't tell you what they were so upset about."

"Any idea who might know?"

Woodall bit her lip. "You can ask their friends, see if they know. But after I broke it up, they scattered, and I didn't give it another thought. Boys will be boys."

Taylor made a note to ask around about the fight. Too much of a coincidence for her taste.

"We'd like to get a list of the kids you'd term Goth," McKenzie said.

"Certainly. I'll pull it together for you."

"Thank you. Did any of the students who were killed have any problems with their classmates? More fights between them, things like that? And are you aware of drugs on campus?"

"We're allowed to do random locker searches, and we find all kinds of things. There's always some drugs—marijuana, Ecstasy and the like."

Taylor leaned forward in her chair. "Can you remember whose locker had Ecstasy in it most recently?"

Woodall went to the filing cabinet and pulled out a manila folder. She flipped it open and perused, taking her time about it. Taylor was getting fidgety, felt like they weren't getting anywhere, until Woodall turned with a smile.

"We expelled a boy just last week. He had pills. I was surprised—he's a lovely young man. Claimed they were his mother's and had gotten into his backpack by accident. Thinking about it, he's one of the quiet ones, like you said."

"What's his name?" Taylor asked.

Woodall closed the file. "Juri Edvin."

Twenty

Raven and Fane had followed Ember, trying to stop her, but she'd been too quick for them. They couldn't go to her house; Raven didn't want to insert himself into the crime scene. He wasn't an idiot. He knew if they showed up—their faces pale, their hair jet-black—the people running the investigation would see them and put it all together.

They'd driven out of downtown in silence. Maybe he could buy a baseball cap and some chinos, try to get in that way. He discarded that thought. No matter what he tried to do to look like everyone else, he was always apart, always separate. They'd pick him out as an imposter in a heartbeat. He had the shadows of the night etched across his face, as permanent as a tattoo.

They spent the rest of the night together, just the two of them. They slept late, then he dropped Fane at her house with a soulful kiss. Back home again, his house was silent, waiting. He took some milk from the fridge and went to his room.

What to do about Ember?

He went to his small altar, the one in the corner on the floor, the one he used for his darkest path work. The small table held a chalice, his athamé and a lidless black box. His implements, his tools. They were waiting for him, their energy rising out of the box in waves.

These were his portable paraphernalia, something he usually carried in his car for times of extreme unction. He'd brought them last night, to the houses of his enemies, for strength. A feather for air, a piece of obsidian for earth, a match for fire and a shell for water, each imbued with spells conducted in the moonlight to give them power and anchor them to him. He didn't need fancy things, didn't need to be surrounded by opulence. He worshipped the earth, and his tools represented that.

He arranged the items in their appropriate spots on the altar—North, South, East and West—lit a candle scented with jasmine and ylang-ylang, then sat on the floor facing the flame, and watched. He ignored the phone when it rang, knowing it was Fane. He needed peace and quiet. Oh, how he wished it were dark out. He could concentrate so much better when there wasn't sun and light.

He relaxed into deep contemplation, meditating on the correct path, until the flame of the candle finally guttered out in the melted wax.

He came back to himself then, knew what he needed to do. He opened his Book of Shadows, searching for the right spell to counterbalance Ember's anger, to draw her back to them.

He found the spell. He went back to his altar, took up the poppet he'd designed two weeks earlier, just in case. As much as he hated to do it, he was going to have to punish Ember. She'd see the path after she suffered. He thought as he worked, molding the wax into a more feminine shape.

The pentacles were a masterful stroke. The police would be off chasing their tails, looking for suspects who fit their stupid profiles, combing the bushes and dark churches for Satanists and such. Satanists. What a joke. They had no power in his world—Satan didn't exist. Dark angels, purveyors of evil, certainly, but with the right spell, the right amount of control and power from Elysium and the netherworld, they too could be cowed into work.

He sent a quick mental thank you to Azræl, felt his skin grow hot as the thought coalesced. Azræl was with him, inside him now. He'd opened his soul to the dark angel, allowed him passage into the deepest recesses of his mind. He was becoming more powerful. Shedding the blood of the nonbelievers gave him a new gravitas. He wondered for a moment just how strong he was going to become, then set the poppet down. It was finished, and at midnight he'd go to the graveyard, speak the words that would finish Ember's independent streak and secure her back to his side.

Raven was counting on the ignorance of the lay community to assure confusion, to buy himself time. He just needed another couple of days to get the rest of his plan in place. Thorn had dropped off the face of the earth; he assumed Ember had been in contact with him and was trying to draw them apart. Ember herself had turned off her phone, wasn't responding. He felt the bits of his life, his world, unraveling, but assuaged himself with the knowledge of what he had left to do. He was almighty, and he had Fane. Fane would never leave his side, would never betray him. That he knew for a fact.

He opened his computer, routing himself through several servers until he was confident the originating address would lead to Japan, then pulled up YouTube. The video was gone.

He felt the fury flow through him, the dark angel's fury. He tapped the keys, searching, then found it again, on a sharing site called Vimeo. He glanced at the comments; they ranged from shock to admiration. He breathed a sigh of relief—the plan had worked. It was going viral, just like he wanted. He looked in a few more places—some had it, some had taken it down. That was fine. People would continue posting it in his stead, until the entire world viewed his masterpiece.

His lips pulled back in a grin and he ran his tongue over his chapped lips. Despite constant exfoliation with a tube of Fane's Philosophy Kiss Me lip scrub, the black lipstick he liked seemed to eat away the top layer of skin on his lips, leaving them perpetually chapped. His nervous licking didn't help, he ended up smothering his mouth in Carmex when he wasn't in public. It was a shame, because he hated looking in the mirror when he wasn't dressed. The makeup gave him strength, helped him hide. He turned off the desk lamp behind him so he wouldn't see his reflection in the laptop screen.

He queued the movie, sat back in his chair and watched.

It had taken him and Fane many weeks to make the film. There had been so many little things along the way—the screenwriting course she took at Watkins, the digital film course he'd taken last summer at The Art Institute, the expense of buying the camera and laptop that would allow him to edit the video down into cohesive footage. They'd pooled their money and made the investment—he was sure it would pay off in the long run. Movie Maker ended up being incredibly simple to use. He and Fane had written the script, taken turns filming the shots. It had taken them three weeks to get everything perfect, to shoot, edit the scenes down, storyboard the sections that weren't flowing right, building the film frame by frame. The music had proved harder than he expected, but once he found Audacity, an online music editor, he was able to get it seamlessly integrated.

Granted, he'd been tinkering with the background music up until yesterday, but that was more an effect thing, deleting out the real names being shouted and dubbing them with the characters'. He had to admit, he'd done a brilliant job. Fane had helped too—they'd gotten so good at the software, so flawless, that when the time had come to load in the actual murder scenes, they were able to do so in less than an hour. Well, an hour and a half—they'd stopped midway through to have wild, unrelenting sex. It was the deepest joining they'd ever experienced, leaving them both breathless and trembling; their hands still covered in the blood of the non-believers.

Yes, the production quality was a bit off, shaky in spots, but they were filming horror, after all. *The Blair Witch Project* was a huge hit and their camera had bounced around through the whole film. It would be fine. Once it was picked up by a studio, a new producer might want to fill in some of the rough spots, but for the most part, Raven felt sure his genius would be appreciated. And he was right. The movie going viral would cement the first part of the plan.

He sat back in his chair. He'd always known he was meant for more. He was meant for much, much more.

Aware of his differences at an early age, Raven had done everything he could to understand himself. Philosophy gave him a respite, the burden of self-actualization allowing him to find out his true motivations. He couldn't help but think dark thoughts—it was his nature. He couldn't help being a natural leader—that was his role in the universe. He devoured Sartre and Nietzsche, Jung and Freud. Plato, Aristotle, Socrates. He filled his mind with great works, delved into a study of mythology, found he had a great affinity for the concepts of the pantheon, the polytheistic religions. One God did not fit all, that was readily apparent to him. He stopped watching television and devoured books. He started at the beginning, with Hesiod's *Theogony,* and *Bullfinch's Mythology,* built from there. His library was extensive. He felt an affinity for the soil, for nature, for the moon and the cycles of the earth, and started openly practicing paganism early in his teens.

Thinking back, he fingered the spine of the Italian witchcraft book he always kept handy on his desk. He felt a true kinship with the Stregheria, the Italian version of Wicca. It was the closest to the Old Ways he could find, the closest to the origins of Mount Olympus, to the beginnings of time. He loved their practice, thought the modern versions of Wicca, the Gardnerian and Alexandrian methods, weren't nearly as beautiful. He'd never felt it was wrong to believe in the Old Ways, never felt he should have to hide himself from the rest of the world, from the austere gaze of the older witches who practiced in Nashville. He preferred to let everyone know his joy, but the traditional covens wouldn't accept him. Too young, too controversial. That mattered not a whit—he'd formed his own.

He was an evangelist for the Strega. Two hundred years ago he would have been burned at the stake, crisping to the merry shouts of local villagers, being damned for having prescient moments.

No more. The Strega were powerful, and he was proud to worship in their ways.

It was only natural that his dark path, his nocturnal tradition, his self-initiations strengthening his link to the divine, would show him the path to the Goths. The Gothic lifestyle—the real Gothic lifestyle, not the smearing on of makeup and black clothes because it looked cool—worked through a path of self-awareness, dedicated observation and worship, mourning for the rest of the world as it collapsed into capitalistic greed, an affinity for individual practice. It all spoke to him. He'd found his place at last.

He took the name Raven and became.

That's when his true awakening began. He was unrelenting in his quest, his Book of Shadows filling with spells and charms, ideas and recipes. The book was a leather-bound journal he'd found at a bookstore, with a rawhide strap that tied it all together. He wound the strap lovingly around the leather, knowing that only he could understand the forces within. The shadows of the spells, the ideas glimmering on the blank parchment, that's where his true power lay.

He researched, and continued his education. He made himself an expert in spell work, using his lyrical words to change things he wasn't satisfied with, writing his own versions of the traditional, and not so traditional, calls. He practiced drowsing—reading minds; path work—finding his way among the ancestors, allowing them into his world.

He honestly believed that if he were open and willing, the Gods and Goddesses would make themselves known in myriad ways. And they did. Signs of his acceptance into their ways were everywhere.

Divination, ways to predict the future through sophisticated spell work, wasn't far behind. He began to play with the thoughts of others. He attracted like-minded individuals, eventually settling on the strongest of those—his three, his Immortals. He taught them the Old Ways, and they worshipped him.

The path was righteous and good. The path would lead him to greatness. The path would show him how to become as powerful as the cycles of the earth, as the rising of the moon, as the Goddess Diana.

It began so simply. He planned, and plotted, knowing he needed to spread the word, to recruit. The Immortals were only four now, but their numbers would grow. His very own army, guided by perfect love and perfect trust. Together, they would change the world. Together, they would make all those who treated them with derision and disdain pay for their sins.

He realized the movie had finished playing. He queued it up again, wanting to pay closer attention this time. It was hard to see a work of such magnificence and not get caught up in the story behind it. He wondered if he should write some sort of liner notes, something to explain what their purpose was, where their heads lay. But the letter was enough, for now.

Screams rang out from his laptop, tinny, life being taken as he stood near, feeding on the souls of the despised.

He wondered what would happen if everyone in the world died.

Twenty-One

Baldwin's conference room was a train wreck. He had the files spread before him, five sets of crime-scene photos, whiteboards full of conjecture. Each seat was taken by someone; the scent of burned coffee lingered in the air. The team was getting tired, wired on caffeine and little sleep, waiting to get the call they all knew would come soon. The call that another girl had been taken.

Never mind the fact that every parent in the tristate area had their kids under lock and key—the Clockwork Killer would find a way. There was always someone who turned the other way in the grocery store or in the playground just long enough for him to slip in and snatch the child.

He was invisible, a chameleon. He blended in so well with the surroundings that no one thought he seemed out of place. His normalcy was his gift. He was able to stalk, to kidnap, to kill and dispose of the bodies, all without being noticed.

It had always been Baldwin's experience that the more normal the unsub seemed on the outside, the more twisted their pathology. The Clockwork Killer was proving to be just that sort of man.

And they were convinced that this was the work of a man. The violence done to the bodies was the key: no physical rape, but the thrust of the knife through the chest was a clear substitute for penetration.

The team had spent the day on the street, interviewing the multitude of possibles their compatriots at Fairfax County Homicide dredged up. They talked to the usual suspects, the local sex offenders topping the list. Alibis were checked, probation officers interviewed, neighbors notified and questioned. The day had grown warm, and they were all cranky by the time Baldwin and Charlotte had reached the home of the creepiest man Baldwin had met in a long time.

His name was Harold Arlen.

Even now, four hours later, in a perfectly comfortable, air-conditioned room, Baldwin broke out in a sweat at the thought of Arlen.

The Clockwork Killer may have had the mundane ability to fit in on his side, but Baldwin had a unique talent for ferreting out the truth. He wasn't psychic—far from it. He just had a knack for seeing past the words being spoken, into the soul of the suspect he was interviewing. He could see when something was out of place. His boss called him the human lie detector. Baldwin didn't know if that was the case, but as he went back through the files, he couldn't help but feel like there was a problem with Harold Arlen. He was a serial offender, yes, but there was more. Something about him had seemed off.

Baldwin had done the interview himself, and it felt… smooth. Arlen was perfectly under control. Politely disinterested. He had all the right answers, every date and time covered. His alibi was perfectly intact. But Arlen's eyes had lightened a bit when he caught a glimpse of the girls' pictures, the pupils contracting, lips thinning, the corners turning up ever so slightly. Baldwin had gotten that chill, the sense that something is wrong that precedes a phone call bearing bad news.

Baldwin flipped through the man's record again, familiarizing himself with all the details.

Over the past decade, Harold Arlen had been repeatedly accused of taking indecent liberties with a minor, and indecent exposure. He was, at his most basic, a tally wagger. Got his rocks off exposing himself to little girls. He used to drive by their bus stops, window down, and ask if they'd like to see his new puppy. When they approached the window, he exposed himself.

His most recent bust was back in 1998, after he was caught with a little girl in the front seat of his car with her hand on his penis. The judge wasn't lenient; because this was the fifth time Arlen had been charged with indecent exposure, and since it had proceeded to what the courts referred to as lascivious intent, Arlen was sentenced to three years in prison and mandatory chemical castration. By all accounts, he was a model prisoner, and had come out of the joint a new man. He registered with the sex offender database, showed up on time for his appointments to get his Depo-Provera shots, accepted that his neighbors sometimes egged his house without complaint. When Halloween rolled around, he turned off all his lights and wouldn't answer the door. All the things he was supposed to do.

Harold Arlen. He fit the profile perfectly—a suspect who was so into showing off for little girls rarely stopped, even if he couldn't function normally.

They had other suspects, men who fit parts of the profile. They wouldn't stop pursuing those angles, but for now…

He knocked his knuckles on the wooden table for luck, then handed the file to Charlotte with a sideways glance. "Take a closer look at this," he said.

She popped it open and began reading without meeting his eyes.

He pushed his chair back and stretched, running his hands through his hair. Everyone took the sign. Geroux started shuffling the files into a neat stack, Sparrow yawned without covering her mouth, Butler closed his laptop. Charlotte alone didn't move. She had been coy this afternoon, only speaking when spoken to, focused too hard on her work, which he took as a good sign. Maybe she'd taken stock of the situation and realized it wasn't such a grand idea to be screwing her boss.

She still had her eyes on the file when she finally spoke. "Did you see his current occupation? He's a photographer at Sears. He's not supposed to be having contact with kids, but I'll bet he is. If it's him, there's a chance that he's been stalking his victims through his job. We should have the Homicide guys run through the list of victims and see if any of them had photographs made in the past six months."

"That's a good thought. So you concur?"

"All of his previous jobs involved children of some kind. And he's a good-looking guy—he wouldn't stand out." She chewed on her lip for a moment, and Baldwin felt a pang deep in his stomach. "Yes, I concur. I think Mr. Arlen is worth having another conversation with."

"Not to mention the chemical castration. That would explain why none of the girls had been raped. We always knew he was using the knife as a substitute."

"We need to give him a second glance." She handed the file back to Baldwin with a curt nod.

"Then let's go meet with Goldman and the Fairfax County Homicide team. Let him know we want to take a closer look. At the very least they can get a tail on Arlen, see if he's doing anything that raises eyebrows."

Their role in the case was tricky. Normally, it wasn't their job to identify suspects—just to give the local police an idea of the kind of person to look for. But the pressure was on, and it was all hands on deck.

The phone began to ring just as he finished, and his heart sank. Too late. They were too late.

Charlotte answered without giving it a chance to ring twice. She listened intently.

"What is it?" Baldwin asked, but she just shook her head and motioned him away. The four of them stood stock-still, waiting for her to hang up.

After an endless amount of time, she did. Her face was pale, her amber eyes clouded with anger.

"The Great Falls Police just got a call. Another girl is missing, name is Kaylie Fields."

Their collective breath let out. Geroux sat back at the table with a grimace. The rest of the team stayed standing, ready, expectant.

"From where?" Baldwin asked.

"Her parents took her and her brother to a nursery to buy some plants for their garden. Right in the middle of downtown Great Falls. She turned a corner and was gone. Of course, there are no cameras at the nursery. He picked his spot well."

"And we're sure it's him?"

"The description of the girl matches. Ten years old, small boned, blond hair. The timing is too perfect. It's him, all right."

Baldwin felt his heart rate rise a fraction.

"We need to make a move on this Arlen guy, quickly," Geroux said.

"Keep looking at everyone, Geroux. We can't put all our eggs in one basket. But, Sparrow?"

"Yeah, boss?"

"While Geroux finishes these files, you see what you can find out about Arlen. Track his every move. I want all the details of this guy's history, credit reports, who he talks to, what kind of soap he's using. He may be using online accounts—you can go work your magic there, too. He started killing five weeks ago. What made him start? If Arlen is our guy, was there something in his recent past that stands out as a good stressor? Talk to Sears—see if he's been disciplined lately. Look at his close relatives, his exes, anyone and anything that you can find."

Sparrow smiled at him, careful not to let her teeth show.

The front two were crossed a bit, and it gave her fits. He thought it gave her an air of mystery, but she hated the perceived flaw.

"Butler, I'd like you to start cross-referencing the databases. See what you can dig up. There was a three-year lag time between Arlen's release from prison and the start of these murders. Check through ViCAP and see what other crimes have been committed in this area, and throw in Maryland and West Virginia too, just to be safe."

"Checking for an escalation pattern, Doc?"

"That's it exactly. Let's make sure we didn't miss anything in the local area." He smiled at Butler, clapped a hand on his shoulder. "Charlotte and I will go talk to the Homicide guys, let them know what we're on to. We've got a few hours of daylight left. Let's make the most of them."

As they left the building, he felt a spark of hope. This might come together after all.

Twenty-Two

Taylor and McKenzie left Hillsboro High School with the files of several students, including Juri Edvin, and a list of the kids the counselors had termed Goth. She was surprised to recognize a name on that list—Letha King was a part of the alternative crowd. Taylor couldn't help but wonder if she was involved.

Could a girl murder her own brother? The answer, unfortunately, was yes. She called Marcus, asked for a meeting with the girl later.

Taylor wanted to go directly to the hospital and have a chat with Juri Edvin, then do a six-pack of like photos and take them to Theo Howell, see if he could pick out the drug dealer he knew as Thorn. It all made sense to Taylor, the idea that Thorn and Juri Edvin were one and the same. And maybe Theo could shed some light on the relationship between his friend Jerry and Jerry's little sister, Letha, and what Jerry and Brandon Scott had been fighting about.

But as they drove back downtown, her cell rang. It was Marcus.

"That was quick. What's up?" she asked, driving with

one hand. They were in Hillsboro Village, passing Vanderbilt, and she sent a quick prayer toward Brittany Carson.

"We've got the man who was at the crime scenes, Keith Johnson? To start, he insists on being called King Barent. And he's claiming he's responsible for the murders."

"Really. Why do you sound so unconvinced?"

She heard him sigh. "I don't know. He knows some details that haven't been released, but he might have seen the video online, too."

"We'll come there first then. Can you check on Juri Edvin's status for me? I'm more convinced than ever that he's the boy named Thorn who's been pushing the drugs into Hillsboro. Make sure there's a guard on his room, too. If he tried to kill Brittany Carson once, I don't want him getting any ideas now that she's in an even more vulnerable position."

"Sure. Hey, speaking of that—at the Carson place? There was a small patch of semen found on the bricks outside the bay window. It looks into the den."

"Semen, huh? My gut was right on the money there. I bet you Mr. Edvin was watching through the windows, masturbating to Brittany Carson's dying body. That nasty little bastard. I should have let Max chew him to pieces."

"You want me to send that over to Private Match as well, get DNA from Edvin to look for a match?"

"Yes, please."

"One more thing. The letter? Tim Davis said to tell you that he thinks the blood came from several different sources. Possibly all the victims. He's matched blood types to them. Several distinct samples, he said."

"Jesus. So the symbols were drawn in the victims' blood?"

"Looks that way."

"Wow. All right. I'll see you in a few."

She hung up the phone and filled McKenzie in. They were nearly to Broadway now, just a few more minutes to the CJC.

"You look exhausted, LT."

"I am exhausted. Aren't you?"

"Sure. But this is an incredibly fascinating case. Witches and vampires and Goths, teenagers possibly murdering their peers, all thrown into a psychotic melting pot. What's not to like?"

She huffed out a laugh. "I'm glad you can find the intrigue in all this. I just want to piece together the case and find who's responsible. Let's go see if the vampire king knows from whence he speaks."

Taylor was surprised by the looks of the man calling himself the vampire king. He was burly in an unfit way, a red-and-blue-striped rugby shirt stretched taut across his belly. His brown hair was mousy and thinned at the top, curling over the collar of his shirt in greasy tangles. His skin was pale and strangely devoid of facial hair—there was no sign of a beard or eyebrows. Brown eyes, not unintelligent, capped off his moon-round face.

She watched him on the video-feed monitor that was running into Interrogation One, assessing. He didn't seem nervous or excited, just bored. One long finger snaked against his chin, then sauntered casually up to his nose. With a furtive glance at the door, he indelicately picked, then examined the end of his finger. Taylor turned away, mildly repulsed.

McKenzie and Marcus watched with interest. "Amazing. His teeth, he has fangs, too. Though I can't tell if it's the mouth from the video. What do you think, LT?"

"Is his finger in his mouth?" she asked.

"No," McKenzie laughed.

She turned around and looked back to the video.

"I'll have to see the movie again to be sure, but it could be him. Though it seems to me that the face on the film was thinner—it had a much sharper chin. I'll talk to him alone to start. You guys observe from here."

Interrogation One was right next door. She entered the

room and Barent jumped to his feet. The movement was so sudden, so surprising that her hand went to her weapon. She unhooked the snap with her middle finger. He backed away from her, hissing.

"Sir, sit down," she said, voice ringing with authority. He feinted at her, going right, then left, still making the hideous noise that sounded like a strangling cat. The room was small—he'd have to go through her to get out. She heard the door open, but she didn't take her eyes off Barent. He was staring into her face like she was holding a knife to his jugular. His eyes finally strayed away from hers, and that moment was all she needed. She pounced on him, flipped him around and smashed him face first against the wall. He snapped his jaws at her and she leaned away while he struggled. Then Marcus was next to her, and Barent was in handcuffs and pushed heavily into the chair. He was panting, frustration bleeding off him in waves. Taylor caught her breath and stepped away, letting Marcus secure Barent.

"What is wrong with you?" she yelled.

"Keep her away, keep her away, keep her away, keep her away." Barent was panicked, sweat dripping off his brow, and she didn't know what to do except listen to him.

"Detective Wade, join me outside," she said, then turned. The panting ceased behind her, the door swinging shut. Two seconds later, Marcus came out. The look on his face made her want to giggle, the adrenaline spilling away.

McKenzie met them in the hall.

"What the hell was that about?" she asked.

"I don't know. He had a completely real and visceral reaction to you."

"He nearly gave me a heart attack. When he jumped at me I almost shot the idiot. Marcus, was he like this at all before?"

"No. He's been completely normal. Well, as normal as someone who claims to be a vampire can be."

They went back to the video feed. Barent was calmed

now, his eyes the only thing moving, roving constantly around the room.

"Was there any record of mental illness in his file?" McKenzie asked.

Marcus shook his head. "Not that I saw. Why don't you let me have a go at him. He's not reacted badly to me yet."

"You up for that?" she asked.

"Yeah, just have the Tasers ready in case he freaks out on me."

They watched him enter the room. Barent started at the noise, but relaxed when he saw Marcus.

"Please, please, please don't let her in here again." His body bowed in supplication, his lips quivering in terror.

"She's just outside, observing," Marcus said. "What's the problem?"

"You don't recognize her? Of course, how could you? You aren't one of us, you don't understand. She's the Bruxa. She's Lilith, Lilitu. She came to me in the night and drank my blood, turned me into one of her kind. She was my mother. She kills me in all my lives."

Marcus warily took the chair across from Barent.

"All your lives?"

Barent warmed to his topic with fervor. "We are the reincarnate, young one. We find each other, our spirits moving across the centuries to find safe haven in corporeal bodies. We are traditionally agents of destruction, but some of us have had a powerful reawakening, have found that love will compensate for our sadistic natures. But Lilitu kills all of that. She wishes for us to return to the Old Ways, to feast on the blood of the children and discard the code of ethics put into place by the Sanguinarium."

"The Sanguinarium?"

"It is our ruling body. Our church. All psy and sang vampires follow a specific code of ethics. We aren't bloodthirsty monsters driven by our desire for death and destruction. Well, not all of us, anyway. I lead the Vampyre Nation, as I told you before. We are but one subsection of the San-guinarium—there are many families across the world."

"Psy versus sang? What's that?"

Barent warmed to his topic, eyes shining as he spoke. "Psychic versus sanguine. Energy versus blood. Many of us don't drink blood anymore, we've evolved. We can feed off energy. But some still enjoy the sanguine lifestyle. There is precedence for it, after all."

Marcus glanced up at the camera, the silent message sent to Taylor and McKenzie. Nut. Job.

Taylor tuned him out, turned to McKenzie. "So I'm Lilith?"

"The succubus. The rumors about you are true, appar-ently. I just didn't realize men could tell that from your aura."

"Oh, you're just hysterical. What do we do with this guy?"

"Listen to him. I don't know what we can glean, but you never know."

"You chat with him then, since you speak the language. I'll stay here. I don't feel that great."

"LT, what's wrong?"

"I feel…like…all my…energy is…gone." She collapsed into laughter, felt better immediately. There were no such things as vampires. There were strange people in the world, and she'd run into a slew of them on this case. Period, end of story.

"You're a riot, LT." He entered the room and she headed back to her office.

A young woman was sitting in the spare chair outside Taylor's door. There were several other people in the small space, detectives going about their daily work, all keeping a safe distance from the woman. Sidelong glances, lots of throat clearing. When Taylor entered the room, the woman stood, her long black skirt swishing with the effort. Black hair glistened nearly to her waist, thick and coiled. She was small, no more than five foot three, and looked up at Taylor with blue eyes the color of the sea. Taylor felt oddly mesmerized, stopped, at a loss for words.

The woman smiled, held out her hand.

"I am Ariadne," she said. "I am here to help."

Twenty-Three

Charlotte paced around the Fairfax County Homicide offices. God, what was taking so long? She had other things to do today.

Baldwin sat quietly, flipping through the file over and over again. She'd tried getting his attention by slipping past him and running her foot up his calf, but he cock-blocked her, clearing his throat meaningfully. She finally caught his eye, there was a combination of desire and exasperation lingering in the clear green. She winked at him, then resumed her pacing.

They'd been waiting for Max Goldman, the commander of the Fairfax County Homicide team, for the better part of an hour. He finally chugged through the door, running his hand through his wispy black hair, combing it back from his prominent forehead. Baldwin jumped to his feet, shook the outstretched hand. Goldman turned to Charlotte second, grasped the tips of her fingers in that bizarrely effeminate way some men had. She supposed it lingered on from the days when a touch of the fingers would lead to a kiss, planted softly on the top of the hand. But this was 2004, for Christ's sake. Like a real handshake was going to give them girl cooties or something. She only took minor offense at being handed the limp fish second; Baldwin's shake had wiped some of the sweat off Goldman's palm.

"Sorry I'm late. Got caught up in court this morning. What can I help you with? You got something for me on this Clockwork asshole? He's running our asses ragged, and we got nothin'. Fucking squirrel. I hate working these kiddy diddlers." As he spoke, he ushered them into his office.

Charlotte measured people on a scale of one to ten, ten being the ones she wanted to fuck immediately, one representing the ones who she wouldn't touch with a ten-foot pole. Goldman fell into the latter category. He had yellow teeth, crowded together in his mouth like they were planning a jailbreak, and he'd eaten onions with his lunch—she could smell him from five feet away. Which is where she stayed, perched on the edge of a credenza near the open door, to help catch a breeze. Baldwin was sitting face-to-face with the man, God bless him.

Goldman was still chattering. "I hope you've got something for me, 'cause I'm getting crucified, Jesus H. Roosevelt on the cross crucified, by anyone with a microphone within a hundred miles."

A colorful man. What a match for that breath.

Baldwin nodded. "We have more for your team to look at, yes. We've refined the profile, and we have someone we think could be a suspect."

"That's fan-fuckin'tastic." He looked at his watch. "Let's go arrest him. We do it now, we can make the five-o'clock news, get little Kaylie home by dark."

"Let's just go over the details first, okay? Charlotte?"

Charlotte swiveled her head toward Goldman.

"His name is Harold Arlen. He's a convicted sex offender, lives in the Great Falls area. We think you should put some eyes on him."

Goldman looked impressed. "What was with that big

song and dance you gave me about not identifying suspects, just pointing us in the direction of a type of person? You do voodoo now, too?"

Baldwin laughed briefly, then got serious. "Not exactly. We've been working on the profile, and he fits many of the top-line points. We believe the man who is perpetrating these crimes is a sex offender, mid-thirties, who needs the privacy of his own home to act out his fantasies. Like we talked about, he'll have an extensive collection of child pornography. This suspect is fascinated by children, but girls only. He was probably abused in his early years, before he was ten or so, by a female babysitter or close relative. He's controlling, manipulative and deceitful. He doesn't have any real friends. There's something about him that makes children unafraid, which means he has no obvious, visible physical deformities. But he's impotent, unable to have meaningful physical relationships with adults or children. Regardless of that, he's charming and fits into society. His car is nondescript, a sedan, probably an import. A high-end Honda, Nissan or low-end Lexus, something that wouldn't stand out but wouldn't look out of place. It would match the demographics of this neighborhood. The median income in this area is about $170,000, so he isn't driving a clunker. He's white, too."

"That's not a lot to go on, Doc. You've described half the country-club set, and three quarters of the folks who hang at the Great Falls Pub."

Charlotte slid off the credenza. She'd had enough fore-play—it was time to get back to work. "Listen, Arlen works at Sears in the photography department, which gives him access to children. How he got the job is beyond me. Our suspect will have a history of violence in his teens, before he learned to control his temper, so I'd advise backtracking Arlen's life. See if he's got something in his juvenile jacket. We'll keep working it from our end."

Goldman gave her legs an eyeful, then turned to Baldwin.

"Can I ask you a question, Doc? How did you narrow it down to this guy?"

"The Depo-Provera. The stabbing is a stand-in for sexual penetration. Arlen is only one of ten in the local files who are on the shot who fit the profile. I've got my people looking for something that might be a stressor, a breaking point that would drive him to start killing. And to be perfectly honest, when I talked to him, he gave me the creeps."

"That's pretty damn scientific, if you ask me. Instinct counts for a lot in this business."

"I know. You can't teach instinct. I tell everyone on my team to follow theirs. So I'm practicing what I preach. Arlen is involved."

"Okay then, if you say so. I'll get the team rounded up, and we'll take a gander."

Baldwin stood, stuck out his hand to shake goodbye. Charlotte just stood by his side, listening, feeling the power surge off of him. He smelled good, warm and clean, like leftover soap and shampoo and the tiniest hint of male sweat squeaking through. He didn't wear cologne, which made her happy. She liked men who smelled like men, not flowers or wood chips or cedar. Her mind drifted back to their earlier romp.

A few seconds later, things were wrapping up. She'd missed something. Wow, she really needed to try and focus. Just being around him made her lose all track of time and space.

"Good. Thanks for your time. We're going to go back to the office, we have more interviews to conduct. I've got my people back tracing the hard copies of Arlen's life. Just give us a yell if you need anything," Baldwin said.

He and Goldman shook hands and Goldman said, "I'll let you know. One little problem—we do need some sort of evidentiary material to get a warrant. Judges up here aren't easily swayed."

"Remind them that we have a missing girl, then. See if they want Kaylie's death on their conscience."

"Yeah, yeah. I hear ya."

Baldwin seemed willing to let it go at that, but Charlotte didn't think he was taking the request seriously enough.

"Mr. Goldman, we need that warrant. We have to find some evidence," Charlotte said.

"Then you do that, girlie. You go find me something that will talk these judges into letting us into the creepo's house."

"It's agent, *sir.*"

"Hmm. So it is. Sorry 'bout that."

He smiled meaningfully. He wasn't sorry at all. Charlotte had spent her life being second to the men around her, and she got damn good and tired of having to prove herself.

Goldman saw them out and Charlotte waited until they were back in the parking lot before she spoke. Complaining to Baldwin about Goldman's treatment wouldn't work. Besides, she'd stuck up for herself. She decided to use a different tack.

"Was it just me, or did the commander there seem to be in a hurry to get the cuffs on someone?"

Baldwin looked at her queerly. "And you think he should be taking it slow? We've got a missing girl out there, plus five already dead."

"Not slow, no. But we need more information about this guy before we arrest him. Goldman was right—we need actual evidence of wrongdoing. We're just going on a hunch. Your hunch."

"Charlotte, you have my blessing to drum up whatever evidence you can on this guy." He held the car door open for her. She ran a hand along his stomach as she got in.

After he slammed the door and turned the engine over, Charlotte leaned over and rubbed his crotch. "What do you say we stop off for a quickie on our way back to the office?"

"Now's not the time. We can wait until later." Baldwin adjusted his sunglasses, pulled out of the parking lot a tad faster than necessary.

Charlotte was getting bored with being told no. She wasn't used to it. Most men she slept with couldn't take no for an answer. Well, she knew just how to fix that attitude. She waited until they hit the highway south before leaning over again, this time tugging down his zipper. He groaned.

"You're not."

"I most certainly am."

She heard the ghost of a laugh from above.

"We're going to get arrested," he said a few moments later.

She stopped and looked up at him, the back of her head tapping the steering wheel. "Just don't wreck the car. I'm not wearing my seat belt."

Twenty-Four

Taylor had never wished so hard for a day to end. Home-made horror films, vampires and now a self-proclaimed witch. She was waiting for a werewolf to come turn himself in, just to complete the ensemble.

Ariadne sat across from her, back ramrod straight, not touching the chair behind her. The woman didn't blink much, and Taylor found her gaze disconcerting. She edged a paper clip around the top of her desk with a finger.

"Okay, go over it again. You're a witch."

Ariadne laughed, a musical, tinkling sound that made Taylor want to smile. "I am a sole practitioner Dianic witch, yes. I have been studying Wicca for many years, but my family is made up of witches, my mother and her mother before her. I found my path in my mid-twenties, when I couldn't ignore the power I'd attained any longer. I was causing change, causing problems, actually, and I needed to find a way to harness the power that was building in me. Extensive practice has allowed me to temper myself, to focus my energies. And I normally wouldn't be found dead sitting in the office of a homicide detective, but the Goddess told me to help you. And trust me, you need my help. You're on the edge of something very strong, evil, and you need a protector." She stopped and gazed speculatively at Taylor, eyes blank. "Though who would have ever thought I would be protecting Athena?"

"Huh?"

"You can't see yourself very well, Lieutenant Jackson."

Taylor abandoned the paper clip. "Listen. This is great, and I appreciate that you want to help. But I don't believe in spells and magic, and I have a lot of work to do." She started to stand, to dismiss this crazy woman who stared right through her.

"Don't you?" Ariadne asked, unmoving. "You aren't the least little bit superstitious? You don't throw salt over your shoulder, or lift your feet when you go over railroad tracks?"

Taylor folded her arms across her chest. "I'm as super-stitious as the next person. But that doesn't mean I believe in witches."

"But you do believe in evil, Lieutenant. You've seen it with your own eyes. I know evil exists. I think you'll find that we can be of use to one another, if you'll let me." She paused, focused on her hands, which were spread across her lap, dainty and manicured. "I promise not to put a wart on your nose."

She looked up and grinned, and Taylor couldn't help but smile back. The woman had a charming laugh and small white teeth—she certainly didn't fit the image Taylor had of a witch.

A flash caught Taylor's eye. She glanced at it, saw the delicately wrought chain of silver encircling Ariadne's neck, and the ornate pentacle that hung just in the indentation between her clavicle and her throat. Without thinking, she drew back slightly.

"Maid, mother and crone," Ariadne said.

"What?"

"You were thinking I didn't look like a witch. We believe in the incarnations. Maid—the young witch, Mother—the fertile witch, Crone—the wise woman. I'm more the maid side of things, as you can tell." She laughed again, and Taylor couldn't help but join her this time. She felt good, reenergized. She sat back down, chewed on her lip.

"Okay, so how did you know what I was thinking?"

"I read your mind."

Taylor immediately squirmed in her chair. Ariadne leaned forward, eyes twinkling.

"I'm kidding. I didn't read your mind, though we can do that. It's not mind reading the way you're thinking of it, it's more drowsing, a way to look into your feelings. Relying on your gut, your emotions, to help you make decisions about what a person is really thinking. You do quite a bit of that yourself, Lieutenant. So do I, and I'm actually quite good at it. I have to be careful not to look too deeply. It's not polite. But I had no reason to look into your head—your face is like a mirror of your soul, transparent. You said it all yourself."

Taylor was taken aback. She'd always thought her face inscrutable; it was one of her strengths. Fitz had taught her that a good cop had to be half actor to elicit trust from suspects—that's what made her so good in interrogations. A spike of pain passed through her. She straightened, tried to make it go away.

"Intuition isn't mind reading," she said.

"Sure it is. You're assimilating others' emotions and putting them into context." The smile fled, and Ariadne's brow creased. "Listen, you may not believe in witches, and that's fine. But these murders, this situation, are very, very serious. This is way more than playing light as a feather, stiff as a board. This is real, and it's dangerous. There is a whole community of people who practice some form of paganism in Nashville, thousands of them, more than you could possibly imagine. It's a peaceful, gentle religion, but there's always the one who wants to pervert the Goddess's power. That's what we're dealing with, and you're going to need my help to stop him."

"Him?" Taylor asked.

"Yes. I don't know his name, but he's powerful, and young. And he's not alone."

Taylor left Ariadne in her office. She needed a sanity break.

She found McKenzie and Marcus standing in the hallway, deep in discussion.

"What's up?" she asked.

McKenzie grimaced. "Barent has asked for counsel. We had to stop interrogating him."

"Well, that's a shame. Did he give anything up before he invoked?"

Marcus rubbed his chin. "Not exactly. I think we have enough to get a warrant for his house—with him claiming to have committed the murders and his attendance at the crime scenes, that shouldn't be a problem. I'm going to write up the warrant application now, see what I can make happen. He definitely knows more than he should about it, but I'm still not convinced that he's really responsible. He's a bit fragmented, personality-wise. I had him moved to a cell and booked, just in case. I didn't want to send him home and have something go down. He seems like he has something to prove, though I'll be damned if I think he killed those kids."

McKenzie leaned against the wall. "He's a true narcissist, that's for sure. And a true believer. He honestly feels he's a psychic, energy-feeding vampire, and that he heads a nation of vampires. He told us he's been at war for the past two years with another vampire king, Laurent. They've got an online media campaign against one another, their followers are viciously attacking each other. It's a brave new world in the vampire wars—cyberspace."

Lincoln joined them in the hall. The confab was starting to draw the attention of several passing officers, who didn't mask their curiosity.

"Are you sure they aren't involved in some kind of LARP?" Lincoln asked.

"A LARP? What's that?" Marcus asked.

McKenzie answered. "Live-action role-playing. A modern-day version of Dungeons and Dragons. LARPs are incredibly intense. It's quite possible that if you already have an unsteady mind, extensive exposure to a LARP world could be a tipping point. It's an excellent suggestion. It wouldn't be the first time. We had a situation in Orlando with a rape role-playing game called RapeAid, with extensive gang-rape scenarios. A couple of the men playing decided to act it out—managed to rape four women before we caught them."

"Is it possible that the murderer was acting out something from one of these LARPs? And that's why they filmed it all and posted it online?" Taylor asked.

"Anything's possible," McKenzie said.

"I have one more component to throw into the mix. I've got a woman in my office, claims she's a witch. Her name is Ariadne."

McKenzie eyed her speculatively. "Ariadne the witch. That's priceless."

"Why?"

"Don't you know the history of Ariadne?" He was met with three blank stares. He shook his head. "What am I going to do with all of you? Ariadne was the daughter of King Minos of Crete. She helped Theseus get through the labyrinth without being killed by the Minotaur, then went on to marry Dionysus."

Taylor raised an eyebrow. "Greek mythology. Now it makes sense. She called me Athena," she said.

"That fits." McKenzie had something akin to amusement glinting behind his steady gaze. "Can I meet her?"

"Sure." They started back to the Homicide offices.

"With any luck, we'll be able to close in on this killer before the end of the day. We're all going to have to get some rest—you guys look kind of rough. Get some sleep this evening. We'll tackle everything fresh in the morning if it doesn't break soon."

"That goes for you too, LT," Lincoln said.

"I know, and I will. But I still need to go talk to Juri Edvin. How is the Internet stuff coming?"

He stopped walking and leaned back against the wall. "It's been a total nightmare. The video gets replaced every time the old one is removed. But they'll get a handle on it—it's only been a few hours. They're doing all they can to trace everything. My contact at YouTube is supposed to call me within the day. Since it's Saturday, they had to pull in some of the senior staff who had the weekend off to help with the situation, and that was taking some time. When we talked last, they thought they might have a lead on the original upload site."

"Good. I'm glad they're so willing to help. That's a nice change. You get to it, and let me know what happens. Marcus, get that warrant in place and let's see what Mr. Vampire has in his closet. Don't get stuck by anything."

Ariadne was where Taylor had left her, sitting in the chair just inside Taylor's office. Taylor suggested they go into the conference room so they could have more space.

Lincoln, staring at Ariadne with openly frank curiosity, excused himself, but shook the girl's hand first, lingering for a moment. Ariadne smiled back at him, and Taylor could swear he blushed.

McKenzie shook her hand with interest as well, but his was most definitely cool and appraising, pure professional detachment. Marcus was the one who held back, and Taylor found that interesting. He mumbled something about the warrant and scooted out of the room.

Taylor and McKenzie settled across the table from Ariadne, and Taylor gestured for her to begin. "Tell us what you know. But first, would you please answer something else for me? Why do you want to help us?"

"Well, that's easy enough. All of us are threatened by the

actions of this warlock. Have you ever heard of the Wiccan Rede?" Ariadne asked.

"No," Taylor answered.

"It's our code of ethics, what all good little witches and warlocks believe in. It's our version of the Hippocratic oath. The Rede itself is long and involved—gives us a guide to the intricacies of spell work on the feast days, these types of things. But it's the last two lines that are the most important. 'These eight words the Rede fulfill—an ye harm none, do what ye will.' We believe that any magick you cast is brought back to you threefold. The law of return, that's what we call it. Which means if you cast a negative spell, that negativity will come back and bite you on the ass."

"So why would a witch ever cast a negative spell?" Taylor asked.

"Some feel they can control it, some don't care. Sometimes it's vital and necessary, like binding. That's what I've been doing, trying to bind the killer, to forbid him from killing any more innocents. But the vast majority of good witches don't go anywhere near negative casting. It's just too unpredictable."

"So according to you, the killings yesterday were the work of a witch?"

"Of a warlock. A young, powerful warlock. Actually, I believe a whole coven was involved. I saw them last night, at Subversion."

"What's that?"

"A coven? It's a group of like-minded witches who want to work together, to draw power from one another."

"I meant Subversion. I've not heard of it."

"Oh, sorry, Lieutenant. It's a club, on Second Avenue. They only operate once a month or so, and on special occasions, like Samhain—sorry, Halloween. When I heard about the murders, I immediately began looking for them. They led me to the club. There were two, a boy and a girl. By the way, not to confuse you, but they're practicing vampirism too, the little bats. A second girl joined them. They had an awful spat, then she took off running. The two older ones followed her. I lost them after that. It was a rough night, actually. So many of these Goth kids think they're psychic vamps, and they go to the clubs to feed. The energy is overwhelming, you see, especially on a feast day. It drains your energy—heck, it even affects me, and I've got a rock-solid shield. Feeding on others without express permission is a nasty, dark habit. We don't approve."

"You called them bats."

"It's a nickname for the Goths. Baby bats. In Wicca we call them Fluff Bunnies. But Fluffs are a bit different—they're more poseurs, wannabes. These bats are for real, they're just too young to be accepted into a traditional coven. Legally, you must be eighteen."

"Bats," Taylor said. "What did they look like?"

"The girl was tall, as tall as you, black hair, pale, of course, with green eyes. They were very green—they might have been colored contacts. She was in traditional garb, her makeup designated her as a RomantiGoth."

"RomantiGoth? What's that?" Taylor asked.

McKenzie finally spoke up. "There are a ton of subsects within the Goth community—fairies and industrials and neopunk, skimpy, gravers. I could go on and on. New ones pop up every day."

Ariadne eyed him with interest. "So you are one of us?" she asked.

"Not anymore," McKenzie answered impassively.

"Hmm," Ariadne said, head cocked to one side. She turned back to Taylor. "It's much more an American phenomenon. Darklings in the European sects don't distinguish themselves so rigidly. We're still so married to our labels."

"Ah. Continue, please," Taylor said.

"The boy was dressed similarly, but in black pants instead of a skirt. They both had corsets on, platform boots that laced high up on their calves, cloaks. His hair is short, cropped, dyed black. They were both made-up, but I'd recognize them if I saw them again. They stood out, made an imprint on me. The youngest was in makeup, but not as elaborately dressed."

"If we showed you pictures?"

"Certainly."

"What's the difference between Goths and Wicca?"

"Oh, lots. Wicca is an earth-based religion. Goths are…well, let's put it this way. Most people don't like to be sad. The world says you have to be happy, to go, go, go. Goths embrace that darkness. They explore their sadness, and the sadness of others."

She glanced at McKenzie, who nodded despite his obvious embarrassment. Poor guy was being laid bare in front of her. She felt for him.

"And the makeup?" she asked.

"A variety of self-expression. They like to disappear, to draw attention away from their corporeal being and to their spiritual side. The real ones are accomplished witches and warlocks—they understand paganism and all its iterations thoroughly. When you find this boy, you'll find his spell book, what we normally call our Book of Shadows. It's our most intimate accessory, full of hopes and dreams, spell work and notes, what worked, what didn't. It's a vital piece of our lives, and his will be full of clues for you. So will his altar."

"It seems like they're drawing attention to themselves by being different, instead of away from themselves," Taylor said.

"Well, that's the outsider's way of seeing them. Most are searching, seeking, looking for their place in the world. They find the Gothic lifestyle and it fits them, like pulling on your favorite pair of jeans and knowing you look fantastic. It's an emotional journey as well as physical."

"But the black dress, the hanging out in graveyards. What's all that about?"

Ariadne smiled. "Because they're sad. But unlike most, they embrace that emotion. If you could stop, look inside, admit to yourself what is really making you unhappy, then try to alter yourself for the right reasons, for your own personal empowerment, you'd be much better off. It's okay to be sad. You don't have to be happy all the time. It's healthy to let some depressive thoughts into your psyche, to think about the bad things that can happen without the judgment of society. Look at the Buddhists. They are a guiding force behind most disciplined Goths. Buddhist teachings tell you not to get attached to your emotions while you experience them. That emotions are simply a reaction to stimuli, that a sensation doesn't define you. That level of self-awareness is the key to the gothic lifestyle. They mourn for mankind, basically."

"They're teenagers. How self-aware can they possibly be?"

"Very. You're looking for an incredibly intelligent person, Lieutenant, one who is well-read, well versed in everything from mythology to naturalism to botany. Someone who has skills, who can be a natural leader. Someone who has learned that darkness carries a current, who thinks that they can feed off the energies of the night, and can scare the hell out of all of us who strive to work for good. And you may want to check his athamé for blood. I assume that's what he used to cut them."

"What do you know about that?"

"The cuts? The pentacles? It was all over the news. It's something to excite, to titillate. To guarantee it's all that's talked about. The killer is exceptionally egocentric—he wanted to leave his signature behind."

Ariadne shifted in her seat, her tone more serious now. "This wasn't some guy shooting from a clock tower, Lieutenant. This was methodical, planned, and it might not be over. You need to be looking for someone with a very special skill set."

"Someone like you," McKenzie remarked.

Untroubled, Ariadne said, "Yes. Someone like me. But I would never kill to further my goals. That is strictly forbidden. You of all people know that. Besides, it's against my own personal code."

"You know an awful lot about this, Ariadne," Taylor said. "I can't help but wonder how. And not through any of these gimmicks, either. You know details, and you've actively interfered in an official police investigation."

"That is true," she said, a small smile playing on her lips.

"We have a man in custody who says he committed the murders," McKenzie said. "He also claims to be the king of the vampires."

Ariadne threw up her hands, her long hair swirling around her like a wave. "*Tcha.* The Vampyre Nation is a joke. They are parasites, vermin. This so-called vampire king is lying. The warlock who did this is too smart to turn himself in." She paused for a moment, then said, "Though he will want to brag, of course. Has he sent you a letter yet? I thought I picked up words last night."

McKenzie gave her a long look. "You'd make a good cop, Ariadne," he said at last.

Taylor leaned back in her chair, eyes narrowed. What was the agenda here? Yes, this was a splashy case, plucking at the heartstrings of everyone involved. And it wasn't entirely unusual to have people surrender themselves, admit to knowledge of the crimes. She'd had self-proclaimed psychics try to horn in on cases in the past, people who claimed they could see the missing, could communicate with their spirits if they were already gone. They'd always ended up being charlatans, glory seekers, redirecting the investigations to suit their own twisted purpose. She couldn't take that chance, not on a case this big. She realized she'd made her decision already.

"Ariadne, I'm going to read you your rights. You understand that I'm going to have to treat you as a suspect— you've really given me no choice. This is for your protection as much as for mine."

Ariadne nodded in agreement. "Do what you feel necessary, Lieutenant. I have nothing to hide—my heart is pure.

You must do what your path tells you. I am not offended in the least. As a matter of fact, if you hadn't, I might have been suspicious."

"And why's that?"

"Because now I know that you believe me."

Twenty-Five

She'd left McKenzie with the witch. He'd be able to ferret out whatever it was that Ariadne was holding back.

Truth be told, Ariadne made her desperately uncomfortable. Mind reader or no, she was entirely too perceptive. Taylor had noticed her eyeing the bouquet of white roses Memphis had sent, wondered if she'd had the audacity to read the card while Taylor had been conferring with her team in the corridor. Probably. Frauds, the lot of them, these people who claimed to use the supernatural as their guide. She most certainly didn't believe the woman was a witch, but she did believe she was involved. And since it wasn't unusual for suspects to inject themselves into cases, Ariadne certainly fell under suspicion.

What was the deal with that creepy Barent man? Claiming he was a vampire, that Taylor had killed him over and over. Marcus had submitted the paperwork to get the warrant, they were playing the waiting game now. She was surrounded by kooks.

And by one clever killer, who had them chasing their tails, looking into the dark shadows for answers.

It gave Taylor chills to pull back into the Kings' driveway, but she needed to talk to Letha before she went further. There were multiple cars in the driveway, well-wishers and neighbors bringing covered dishes and morbid curiosity.

Taylor had always felt vaguely uncomfortable with the southern tradition of the wake—too many people seemed to live for tragedies, were surrounded by death and sickness. They were the first in line to comfort strangers, to offer help when victims' families were more interested in battening down the hatches and healing themselves. This scene was being repeated all over Nashville this afternoon.

She knocked on the door, surprised when Letha herself answered. Her face had been scrubbed and her hair was clean, the black polish gone from her nails. Her eyes were clear.

"Letha, Lieutenant Jackson. We met yesterday. I'm so sorry about your brother. Can I come in?"

Letha glanced over her shoulder. "Do you mind if we talk out here? It's really crowded inside."

"Certainly."

The girl came out and closed the door behind her softly, as if she didn't want to alert anyone of her actions. Taylor stepped to the porch railing, leaned against it.

"So. I was at the school this morning, and your name came up. You hang out with the Goth kids?"

Letha bent and picked up a broken limb that had fallen on the stoop. "I don't hang with them, not really. I was just…experimenting."

"Who do you hang out with?"

"I'm a floater. I don't belong to any of the cliques."

"Theo Howell told us that you found Jerry yesterday, and called him and his sister to come over to help. You must be friends with them if they were your first recourse."

"Theo and Jerry are friends. Were friends. I didn't know who else to call."

"What about the police?"

She shook her head. "I didn't want to get Jerry in trouble."

Taylor tried not to groan aloud. The logic of teenagers.

"You should have called 911 as soon as you found him. You know that, don't you?"

"Yes, ma'am. I'm sorry."

"Don't apologize. So you aren't part of the popular crowd?"

"I told you. I don't hang out with anyone in particular." She tossed the branch out into the lawn. Taylor could see the lines of anger in the girl's shoulders.

"What do you know about drugs at school?"

Her eyes darted away, and she mumbled, "Nothing."

"Vi-Fri? You're sure you don't know anything about it?"

Now she was truly discomfited. "How do you know about that?" she asked.

Taylor nudged a fallen leaf with the toe of her boot. "Theo told me. Was Jerry doing drugs?"

She nodded meekly.

"Were you?"

"Maybe a little X, here or there, but nothing major. Just on weekends. Like Jerry. He gave me some of his, if he was in a good mood. Please don't tell my parents. They'll be really mad at me."

"Only if you tell me who Jerry bought the drugs from."

The girl hung her head. "His name is Thorn. He's a freshman."

"What's his real name?"

"I don't know. It's something foreign. I don't remember. Can I go back in now? My mom's going to notice I'm gone."

"Juri Edvin?"

She looked startled—she knew the name. "Maybe. I really don't know."

"What does Thorn look like?"

"I don't know. Short, like me. Kinda heavyset. He's really part of the Goth crowd."

Taylor watched the girl. She was biting a thumbnail, obviously upset. Was she lying? Or just not telling the whole truth? Taylor didn't think so, but it never hurt to ask.

"Letha, your brother and Brandon Scott had a fight last week. Do you have any idea what that might be about?"

"No," she said, quick and sharp. She clamped her lips together, leaving Taylor to think the real answer was yes.

"Letha. Was it the drugs? Were they fighting about Juri Edvin? Thorn?"

"I really don't know," she said.

"Is there anything else you can think of that might help me catch your brother's killer?"

She shook her head, mute.

"I figured as much." She gave the girl her card. "If you think of anything, please let me know." She turned to go.

"Ma'am?"

She faced the girl again. "Yes?"

"Is it true, about Brandon? That he was…mutilated?"

"Where did you hear that?"

"Umm…I saw the video online. Was that real?"

Taylor wrestled with her answer. Brandon had been a very good-looking boy. She watched the girl sweat it; she was genuinely concerned. There was the link.

"It may have been. Letha, do you know Brandon?"

The girl's eyes flooded with tears, all her stoic walls crumbling. "We used to date. We broke up a while ago though. He was…seeing someone else. Jerry was so mad at him, so mad for hurting me. That's what it was about, I'm sure. They'd been arguing a lot lately." She sounded much too bitter to be fourteen.

"I'm sorry," Taylor said.

Letha just nodded, then slipped silently through the front door into the house, closing it firmly behind her.

Strikeout. The girl didn't know anything more. Taylor could tell that she'd been telling at least most of the truth. Time to call in the big guns.

Twenty-Six

Jessamine Sparrow was sorely misnamed. Baldwin thought she should have been called bulldog—her tenacity was one of the things that he was most impressed with when he hired her. So when she said, "Hey, boss. Come take a look at this," with an indefinable note of curiosity in her voice, he dropped his files and mentally crossed his fingers.

Baldwin stretched and stood, shaking away the cobwebs. He'd been staring at evidence files for the better part of two hours and his head was aching with all the tiny print. He didn't need glasses, not yet anyway, but the words were swimming before his eyes, refracting in the harsh fluorescent light of the conference room.

Sparrow couldn't have felt much better. She'd been cruising the online world for nearly twenty hours.

Her computer screen was a mess, with open windows of every conceivable size, shape and color. She clicked one of the windows on the top left, made it fill the screen. It was an obituary notice from *The Washington Post,* dated January 12, 2004. A small face smiled sadly at him, a little girl, maybe eight, nine years old. She had no hair—his first thought was cancer.

"What's this?" he asked.

"Her name is Evie Kilmeade. Nine years old. She died this past January after a battle with leukemia."

"That's terrible."

"Yes, isn't it?" Sparrow spoke without the conviction many women would have given the statement. Though only in her late twenties, Sparrow was unmarried, with no real prospects, and no burning desire to populate her life with either a man or a baby anytime soon. She could still look at children and their suffering with a dispassionate eye. Baldwin had wondered if she was gay, then pushed it out of his mind. Her sexual orientation had absolutely no bearing on her ability to kick ass at her job, and Sparrow was one of the best hires he'd made in a long time.

"So what's the catch?"

"Well, the name sounded familiar. Kilmeade isn't terribly common, and when we did interviews with Arlen's neighbors, it stood out to me. Then I see this, and when I put it all together, I found her address. Guess where little Evie lived?" She glanced over her shoulder to make sure he was watching, then popped it up on the screen.

Baldwin read it three times in disbelief. "You're kidding," he said finally, mind whirling.

"Nope. She spent her last days on this earth living across the street from the big bad wolf."

Baldwin thought back, grabbed a mental image of the house across the street from Arlen's. That's right. He'd talked to them briefly two days earlier. The Kilmeades had been an open, friendly, caring couple, with two young boys. They'd never mentioned a little girl, and they were the only people who showed any sort of empathy toward their perverted neighbor. Kilmeade was some kind of psychologist, and he worked with prisoners.

"What color was her hair?" Baldwin asked.

"Funny you should ask. After some serious prodding

and a probable-cause warrant, Sears sent over all the negatives from every one of Arlen's shoots. You can thank Butler for that later. Evie Kilmeade has a file with them. When she still had hair, it was blond."

"Let me see."

Sparrow clicked her mouse a couple of times, and a full-color photograph came up. It was the same girl, though in this picture, she was healthy and happy, with long, cascading blond hair.

"So she physically fits the victim profile, she lived across the street from our main suspect and she's dead. But there's no evidence of murder—she died from leukemia complications, right?"

"Yes, she did. Six months ago."

"The connection, Sparrow? I need something more."

"I looked back through the online obituary guest book. There was a note from Arlen. I've printed it out for you."

She handed him a piece of paper. He got chills when he read the words.

Dear Evie,
I will miss your bright smile, your inquisitive nature, your charming laugh and your long hugs. Rest in peace, little one. You deserve a break.
Love,
Your Harry

"Son of a bitch. *Your Harry?* In his own words, he's admitting a relationship. Sparrow, you know what this means, right? He had personal and physical contact with a minor. That's breaking his probation. At the very least, Fairfax County can pick him up for that. We can sweat him ourselves if need be."

Sparrow nodded. "On the surface, at least, it looks like Evie and Arlen were friends. I'm thinking her death might have been the trigger. He loses Evie, then starts to re-create her, acting out all the horrible fantasies he's been having about her all this time. Finally, the fantasies weren't enough, and he started to kill."

Baldwin turned back to the image on the computer, traced his finger over the little girl's sharp chin. Of course. If Arlen had found a compatriot, a little girl he could act out with, and she betrayed him by dying on her own...well, that could easily have caused the break that got him started. If Arlen was their suspect, they had a good basis for motive. Baldwin ran his hands through his hair like he was pushing all the thoughts back in, and breathed a deep sigh.

"Nice work, Sparrow. That most certainly could be the case. Now let's go talk to her parents, find out just how close their daughter was to the local pedophile. Where's Charlotte?"

Sparrow didn't look at him, just started shutting down all the windows on her computer. "She's at the crime lab, I think. Something about double-checking one of the evidence tags."

"What?"

"I don't know. Sorry, boss, I wasn't really paying attention."

"It's no problem."

They started from the room. Baldwin held the door for her, let her go out before him.

"Hey, boss?" Sparrow's wide, clunky heels clacked on the linoleum floor.

"Yeah?" Baldwin answered, distracted. Could this be it? Could they have found that little link that explains everything?

"Speaking of Charlotte?"

That brought him back to the conversation. He warily answered, "Yes?"

Sparrow bit her lip, then dropped his gaze and shook her head. "Nothing. It's nothing, boss. Never mind." She walked out ahead of him, and Baldwin felt all the breath go from his body. They knew. They probably all knew. Son of a bitch.

And that little bit of uncertainty from Sparrow was all he needed to help him make his decision. He knew what he had to do. He must put the team first. They were in his charge in more ways than one.

Twenty-Seven

The hospital corridor was too bright, glaring and overly white to Taylor's tired eyes. She was heading to Brittany Carson's room first, then planned to sit down with Juri Edvin. His surgery had gone well—he was out of Recovery. Ready to be grilled. She was going to have answers before she left this hospital, no matter what it took.

Vanderbilt University Medical Center was always busy, packed with people young and old, in varying degrees of sickness. She'd been here many times—visiting the psychiatric ward to interrogate suspects deemed too violent or too insane to be booked into the regular system; attending to vicious wounds in the emergency room; even riding along on LifeFlight from a scene once, a desperate and frenetic evening that ended in tragedy despite their best efforts. It always smelled the same, bitter and astringent, overlaid with the sickly sweet smell of premature rot that emanated from the most dire cases. She hated hospitals.

Visiting hours were specific and militant in the Intensive Care Unit, but her badge allowed her access. A nurse manning the station shook her head, hurriedly explained the girl wasn't doing well, then went back to the multitudes of patients who could be helped.

Taylor took a deep breath, stepped through the doors. She wanted a chance to, well, do something. To say goodbye to a girl she'd never known. She stopped in front of Brittany Carson's room in the ICU. A patrol was seated three feet away. She motioned to the badge on her belt; he nodded and went back to his *Sports Illustrated.*

She looked through the glass wall at the girl, dwarfed by the machines keeping her alive. Tubes snaked into her mouth, the ventilator helping her breathe hissing with purpose. It didn't know its work was for naught—it reliably pumped, over and over and over, oxygenating the girl's lungs, forcing air into dead, gray flesh.

A voice sounded in Taylor's ear, sour and worn.

"She's brain-dead."

Taylor turned. Brittany Carson's mother, Elissa, was still wearing her red blouse. Suspicious dark streaks leaked across her breast and shoulders. Her highlighted hair, crumpled from her constant worrying, lay flat against her small head. Her eyes were dry. There would be time for crying after.

"I'm sorry," Taylor said.

"I'm sorry, too. She's a delightful girl, the light of my life. Since her father left, it's just been the two of us against the world. We'd had a conversation about this once. She read a story about a little girl who received a heart from a car-crash victim and declared on the spot that she wanted to be a donor." She looked into the room, swiped a finger under her eyes, gave Taylor a bittersweet smile. "I've just signed the organ donation forms. If I have to lose her, at least a few others may find life through her sacrifice. God works in mysterious ways, as they say."

"Yes, ma'am, He certainly does."

Taylor watched her trace a hand along the glass, caressing the shape of her daughter's face in the air.

"I'll miss her so much."

Taylor bit back unexpected tears. The horror of what Elissa Carson must be going through, the strength she showed, all humbled Taylor. She doubted she'd be as forgiving if it were her own daughter being forced to respirate, the beating heart inside withered and slow, limbs like broken sticks under the white sheets, all because of the whim of evil.

"When?" she asked, not knowing what else to say.

"Within the hour, they tell me. They're making notifications to the various transplant teams. They have to keep her like this until they're ready to start the harvest. Then we'll turn the machines off and let her go."

Dear God. Taylor couldn't stand this. She must find this killer, must give Brittany Carson justice. It was all she could do. She turned and embraced the woman, unsure of her own voice. Carson squeezed her hard around the waist, a silent sob shaking her, then stepped back, hand to her mouth.

"Find him," she commanded, then fled down the hallway.

Taylor looked back at the dying girl, waxy in the harsh hospital lights.

"I will," she whispered.

Juri Edvin was on the surgical floor. Taylor fought the fury that drove each step she took as she walked to his room. She tried to force the anger away—she had no proof. She needed hard evidence. But her gut was telling her Edvin had a role in Brittany's demise, and damned if she was going to let him get away with it. Whether he'd given Brittany the drugs, carved the pentacle in her stomach or simply stood by, watching from a perch outside as she fought for breath, he'd been there as she struggled. Taylor knew that in her bones. She wanted to nail his scrawny ass to the wall.

A young doctor, brown-haired and obviously tired, was emerging from Edvin's room, stethoscope draped like a stole across his shoulders, a chart in one hand and a beeper in the other. His nametag read S. Pearson.

He wasn't watching his way and collided with Taylor. She grasped his arms to steady him.

"Doctor, sorry. Lieutenant Jackson, Metro Homicide."

The doctor gave her a casual glance. "He can't talk to you. He's just had a serious surgery. He's sedated." He started to walk away, she grasped his right arm tighter.

"Is he awake enough, Doctor? Because the girl he may have killed is being prepared for the transplant teams upstairs. I'd like to have a go at him, just in case. I'd like to see some justice done, for Brittany Carson, and for the seven other children."

Pearson stopped then, looked her in the eye. "I heard she wasn't doing well. The decision's been made, then?"

"Yes. I just talked with her mother."

"Ah. Well, I can't promise anything for you with Mr. Edvin. He's had a trauma, and the medications are going to make him incoherent. But try if you like. Unfortunately, I'll have to leave you. I've just been called back into surgery. Don't push him too hard—I don't need him going into shock."

She released him, and he hustled away. She had the strangest sensation—people fleeing from her in these bright corridors, as if she were the cause of the agonies within. She shrugged it off, signaled to the patrol guarding Edvin's room.

"Have you seen the parents?"

He flicked the edge of his magazine in annoyance—the interruptions were impeding his relaxation time. "They're getting coffee. They asked to speak with whoever wanted to question their son before you talk to him. I guess you're nominated."

"Where are they?"

He pointed down the hall. A door labeled Family Room was on the left, just past the nurses' station. She thanked him, went down the hall and entered the room. She saw a television, a couple of couches, numerous chairs and a refreshment table with coffee and tea in labeled urns, a small basket of peppermints. Two empty wrappers sat nearby, curled in on themselves.

A man and woman stood a few feet apart from one another, staring at the television. It was on Channel 50, the cable version of the local CBS affiliate. Taylor tuned out when she heard her name from the tinny speakers.

"Mr. and Mrs. Edvin?"

They turned and faced her. Both had short blond hair and square black glasses—so similar that Taylor immediately thought them brother and sister rather than husband and wife.

"We have no comment," the man said, turning his back to Taylor. His arm snaked around his wife, pulling her closer.

"Sir, I'm not a reporter. Lieutenant Jackson, Homicide. I need to speak with you about your son."

The wife snapped at Taylor. "About what? Your people are the ones who put him in here. He nearly died, and you want us to let you talk to him?"

"Now, now, *mijn beste.* Juri said he ran, that's why they chased him. I apologize for my wife, Lieutenant. She is very upset by the incident." His English was accented, the broad, flat Scandinavian vowels pronounced.

"I'm sorry about that. Juri did run, refused to stop. We had no choice but to send the dog after him. Has he told you why we were chasing him?"

"He says you thought he was someone else," Mr. Edvin said.

"That's not exactly true. He was present at the scene of a homicide. He claims to have been trick-or-treating, but he was miles from home, with no costume." She had to be careful. The Edvins looked like they were softening, and she didn't want to lay it on them all at once and lose her chance to speak to the kid without a lawyer telling him to clam up.

"I need to ask him a few questions. If he hasn't done anything wrong, then it shouldn't be a big deal, and you'll receive a full apology from me and from the department."

"And if he has done something?" Mrs. Edvin's accent was stronger than her husband's. "Will you send him away?"

"That depends, ma'am. Why don't we cross that bridge when we get to it? Is Juri a good kid? Has he been giving you any trouble?"

"Oh, no," she said quickly, but her eyes were clouded. The edge of her left eye was the tiniest bit yellow—a fading bruise. Taylor glanced at Mr. Edvin. His face was screwed into a frown. She could see the pulse at the base of his jaw jumping. He looked like a rabbit about to bolt, the whites of his eyes showing as he calculated the distance to safety.

So that's how it was.

"I know how hard it can be," Taylor said softly. "Being afraid of your own son is terrible. Will you tell me more?"

The Edvins' eyes met, and they seemed to shrink a little bit. They sat down on the closest couch heavily, all of a piece, sudden and breathless.

"We just don't know what to do with him anymore," Mrs. Edvin wailed. "He was never like this before. He's always been such a sweet boy. We move to the United States when he is ten, and he changes. He sneaks out. I find marijuana in his gym bag last year. He is never coming home at night. And now he is seeing some little *wijfje* who glares at me when she comes over. They go into his room and he blocks the door. When I tried to stop them last week, he hit me. He has not been home since."

"Did you report him missing?"

They shook their heads. "He's done this before," Mr. Edvin said. "We think moving back to Finland is a good idea, but he raised such a fuss we must back away. He says he'll kill us in our sleep before he lets us take him. We lock our door at night, afraid he means to murder us. We don't know what happened to our boy."

"Do you know his friend's name?"

"He calls her Ember. We don't know her whole name. She brings him the makeup, and they dress like ghouls and run around downtown. We have no more control of him than we do the wind."

That was as apt a description of a troubled young man as she'd ever heard.

"Will you allow me to question him?" Technically, she didn't need their permission, but parents usually lawyered up their kids the moment they realized they were in real trouble. She held her breath—she thought she had them, but she never knew. The Edvins looked at one another. She could see the conversation going on in their silent gazes. Finally, Mr. Edvin pulled away from his wife.

"Yes. You may talk to him. We would like to be there, too."

"Okay. But I may need to ask you to step out if he won't talk to me with you in the room. Let's go."

She led them back to their son's room. The patrol stood when he saw them barreling down on him. Taylor motioned for him to join them.

"Come in and witness for me, okay?"

The patrol set down his magazine, silent as the grave. She'd met him before, once or twice, a man named Rob, quietly suspicious of his female fellow officers, but efficient and solid. He opened the door for them. Taylor let the Edvins go first.

Juri Edvin's eyes were open, glazed, but he recognized Taylor. With no place to go, he shrugged and turned his head to face the window. If he saw his parents, he gave no indication at all.

"Juri, we need to talk," Taylor said, pulling a chair closer to the bed. She was damned tired, and the idea of sitting was most welcome. She hoped it would disarm the boy too, looming over him would remind him of her authority. If they were eye to eye, he might relax a bit. The chair screeched on the linoleum floor, the shriek making a chill run up Taylor's spine.

"So talk," Edvin said, still facing away. He sounded groggy, but coherent enough.

"You are quite the little smart-ass, aren't you? Okay then, I'll talk. Tell me why they call you Thorn."

She had him. His eyes popped open, the whites flaring. He started to struggle, quickly realized he had no strength and nowhere to go. He collapsed back against the pillow.

"So you're the dealer, huh? I've heard all about you. Why'd you kill them, Juri?"

"I didn't kill anyone," he said, hot tears starting to course down his face. "I have no reason to kill anyone. Mama. Papa. Help me!"

Juri had obviously never heard the tale of the boy who cried wolf. Taylor was impressed by the Edvins—they stood their ground. His father set his shoulders a little straighter.

"You must tell the lieutenant what she needs to know, Juri. If you have done something wrong, you must answer for it. We've always tried to teach you that."

"Oh, fuck off, you freaks."

Mrs. Edvin began to cry. Taylor barely resisted the urge to slap the boy. She turned to them.

"Maybe it would be better if we talked without you for now."

Mr. Edvin met her eyes, bleak and hopeless. "Maybe."

Juri became incensed. "You can't just leave me with the cops. What kind of parents are you? You're supposed to love me, and you throw me to the wolves instead? Thanks a whole hell of a lot."

Taylor popped out of her chair and grabbed ahold of Mr. Edvin before he could cross the room and strike his son. She propelled them toward the door.

"Go," she said. "I'll come find you when we're done here."

The two left, the soles of their sneakers the only noise to compete with Juri's snuffled whimpers.

Taylor took a deep breath, turned back to the bed. She heard a squeak behind her, glanced over her shoulder at the noise.

The door to Juri's room slid open. A small girl, pale, with wide, liner-blackened eyes, slipped inside, closing it carefully behind her. She glanced back out the door, then whispered, "Thorn, your parents are gone, and the guard left. We can go now."

She turned and saw Taylor, jumped and screamed. The patrol grabbed her by the arm. She spit and snarled, sank her teeth into his hand. He yelled and let go. The girl took the opportunity to scram, throwing open the door and bolting down the hall toward the stairwell.

Taylor shouted, "Stay here," to the patrol and took off after her.

The girl was quick, athletic, built like a fireplug, or a gymnast. She was a powerful runner. She made it all the way to the stairwell, threw open the door. She miscalculated—instead of continuing to run, she tried to pull the door closed behind her. Taylor burst through the door, knocking the girl over. She scrambled to her feet and headed down the stairs. She made it down a whole flight before Taylor, longer legs making up precious time, caught her. She grabbed a fistful of the girl's hair and yanked, drawing her up short like a wild horse. She was breathing heavily, struggling. Taylor clamped another hand down on her shoulder, spun her and slapped cuffs around her wrist.

"Bitch," the girl screamed.

"Nice to meet you, too. What's your name?"

"Fuck off."

Taylor was getting sick and damn tired of being told nasty things by children. She was so much bigger, it took nothing at all to pin the girl to the wall.

"Listen to me, you little brat. You'll show me some respect or I'll haul your ass to jail. Get it?"

"You can't arrest me. I'm a minor."

Taylor laughed. "Watch me."

She hauled the girl by the arm up the stairs and back into the hallway. She thumbed her radio as she strode down the hall, dragging the struggling girl behind her. "Dispatch, I need backup, my location. Vanderbilt surgical floor. I need to transport a prisoner."

"You can't do that. I didn't do anything," the girl screamed. "I want my parents."

"Oh, we'll get your parents, sugar. Though you'd be better off talking to me right now. For all I know, you've done nothing wrong except try to come see your boyfriend. I do assume Juri is your boyfriend, right?"

They were at the Family Room now, and Taylor opened the door, pushed the girl through. The Edvins weren't in the room. Good. She sat the girl on the couch, arms stuck awkwardly behind her, and glared at her. The girl wasn't stupid—she could see she was beaten. She'd have to go through Taylor to get away, and with the handcuffs… She sagged back into the couch and pursed her lips.

Taylor crossed her arms across her chest, leaned against the door.

"Is Juri your boyfriend?"

Silence.

"Answer me, damn it. I'm not in the mood for games."

The girl was pretty in a sullen, troubled way, her lips overfull right at the top center, making them overtly lush, freckles sprinkled across her forehead and cheeks. She was fighting tears.

"His name is Thorn," she said finally, somewhat mollified. "And yes, he is my mate."

"There, that wasn't so hard, was it? Where were you two planning to go?"

The voice was stronger now. "Anywhere but here. Away. We need to go away. It's not safe."

"Safe from whom?"

The girl's eyes flashed, but her lips stayed together. Okay. Taylor tried again.

"What did Juri have to do with the murders in Green Hills last night? And what's your role in all of this? If you were involved, in any way, you'll pay just as dearly as if you wielded the drugs or the knife yourself."

"I had nothing to do with it. *Nothing.* Neither did Thorn. He was with me the entire night."

"Really? He wasn't with you when I chased him through the woods. Let's try that again. Where were you last night?"

A gaze full of derision lasered into her. "Packing. Thorn went for supplies."

"So we've established that Juri is Thorn. Good. You realize he's broken a number of laws, and we're holding him as a suspect in the murders of seven people?"

"He. Did. Nothing," she hissed. Taylor felt a warmth begin in her chest, noticed the girl's lips were moving. She stepped to the side, broke eye contact. The warmth ceased. Taylor thought about Ariadne for a brief minute, wondered what she'd make of that. Being around Ariadne made her feel good, even though the woman was certifiable. Now she felt angry, drained. She chalked it up to exhaustion, went back to the girl.

"That's not what the evidence says. And what about your parents? Wouldn't they worry if you ran away?"

She tossed her head, then gasped a little when her shoulders pulled tight. She'd forgotten she was handcuffed. She licked her lips. "They don't care about me."

"I'm sure they do. What's your name?"

She didn't answer, so Taylor took a guess. "You're Ember, right?"

She stiffened.

"Ember, what's your real name?"

The girl drew herself up straight. "The only name I have is Ember. And I'm through talking to you. Get me a lawyer, or let me go."

When did kids get so damn cognizant of the law? Taylor sighed, pulled her hair down and massaged her temples. A voice crackled on her radio—her backup was here. They came through the door a moment later, Paula Simari and Bob Parks.

Parks nodded at Taylor, said, "What have we here?"

"Hey. Girl claims her name is Ember, but that's an alias. She just invoked. Mirandize her, take her downtown, find out her real name and call her parents. Do whatever it takes," she said, eyebrow raised. Intimidating children just wasn't her idea of fun, but she needed answers, and she needed them now.

Simari cracked her knuckles, and Ember jumped. Taylor wondered what made her so anxious. They got her on her feet. As they were walking out, the girl turned back to Taylor, a knowing grin playing on her lips.

"Call Miles Rose. He's my father's lawyer."

She looked Taylor straight in the eye, defiant to the end.

Taylor edged closer. "Miles Rose is a defense attorney, and a smarmy one at that. Why does your father need a defense attorney?"

"He hired him after my brother was killed. We know how justice works in this country. The innocent stand accused and the guilty walk free."

"Your brother?" Taylor asked, confused.

Ember shook her head. "By the Gods, you are stupid, aren't you? You've already talked to my parents. My brother's name is Xander."

"Xander Norwood?" It finally dawned on her who Ember really was. "You're Susan Norwood, aren't you?"

The girl's face closed. "My name is Ember. That is all you need to know."

Taylor went back to Juri. Maybe she could leverage this new information.

His parents were back in the room, trying to coax him into being the good little boy he should have grown into. He wasn't falling for it, had turned the other cheek and was ignoring them.

Taylor tapped Mr. Edvin on the shoulder. "May I?" she asked.

His face was haggard, the lines between his forehead deeper, grooves cut in the flesh. "By all means, Lieutenant. I believe Helga and I are going to get dinner. Take all the time you need. I assume our boy will not be coming home right away?"

"Perhaps not, Mr. Edvin. He's certainly not leaving the hospital for the next few days. The guard will stay on the door in the meantime. Thank you for working with me. I appreciate all your help. We'll be by your house to talk more later. Here's my card. Please, call me anytime, day or night, if you have any questions or concerns."

Taylor opened the hospital room door for them, motioned for Rob to come in again. He slid in and leaned against the wall, out of the way.

The door closed softly behind the Edvins. Taylor took her time getting settled in the chair next to the bed again, weary. She propped her boots on the rail, legs crossed at the ankle.

"So, Juri, it's just us. Would you prefer me to call you Thorn?"

A small sound of concurrence rose from the bed.

"Thorn, where do you get the drugs? Who's your dealer?"

He turned to her then, his face so tight as he tried to control his emotions that his cheekbones strained hard and white, nearly cutting through his skin. She could see the tracks of tears as they slid down to his chin. "Is Ember okay? Can I see her?"

"She's being taken down to the Criminal Justice Center. She'll be questioned, and we'll go from there. Where were the two of you trying to go?"

"Away."

"Okay. I understand. You weren't happy at home, wanted to run away. But I really need to know where you got the drugs."

He was quiet for a moment, then said, "A friend."

"The friend's name, Thorn. Come on, man, let me help you."

He shook his head. "He'll kill me. He'll hunt me down and kill me. I can't tell."

"Okay. Talk to me about Brittany Carson then. What were you doing at her house?" He started to say something but she held up a hand. "No, don't even try. I've got your

DNA being analyzed right now, and I'm betting it will match
the semen stain we found outside the den window. Were you
standing out there, masturbating, watching Brittany?"

Slowly, he nodded, face aflame.

"Thank you for telling me the truth. That's a start. Did
you give her any of the drugs?"

He nodded again. Taylor felt the breath leave her body.
She glanced at Rob, saw him staring at the boy with interest.

"Thorn, I know you've been read your rights already, but
I'm going to do it again, okay? Because I have to place you
under arrest for murder."

"I didn't murder her! It was Ember's idea—she hated her.
Hated her. I was just going along with it because she wanted
me to." He started struggling in the bed, this time managed
to pull an IV loose and detach his heartbeat monitor. The
machine began its claxon call and Taylor knew they were
done. Two nurses burst into the room, shoving Taylor out
of the way. She stepped back, watched them reattach the
line, fix the feeds, get the boy settled.

When they were finished, she read him his rights again,
made Rob handcuff the little bastard to the bed and walked
slowly down the hall to the elevator. She glanced at her
watch—7:00 p.m. Brittany Carson's harvest would have
started. She choked on the sorrow, pressed the button on the
elevator.

One down. So why did she feel like this was just the beginning?

Twenty-Eight

Northern Virginia
June 16, 2004
Baldwin

Baldwin drove, drumming his fingers on the steering wheel while Sparrow worked frantically on her laptop. It only took an hour door-to-door—lucky, considering the time of day and the usual traffic congestion in suburban D.C. They'd sailed up 95, got on the George Washington Parkway, skirted through the western edge of D.C., up the Potomac River and out to McLean, then took Georgetown Pike straight into Great Falls. Baldwin couldn't help but notice when he passed Spring Hill Road; he'd dated a woman who lived in a neighborhood down there. It was beautiful in this part of the suburbs, ancient trees and horse farms and glens led to stunning houses situated far off the beaten path. Not the usual tableau when one considered murder, unless you counted the infamous story of the headmistress of the Madeira School, Jean Harris, who'd murdered her ex-lover, Scarsdale Diet pioneer Herman Tarnower. That had caused a bit of a scandal. Or the twisted Edward Chen, who'd murdered his family, then left them in their house to rot for four years before he and a friend cut them up and dumped their body parts in the Chesapeake Bay. Baldwin remembered that case vividly—he'd been working with the detectives who broke the case at the time.

And now the Clockwork Killer was adding his name to the mix. He would most likely overshadow any and all previous murder stories, and those to come in the future.

The Kilmeades, and Harold Arlen, lived off Walker Road, before the turn for River Bend Country Club. The houses were generous, both in structure and land, but the neighborhood they lived in was a cloister, allowing the houses to lie closer to one another, with garages below the living spaces. The architect had been going for a style similar to a British mew, and the environs reminded Baldwin of Notting Hill.

The sun drilled into Baldwin's eyes as they got out of the car in front of the faux Tudor-style houses. He couldn't help but steal a glance at Arlen's front door, closed and locked, seemingly unaware of the storm that was about to batten its hatches.

They mounted the stairs to the Kilmeades' neat, clean porch. Baldwin rang the bell, and a few moments later, Mrs. Kilmeade answered the door in a flour-covered apron à la June Cleaver. The delicious, yeasty scent of baking bread spilled out onto the porch.

"Oh, hello there. Can I help you?"

"Mrs. Kilmeade, I don't know if you remember…I'm Supervisory Special Agent John Baldwin, and this is Special Agent Jessamine Sparrow. We spoke briefly two days ago—"

"Yes, yes, I remember. How could I forget? Such a terrible time for those poor families."

"It is, ma'am. We were hoping to steal a few more moments of your time, if you're available. We need to ask you a couple of questions about your daughter, Evie."

Her face fell, then she pulled herself together. "Certainly. If you don't mind me working while we talk, I'm in the middle of a project with my boys. We make our own bread weekly—we've got three loaves done right now."

She allowed Baldwin and Sparrow into the house, her natural graciousness only barely hiding her perplexed look.

As promised, the boys were in the kitchen, quietly kneading dough. In the attached eating area, Mr. Kilmeade was reading a book so thick Baldwin's first thought was encyclopedia. Mrs. Kilmeade leaned down and whispered in his ear; he turned and met Baldwin's eye before standing.

Baldwin's guess was close. When Kilmeade came into the kitchen, he brought the book with him—it was a world atlas.

"Some light reading?" Baldwin asked, trying to break the ice.

"Something like that." He set the book on the counter. "We homeschool, you see. I was planning tomorrow's geography lesson."

The boys groaned in unison, but smiled at their dad.

Baldwin had a moment's flashback of his own father helping him with his schoolwork. His dad always seemed to have time to help him; now he understood that he made time. Of course, that was before. Before Baldwin's life got shaken into a million pieces.

His parents were killed in a car accident when he was just sixteen. His mother's sister, Agatha, was his only living relative, and she was much older. He'd gone to live with her, on the west side of Nashville, attended a school of her choosing, Father Ryan. He'd hated most every moment of it. Though nominally a Catholic, even now Baldwin considered himself one of the fallen.

Memories started to flood in, but he wiped them from his mind. He had work to do, and revisiting the painful parts of his past wasn't on the agenda.

He cleared his throat. "I understand completely. Would you mind if Special Agent Sparrow and I talk to you and Mrs. Kilmeade alone?"

Kilmeade looked startled for a moment, then nodded. "Boys, why don't you go look through that geometry lesson we abandoned earlier. I'll come quiz you in a few minutes."

Polite and respectful, the Kilmeade boys rose from the kitchen counter as one and disappeared from the room. Kilmeade listened with a practiced ear until the soft noise of a door closing reached them, then turned to Baldwin with a smile.

"So, what's happening? Julie said you needed to talk about Evie?"

"Are you up for a few questions?"

"Of course. Evie's been gone for months. We've battled through as best we can with God on our side. He's helped us stick to the path. She was a special little girl—we weren't surprised that He decided to take her from us. She always was an angel on earth."

The words sounded good, but Baldwin could hear the note of despair that lingered beneath them, saw the brief flash of pain in the man's eyes. Kilmeade was a man, a provider, a father, and he obviously took those responsibilities very seriously.

"Besides," chimed in Julie Kilmeade, "we're working on adding to the family." She touched her belly reverentially; Baldwin could see the slight swelling there, covered by the apron. Replacing their dead child with a living, breathing proxy?

The Kilmeades struck him as a happy family, solid and close, but with little brown edges like spoiled roses. Hardly surprising, considering the devastating loss they'd sustained so recently. Interesting that they hadn't mentioned it when they talked before.

"Congratulations," Baldwin said.

"Thank you." Kilmeade reached out and took his wife's hand. "Now, what can we help you with?"

"We need to talk about Harold Arlen."

"Harry? Whatever for? Why would the FBI be interested in Harry?"

Baldwin took a seat at the kitchen table. "I have to ask you some difficult questions. Would you mind joining me?"

Everyone got seated, then Baldwin continued.

"We found a note on your daughter's obituary page from Harold Arlen." He pulled the piece of paper out of his pocket, smoothed the wrinkles out and placed it on the table.

"Well, sure. They were buds, Evie and Harry. She adored him. He was quite crushed when she passed."

"Mr. Kilmeade, you were aware that Harold Arlen was a sex offender, correct?"

"That was a part of Harry's past. He was fully rehabilitated. He ran a group for those less fortunate than himself, those who still struggled with their urges. But Harry, no, he is one of the good guys. He hated that he'd done those things, and was so happy to be on a clean path. God smiled upon him in prison, you know."

Doesn't He always? If Baldwin had a dollar for every convicted felon who told him he'd found Jesus, he could retire.

"Mr. Kilmeade, you're a psychologist, correct? You work with the incarcerated?"

"That's right. I'm finishing my dissertation now. I'm planning to open a private practice specializing in criminal rehabilitation."

"So you understand, on an empirical level, that sex offenders rarely change. They simply disguise their behavior."

Kilmeade bristled, sitting forward in his chair and narrowing his eyes. "Are you insinuating that Harry did something to Evie? Because I'll tell you, that isn't the case. He was never alone with her."

"Never? You're absolutely sure of that?"

"Yes, I am. Listen, you may have some preconceived notions about Harry, but he is a good man. He loved Evie like she was his own daughter. When she died…" His voice broke, and he cleared his throat viciously. "When she died, he cried for days. He was right there the whole time, helping us. I know Harry. He could never hurt Evie. Or anyone else, for that matter."

Sparrow had about enough at this point, and jumped into the interview. "You didn't find it at all alarming that a grown man with a history of sexual deviance was taking such an interest in your underage daughter?"

"Sparrow," Baldwin said in an undertone.

Kilmeade waved Baldwin's warning away. "No, that's fine. I'm sure to an outsider this would look very strange indeed. But Harry is changed. He'd done some stupid, awful things in the past, but he really was changed by life in prison. He would never do anything, *anything,* that might jeopardize his freedom. I'm not an idiot. I'm a trained professional. My job is to help people like him. If I thought he was a threat, I'd have tossed him out on his ear. Like I said, he was never alone with Evie. Either her mother or I, or one of her brothers, was always in attendance."

"Ralph?" Mrs. Kilmeade had been silent up to now, but her eyes were rimmed in red from the pressure of the tears she was holding back.

"Yes, honey?"

"May I be excused? I'd like to go lie down for a few moments."

"Goodness, my dear, of course. I'll come to you in a moment. I'm just going to see the agents out. We're finished here, correct?"

There was a note of finality to the question. They were done, whether Baldwin wanted to be finished or not.

Baldwin nodded. Everyone hastened to their feet as Mrs. Kilmeade exited the room. Sparrow met Baldwin's eyes, and he felt the message being sent. There was something very wrong with this picture. He couldn't agree more.

Regardless, Kilmeade had said all he was willing to on the subject. They had what they needed anyway. Little Evie's death could certainly be interpreted as a stressor for Arlen.

At the door, Kilmeade left them with a final thought.

"I'd appreciate it if any future conversations be conducted at my office. My wife is having a difficult time with the pregnancy, you see, and with all the hubbub still lingering over Evie's death, it's been terrible for her. You understand." He shook their hands and shut the door behind them softly, leaving Baldwin and Sparrow on the porch, staring across the street.

What sort of monster lived behind those four walls?

And what kind of father let his dying daughter play with a sex offender?

Charlotte

It was late. Charlotte was hungry and thirsty, but she stayed rooted in her chair at her desk. She chewed on the end of a pen, thinking hard. She agreed with Baldwin that Harold Arlen was their suspect. The problem was, they still had exactly zero proof. Where was the evidence? And where was that warrant they needed so desperately? Maybe she'd have to take a trip down to the courthouse later, lean on some doors. See if that shook things loose. She hated having to take matters into her own hands, but they needed to get this case wrapped up. Child murderers gave her the creeps. She didn't know how Baldwin could stand it.

Speak of the devil. Charlotte saw Baldwin approaching and felt her pulse race. She was always struck by his looks; he epitomized the very being of tall, dark and handsome. Now that she was in, she didn't plan on letting go anytime soon. He was the perfect catch, the perfect man. Attentive and loving in bed, willing to take a few risks and not afraid to show his own feelings. He didn't even snore. What a combination.

He was getting attached. She could feel that. Every look, every touch, screamed, *you're mine, woman.* It made her feel all warm inside. She had to admit, she'd had him pegged from day one. He was a natural savior, a white knight, the kind of man who hated to see a woman cry, who was instantly drawn to fragility. She'd have to keep it up just a bit longer, then he'd be on the hook and she'd be set.

She hadn't given a great deal of thought to settling down with one man, or one woman, for that matter, until recently.

It seemed…an interesting concept. One person, for a life-time. She wondered how long it would really last.

She may have to switch departments when they got married, but that was fine. She could easily lead in other areas. That might not be necessary after all: Baldwin was sure to be promoted out of the BAU—he was too good at his job, too adept, too thorough. He had Director written all over him. Oh, the power he would have. And she'd be at his side, the perfect helpmeet.

They would have to get a new place—his apartment wasn't anything to write home about. There were plenty of lovely suburbs in the area north of Richmond, providing for a short commute. And they'd certainly need a place in D.C., preferably in Georgetown, so she could rub elbows with the real money. There was power in D.C., that's what attracted her to the feds in the first place.

Oh, it was so nice to be with him at last. She'd been so careful, so subtle. And he'd always seemed so sad. Now, despite the horrific case they were working, he seemed almost chipper. Downright happy.

When he entered her office, Baldwin gave her a heart-stopping grin.

"Guess what we have?" he said.

"Herpes?"

He stopped in his tracks, eyebrows creasing. "What?"

"I'm kidding, silly. What do we have?"

"Oh. God, Charlotte, that's not remotely funny. Goldman just called. They got the warrant for Arlen's place signed five minutes ago. The Kilmeades admitted that Arlen had regular contact with their daughter. That's a probation violation, which is enough for the judge. We're in."

Waning Crescent Moon
Twenty Percent of Full
Feast of Odin
(All Souls' Day)

Twenty-Nine

Nashville
Midnight

Taylor was in bed, watching a replay of the late local news. She was fighting sleep, but would succumb at any minute. She'd been awake for thirty-six hours, and even by her insomniac standards, it was time for a rest.

Nashville would never get used to news about dead teenagers. Especially around the holidays and graduation, the nightly news brought stories packed with grief and remorse. Brave girls fighting meningitis. Silly young boys who drank to excess then wrapped their cars around trees. Cheerleaders text messaging their football-hero boyfriends and crashing into oncoming tractor-trailers.

But Nashville had never seen coverage of a tragedy of this magnitude. It was made worse by the extended horrors—nearly two days into the news cycle, when the gaping holes in the collective hearts were beginning to clot and crust, the sweet young face of Brittany Carson, smiling to the masses through the television screen, ripped them open all over again.

Her death had first been reported in a breaking news

alert by a teary-eyed rookie reporter, one too young to have hardened to the nearly daily depictions of death and violence that roamed Nashville's streets. On the 10:00 p.m. news, Brittany's organ donation was the lead story—some vulture inside the hospital reported that she'd signed a donor registration card during a school campaign and the media seized upon it, getting a confirmation quote from her mother, Elissa, still dressed in the red blouse streaked with her daughter's blood.

She wasn't the only one; the entire city had been holding out hope that one of their children would make it through this tragedy alive. Sons and daughters, brothers, sisters, couples, loners, all marked for death. There seemed to be no real rhyme or reason to the victimology, not yet. They had nothing concrete, nothing except the knowledge that a teenage boy gave a teenage girl a pill laced with poison designed to kill her, then masturbated while he watched her die.

Taylor sighed, rolled onto her back to stare at the ceiling.

The images on the screen had been littered with smiling faces, full of hope. It was near impossible to imagine those same boys and girls lying on stainless-steel trays at the medical examiner's, brutal Y-incisions demarking their virginal flesh.

The ME's office was overwhelmed. Parents who'd been out of town returned with the knowledge of their children's deaths weighing heavily on their consciences, needed to say goodbye. They had been camping in the lobby of Forensic Medical until their time came, were ushered one by one into a side room with a closed-loop video feed to identify their dead.

The first official comprehensive toxicology screens were rolling in. All eight victims had high levels of Ritalin, codeine, PMA, MDMA and Valium in their systems, disguised in the small, benign tablet of Ecstasy that Juri Edvin had sold them.

Taylor couldn't stand it anymore. She flipped the television off. She wished Baldwin was with her, imagined him encircling her with his arms. The blank of darkness enveloped her, and she fell asleep.

Thirty

Midnight

Ariadne glanced at the police car parked in front of her house and sighed. At least they'd let her come home. For a moment there she thought the lieutenant was going to arrest her and toss her in a cell overnight. Instead, she'd been escorted home and instructed not to leave until summoned. That was fine—she had plenty of work to do.

She shut off the lights in the house and prepared herself, taking a long, cleansing bath, rubbing herself with fragrant herbs, allowing her mind to be open and accepting. Once the ritual bath was complete, she went to her drawing room. She built a fire, lit the candles, opened her Book of Shadows and got down on her knees in front of her altar.

"Be true to me, as I am to you. Honor that which I have created, as I honor you. Goddess, hear my prayers. With harm to none, so shall it be."

She stopped for a moment, let the impact of the words charge through her body. Her deity, the Goddess of the Moon, Diana, was insistent, and she answered. The pulsing energy filled Ariadne, making her gasp.

She'd been chosen early in her practice, when Diana revealed herself during a divination spell. Once Ariadne knew her path, she became stronger. Strong enough to rise to the position of High Priestess of her coven, before she left.

Sole practice worked better for her. She loved to teach the Old Ways, so she maintained a blog, with thousands of daily followers, and kept herself out of the politics that governed their kind.

But the matters of the past two days were too important for her to ignore. While the rest of her followers gossiped and prayed, she felt compelled to help.

Truth be told, the lieutenant fascinated her. She had no idea just how dominant she really was. If Ariadne could only spend more time with the woman, alleviate her skepticism. But no. Taylor Jackson was an empirical being, solid to the core with belief and justice. Even with proof of the other-world, her mind would find a rational response.

Ariadne lit a candle, stared into the flickering flame, conjured a mental picture of Taylor Jackson. The eyes were what stood out. Athena's eyes, the gray of a stormy afternoon, clouds roiling in the sky. The right darker than the left, the variation even more pronounced when she'd gotten angry. Her nose, slightly off, and that wide, mobile mouth. There was power, hidden behind the fringe of dark lashes. Power that the woman wasn't aware she possessed. She was fair without being judgmental, skeptical but willing to accept help. So rare to find in any person, much less a cop.

Ariadne's cat slid sinuously around her legs, drawn to the energy she was putting out. She picked her up, cuddled her face for a few moments, then blew out the candle. She'd invited her subconscious to bed, would let her dreams tell her what she needed to know. She'd felt dread this afternoon, strong and vivid, and was afraid of the consequences.

Still, she must try.

She must.

Thirty-One

Midnight

Raven stood in the cemetery, Fane at his side. They'd drawn the circle, called the corners, done their spell. They had bound Ember, both from saying anything about their actions, and from leaving. It was a very powerful spell—Raven felt sure Ember would be at his house when they returned.

Raven was worried about Thorn. No word from him, and he was the lynchpin. They'd bound Thorn to them, as well.

Just to be extra safe, they'd buried their witches' bottle in their sacred circle. They'd originally made it a year earlier, and Raven had stored it on the shelf in his closet. Full of dark essences, the special herbs—chamomile and sage, belladonna and mandrake, peppercorns and rosemary—for protection and balance; shavings of their favorite Crüxshadows CD; crushed eggshells and the discarded claw from Fane's cat; tacks and nails, razors, the shards of a broken plate. Once the pieces were in place, they'd filled it to the brim with first-morning urine collected from both of them. Raven added in his semen, then they'd cut their arms and dribbled their blood into the bottle. Sealed tight with black wax and then electrical tape, it was an incredibly powerful deterrent of negative energy.

They'd been forced to make the bottle after one of their classmates had beaten Raven up. That threat was neutralized now, soon to be rotting in the earth, but it seemed sensible to charge the bottle and bury it, deep into the earth, far away from their daily lives, to draw any negative forces away from them.

Wiping sweat from her brow, Fane asked, "What are we going to do if it doesn't work?"

Raven turned to her, drank in the beauty of her face, shining in a sliver of moonlight.

"That's easy, my love. We'll kill them."

Thirty-Two

Taylor woke with the sun, her mind already deep into her case. She'd dreamed of the dead last night, the ghosts of the children sitting on the edge of her bed, staring at her.

Eight dead. How would a troubled teenage boy master-mind such a crime? Her gut told her he hadn't, that there was someone else, someone older, more devious, who was the guiding hand behind this. The vampire king, Barent? The so-called witch, Ariadne?

She wondered when the funerals would begin.

That was enough to drive her out of the bed. She show-ered, dressed in her most comfortable pair of Tony Lamas and Levi's, pulled on a black turtleneck against the chill. She wound her wet hair in a bun, taking care that all the strands were caught back from her face. The nightmare washed from her body, she went downstairs to make some tea.

She sipped the fragrant Earl Grey, staring out into the backyard. It was raining; the soft pattering on the leaves of the river birch made her want to go right back upstairs and get into the bed. She poured some cereal in a bowl and ate it without tasting, peeled a banana, knowing she'd need energy to get through the day.

She had just attached her gun and badge to her belt when the phone rang.

Baldwin.

She answered with a smile, just happy for a chance to hear his voice.

He caught her up on his hearing in the most general of terms. She could tell there was something bothering him.

She filled him in on the killings in Nashville, expecting him to be more interested. She finally said, "Hey, what's wrong? You are a million miles away."

"No, I'm right here. I just have to tell you something. I got a call from North Carolina a few minutes ago."

Fitz. She felt the dread course through her. She missed him so much. Not having Fitz around was like having a piece of herself missing. He'd always been the grounding force in her cases, the sounding board. He kept her focused, and stable. She wanted to throw everything to the wind, get in the car and drive to North Carolina, help search for him. God, if something had happened to him…

Baldwin was quiet, and she felt the agony begin to build, her heart racing as adrenaline showered her system, the very real sense that her blood pressure had spiked, the pit of her stomach gone to water. She heard her heartbeat in her ears, felt it in the back of her throat. She swallowed, hard.

"No. Please, no. Tell me they didn't find his body." Her voice sounded far away, not her own.

"I'm so sorry I can't be there with you right now, Taylor. I know this is hell for you. They didn't find his body, honey. But they did find something. It's relatively recent, within the past week. An RV, left unattended in a campground up near Asheville. They're tracking the rental records right now."

She spoke between clenched teeth. "What did they find, Baldwin? Tell me."

"They found a note. Addressed to you. It said, *'Ayin tahat ayin.'*"

"What's that mean?"

"It's Hebrew. It means an eye for an eye."

"An eye for an eye? Do you think it was from the Pretender?"

"He signed it that way, yes."

"What the hell kind of game is he playing? An eye for an eye?"

"I don't know." He stopped talking again. Taylor heard him swallow, followed suit herself, trying to contract the muscles of her throat to force the gorge down.

She felt a calm steal over her, that sense of disbelief, the out-of-body feeling she got when she was about to receive bad news. "What is it, Baldwin? I can tell you're leaving something out. What else did they find in that RV?"

"Honey, it's... They found an eye, Taylor. They found what they think is Fitz's eye."

Thirty-Three

Once she calmed down, she'd forced Baldwin to call his friend at the NCSBI back so she could talk to him directly, gleaned every tiny detail she could from the man. They were changing the scope of the investigation, were on a search-and-rescue mission now, tracking the man they only knew as the Pretender. Hoping they could get Fitz back in one piece, instead of twenty.

We have a strong team in place, ma'am. We promise, we'll find him, ma'am. We're sorry we went in the wrong direction for a while there, ma'am.

She had to believe them. Baldwin assured her his friend was one of the best.

The thought of Fitz in pain, being tortured, made her want to scream, to tear her hair out. But that wasn't going to solve anything. It wouldn't bring him home.

Baldwin was quiet on the other end of the phone, letting her work through her thoughts without interruption.

"Tell me the quote from Exodus again," she said.

He shifted toward her. "Exodus chapter twenty-one, verse twenty-three through twenty-seven—*'If any harm follows, then you shall give life for life, eye for eye, tooth for tooth, hand for hand, foot for foot, wound for wound, stripe for stripe.'*"

She moaned softly. "He's going to kill him."

"I don't know, Taylor. The verse goes on. '*When the slave owner strikes the eye of a male or female slave, destroying it, the owner shall then let the slave go, a free person, to compensate for the eye.*'"

"What are you saying? You think he's been set free? Then where is he? Why hasn't he been in contact?"

"I don't know what to think, Taylor. The Pretender is still hell-bent on you, that's for sure. He's doing things he knows will hurt you directly."

"I have to focus on these murders in Nashville. But as soon as I'm done, I'm going to go join the hunt."

"Do you think that's wise, Taylor? These men and women know what they're doing."

"It's not like I'm going to get in the way. I'm a law enforcement officer, too. I know the protocols. I can help."

Baldwin sighed deeply. "Taylor, that's what he wants. That's what the Pretender is counting on. He knows you, too damn well for comfort. He knows that if he leaves you a bit of bait, you're going to run headlong toward it."

Her chest tightened, frustration making her stomach clench. She knew she was responsible for this. She knew she'd gotten Fitz hurt. It was her fault. She didn't need to be reminded.

"Low blow, Baldwin."

"I don't mean it as one. If it were you out there, and the police were finding pieces of your body, you don't think I'd do the very same thing? I would hunt him down, tear the bastard limb from limb. But you can't do that. You're his target. You are what he wants. We need to keep you in Nashville. On your own turf, with your force to back you up. If you ever go out on your own, you're vulnerable."

"I'm not that vulnerable, Baldwin. I have a gun. I know how to fight."

He raised his voice. "You knew how to fight on our wedding day too, and where did that get you? Tied to a bloody chair in a warehouse in New York." She could practically hear him gritting his teeth, biting back the caustic

words he'd never be able to take back. Her own temper rose
unbidden.

"Don't you *dare* yell at me. I wasn't on my guard then.
Who would have been? I was in a fucking wedding dress,
on my way to marry *you*." She was feeling hot, furious and
uncomfortable. They'd never had this argument before; she
didn't know he considered her weak for being captured.

"I know, Taylor. Jesus God above, I know. If it weren't
for me, none of that would have ever happened."

"Oh, don't be stupid. You weren't the cause, any more
than I was. It was a situation, and I mishandled it. Believe
me, I'll never make that mistake again."

The moment the words were out, she regretted it. "That's
not what I mean," she said, softer now. "I mean I'll always
be on my guard. I'll always be watching for him."

"So you do still want to marry me?"

She tried to calm her breathing.

"Of course I do. I'm wearing your ring, aren't I?"

His voice was bleak. "When all I bring you is danger?
You're a hard woman to keep safe, Taylor. What I do, the
people I have to associate with, all of it brings you into
harm's way. Look at Aiden. If the Pretender hadn't killed
him, where would we be?"

"I don't know. We'd—"

"Be running from the bastard, that's where!"

She modulated her voice carefully. This could easily
spill out of control, and she didn't want that, not now. Not
over the phone, where the smallest turn of phrase could be
misconstrued.

"Stop shouting at me, Baldwin. You have no idea where
that might have led. Stop imagining the worst and let me do
my job."

"Your job is to stay in Nashville, or have you forgotten
that? Your caseload, your team. You have responsibilities
there, Taylor. You can't just run off willy-nilly on a wild-
goose chase."

He huffed to a stop, biting back the words.

Taylor had learned the hard way that fighting with someone you love has rules of engagement. She'd learned never to say the first thing that popped into her mind. Or the second. Or even the third, for that matter.

Finally, she took a breath, calmed herself, then said, "You think Fitz is dead, don't you?"

"I don't know. But I do know that if you fall for this, if you run off after him, you might be. And I can't lose you, Taylor. Not like that. Not to someone like him."

"So are you going to forbid me to go? Put your foot down, assert your rights over me?"

"No. I'd never do that. But I can ask, can't I? I can ask you, beg you, to stay away from this case. To stay in Nashville where I can breathe easier, knowing you're surrounded by people I trust to help keep you safe. All I can do is ask that you'll keep me in mind before you do something reckless. Will you, Taylor? Will you please, please think about what you're doing before you do it?"

Could she do that? The other thing about love, she'd quickly learned, was that you had to think about the other person first, then think about yourself and your own desires. Every bone in her body screamed to get in the car and drive, to get to that campsite, to see what was happening, to make sure they were doing everything right. But Baldwin had a point. The Pretender was trying to draw her out, to get her off balance. She would be no use to Fitz if she were captured or dead.

"Okay," she said finally. "Okay. I'll stay here."

"Thank you," he said, voice barely above a whisper. "You know I'll do everything in my power to keep you safe. You're my own heart, Taylor."

There was a puddle of water forming at the base of the driveway. A cheap penny saver, delivered to the wrong house by accident, floated in its plastic bag. She drove over it, out of the drive, up the street, wipers on, lights on. Mind completely and utterly off.

Poor Fitz. Being used as a tool in this ridiculous game. Knowing she'd caused him to suffer was overwhelming, and she realized that's exactly what the Pretender had in mind. The suffering of those she loved was to be her penance until he was ready to face her.

She picked McKenzie up from his house, grateful that he could recognize she had her mind on things. He stayed silent until she finally spoke.

"Where are we on the case?"

He flipped open his notebook. "I think we're very close. We've got all the players. Juri Edvin will be booked for the murder of Brittany Carson. His girlfriend, Susan Norwood, is cognizant of his actions—she was trying to help him run away. We get a confession out of him today about the other seven kills and we can wrap this all up."

"I still think there's something else going on."

"Like what?"

"This is all too sophisticated for a teenage boy to pull off. I think we should look harder at our vampire and our witch. Marcus applied for a warrant to the vampire's house. I want to see what he had stashed there."

"Ariadne's not involved," McKenzie said, a note of finality in his voice.

"How can you know that? She's completely out there. How do you know she isn't leading us down the primrose path?"

"A gut feeling about her, that's all. I did a little research into her last night while you were at Vanderbilt. She has no history of interjecting herself into cases. She was a very powerful political figure in the Wicca movement, a high priestess who doubled as a judge on a disciplinary committee. But she dropped out several years ago, citing personal conflicts with the direction of the religion."

"Then she may have a grudge."

"I don't think so. I think she's telling the truth."

"You think she can read minds and conjure energy?"

"I don't know about that. I think she believes she can

help, though. Just do me a favor and listen to what she has to say. I asked her to come in later this morning."

Taylor parked the car, and they crossed the street together. As she swiped her key card in the back door, she turned to him.

"Okay. I trust you."

A small smile gleamed on his face, but he didn't say a word.

Paula Simari was sitting in the Homicide office, chatting with Marcus Wade when Taylor and McKenzie walked in. She was on a roll, gesticulating wildly to make her point.

"You can always judge a man by how he treats his dog, Wade. All you have to do is watch. Does he jerk its head to keep it in line? Does he yank a little too hard when he's training, or is it justified? Dogs like to work, you know. They like to have a purpose, a job. Max knows what his job is, and he's happiest when he's working. But I'll be damned if I'll yank his head like that."

"Morning, you two," Taylor said. "What's up?"

Simari turned with a grimace, deep black circles under her eyes. "Animal cruelty case rolled in overnight—I got stuck with it. I hate these bastards who chain their dogs and claim it's good for their character. Asshole was training his Rottweiler, yanked a slip chain around the dog's neck so hard that his neck broke. Didn't kill him, the poor thing, we had to put him down after we got there. I'd like to put his owner down, I'll tell you that much."

"God, Simari, sorry. That's awful."

"Yes, well. It's not your problem. I actually came to tag along on your warrant. Wade requested Max and I ride along."

"Are you up for it? You've been on shift all night?"

"I am. It's all good. We'll rest after."

"So Marcus, we have the warrant?" Taylor asked.

"Signed, sealed and delivered. Mr. Johnson was the guest of the county last night."

"What about Susan Norwood, the girl who calls herself Ember?"

"Released into her parents' custody at midnight."

Taylor slammed her hand against the desk. "Shit. I wanted her held. What happened?"

Marcus shook his head. "Nothing to charge her with. Sneaking into a boy's hospital room wasn't enough. Miles Rose, slippery bastard, talked her right out of the cuffs."

Taylor chewed on her lip for a moment. "I want an officer on her at all times. She's involved in this."

Marcus waved his hand at a pile of papers, what she assumed were the guardian orders. "Already done. Juri Edvin passed an uneventful night at Vandy. They think he'll be ready to be released into custody tomorrow. Lincoln's in, he's still working with the video-sharing sites."

"Excellent. Thanks for running all that down for me. McKenzie, what time is Ariadne supposed to be here?"

"The escort is supposed to bring her back at 10:00 a.m."

"Then let's get moving. Simari, Marcus, you're with us."

They left a few minutes later. Taylor drove, McKenzie rode next to her. Marcus was in the backseat, working his phone. Simari followed in her patrol car, Max sticking his nose out the open window, a channel of crisp, fresh air running straight up his black nostrils.

Rush hour was ending, but the streets were still congested with latecomers and two fender-benders. The ride up to Joelton would normally take thirty minutes; they'd already been gone an hour and Taylor was getting frachetty. She hated traffic.

Lincoln called just as they took the exit off the highway. Marcus spent a few minutes listening, then slapped his phone shut.

"Good news," Marcus said "One of the video sharing sites found a match to the address. They're tracking it down now."

Taylor looked in the rearview at him. "What do you mean, a match to the address?"

"Remember Lincoln said yesterday that there was a ghost in the IP address that showed him the uploads were being rerouted? There were multiple IP addresses for the uploads, but he's found a pattern."

"Honestly, no. That one slipped by me."

"Well, there've been other videos posted by the person who posted the original video. They're tracking the IP addresses now. They think they'll have something concrete by noon."

"Big Brother is watching," McKenzie said wryly.

The morning had become glaring and hot. Taylor slipped on her sunglasses. She looked back at Marcus again, amused by the excessive floppiness of his brown hair this morning. The kid hadn't slept much, looked like when he did, it was face-first. "Well, thank goodness for Big Brother in this case, because it may be our only credible lead. Nothing showed up on Juri Edvin's or Susan Norwood's computers, I take it?"

"Susan's hasn't been looked at—her parents are being a bit difficult. But the Edvins were quite forthcoming, dropped Juri's laptop off with Lincoln late last night. He didn't find any links, but he's still looking. The kid was into all kinds of crazy stuff though. His history reads like a who's who of creeps and illegal stuff—some bondage footage, a guide to bomb making, cyanide poisoning, neck breaking. He's studying violence, and violent means of death. He fits the profile we have to a T."

"If we can tie him to Barent we'll be set. Any correspondence between the two?"

"Not that we've found yet. We dumped his texts and are going through them, but that's going to take a while."

"Anything off the personal security video cameras at any of the houses?"

"The only one that had a camera was the Norwoods', but it was turned off. The rest were pointed away from the scenes, so nothing of use."

"Well, if little Miss Ember was sneaking out at night to

see her boyfriend, Thorn, she may have jury-rigged the camera to cover her tracks."

"We'll have to ask the Norwoods to get the whole story. The security firm said the camera was turned off sometime during the first week of September because Mrs. Norwood felt it too intrusive."

"Too intrusive? I will never understand why people spend oodles of money on these elaborate alarm systems then don't use them correctly."

"Maybe Mrs. Norwood was aware of her daughter's proclivity for running around after hours and approved," McKenzie said.

"Do any parents approve of their child seeking nocturnal activities?" Marcus asked.

Taylor glanced at him in the rearview. "You'd be surprised. I've seen parents do crazy things. If the Edvins were feeling so terrorized by their son, what's to say the Norwoods weren't feeling that from their daughter? Maybe it was self-preservation."

"Do you think she could kill her own brother?"

"I don't know, Marcus. I just don't know."

McKenzie pointed to an ornate mailbox. "Hey, this is it."

Taylor braked, hard, skidding a little bit on the rough asphalt. There was a gated entrance, harled stone stacked six feet high on either side of a dirt driveway. The black wrought-iron gate was conveniently open.

Taylor backed up a bit, then drove through, dust swirling around the Lumina in choking waves.

The drive was about a mile long, with a hedge running along each side that blocked the view of the land.

"He's got a decent bit of property out here," she said, gritting her teeth as she hit a dip in the road unexpectedly, jarring all of them. "Sorry."

The road curved then, and opened into a beautiful cobblestone parking area. The house beyond sprawled the length of the circular turnaround, a three-storied Gothic Victorian, columned, gray with white trim, complete with a turret. It was a lovely house, double balconies, in good shape, no peeling paint, no cobwebs. If it were run-down, then she could get the sense that the king of the vampires lived there. As it was, it was downright cheery. She snorted to herself at the thought, threw the car into Park and climbed out.

Simari pulled in behind, left Max in the car and joined them.

Marcus stared in admiration at the surroundings. "Used to be a farm, I'd bet. See how the land rolls away? It would make a good vineyard."

"Lots of good farmland up here. Cotton and corn. Some tobacco, too."

They jumped at the voice, turned to see a small man in coveralls advancing on them, brandishing a rake.

"You're trespassing on private property. Can I help you folks?"

Taylor took a step back, tapped her badge on her belt. "Yes, sir. My name is Lieutenant Jackson, Metro Homicide. Detective Wade, Detective McKenzie and Officer Simari. We have a warrant to search the premises."

Max began barking in the backseat, Taylor shot Simari a glance. *No sense getting this guy riled up. Go calm the dog.* Simari turned and went to her patrol car. Max's throaty growls lessened.

The man used the rake like a cane, leaned on it and scratched his freckled, balding head. He had tufts of white hair pouring out of his ears—it made him look like a party favor.

"Now, what in the world? A warrant? For what? Why do you need to search my home?"

"Your home? We were under the impression that it belonged to a Keith Barent Johnson."

"Ha!" The little old man laughed. "That's me, and this here's my house. But I've done nothing wrong."

"Sir, we have a man in custody who says his name is

Keith Barent Johnson, and lists this address as his residence."

The man shifted the rake to his other side. Taylor could see him thinking. He finally sighed deeply, mopped his forehead with a red bandanna and waved them to the porch.

"You're probably talking about my son, Barry. Come on in the house, I need some coffee. We can talk."

Mr. Johnson poured the coffee, so thick it practically slid into the cups.

"Barry's a good boy, you mind. Just a wee bit messed up in the head. He was a soldier, don'tcha know. A damn good one, from what I hear."

"What branch of service was he in?" Taylor asked. She pretended to sip from her cup—coffee wasn't her favorite thing in the world.

"Marines. First Gulf War. He's a chemical engineer by training, but he ended up in the infantry. Boy can handle a weapon—I taught him young, they buffed him up. Parris Island, then SOI at Camp Geiger."

"SOI?" Taylor asked.

"School of Infantry. He came home in one piece, but the mind wasn't all there, if you know what I mean. Gulf War syndrome, they call it. He's on a full disability discharge and gets regular checkups at the VA hospital. They've been doing a nice job keeping up with him, actually. Once his momma died, God rest her soul, it's just been the two of us. He gets lonely, I know that. I try to keep him busy, but he spends a lot of time on his computer or out in his sheds."

"You weren't concerned when he didn't come home last night?" McKenzie asked.

Johnson poured himself another cup of sludge. "Naw. He likes to carouse, sometimes. He's got himself a widow woman up near Pleasant View. She was the wife of a friend in his old unit. He goes up there to see her at night, once in a while. She's a nice girl, churchgoing. Bit soft in the head herself, but they manage. When I came home from the grocery yesterday and he wasn't here, I just assumed he was up with her. Guess y'all had come to take him away though, huh."

"That's right."

"So are you going to tell me what he's done, or do I need to guess?"

Taylor hated giving bad news to parents, regardless of the age of the child or their misdeeds. "Sir, your son has claimed that he was involved in the murder of seven teenagers in Green Hills on Halloween night."

He shook his head. "Nope. Wasn't my boy. He was here with me on Halloween." The small mouth shut firmly.

"He also claims that he's the king of the Vampyre Nation," McKenzie said.

The old man closed his eyes briefly, shook his head. His voice was soft. "That's just his sickness. He came back from that war all kinds of messed up in the head, talking about vampires sucking the blood out of his body. Started sleeping all day and roaming around at night. Filed his teeth into them stupid fangs. I never saw no harm in it—he doesn't do anything. He talks to some of his kind on the computer some. They have themselves a fine old time. But he'd never hurt a flea."

"Sir, you understand that we will have to execute this warrant regardless. Your son knew details about the crimes that weren't released to the press. And he was caught on film at several of the crime scenes. So we know he wasn't home with you."

"Must've left after I went to sleep. I have a scanner in the living room. He likes to listen to it. I'm sure he heard about it from that and decided to go check it out."

"Sir, I appreciate that, but we're going to have to search the house anyway. We'd best get on with it." She stood, plunked her cup in the kitchen sink. "I'll just go get Simari."

McKenzie stayed put with the old man. She knew he was going to pump him for more information, left him to it.

Marcus and Simari were ready to get going, both leaning

impatiently against Simari's patrol car. Max was leashed and had his nose to the ground, quivering.

"Marcus, why don't you start in the house. Mr. Johnson mentioned his son likes to putter in the sheds. I thought Simari and I could take a look at them."

He nodded and pushed off the car, taking a set of purple nitrile gloves out of his pocket as he left. Taylor watched him go, then turned to Simari.

"So, think Max can do a little snooping for me while we're here?"

"Of course. Drugs?"

"That's what I'm hoping. Let's go look around."

They took a path that led to the right of the house, curving back toward the hills. The backyard was as tidy as the front—azaleas and hydrangeas and crepe myrtles cut back for the winter, dogwoods and tulip poplars spread across a vast expanse of still-green lawn.

"Man, he must spend hours on this," Simari said. Max had his nose to the pea-gravel pathway, snuffling.

"I bet it's beautiful in spring. I love dogwoods."

"Why, LT. How romantic of you." They shared a laugh, the gravel crunching beneath their boots as they walked. The sheds were one hundred yards ahead, three of them, low to the ground, painted red with white trim, like the side of a barn.

They passed a small fire pit, the scorched remnants of leaves and twigs gathered at the edges, like someone had stuck a stick into the hole and stirred. Simari held up, let Max smell it. He didn't hit, so they kept going.

When they were twenty yards from the sheds, Taylor saw Max begin to vibrate. "Something here," Simari said.

"Yeah, no kidding. Does he have different signs for different kinds of drugs?"

"No, but he'll bark when he hits something he knows. He's great with pot and cocaine."

Taylor could smell the acrid scent of acetone, and

stopped. "How's he do with meth?" she asked, just as Max let out a vicious howl.

"He's pretty good with that, too," Simari said, eyebrow raised in a dry salute.

Thirty-Four

MAX had been right on the money.

The three sheds in the back of the Johnsons' property held a sophisticated methamphetamine lab. After a quick glance inside, Taylor pulled back and got the warrant amended, called in the experts from the Narcotics Unit to come and take the lab apart. Meth labs were tricky, dangerous territory for those who didn't know what they were doing—and not much better for those who did. She glanced into all three sheds carefully. Two held all the tubes and barrels she recognized, all flammable, with box after empty box of pseudoephedrine thrown into the overflowing trash cans. The last shed was equipped as a chemistry lab. For cooking up batches of dosed Ecstasy, perhaps? She put a priority rush on everything.

Mr. Johnson had said his son was a chemical engineer. He obviously wasn't too soft in the head if he could still cook meth.

She went back to the house. The commotion had Mr. Johnson upset—McKenzie was trying to get him calmed down. Taylor caught his eye and signaled for him to come join her.

A few moments later, they were standing on the porch of the Johnson house.

"Meth lab in the back," she said. "Has he given anything more on Barent?"

"Either he's a twisted old man and a brilliant liar, or he really does turn the other cheek."

"Probably a bit of both. Marcus find anything?"

"Yeah. You should probably go on up there. I'll keep Mr. Johnson from getting in the way. We're going to be late for Ariadne."

Two large, white vans were pulling into the driveway. The drug boys were here. Taylor hoped they didn't all get blown up.

"Lincoln can handle her for the time being. I'm willing to bet money that this is the source of our tainted drugs. The third shed looks like a chemistry lab. I'll bet that's where the Ecstasy came from."

"That would be a nice coup, wouldn't it?" He smiled at her, and she smiled back.

"But why in the world would he turn himself in, knowing we'd come up here and find all this?"

"Honestly, I think the man is in a bad way. From what his father tells me, he's had a terrible time since he got back from the war. Apparently, he was the sole survivor of a tank explosion—the tank got hit by a SCUD missile. They were providing cover for his unit and it all went to smash. He mustered out after the war, but he's never been the same since that event. He went steadily downhill from there. Gulf War syndrome is tricky—they don't know if it's caused by something that was in the air over there, a bacterial infection, heavy metals, chemical weapons or what. It can manifest physically or emotionally.

"If he was simply unstable to start with, the loss of his comrades could be the precipitating event. He's so far into the vampire world now that I doubt anything could pull him free. He must have had a fit of conscience, knowing he sold the drugs that killed those kids. He could have wanted to be a part of it all. I don't know. I'll have to get his VA records pulled and talk to his treatment doctors there to get a full picture."

"So where is his tie to our suspects?"

"That's what we have to find out. Juri Edvin got his drugs from somewhere."

"Possibly Barent? They run in the same crowd, most likely, if they're both into the vampire scene. It can't be that expansive here in Nashville."

"Probably. You'd be surprised at just how pervasive these countercultures are."

"Okay. I'm going to go see what Marcus has, and then we can start heading back into town."

She went inside through the kitchen to the foyer. She took the stairs to the second floor two at a time. She could hear Marcus, followed his voice down a long hall to the third bedroom on the right. She turned in and stopped dead.

The room was draped in black-and-red velvet, with photographs of wide, gaping mouths, fangs dripping with blood, throats thrown open in a scream, every few inches. The effect was startling. She felt like she was about to be bitten, eaten, from every corner. A huge canopied tester bed—probably brass once, but painted black—with black sheets and pillows, stood in the center of the maelstrom of mouths. She risked a quick glance under the canopy—yes, more mouths there.

The room smelled like old things, rotting blood and moldy leaves, overlaid with some sort of sickly sweet incense. Taylor breathed through her mouth, looking around.

Marcus was sitting at a desk that was covered in a shaggy black fur throw, the computer on and running.

"This is…interesting," she said, chills running up and down her spine. "It stinks in here."

"No kidding. I feel like I need a shower, and I haven't touched anything but the keyboard. I've got the creeps sitting in here. We should just take the computer with us—it's loaded with information. Looks like Barry is a first-class drug dealer. He keeps transactional analyses of what's working and what isn't, listings of buyers and resellers. And lots of vampire shit."

"Did you see any familiar names on that list?"

"Yep. Juri Edvin's on there. So's Susan Norwood, though they both go by their nicknames, Thorn and Ember."

"Bingo," Taylor said. "That should be enough to rearrest Susan Norwood, right?"

"We'll have to prove that Susan Norwood and Ember are one and the same, but yeah, there's enough here to send her away for a long time."

"Excellent. That's easy enough—the Edvins only know her as Ember. They should be able to ID her with no problem. Is Barent making all of his own drugs, or is he buying, too? It would be nice to give the Specialized Investigative Unit a cut of this."

"I can't tell that. This is just what he's selling and to whom. I've already called Gerald Sayers—they're waiting for us. He wanted in."

"Great. This is right up his alley. Okay, grab the computer. Do we need to amend the warrant to include anything else?"

"No. I've already called Tim Davis, asked him to ride on up here and do a search. He can bag and tag anything else that we need. I think we need to get back and get to work on this. We're awfully close."

He flashed her a grin, looking younger than his years, and she felt herself grinning back. A good morning, all in all.

Thirty-Five

Baldwin hated fighting with Taylor.

Having to tell her about Fitz over the phone was a catastrophe. He should have called Sam first, had her there. He'd heard the cracks form in Taylor's otherwise rock-hard shell, and it made his heart break. She was the strongest woman he knew, the bravest. And the most foolhardy when her dander was up. He hoped like hell he'd gotten through to her, that she would actually listen to him and stay in Nashville. She'd promised, but he wasn't convinced. Knowing her friend was out there in need may prove too hard for her to hold back on.

He needed to get this hearing over with and get back to her before she did something stupid.

He checked his watch. They were due to reconvene in twenty minutes. He needed to get a move on.

Reever was waiting for him when he arrived.

"What took you so long? I thought you weren't going to show."

"There's some role reversal for you, Reever. That's how I felt yesterday."

"Touché."

"Listen, how much longer do you think this is going to go on?"

"Depends, Doc. How much more do you have to tell them?"

Baldwin looked at his friend. How much more indeed. He could just sacrifice himself, fall on his sword, give them everything right now and walk away. It wouldn't be the first time he'd considered leaving the Bureau.

But with the Pretender on the loose, he needed the full force of the FBI behind him. No, he needed to continue to tread delicately, not giving them anything that wasn't absolutely necessary. He still didn't know what they had hanging over him, though he was starting to get an inkling. And if he was right, he was in more serious trouble than even the disciplinary board realized.

"Baldwin, time to go in. You ready?"

"Yeah."

They got settled at the table. Tucker entered the room like a judge; Baldwin waited for the cry of "All rise." Instead, Tucker actually flashed him a smile, which disconcerted Baldwin to no end. It wasn't friendly, that was for sure.

Tucker made sure his minions were ready, then looked down his long nose at Baldwin.

"You may continue where we left off yesterday, Dr. Baldwin."

"All right. We executed the search warrant at dawn. We had such hope that we would find Kaylie Fields alive."

Northern Virginia
June 17, 2004
Baldwin

Harold Arlen came to the door outrigged in a terry cloth robe over short blue-striped pajamas, moose hide slippers and a glass of orange juice. Every piece coordinated, he looked like any other suburban guy who'd been startled out of his morning routine.

"What the hell is this?" he demanded.

The Fairfax County detective held up a sheaf of papers. "We have a warrant to search the premises. Please stand back, Mr. Arlen."

"Search? For what? I haven't done anything. What the hell is this about?"

"There've been a number of little girls gone missing over the past few weeks, and—"

Arlen's mouth fell open. "You think I'm the Clockwork Killer? Are you daft, man? That's the most ridiculous thing I've ever heard."

The air crackled, the situation's intensity ratcheting up. Baldwin and Charlotte stayed back. This was the Fairfax Homicide boys' show. Goldman was there, overseeing his detectives as they served the warrant. Arlen's probation officer was there, too. When they pushed into the house, moving Arlen out of the way, his PO grabbed him and held him aside. That didn't help his temper at all—his fury and indignation continued to explode. He met Baldwin's eye like he knew who was behind this, and Baldwin felt the implicit threat. He just smiled. They were going to wrap this up today. Maybe, just maybe, little Kaylie would be found before it was too late.

A deep rumble of thunder sounded in the distance. Baldwin couldn't see very far. They were sandwiched in the cloister of houses, but the weather forecast called for severe storms today. Just what they needed—rain to hamper the search efforts.

Baldwin saw the curtains twitch across the street at the Kilmeades' house. The door opened a few seconds later. Mr. Kilmeade came out onto the porch, fully dressed despite the early hour, the scowl on his face evident from a distance. He started down the stairs, intent. Baldwin broke away from the group to head him off. He met him at the bottom of the drive. Kilmeade had built up a head of steam, Baldwin actually had to put out an arm to stop him.

"Whoa, whoa, whoa. You can't go over there."

"What's happening? Is Harry being arrested?"

"They're executing a search warrant. Arlen broke his parole when he had contact with your daughter. They have to look at every angle in this case, and Arlen fits."

Kilmeade was shaking in fury. "That's a lot of preconceived bull. I told you, Harry wouldn't hurt a child. It's not in his nature. And how dare you use my dead child in this case? What is she, just a means to an end? She's not alive to defend herself, to explain. How dare you?"

"I'm sorry this upsets you, Mr. Kilmeade. But right now, we need to stay back and let the police do their job. Why don't we go back into your house and have a cup of coffee?"

Kilmeade shook his head. "No. You're not welcome in my home. You've used me and my family to further your sordid goals. I'm going back in and calling a lawyer. You don't have the right to come in and railroad Harry just because he fits your idea of what a killer should look like."

"Mr. Kilmeade," Baldwin started, but the man ripped his arm away and stormed back into his house. Great. Just what they needed, more lawyers involved.

Baldwin went back across the street. Charlotte met him at the door, a huge grin on her face.

"What is it? Did you find Kaylie?"

"No, we didn't. But he's got kiddie porn galore on his computer. It was open—we must have interrupted his morning constitutional. More than just dabbling, it looks like he might be trafficking, as well. And there's pictures of all of our victims too, including Kaylie, and several other girls we don't recognize."

"Then we've got him!" Baldwin had to resist sweeping Charlotte into a hug. He settled for squeezing her hand. This was fantastic news.

"But there's no sign of Kaylie, or where he might be holding her?"

"No. This is going to take a while. They've Mirandized Arlen. Goldman is having him transported back to Fairfax County for interrogation."

"Has he lawyered up?"

"Not yet, though his PO is going insane. He insists he's innocent. Arlen says he has nothing to do with any of this."

"Don't they all. Kilmeade, from across the street? He's pretty fired up, said he was going to call a lawyer on Arlen's behalf. So be prepared. Homicide is taking care of the families, right? Do we need to be along for that?"

"No, we're good there. They've got it covered. We can keep focused on helping find Kaylie."

Baldwin nodded. "Okay. I want to do a walk-through of the house, get a feel for things, and I want to be there when they do the interrogation. There's still something we're missing."

"I figured as much. Goldman said he'd give you a ride whenever you're ready. It's going to take a bit to get Arlen processed anyway. I'll stick around here, if that's okay with you. I want to see what else they might find."

"That sounds good. I'll see you back in Quantico, then."

Thirty-Six

The mood on the ride back to the CJC was triumphant. Taylor called Commander Huston and told her about the morning's events, got a nice attagirl that left her feeling good. They were getting close, getting very, very close.

Lincoln met them at the door to Homicide, his grin ear to ear. Even the space between his two front teeth looked cheerful. He had a sheaf of papers in his hand. "Got it," he said.

"Got what?" Taylor said, discarding her leather jacket behind the door to her office.

"The IP address of the video uploads. I cross-referenced the IP addresses the video-sharing sites gave me and got a match to one here in Nashville. Right now, I'm looking for the actual place where the movie was uploaded. It came from Davidson County, that much I know. I'm waiting on BellSouth to give me an exact location."

"Oh, that's great news. How long, do you think?"

"Within the hour."

"Fantastic work, Lincoln. Really."

"I'm also collating some reports for you from the autopsies. Hang tight, I'll be there in five minutes. Sam wants you to drop by her office this afternoon when you have a chance. She has something to show you."

"Gotcha, thanks. We've got too much stuff to cover to handle it in my office. Move everything into the conference room."

She felt good, that high that comes when a case is about to break free. They were forty-eight hours in and had almost all the pieces together. Good old-fashioned police work, not mind reading and other bunk.

Ariadne stepped into the Homicide offices, the patrol escort at her elbow looking nervous. Ariadne seemed to have that effect on men, Taylor noticed.

Taylor nodded to her, thanked the patrol, who wiped his hand surreptitiously on his blues and backed into the corridor.

"I'm sorry we're so late. Why don't we go in my office," Taylor said.

"All right," Ariadne responded.

Taylor led the woman in, then shut the door behind her.

"You're looking very pleased this morning," Ariadne said.

"It's been a productive day so far. Listen. I have what we call a six-pack of photos that I want you to look at. You tell me if any of the men in the pictures match the one you saw at Subversion Halloween night, okay?"

"Certainly. Anything I can do to help."

Taylor laid the hard sheet of paper on her desk, facing Ariadne. Six sets of eyes glared up from a white background. Ariadne sat forward, running her finger along the pictures, absorbing.

She finally sat back. "I'm sorry. No one in those pictures is the boy I saw."

Taylor shook her head slightly. "Look again." She couldn't lead the woman, but Juri Edvin was the second from the right, top row. If she was telling the truth at all, surely she'd recognize him.

"I'm sorry," Ariadne said. "The boy we're discussing isn't in these photos."

Taylor felt the wind go out of her. She pulled the sheet with the females on it, handed it over.

"What about this?" she asked.

Ariadne was quick this time. "That's her. Bottom right. She's the one I saw at Subversion, the one that slapped the boy."

A little relief bled into Taylor's system. At least they had a positive confirmation on Susan Norwood.

"Okay. Would you be willing to sit down with a sketch artist to help us draw up something with the boy and the other girl that you saw?"

"There's really no need for that, Lieutenant." She reached into a capacious velvet bag and pulled out a roll of parchment. "I've drawn them for you."

She unrolled the paper, the stiff vellum crackling. It was a scene from a bar, happy faces, laughing and jumping in the background. Taylor could almost hear the music that made them sway to and fro. In the center were a boy and a girl. The girl was tall, willowy, the boy ramrod straight. They looked like they were wearing masks.

"You're an excellent artist," Taylor said. "These are the two you were talking about?"

Ariadne nodded.

"There's just one problem. It's going to be hard to figure out who they are with all this makeup on them."

"I took the liberty of trying it without, as well," Ariadne said.

She flipped the paper; a second drawing was below. This captured the exact same scene, but none of the children were obscured by makeup.

"Ah," Taylor said. "If this is them, we can work with this."

"That's them. The little girl from the photograph slapped the big boy here, then they chased after her. I'm sorry, it's the best I could do under the circumstances."

Taylor was glad they'd decided to let Ariadne go home last night, with a patrol on her house to assure that she didn't try to leave. Taylor imagined it hadn't been a fun night for her. Regardless, the drawings were as good or better than any of their artists could have done with an Identi-Kit, that was for sure. Taylor looked them over one more time.

"I'm going to take these pictures with me, okay? I need to see if anyone who knows these children might recognize them. What do you plan to do?"

"Pray. I plan to pray to the Goddess for your success."

Taylor stared at the picture for a few more minutes, then looked Ariadne straight in the eye. She weighed her words carefully.

"My detective thinks I should trust you."

"He's a very smart man."

"Then tell me the truth. Do you honestly believe in all of this?"

Ariadne didn't blink, but the pupils of her eyes grew larger. "I do, Lieutenant. With all my heart. It is who I am. I know that's hard for you—you're a very black-and-white person. There's nothing wrong with that, nothing at all. I imagine in your line of work it can be quite useful. But me…I see all the colors of the universe, and then some. I find the path between the markers, and set upon that. What's happened over the past two days is evil. It's bad. It's wrong. No true witch would consciously seek such power over others. Psychic vampires, yes. But Wicca is the way of the light, of good. It wasn't one of ours, I promise you that."

Taylor had to admit, Ariadne was at least partially right. She did see the world in black-and-white. It was how she slept at night.

"Okay," she said, finally. "I can respect that."

"Good. Then we can be friends." Ariadne stuck out her hand, and Taylor shook it.

"You have a huge burden on your shoulders, Lieutenant. May I ease it for you?"

"What are you talking about?"

Ariadne waved toward the roses, toward Taylor. "There's a storm brewing behind your eyes. You're suffering, trying to make a major decision. On one hand is your true path. The other leads to pain and suffering. You'll choose the correct path, and you already know which that is. But a sacrifice must be made. Use your strengths to divine your way."

Fitz? Or Memphis. Who was the witch talking about? And where did she get off prophesying?

"My path. What do you know of my path? Of my responsibilities? Of the people I care for, and who care for me?"

Ariadne looked at her with sympathy. "It's all written on your face, and in your aura, Lieutenant. And I may have done a tarot reading last night, just out of curiosity. If you give me your palm, I can direct you. The key to the occult is applying what works for you. You must seek your own truths."

"Ariadne, now you're getting into the silly stuff. Tarot cards and palm reading? Come on. Give me a break."

She smiled, an impish grin. "Aren't you the least bit curious, Lieutenant? Just the tiniest bit?"

"No, I'm not. I have absolutely zero desire to know what's coming."

Fitz flashed into her mind again, bloody, hurt. She couldn't help but shut her eyes and swallow.

"I can tell you what will happen to him, if you want to know," Ariadne said softly.

Taylor opened her eyes and stared into the deep blue of the witch's soul. Yes, she probably could hazard a guess. She had a fifty-fifty chance of being right, too. There were only two outcomes for Fitz—life or death. Taylor didn't know if she wanted to think about the possibility of the latter.

Ariadne didn't budge, didn't breath. They stood, locked in each other's gaze, until Taylor broke away.

"He's going to live," Taylor said with finality, then swept from her office, leaving the witch behind.

Dear God, I hope I'm right.

Thirty-Seven

Northern Virginia
June 17, 2004
Charlotte

Charlotte watched Baldwin leave with the Fairfax County folks, then started her own walk through Harold Arlen's house. She was deeply unsettled by the whole incident. Arlen really had seemed sincere when he claimed he wasn't responsible, that the photos on his computer were planted there. He admitted to looking at some porn now and again, but just looking. My God, he couldn't have done anything, the shots took care of that. Where was the fun in that? He couldn't explain how photos of the dead girls got on his computer—was in tears by the time they carted him off.

She could hear the storm getting closer, the thunder booming. There was a sense of urgency to everyone's movements; dragging evidence through the wind and rain was the last thing they wanted. She could hear the muffled shouts of people trying to set up some sort of shelter between the crime-scene vans and the front door. Arlen was being transported—for the time being, she felt like she was practically alone with the man's thoughts.

She went through his bedroom carefully. He was organized, methodical. Shirts in the closet were arranged according to color, and he only had white and blue long-sleeved button-downs. There were five pairs of chinos plus one empty hanger, three pairs of brown loafers. His bathrobe had been securely hung on the back of the bathroom door. His medicine cabinet had inconsequential items—shaving cream, aspirin, all the same brand, Kirkland. He did his shopping at Costco. The shower was clean, not a surprise. His house bespoke the worst about him—controlled, and controlling. Everything in its place. Another check mark on the profile.

Charlotte trailed through the house, looking at everything. The preternatural organization was evident in every room. Finding physical evidence was going to be tough—he was meticulous. And they needed the physical evidence to tie Arlen to the Clockwork Killer case. Somewhere in this house, there was a knife with a ten-inch blade, and ligatures, and some sort of bat or bar used to break the girls' legs. The medical examiner had been relatively sure the girls had been lying down when their legs were broken, a rounded instrument used to crack their tibias and fibulas cleanly.

So where would he have done it? A bed? The floor? Some sort of table? Charlotte tried to get into Arlen's mind. What would she do if she needed to restrain a young girl?

She shut her eyes and let the terror overwhelm her.

She would put her somewhere scary. In the dark. Away from any sort of light. With creepy, crawly things, rats and spiders and the cold, dark, dank air that signaled you were underground.

A memory rose unbidden to the surface. Her father, a tyrant on the best of days, locking her in the wine cellar below their house, punishment for some perceived transgression.

She shuddered at the thought, then went looking for Arlen's basement.

Thirty-Eight

The conference room was set up just the way Taylor liked it—whiteboards overflowing with information, victims' photographs at the top, so they could fill in any and all information on the victimology. A separate board was kept for information about the killer. Taylor went to that, unfurled the drawing Ariadne had given her and pinned it up.

"Who's that?" Marcus asked.

"This is the drawing Ariadne did of the kids she followed Halloween night. Her view of the killers. With and without makeup. She didn't recognize Thorn, but she did pick Susan Norwood out of a six-pack. I want that girl back here. She's involved in the killings and the drugs."

"I'll get on it," Marcus said, stepping from the room.

Lincoln was tapping away at his laptop. She heard him whistle, low and long, then he got up and stared hard at the drawing. He went back to the laptop, tapped a few times, then said, "Come here and look at this, LT. I've got something."

Taylor joined him, looking over his broad shoulder at the laptop's digital screen. He was on a video-sharing site.

"Please tell me this isn't the movie again," she said.

"Nope. This is from the address that was part of the ghost IP. Another upload from the same place."

He hit Play on the video.

A horrendous racket launched from the speakers, clanging, industrial noises overlaid with some sort of melody. A deep screaming emanated, words hardly recognizable. The subtitle read, A Goth Makeup Tutorial. The screen went black for a second, then a girl's face filled the space. She was pretty, high cheekbones, wide eyes that were very, very green. Taylor knew in an instant they were colored contacts—Baldwin had naturally clear-green eyes that were just as bright, but much more beautiful. The video accelerated, double time, the girl covering her face in pearly makeup, applying blush, penciling in eyebrows, then going to work on her eyes.

The black rings grew and grew, each swipe applied with a steady, practiced hand. She built a foundation around the eye, each stroke making it deeper, wider, layering on coat after coat of mascara until the green stood out like an emerald and the rest of her face disappeared. She moved to her lips, outlining them in black, then filling the pillows in. A small white line was drawn above the cupid's bow. Then she went back to the eyes again, adding long, draping tendrils of black in perfect swirls down her cheeks.

Finished! The subtitle screamed, then the shot went back to the girl, a quick before-and-after. When she smiled, her teeth were white against their black background; the long fangs in place of her bicuspids made Taylor think about the gaping mouths in Barent Johnson's bedroom. Then the video was over, the grating noise ended.

"What do you think about that?" Lincoln asked.

Taylor smiled at him, then went to the whiteboard and brought Ariadne's drawings to him.

"That's her, isn't it?" she asked.

Lincoln nodded. "I think it is. It certainly looks like her."

"Please tell me that video has a name attached."

"It does. The credits say, 'starring The High Priestess Fane, as herself.'"

"Fane. Fane. Why does that name sound familiar?" McKenzie said.

Taylor went to the conference table and grabbed the file folder from Hillsboro High School, held it up triumphantly.

"She's in here. On the list of Goth kids at Hillsboro."

Taylor flipped it open, scanning through the names until she saw what she was looking for. She read aloud from the folder. "Here we are. Fane Atilio. She's a sophomore. Hangs out with the Goth crowd, straight-A student, excels in English and history."

"Does she have a boyfriend?"

"It doesn't say. The information is sparse on her. It looks like she flies under the radar. She's never been in trouble, never been disciplined."

"Is there an address for her?" McKenzie asked.

"Yes, there is. Feel like taking a ride? I'm going to bring a few extra patrols, just in case. Maybe we'll get lucky."

"You bet."

Thirty-Nine

"I wrote something for you, my love."

Raven was laying on Fane's bed, head hanging off the edge, watching her study a book on ancient runes. She looked up, set the book down and crawled across the room to him, tearing her stockings further as she scraped along. When she reached him, she slid her tongue into his mouth, sucked on his upper lip, then sat back.

"You did? What is it? A spell?"

"In a way. For you to have endless beauty, and my love, always. Say it thrice by the full moon, and your deepest desires will come true."

"Don't tease, Raven. You are my deepest desire, love. Only you. Let me see it?"

He handed the paper to her. She scooted up alongside him, and he watched her lips move slightly as she read his words.

"'Ode to Antigone'
Black boils beneath thin pink flesh
Molten emotion devouring rational thought.
Carrion attacks the filial bonds of lust
Which lie exposed, faultless in
Oedipal wantonness, broken by greed,
Damned to an eternal external hell

For another's unknown sins.
The saving grace of a bleeding hand
Reaches through earthly bounds to
Experience the afterlife.
Hades, Creon, Zeus be damned,
Simple Antigone is drawn beyond
Where a silken sash has unforeseen power:
Haemon's love cannot penetrate
The bridal tomb but for layer
Upon layer of pounded metal thrust
Through a rib as life ebbs onto
The musty gray floor.
Bound forever in the deathly marriage
Of two minds transgressing mortal thought,
Drawn to immortality in legend,
Farther and deeper that bloodless
Purity bound to bloody passion."

Fane hugged him hard, wiping tears away from her cheeks. "Oh, Raven. It's beautiful. You wrote that for me?"

"I did. I wanted you to have something special, just for you. Now that Ember and Thorn are...gone, I wanted to give you my soul."

She slid back down to the floor at his feet, caressing the inside of his calf. "I'll take your soul, and damn them. How dare they run off like this? No, I can't believe they would betray us, Raven. It must be something else. Ember's parents might have taken her phone away, and you know Thorn is going to be somewhere close to her."

He slipped to the floor next to her, put his arm around her thin shoulders. He loved to feel the bones sliding under her skin, so close to the surface he could practically see their edges.

"I do know that, love. I have to believe that they are being kept away against their will. The spell we did last night was so strong, the only thing that could keep them away is if they were being held somewhere. I should go, actually—see if I can find out what's happening. It's been entirely too quiet out there."

"Where will you go?"

"Back to my house. I can look into the mirror, see if I can find them." He stood, and she scrambled to her feet.

"I'll come with you," she said.

"No. I must do this alone. You know I need all my concentration to scry, and you're too much of a distraction, my dear. A good distraction, but one nonetheless."

He kissed her deeply, running his hands along her body. When she put her arms around his neck and drew her to him, he felt that incredible high that no drug could ever bring him close to. She slipped her hand into his pants and brought him to readiness in an instant, running her tongue along the edge of his collarbone as she wormed her way farther and farther down his body.

He stepped out of his pants and guided her mouth to his cock, let the warm ache begin inside his balls as she suckled. When he started getting close, he reached down and brought her to her feet, face-to-face, and took her mouth. He loved to taste himself on her lips. Kissing her, he slid up her skirt. She was wearing his favorite garters and panties, the black-and-silver striped ones. They were crotchless, and she was wet, ready for him. He lifted her off her feet and onto the bed, pushed into her body with a single thrust, his hands beneath her buttocks so he could get as deep as humanly possible. They writhed together, becoming one, building to a climax quickly. No spells, no potions, just their love, exploding between them.

He came back to himself, realized he must be crushing Fane, though she didn't complain. He sat up, stroking the length of her, then smiled.

"I'll be back in an hour," he said.

Forty

Baldwin watched Harold Arlen through the two-way glass. Goldman was going at him hard. Arlen just sat shaking his head, repeating over and over, "It's not me. I didn't do this."

Baldwin watched the nonverbal cues, looking for the lie. Looking for the trail Arlen had left for himself, the winding, narrow path back to reality. Back to the broken body of another little girl.

The cues were all there. It wasn't the obvious things he usually saw when interviewing child killers: the leering face during the interviews, the preening, the giggles. The dead eyes that got lively only when the crime-scene photos appeared under his nose. No, Arlen was much more subtle than that. It was all but invisible, masterfully contained below the surface.

Arlen talked in rapid-fire denials, getting angrier and angrier the longer he was kept in the interrogation room. Baldwin was utterly shocked that he hadn't asked for a lawyer. There was something wrong with that.

They still had a young girl missing. There were no signs

of her whereabouts found at Arlen's house, no clues where she might be. If he'd stuck to the pattern, she was already dead, though they hadn't told the parents that. Baldwin thought it was cruel to let them have hope when the whole team knew there was none, but that wasn't his call. This wasn't his investigation—he and his team were simply support.

In the meantime, Sparrow was scouring property rolls and tax records, looking for anything that could be tied to Arlen or anyone close to him. So far, she'd come up with nothing. Butler was in the same boat—he hadn't found any matching cases within a three-hundred-mile radius. Geroux was still working the other potential suspects, but they were all checking out. Arlen was their last real hope of ending this.

Baldwin was trained to get into the mind of a killer, to anticipate based on the previous kills. Arlen was so squeaky clean that another thought started to form.

Could there be two of them?

A motion caught Baldwin's eye, chasing the vision of a team away. He watched Arlen's hands. He was stroking his index finger with his thumb, over and over. Baldwin leaned closer to the speaker to hear better. Goldman was asking about Kaylie Fields. Arlen's body was completely still except for that repetitive caress. It was almost as if he was fondling...Baldwin realized Arlen was mentally masturbating, using the descriptions of the missing girl as fodder for his disgusting imagination. Since he wasn't physically capable of having sexual reactions, he was using the hand gestures as a surrogate.

"We have exactly nothing, sir." The voice made Baldwin jump.

He gave Butler a sheepish grin. "You startled me."

"Sorry, boss. I'll give you more warning next time."

Butler was small, only about five foot seven, lithe and wiry. He had a very slight British accent, a leftover vestige of two years in England when he was a child. He didn't have the usual look for the Bureau—sandy-blond hair a little long, covering a piercing in the upper left flange of his ear, jeans instead of a suit. Baldwin didn't care what he looked like—the man was a genius with forensics.

"You were saying?"

"The Fairfax County crime-scene techs got nothing. Not a single hair, a minuscule fiber, a shred of mitochondria. Nothing. His house was completely clean. There is no evidence at all to support the theory that any of the girls were kept there. And now the power is out in his neighborhood, so they had to wrap it up. The storm is really bad. Over an inch of rain so far."

Yes, he'd heard the wind whipping trees against the bricks, saw the torrential downpours. All he could think about was Kaylie, alone in the vicious rain. Baldwin turned back to the window. He'd missed the last exchange. Gold-man was flushed with anger, Arlen grinning slightly. Oh, no. What had just happened?

Goldman came bustling out the interrogation room door.

"Fucking squirrel lawyered up."

"Now?" Baldwin asked. "It's been hours. Why now? What did you ask him last?"

"I asked about Evie Kilmeade. He shut down like a freight train ran him over. Smiled that creepy-ass smile and said 'lawyer.'"

Baldwin looked back through the glass. Arlen had resumed his finger sex, eyes closed, a small smile on his lips. Why now? After hours of being interviewed, after all the games, the denials, why did the name Evie Kilmeade make him put the lid down?

Because he was playing them. And he was doing a damn good job of it.

Forty-One

Taylor and McKenzie rolled up to Fane Atilio's address. Bob Parks was behind them, and another patrol car was on its way. Taylor didn't anticipate trouble from a fifteen-year-old girl, but if her boyfriend was around... She had to wonder, who was she relying on now? Ariadne's impression of a couple of teenagers at a rave? Or her own gut, which told her there was more to come?

So far all the kids she'd talked to in this case fell along the clique lines—the good kids, the athletes and high achievers—were pleasant, easy to deal with, cooperative. Probably lying through their teeth to save their own asses, but at least they were respectful about it. The bad seeds were living up to their reputation as well—Juri and Susan were nasty, ill-tempered children.

The exception to all of them was Theo Howell. The clean-cut kid, holding his friends' drugs to keep them safe. He was due into their offices at noon today. McKenzie told her Theo's parents were back in the country, would be accompanying their son. She wondered what he was hiding. Self-preservation taken into account, he'd been a little too forthcoming. Was he truly the good kid as he depicted himself, or was there a dark side, a silent specter of the truth waiting to come out?

She pushed it all away. The Atilio house looked deserted. A two-story, it was tan brick with powder-blue shutters, a terrible combination. Taylor stepped out of the car, stared up at the windows. Was this it, then? Would this girl be the key?

She went up the five stairs that led to the front door. She rang the bell, then stepped to the side. At her signal McKenzie and Parks took up positions to her right and left.

She could hear footsteps. She touched her Glock briefly, unlatching the snap so she could unsheathe it from its holster quickly if needed. The door swung open. A sultry voice rang out.

"Silly, why didn't you use your key?"

Taylor stepped into line of sight to the door. A young girl stood there, mussed, hair askew, half-dressed in a bustier and skirt. Long black hair. Green eyes. Their girl.

"Who are you?" she asked with such a note of horror Taylor nearly laughed out loud. She bit her lip and said, "Fane Atilio?"

The girl straightened—she was eye to eye with Taylor.

"Who's asking?"

"Lieutenant Jackson, Metro Homicide. I—"

She didn't get to finish. The girl started to slam the door, face full of panic.

Taylor got the toe of her boot into the crack just in time, but paid the price. She'd have a bruise for a month on the arch of her foot after that.

"Ouch!" she shouted, shouldering the door open. "Stop right there, Fane."

Not surprisingly, the girl didn't listen. She bolted up the stairs, her long legs moving gracefully. Taylor took off after her, heard a door slam.

She made it to the top of the stairs just in time to see the wood still quivering. She tried the knob, it was locked.

"Come out of your room, Fane. Right now. Unlock this door," Taylor yelled.

There was no sound from within. Parks and McKenzie had caught up to her now. Parks whispered, "We're clear."

Taylor nodded, then said, "Fane, I'll force it if you don't open the door. You have three seconds. Three, two, one."

Nothing. Taylor stepped back, kicked the door open. It swung back and smashed into the wall, rebounding nearly closed again. Taylor pushed it open with her left hand, Glock pointing into the room.

Fane Atilio was trying to go out the window, one leg over the sill and an arm in a tree outside, calculating the drop. Taylor holstered her weapon, crossed the room in three strides and grabbed the girl by the wrist.

"Stop that. Get back in here right now." She half dragged the girl away from the window. Though thin, she was still heavy. She collapsed onto the floor and refused to look up, a low, keening moan escaping her lips. Taylor nudged her with the toe of her boot.

"Get some clothes on. We need to talk."

"I have nothing to say to you," Fane said. She looked up at Taylor, eyes haughty behind their makeup.

"Oh, really? Well, just you wait and see, little girl. Because I think you have more to tell me than you can possibly imagine."

Forty-Two

Taylor took the struggling girl to the Criminal Justice Center, read her Miranda warning, snapped a Polaroid of her and threw her into an interrogation room. Ariadne had identified Fane instantaneously when the six-pack was put together.

Taylor tried to look at the bright side of things. They had a positive ID on two women, a drug dealer with a chunk out of his leg and a missing teenage boy, possibly the mastermind behind the whole shebang. The Specialized Investigative Unit had confirmed that Barent Johnson was making methamphetamine and Ecstasy, so they had their drugs covered. How they all fit together—that was something she was still working on.

Ariadne insisted that Juri Edvin was not the boy she'd seen at Subversion. Her drawing of Fane Atilio was right on the money, both with and without the makeup. So maybe she was right about this mysterious fourth.

Regardless, Fane Atilio was not cooperating. It was getting close to dusk, the day bleeding away. Taylor was hungry and getting frustrated.

She took a deep breath, tried again.

"Fane. Where are your parents?"

Nothing.

"Fane, where were you on Halloween?"

Blank, soulless stares that never met Taylor's eyes. Nothing.

"Fane, your boyfriend. What's his name?"

They continued in this vein for a good thirty minutes before Taylor finally got huffy, stood and left the room.

McKenzie was in the video-feed room, watching.

"Stubborn brat," Taylor said.

"She is at that. But a true believer. Want me to have a go at her?"

"Sure. Why not. I'm getting nothing. She's giving me the creeps, really. How do these girls get so much attitude?"

"You didn't have attitude when you were fifteen?"

"All in a good way—not like this," she said, but blushed. He was right, she'd been just as sullen and noncooperative when she'd gotten picked up for underage drinking when she was thirteen. She wasn't the one doing the drinking at the time, it was the friends she was with. The patrol officer who arrested her friends believed her. That cop had been Fitz, and he'd let her off with a warning. He'd treated her with respect, actually listened to her when she said she wasn't involved. She'd been struck by the fairness of his actions, and it had started her thinking. The next thing she knew, she was obsessed with becoming a cop, with being fair and just. She'd not seen such actions before, and she liked it.

"You okay?" he asked.

She dragged herself back to the present, forcing the vision of Fitz's eye sitting on a table in North Carolina out of her head.

"Yeah, fine."

He looked at her sideways, but she busied herself with her ponytail until he said, "Lincoln got a warrant for Fane's phone and laptop. He's getting ready to delve into that. Ariadne ID'd her, right? That should be solid enough to start."

"Yes. Though I can't tell you how much I'm looking forward to going to the A.D.A. with this testimony."

"LT, she's credible, no matter what her beliefs. You won't have any trouble there. I just saw Theo Howell and a couple who I assume are his parents. They're waiting on you."

"I'll stick here for a few minutes, if that's okay. I'd like to see you work your magic."

He smiled at her. "Your foot okay?"

"It's a bit sore. I'll live."

"Good. Here goes nothing." He went into the interrogation room.

When McKenzie walked into the room, Fane Atilio sat straight up in her chair, eyes wide. Taylor watched the tiniest bit of a smile curve her lips upward, and then she got it. Fane glanced at the door, saw no one else was coming through it and promptly began to cry. She looked like a wounded kitten, eyes moist and round, the long black lashes filling with salty dew. She cried prettily, demure and low, with glances up now and again to judge the effect.

Taylor turned the volume up on the tape. She'd seen women like this before. The ones who played men, who acted completely vulnerable just to get the attention. Taylor had watched many a strong man fall all over himself to help a girl like this, a true damsel in distress. A girl who needed.

Taylor wasn't like that. She'd always been a hoist yourself by your bootstraps, put on your big girl pants and deal with life kind of person. She detested the very idea of a man rushing to her rescue. Hell, that's what caused half the friction between her and Baldwin in the first place—his desire to protect her and her stubborn refusal to allow it.

But as she watched, she quickly realized that Fane was her complete opposite. Fifteen and already well-versed in the art of fragile seduction. She was peeking out from under her lashes to gauge the effect her crying had on McKenzie. My God, the girl was just like Taylor's mother, Kitty. She was Kitty, to a T.

McKenzie, bless his soul, wasn't falling for it for a second, but was using it to his advantage. Fane was being played by a player, and didn't even know it.

"She's quite a piece of work."

Taylor turned. Joan Huston stood at her elbow, gazing speculatively into the video monitor.

Taylor gave her a wry nod. "Yes, she is. But at least she's starting to talk. I was in there for half an hour and she didn't do anything more than grunt."

"This is your suspect?" Huston asked.

"One of them. We can't find her parents, and she's not cooperating anyway, so we're going to have to sit on her for a while until we clear it up. We're missing one more, but I'm pretty sure they are all in league together. Our eyewitness drew a likeness of this girl and Susan Norwood, and they matched exactly."

"What's her agenda?"

"That's a good question. I'm looking for it. She talks a good game, but who knows? We've tracked the drugs back to the dealer. I'm waiting to hear if the lab results from this morning's bust match what we took from the Howell boy last night. If it does, we have Keith Barent Johnson and Juri Edvin dead to rights for murder one, for Brittany Carson. What I'm trying to figure out is where these girls fit into the picture—Fane Atilio and Susan Norwood—and how the other seven victims are tied in."

"The Norwood girl's brother was a victim, correct?"

"Yes, ma'am. He was found with his girlfriend, Amanda Vanderwood. When I spoke to the parents at the crime scene, they said their daughter was at home with her nanny. They didn't seem to know that she was out of the house. And Xander's best friend is Theo Howell. He was the last person to talk to Xander. We've got a lot of loose ends, I'm afraid."

"Speaking of the Norwoods, they're here now, making quite a fuss. I'd suggest you go have a conversation with them, get them calmed down."

"I'll go in just a minute. I want McKenzie with me. He's got insight into these kids. His impressions have been invaluable."

"He's a good detective, isn't he?"

"Yes, he is."

Huston flashed her a horsey grin. "Tell me, Lieutenant. Is it true that you have a soothsayer on board this case?"

Taylor turned away from the video feed. "A soothsayer? I don't know about that. Her name is Ariadne, and she showed up yesterday and fingered these kids for the crime. I'm not sure how much I believe her, but she does claim to be a witch."

"Hmm," Huston said. "Maybe I should go ask her to read my fortune."

Taylor realized she was teasing, smiled back. "We're close, ma'am. Very close."

"Good. Keep me informed. Good work, Lieutenant."

She strode off and Taylor looked back into the room. She turned the volume back up. McKenzie's face was twisted in alarm—she had missed something. Fane was talking again.

Taylor felt her blood chill when she heard the girl's words.

"You know nothing. He's going to kill them. He's going to kill them all."

Forty-Three

*Quantico
June 17, 2004
Charlotte*

Charlotte was fascinated by death. She felt at home, comfortable, at ease when staring into the abyss. Her job gave her the best of all possible worlds, an overwhelming supply of killings to analyze, hypotheses to form, and perpetrators to trace down. She knew empirically that they were monsters, but she was mesmerized by their actions, the sense of purpose that drove them to satiate their desires by exterminating their prey. Predators were her specialty. Knowing inside of them, their dirty little secrets, the twisted, rotted parts that made them tick—that's what she was good at.

She hadn't told Baldwin about the basement yet. Arlen's basement. The crime-scene techs had gone over it and found nothing. It was empty, with no real indication of use outside of a lack of spiderwebs and dust, not surprising considering how organized and clean the rest of the house had been. But she'd felt something down there in the cold, dank dark. Something evil and wrong. Something she hadn't told Baldwin about, because it wasn't visible to the naked eye. And she knew bringing her theory to Baldwin, trying to explain her thought process, would lead to an exploration of her own past that she wasn't ready to divulge, not just yet.

She had the Clockwork Killer file open on her lap, a glass of Scotch with just a splash of water sitting next to her elbow. Baldwin's couch was extremely comfortable. Heightening this feeling was the fact that Baldwin himself was at the other end, staring into space.

She wondered what he was thinking about. The case, sure, of course, but was there something else in his face? A sense of tenderness, perhaps? Could he possibly be thinking of her?

They'd been distracting each other terribly. Sparrow knew; Charlotte could tell in the way the woman shrank back when Charlotte tried to stroke her arm. She was surprised to learn Sparrow wasn't inclined to share. That was fine. She had more going on here with Baldwin anyway. A future. A life.

Baldwin took a deep breath and turned to her. "Charlotte, we need to talk."

"That sounds ominous," she said lightly. She didn't want to scare him off, not now. Not when things were going so well. She had everything planned to perfection—she didn't need him growing a conscience and ruining it all.

"Not ominous. Just…necessary. This affair needs to stop."

Charlotte closed the file in her lap and sat very still.

"I thought we were having fun," she said.

"I know. We are. But Charlotte, I'm your boss. I'm responsible for you, for the team. I can't be sleeping with you. It's not right."

"I could transfer."

She felt him tense. "You'd do that? You worked so hard to get into the BAU. You'd be willing to leave for me?"

"Yes, I would." She tucked her feet under her and faced him. He was obviously surprised by her statement. She went all in. "You're the best thing that's happened to me in a long time. I want to be with you more than I want to be in the

BAU. I'll happily transfer out if it means we can continue seeing each other."

"I'm not sure what to say. I never thought—"

"Would you rather I stay and we stop seeing each other?" There, she'd thrown down the challenge. Now she'd know just how serious he was about her.

Baldwin didn't answer right away. Shit. That wasn't the reaction she'd hoped for.

"Forget I said anything," she said, injecting as much ice into her voice as she could. She stood up, dropped the file on the coffee table. It knocked into her Scotch, splashing some on the edge.

"Whoa, Charlotte, hold on." Baldwin was on his feet too, his hands gripping her arms like a vise. He was so damn strong, even if she wanted to get away, she wouldn't be able to pry herself loose.

He leaned in to kiss her. She tried to hold very still and not respond, but that only lasted a moment. She felt his tongue flick at the edge of her lips and opened her mouth, accepting him. He tasted like Scotch and honey, and she kissed him greedily, unsure whether this was the last time, or just the beginning.

When they finally broke for air, Baldwin gave her a smile.

"We'll talk about it again in the morning."

Forty-Four

Nashville
5:00 p.m.

McKenzie leaned across the table.

"Who is he, Fane?"

The girl just shook her head, eyes darting toward the door.

"Talk to me, Fane. Who is going to kill everyone?"

She glared at him, lips closed tight together. McKenzie tried a few more times, then shook his head at the camera. He stood and left the room, met Taylor in the hall.

"At least she didn't lawyer up, like Susan Norwood."

"That's a plus. Her parents are nowhere to be found."

"Crime Scene find anything at her house?"

"Nothing that I've heard of yet. I'll put a call into Tim, see if he's got anything. I need to go talk to Susan Norwood's parents. Want to come?"

"Yeah. When are you heading over to Forensic Medical?"

"Oh, damn. I forgot Sam needed to talk to me. I better call her." She flipped open her phone and speed-dialed Sam. She answered, gruff and impatient.

"About damn time you called me back. I've got some stuff for you."

"Sorry. It's been a crazy morning. Can you cover it on the phone or do I need to be there in person?"

"I'll just tell you. Brandon Scott? Anal tearing, evidence of extensive sexual abuse. Recent and past traumas."

Taylor felt her heart drop. "You're kidding."

"I wish I were. Either he's an active homosexual, or he's been raped repeatedly."

"How recent? Was there a PERK done?"

"Yes, and the physical evidence recovery kit got us exactly squat. I cultured some blood, but it ended up being his. There were no other bodily fluids. There was lubricant, probably from a condom. I couldn't tell you the last time it happened definitively, but it was recent enough. One more thing—his tox came back clean, just like we thought. He was killed outright, overpowered and beaten to death. COD is blunt force trauma and attendant exsanguination. The rest are drug overdoses.

"He died first too, before the others. His liver temp and vitreous fluid confirm it. He was dead between 12:30 and 2:00 p.m. on the thirty-first. The others are in the two to three range."

Damn. This was why she liked to attend the posts herself; she could have used this information in her earlier interrogations. No matter, she had it now.

"The dosed Ecstasy was the cause?"

"That's the most likely scenario."

"Okay, Sam. Thank you for this. I'll toss it into our mix. Do you need anything else from me?"

"Just stop sending lab work to my husband. I haven't seen him in two days." But there was a smile in her voice.

"I'll owe you both a nice dinner. We're close here, so hopefully we won't keep Simon hopping for much longer. Have a good afternoon, okay?"

"You, too. Don't work too hard." She clicked off and Taylor told McKenzie about Brandon Scott.

He looked pained. "Really? I wonder…" He ran his hands through his hair, got a faraway look in his eyes that Taylor was starting to recognize. He was about to take a leap of faith.

"You wonder what?"

"Remember Ms. Woodall, at Hillsboro, said Jerrold King and Brandon Scott got into an argument last week? There were some threats made?"

"Yes, I do. Letha King figured it was about her—she and Brandon used to date, and Jerrold was upset that Brandon had dumped her. You think it was something else?"

"Maybe Jerrold and Brandon were lovers."

"Wouldn't Sam have found evidence of that on Jerrold King's body?"

"Depends on who was pitching and who was catching, if you get my drift."

Taylor thought about that for a minute. "So Jerrold King kills Brandon Scott in some sort of fit of rage, then goes home and kills himself with a lethal dose of Ecstasy? It would sound perfect if there weren't six other kids dead."

"Good point. Still, it's something to ask around about."

"I agree. I wonder if Theo Howell knows anything about it? He seems pretty tied into this group."

"Well, why don't we ask him?"

The Homicide offices were jam-packed with people. All the interrogation rooms were occupied—the Norwoods, with their daughter and her lawyer in Interrogation One; Fane Atilio in Two; Theo Howell and his parents in Three. Lincoln, Marcus and Renn were all in the offices proper, having a deep discussion. Taylor cleared her throat and they jumped.

"What's up?" she asked.

Lincoln rubbed his dreads. "Nothing good yet, LT. The video was definitely uploaded from Fane Atilio's laptop. There's a ton of correspondence—it's going to take ages to get through. One address pops up most often, and the back-

and-forth has got some seriously graphic content, NC-17 all the way."

"Not underage porn again, I hope."

Marcus blushed. "Close enough. It's sex talk, between Fane and a boy. She never uses his name, but it's pretty explicit. I felt like I was reading an erotic novel."

"Can you trace the e-mail address?"

"I'm on it," Lincoln said. "There's something strange about it though. It's part of a single account."

"What do you mean?"

"You know how when you set up an e-mail account, you can set up multiple addresses—aliases, they call them. Say you and Baldwin got a DSL connection through BellSouth, and you both wanted separate e-mail addresses, but didn't want to pay for separate accounts. You could set up to fifty aliases on that particular account at no extra charge."

"And who is the owner of the account?"

"Jacqueline Atilio."

"Is that Fane's real name? Jacqueline?"

"No, her legal name is Fane Rebecca Atilio."

"So Jacqueline might be her mother, who we can't find?"

"That's what I'm thinking. I've looked into her accounts, and I've seen almost no activity outside of ATM withdrawals for the past three weeks. All from the same U.S. Bank branch in Green Hills, one each day for the past week, for the maximum daily limit on the account, three hundred dollars."

"That's odd. Let's get the tapes from those ATM withdrawals."

"On it."

"Lincoln, what else do you have?"

"I'm overloaded with text messages and IMs to decipher. I've been going through all the laptops and phones, looking for anything that stands out. These kids spend a lot of time online, that's for sure."

"What about Facebook and MySpace, Twitter accounts? Are they talking about it anywhere?"

"We're about halfway through everyone's profiles. Nothing's leaping out just yet."

"Be sure you check out Fane Atilio. See if she's got any ties anywhere. And let me know about the ATM withdrawals as soon as you can."

"Will do."

McKenzie caught her eye. "The Howells are here—you saw that, right?"

"I did. I'm about to go talk to them. And the Norwoods."

"Good. Umm, about the Scott boy's autopsy? I'd like to look through all of his files for anything that might lead us to an answer for his…condition." McKenzie said the word with a delicacy that she knew was difficult for him.

She looked him deep in the eye. "Good. I'm counting on you to find something there. I think it's important. I still think Brandon Scott was the target of these attacks. Find out why for me, okay?"

"Yes, LT. I'm on it."

"Marcus, where are we with Crime Scene? Any links?"

"We've got fibers and fluids and fingerprints galore. It's taking some time to isolate."

"Anything that points in the direction of our suspects?"

"Not yet. I'll get a call in to Simon Loughley at Private Match. He said he was going to fast-track that DNA from the wounds. Maybe he's close. And there are no matches for that dark hair found at the Vanderwood crime scene."

"Okay. Y'all scatter. I'm going to talk to the Howells first, I think."

They didn't move. "Taylor," Marcus said, then broke off.

"What?"

"Ariadne said something happened to Fitz. Do you know anything about it?"

Taylor froze. How dare she? How dare she talk to them without Taylor's permission? Where did that woman get off? This was none of her concern, and she knew nothing anyway.

"What did she say?" she asked, her voice hollow.

Marcus looked very young. "That he'd been hurt and you were terribly worried for him."

Taylor pulled her hair down with a vicious tug, the blond spilling over her shoulders. She didn't want to have this conversation right now, she needed to keep them focused. *She* needed to keep focused.

"Ariadne knows nothing about Fitz's case. Baldwin called me this morning with some news. The SBI believes they've found his trail. The good news is the North Carolina police are ramping up the search. We've had unsubstantiated reports of an...injury...to his eye, but that's all we have right now. I'll let you know the minute I know more, I promise."

It wasn't an outright lie, at least. She hated to deceive them at all, but she couldn't have them drawn away from the case at hand, not yet. Not when they were so close.

"That's good news though, isn't it?" Marcus asked.

"I hope so, puppy. I hope so. Okay, let's get to work. Who has an eye on Glenda the Good Witch? Or did she wrangle her broomstick home?"

"I'm here, Lieutenant." Taylor jerked around—she hadn't heard the woman walk into the room. Ariadne had her usual beatific smile in place, appearing completely unperturbed by Taylor's barbs. Taylor wasn't sure she particularly liked the access this woman had to her. It was making her very uncomfortable.

"We don't really ride the brooms, you know," she said.

"She was in your office, LT." Lincoln had the good sense to look chagrined. "It was the only place to stash her, outside of the conference room."

"And you don't want me in there, near all those piles of information. You never know what might go missing." Ariadne smiled sweetly at Taylor.

Taylor narrowed her eyes and said, "My office, please. Now." She turned to her team. "The rest of you, get to it."

She crossed the room to her office, felt Ariadne behind her. She stepped inside and went to her desk, signaling for her to take the chair in front and close the door. Once she was seated, Ariadne dropped the smile.

"Lieutenant, I'm feeling a great disturbance—"

Taylor cut her off. "Listen to me. You've done us a great service, pointing us in what seems to be the right direction on these murders. But I'm going to have you taken home now. We can take it from here."

"No, you can't," she said simply.

"Actually, yes, we can. We've got all the components now, it's just a matter of unraveling the evidence. We're almost there."

Ariadne shook her head. "You just don't get it, Lieutenant. It's not over. You're still missing the warlock who is at the heart of this."

"Do you know where he is?"

Ariadne shook her head. "But—"

"Then you need to go home and let us do our jobs. We're actually quite good at finding people, you know."

"Not when they've got cloaking spells in place. You won't see him until he wants you to, Lieutenant. And by then it's going to be too late."

"Cloaking spells. Come on, lady. You're starting to sound flat-out batty. It's time to go." Taylor stood. Ariadne's face was a mask—she didn't move from her chair.

"Do you know how many of us are out there, Lieutenant? In and out of the broom closet?"

"The broom closet?"

"Some coven members like to keep themselves hidden from their secular lives, Lieutenant. They don't want the rest of the world to know that they're practicing. We call that 'in the broom closet.' Samhain, Halloween, is the only night of the year when we can publicly flaunt ourselves. Christians, Jews, Wiccans, Goths, pagans—all the alternate religions, and most of the mainstream ones, recognize this night. Harmless activities have replaced the pagan rituals—dressing up, trick-or-treating, jack-o'-lanterns. By recognizing these symbols year after year, the associations are made.

You have granted this date significance, and its power comes from that. It is the one holiday that we all have in common, religious and secular, throughout the world, and that makes it twice as powerful. When someone recognizes us on Samhain our spirits reincarnate, because we believe that we will live on long after our deaths. We have a great deal of power on Samhain. These children know this. They've utilized the symbolic to help their purpose. They're perverting our ways, and I want them punished."

"That's for the courts to decide, Ariadne."

"Not entirely true, Lieutenant. We are responsible for these children's actions, just as surely as they are."

"Ariadne, really. I appreciate your help so far, but I've got to go back to the practical world. I'll have a patrol get you home safe."

The note of finality in her voice was enough, at last. Ariadne bowed her head, stood and said, "As you wish."

Forty-Five

The phone startled Baldwin awake. He saw the number and cursed. Goldman. He put the phone to his ear and pretended to sound alert. It was only 6:00 a.m.

"This is John Baldwin."

"We found her."

Three little words. Baldwin felt his heart sink. They'd failed, again. For the sixth time, they'd failed.

The forest was silent. The rain had made the path sloppy, it was slow going. The birds knew they were coming and after a flurry of wings and warning cries, had clammed up. All Baldwin could hear was the sound of the team's feet on the gravel path, the soft layer of fallen leaves cushioning each step. The cycle of life was never more apparent to him than when he was surrounded by trees. No matter the season, shedding occurred.

Charlotte was breathing heavily behind him. They'd been hiking uphill for the better part of an hour now, and she was getting winded. At least she'd worn boots, although he could tell they were brand-new and bet she'd have some seriously impressive blisters by now. He'd never seen her in anything but the highest of heels. And barefoot, of course.

He glanced back at her, red hair billowing out of a ponytail, a small moue of distaste on her lips, and felt his breath catch when he thought of that hair lying across his thighs. She'd been at his place every night this week, and he was starting to enjoy not waking up alone. She'd become a comfort, in addition to a bedmate, and he knew he was getting in way over his head. The two halves of his brain had been arguing in the background, creating a fuzz of noise like an out-of-range radio station. He'd been trying very hard to ignore the fight, but in the quiet of the forest, he couldn't tune it out. Now she wanted to transfer out of the BAU so they could be together. The thought frightened him more than anything. He wasn't ready.

It's just sex, for Christ's sake. What are you so twerped out about?

I've been alone for too long. That's what. I might get too comfortable with the situation, and you never know where it will lead.

That's your hormones talking. She's worth lusting over. She might even actually like you, dummy. Did you ever think of that?

He hadn't. Not really. He just assumed he was a tool, a rung on the career ladder for her. What if he was wrong? What if she had real feelings for him? What if he had real feelings for her?

Get your head back in the game, damn it. You're about to see a dead girl. One who died because you were too busy fucking Charlotte to catch the killer.

He breathed deeply, synchronizing his breath with the breeze cascading through the fragrant pines. Sunlight dappled the thick branches, turning the path gold. Physically, he was fine. He'd been training for the Marine Corps Marathon for the past few months and was in the best shape of his life. Emotionally, though—that was another story.

He'd never been so sure of his gut instinct before. Harold Arlen was their suspect. He was the Clockwork Killer. Every law enforcement officer, every neighbor, every member of the media, everyone, everyone thought Arlen was responsible. The pictures on his computer, his interactions with Evie Kilmeade, all of his actions led them to that conclusion.

But there was still absolutely zero physical evidence to prove that. They had no semen, saliva, hair, blood, epithelials, fingerprints. Nothing. He'd violated his probation, but at the arraignment, the judge had unfathomably let him out on bond.

A decent defense lawyer would make mincemeat of their case, and Arlen knew it. He had covered his tracks too damn well.

Baldwin felt like he had gotten to know Harold Arlen, better than he'd known most suspects he'd hunted. Kilmeade had been right. On the surface, Arlen was the poster boy for reformed sexual predators. The nicest touch was helping to run the group for reformed molesters who met and worked their way through a specific twelve-step program designed just for them. No one could get inside his head, though—into the tiny, nasty little crevices that housed his innermost desires. Baldwin had caught a glimpse or two during the interviews, when Goldman had struck a nerve and Arlen had reacted. But for the most part, Arlen had taken the accusations in stride, shaking his head and occasionally quoting his "sponsor."

They'd had people on him 24/7, tracking his every move. Yet here they were, hiking deep into a forest to see the body of the latest little girl who'd disappeared, exactly one week ago today. Like clockwork.

Forty-Six

Taylor saw Ariadne safely out of the building, then joined Marcus to talk to the Howells. The Norwoods already had counsel present and were making noise—there was no sense in forcing them to wait too much longer. But Taylor needed to ask Theo Howell a question before she went any further.

He and his parents were sitting calm and quiet in their interrogation room. Blake Howell was a well-built man, clean shaven, wearing a black suit, white shirt and orange silk tie. His wife was equally decked out, a beautiful spice-colored Turkish pashmina draped across her shoulders. Her blond hair was carefully highlighted and shellacked into place; his was salt-and-pepper, with the salt winning the race. They both stood and introduced themselves when Taylor entered the room.

"Mr. and Mrs. Howell, it's good to meet you. Thank you for being so patient with us this afternoon—we have a lot of ground to cover, as you can imagine. I only have a moment, and we'll be right back to you. But I need to ask Theo a question."

Mr. Howell took his seat. "Wait just a second, Lieutenant. Is Theo in any sort of trouble? Do we need a lawyer here?"

"That's certainly your right, sir. But we're not seeking charges against Theo at this time. We just need some information."

"It's okay, Dad." Theo turned to Taylor. "I've already told them everything we discussed last night. I'm grounded."

"I'll bet," Taylor said. "Okay, I need you to think about something for me. Do you remember Jerrold King and Brandon Scott having a fight last week?"

Theo creased his brow for a moment, then said, "Oh, yeah. They got into it before practice. I figured they were arguing over Letha."

"Letha King, Jerrold's little sister?"

"Yeah. She and Brandon had dated earlier in the year. She broke up with him, though, beginning of October. Said some pretty raunchy things about him, too. He went back and called her some names, they had a little war online, saying nasty things back and forth. But it stopped weeks ago."

Weeks ago. Ah, how quickly time flies to the young.

"So why would they be fighting now?"

"Like I said, Letha said some…things about Brandon." He glanced at his parents, tips of his ears red. "She called him a faggot."

"Was Brandon a homosexual?"

"I don't know. Maybe. He went with a lot of girls, was really popular, but never seemed that into it, if you know what I mean."

"Are there any boys that you know he might have dated?"

"Well, not really. That's not the kind of thing we all talk about openly, you know?" He began fidgeting in his chair. Theo Howell wasn't a very accomplished liar.

"Is there any chance that Brandon and Jerrold were dating?"

Theo laughed. "No way. Jerry was very much into girls. He was furious that Brandon was using Letha as his beard."

Evelyn Howell touched her son's arm. "Theo," she said, the note of warning enough for him to start talking again.

"Sorry. Definitely not Jerry. But he might have gotten together with this guy Schuyler a couple of times. That's what the rumor was, anyway. But Schuyler doesn't go to Hillsboro anymore. His parents sent him to reform school or something, up in Virginia, a couple of semesters ago, so I have no idea. And it was only gossip."

Mrs. Howell's eyes popped open. "Schuyler Merritt? That's who you're talking about? Jackie Merritt's boy?"

Theo nodded.

"Why, I had no idea. The Merritts are friends of ours, Lieutenant. They sponsored some of the events at the bookstore. Or they used to. They split up last year. The divorce was just finalized a few months back. Jackie remarried lickety-split, the ink was hardly dry on the forms, you know. Her new husband is a marine, was shipped off just a few weeks after they got back from their honeymoon. Sky Senior took it all hard, started drinking. He hasn't been worth much these past few months. Hard on the kids too, they split them up."

"The kids?" Taylor asked.

"Schuyler has a sister. She's still at Hillsboro, right, Theo? What's Jackie's new married name, Blake?"

"Let me think. At-something."

"Sky's sister's name is Fane," Theo said helpfully. "Gorgeous girl, at least she used to be. She and Sky were close. It tore her up when he was sent away. She started hanging with the Goths, wearing all that crazy makeup."

"Fane Atilio?" Taylor said. Her voice sounded hollow in her ears.

"That's it. Atilio," Evelyn Howell said, smiling.

"Son of a bitch," Taylor said. "I mean, sorry. Excuse me."

"Was it something I said?" she heard Mrs. Howell ask her husband, their tones growing lower as they realized something was going on. Taylor let the door shut behind her. McKenzie was waiting for her in the hall.

"We need to go have another chat with Fane Atilio."

Fane smiled winningly at McKenzie, then shot Taylor a hateful glance. Taylor was having none of it. She walked around the table, jerked the back of Fane's chair, making the metal screech along the linoleum floor, then sat down right next to her.

"Fane, you have a brother. Schuyler. Where is he?"

Fane looked down her nose at Taylor, then looked away. "Virginia."

"We need his number. Right now."

"I don't know it. It's at the house." She managed to look bored. Her makeup was flaking off. She'd obviously been crying at some point since they'd been gone. Black smears ringed her eyes. Her skin, pale as an opal, blanched further.

"It's not on your cell?" Taylor asked.

"No. I wasn't allowed to call him there."

"Is Schuyler really in Virginia? Or is he here in Tennessee?"

The eyes clouded. "I don't know what you're talking about. I haven't seen him."

"You're lying, Fane. We called your mother's work. They said she'd been out sick for a couple of weeks. She wasn't at your house. Where is your mother? We know your stepfather is overseas, but where's Jackie?"

Fane bared her fangs at Taylor, then licked her lips.

"Wouldn't you like to know," she said, then shut down, arms crossed, eyes closed.

Taylor let her sit that way for a moment. She had a bad feeling about Jackie Atilio.

Something Ariadne said popped into her mind, about the coven. The bond these children had was strong, no doubt about it. Divide and conquer, that was the way in. Turn them against one another, let them think the others were talking. That was how she was going to reach into their minds and draw out the truth, not through threats or cajoling or promises. She stood up, cleared her throat. Spoke softly.

"Fine. We'll just go talk to Thorn again. Between him and Ember, we have most of the story anyway. We know all of you participated in the murders."

The effect was immediate, violent. Fane lunged upward, out of the chair, hand raised like she was going to slap Taylor.

"Liar," Fane screamed. "They would never betray us. The penalties are too steep."

Taylor grabbed her by the arm and twisted, forcing the girl back into the chair. Fane was panting in her fury. Taylor could see her starting to unhinge.

"I beg to differ, little girl. How about you tell me about the movie you and your boyfriend made. The one of the murders?"

Fane looked at the floor, breath coming in short gasps. "What movie? I don't know anything about a movie."

Taylor released the girl's arm. "Look at me."

Fane glanced up at her.

"Stop lying, Fane. It was uploaded from your computer. My tech is going over your laptop now—they found the original."

A beat, the girl gathered her thoughts. "Oh, that. That's all fake. Playacting."

"How could you possibly expect me to believe that, when you've shot the film at all the crime scenes and you have Brandon Scott's murder on tape? You want me to believe that it's a coincidence? Do you think we're stupid, Fane?"

Fane had calmed herself, was sitting straight again, composed. "Yes, well. We've gotten very good. None of that is real."

"Right. And how about the letter you sent to *The Tennessean?* Was that fake, too?"

"Isn't *he* going to say anything?" Fane turned to McKenzie, eyes pleading. "You can't let her talk to me like this."

McKenzie leaned forward, voice deep and grave. "Fane,

I'm very disappointed in you. We talked about this earlier. The more you help us, the less you'll be punished. That's how this works. We know you're involved. You hold the key to this mystery. We want to help you, but you have to help us, too."

"Don't give me that crap. I'm not going to help you. You don't care. You said you cared, and I know you don't." She started to cry again, McKenzie rolled his eyes at Taylor.

Taylor handed Fane a tissue. "Blow your nose. You're not going to get any leniency because you're crying. Tell us what we need to know now."

Fane snuffled into the Kleenex. "It wasn't me. I don't know what you're talking about. And I think I'm done answering your questions. I want a lawyer."

Shit. They'd pushed her too hard.

"That's your right, Fane. Though if you had nothing to do with all of this, you shouldn't need a lawyer. But we'll go arrange for that. One little issue—we need to inform your parents. I wasn't kidding before, I need to know. Where is your mother?"

"In hell, probably," she said, then closed her mouth tight and laid her head on the table. They would get nothing more from her.

They left Fane alone in the room. The hall was bright. Taylor felt like she'd spent half this case standing in the hallways of the CJC, trying to interpret the lies spilled in the interrogation rooms. She itched to get outside, back to the scenes. That's where the answers were going to come from, not this merry band of misguided Goth children, lying and cheating their way through life.

"We need to find this mysterious brother. My gut says he's involved," McKenzie said.

Taylor leaned against the wall, one boot propped against the painted cinderblocks. "I want to find her mother. I don't like any of this."

"What do you think is going on?"

"I think we're looking at an unhealthy relationship between a brother and sister who were separated when their parents got divorced. Being together was paramount. When they were split, they started doing anything they could to get back together. I think we need to comb through the Atilio's house, get word to the husband, see if we can find the mother. She's too conspicuously absent for anything good to be happening."

"You may be right. The separation could be a precipitating event. Fane shows definite sociopathic tendencies. If she's practicing Wicca, she could think she's got control, that she can change the course of her life according to her will. Happiness would be anathema for her—she'd strike out against anything she saw that reminded her of what she used to have. You noticed that the families we've talked to have all been relatively happy, with two parents. That could have been the impetus for choosing the victims."

"So she arranges with her friend Thorn to have the party kids' drugs tainted, then sneaks into their houses and carves pentacles in their stomachs? That's as good a theory as any I've come up with, except for one thing. How did she know who would take the pills and who wouldn't? Theo Howell said he sent word to everyone. Would there have been more? And how would Fane have known?"

"Eight victims. At least three involved. I don't know, LT. Maybe she was there when they took the drugs."

"And Brandon Scott? He didn't take the drugs and was beaten to death because of it. I think we're going about this the wrong way. These crimes are all related, but it's still too much of a fluke that some of the kids with the drugs took them and some didn't. I think the ones who died were forced to take the drugs."

"Which would mean Fane was at each crime scene. Or…"

Taylor slapped her forehead. "They split them up. Fane and Juri Edvin and Susan Norwood, they split the targets and each handled a few. They must have gotten in under the guise of delivering the drugs. Remember there was no sign of forced entry? So they show, drugs in hand, with some sort of weapon, then force their victim to take the pills. The OD effect would kick in almost immediately, and they'd die quickly. They waited around until the victims were fully unconscious, arranged the bodies, carved the pentacles, shot the film and left."

"Three kids, eight victims, including Brittany Carson, would be pushing it in the time frame. But four kids, that would even the odds," McKenzie said.

"And Brittany's murder was last. According to Juri Edvin, she and Susan Norwood have a history. The Carson girl dated Norwood's ex-boyfriend and it pissed her off. Juri said Susan wanted him to kill Brittany, that it was her idea. Well. That answers that."

She stopped. McKenzie was grinning at her—they'd come to the same conclusions at the same time.

"But what about this brother? We still need an ID on the boy from Ariadne's drawing. Think it's Schuyler Merritt?"

"I bet it is. Why don't we go show his picture around? Let's try Susan Norwood first, see what she does. She's the vulnerable one in all of this."

Forty-Seven

Ariadne crumpled the herbs between her palms, rubbing them back and forth so the fragrant sprigs fell into the fire evenly.

"Isis, Astarte, Diana, Hecate, Demeter, Kali, Inana."

She repeated the Goddess chant four more times, calm, monotonous, stringing out the last long *A* on Inana, feeling herself become one with her pantheon. Scrying with fire was her specialty, a favorite, and she was sure she'd be able to trace the movements of the warlock now that the bond to his coven had been interrupted. He would be flinging his emotions around on the wind, searching for ways to bring them back together, and Ariadne felt sure she could connect with him.

The flames rose high before her, scented with rosemary for remembrance, and jasmine, because that was the warlock's scent. She allowed her eyes to close and she fell deeper and deeper into her trance, then opened them, staring into the flames, seeking. Seeking.

She saw an altar, simple, crude, even, and a black-handled athamé. Two bodies, male and female, writhing in the Great Act. Then she saw the female crying, and the male disappeared. There was nothing else.

She drew back and sketched the altar she'd seen. It was a feminine deity being worshipped. There were useful identifiers scattered among the lares and penates on the altar. She tried to make sense of it all.

She knew the male in the flames was the boy she'd seen at Subversion. She just didn't know who he was, or what role he was playing. The female seemed the stronger of the two, but perhaps she was misreading it. Men sometimes withheld their strength in the presence of a female they loved, treated them as equal. When she'd seen them downtown, the boy seemed the stronger half. One thing was certain; their bond was very intense.

She didn't know what else to do. She'd put the word out among her brethren. They were all looking for the mysterious warlock, as well. She finally drifted off into a light sleep, notepad nearby, hoping that perhaps the pantheon would show her the way in her dreams.

Forty-Eight

Kaylie Fields was smaller than the others. Nestled gently into the base of the tree, the ropes holding her in a loving embrace. Her hair was plastered against her face—she'd been out here during the storm, just like he'd been worried about. Sorrow welled in his chest. He'd been afraid of storms as a child; he wondered if she'd been scared. But that was silly—she'd been dead and lashed to the tree long before the storm broke. There was no way for her to be scared, not anymore, and really, what was a little thunderstorm compared to being kidnapped, beaten and murdered? Her legs were obviously broken, a cruel act Baldwin assumed happened almost immediately after the abductions so the victims couldn't run away. None of the autopsies had shown ligature marks on the bodies—why tie someone up if you could incapacitate them?

Baldwin heard one of the Fairfax County guys stumble off, retching. His first dead body, probably, or his first child victim. Kaylie looked to be peacefully asleep, a vision marred only by the slight scarlet stain spread across her naked torso and the awkward bend to her shins. Stabbed through the sternum, just like the previous five girls. The Clockwork Killer had struck again.

There were a few differences in this kill from the others. One was the distance from the previous dump sites. The first five victims had been found just off the main hiking trail. Kaylie was deep in the forest, discarded like leftovers from a camping trip. They wouldn't have found her so quickly if it hadn't been for a phone call the parents received detailing the dump site. Another shift in the MO—the call had come from a pay phone in a dark alley in downtown D.C., possibly the work of the killer, or someone he'd paid off to make the call for him. They were scouring the tapes of the cars coming in and out of the park, with no luck. They still had no idea how the bodies were being transported into the park.

He'd never felt a case so far out of his control before.

Charlotte sighed deeply, and Baldwin turned to see her scratching notes.

"It's different," he said.

"It's him," she replied. "He's just making us dance."

The day had not improved from there.

The crime-scene techs had worked Kaylie's body to no avail. There was no evidence on the body, nothing in the crime scene, the dump site. The storm had washed away the microscopic evidence they might have otherwise found. Baldwin had them take the soil from around the body, hopeful that they could find something in the alluvial muck that pointed them in the right direction. None of the Great Falls Park Rangers had seen anything. The video cameras had a multitude of cars coming in and out of the park, but all of them checked out. It was as if the killer had flown in, dropped the body at the base of the cliff and flown out again.

Of course that wasn't the case. He had been there. But how? They'd been watching Arlen's house. There was no movement, in or out, all last night. He must have dumped the body before they'd started watching him—that was the only way.

Unfortunately, another round of interviews with Harold Arlen had been preempted by the expensive defense lawyer that had been retained by Arlen's twelve-step parent organization, who vociferously claimed he was being unfairly railroaded. He used their own work against them—they were watching the house, they knew he wasn't able to leave and deposit a body. Add to that the nagging little question of the lack of physical evidence. The pictures on the computer just weren't enough. Arlen insisted he didn't know how they got there, and if this went to trial, it was possible for the attorney to claim the photos had been planted, or accidentally downloaded. All it would take was one juror who agreed, and poof, no more case. Without corroboration, they just didn't have enough.

The media was losing faith, accusations were starting to fly. And if the pattern was followed, another girl would go missing tonight.

It was late when Baldwin had dismissed the team to get some rest, as if that was possible. He and Charlotte had stayed in the office for a while, waiting. When no call came, they relaxed a fraction, and Baldwin decided that they should get some food, recharge and start fresh in the morning. Sleep had been his enemy this week—he was running on caffeine and takeout, and his body was rebelling. Added to the mix was Charlotte, who jumped him every time they got a few minutes alone. Intense and powerful as the sex was, he was getting worn-out from all the pressure. There was a bit of desperation in their lovemaking now, coupled with a sense of insecurity and fallibility. He was beginning to sense Charlotte would bleed him dry if given the chance.

Yet here he was, spent and gasping on the bed again.

Charlotte was pacing the bedroom. She was naked, her hair flying out behind her with every turn.

"It's him, goddammit. We know it's him. There's got to be something there. Something that tells the story. Where is he keeping them? How does he disappear with them so easily? Everyone is on the lookout. We've had units on Arlen for days now, there's no way he slipped out without our notice. We're chasing a fucking ghost."

"He's not a ghost. He's right there in front of us. We're just missing the clues."

She turned on him, small white teeth bared in a grimace. "What could we have missed? We've been in his house. We've watched him. He's the single most perfect reformed child molester I've ever seen."

"Exactly. That's what's wrong with him. He's too perfect. He *will* slip up, Charlotte. We are running out of time, yes, but he will make a mistake."

"How many girls need to die before we figure out what that is, Baldwin?" Her voice caught. Add vulnerable to the list of qualities he never thought he'd see from her.

"Come here," he said.

Obediently, she walked to the bed. "Again," she said, husky, demanding, and he almost laughed.

"Charlotte, I'm only one man. I don't think it's possible for me to—"

She proved him wrong, once more.

Forty-Nine

Susan Norwood was meek and docile in the presence of her parents. Taylor wondered if her mother knew about her alter ego, Ember, and her boyfriend the drug dealer, Juri Edvin, aka Thorn. If they didn't, they'd find out soon enough.

Mr. and Mrs. Norwood looked smaller today, shrunken with grief. First their son murdered, then their daughter accused. They didn't smile when Taylor and McKenzie entered the room. Miles Rose got to his feet and shook Taylor's hand, pulled her out of earshot of his clients.

"This better be good, Lieutenant. Her parents are squawking about having your badge for holding a minor against her will without bringing them in."

"Quit posturing, Miles. You know as well as I do I'm allowed to talk to her without her parents around. Besides, said minor ran from me, tried to hit me and was read her rights before a word was spoken. She's being charged with murder, assaulting an officer and fleeing the scene. This isn't some sweet little innocent you're trying to protect."

He showed her teeth in a semblance of a smile, a rat on a floating barrel, then went to his clients and sat down. He ran his hands through the fine black strands that raked across his balding pate. She always felt like she needed a shower after shaking hands with Miles Rose.

Taylor sat across the table from them, introduced McKenzie to the Norwoods. The niceties observed, Mrs. Norwood asked, "Is there news on our son's murderer, Lieutenant?"

Taylor said, "Good question. Why don't we ask Susan that? Susan, what do you think about all of this?"

The girl glared at her, and Taylor raised an eyebrow. Still under her parents' control on the surface, at least.

"Why in the world are you asking Susan? She had nothing to do with any of this. And I want to know why she was taken and held last night, Lieutenant. What exactly is going on here?"

Taylor sat back in her chair. "Your daughter is dating a drug dealer, for starters. He's implicated her in a murder he committed."

"What in the world? That's it. We're leaving." The Norwoods jumped to their feet.

"You can go, but Susan stays. We're charging her with first-degree murder."

Laura Norwood started to sputter, and Susan let out a howl. Miles Rose leaned back in his chair and crossed his hands across his belly, visions of dollar signs dancing in his eyes.

Mr. Norwood said, "But she's a juvenile. Surely you can't charge her. She's done nothing wrong."

"That's right. I haven't done anything. I'm not involved in this." Susan glowered at Taylor.

"Let me tell you a little story, okay? You can correct me where I'm wrong. You've been hanging out with a boy named Juri Edvin, also known as Thorn, who is supplying half of Hillsboro High School with drugs. Vi-Fri ring a bell? Your boyfriend gave a dosed pill of Ecstasy to Brittany Carson, then stood outside her window watching her die. He left his DNA on the wall of her house, there's no mistaking it. Aren't you and Brittany friends? Juri said something to that effect yesterday."

"This is bullshit," Susan said.

"Susan!" Mrs. Norwood thundered at her daughter. "Where are your manners? Apologize to the Lieutenant this instant." She fumbled for a tissue in her capacious bag. "This is obviously some kind of mistake. Susan and Brittany *were* friends. They used to babysit together. Then Brittany started attending St. Cecilia's on a scholarship, and the two of them stopped hanging out as much. Brittany started seeing one of Susan's old boyfriends, and they had a little falling-out. But you were still in contact sometimes, right?"

"Shut. Up. Mom." Susan's jaw was clenched so tight Taylor was afraid she'd break her teeth.

"You were the one who gave her the drugs," Taylor said, incredulous. "You killed her."

"That's not true. It was Thorn. He gave her the drugs. I had nothing to do with it. With any of it." She looked around wildly, seeking support. Her parents were staring at her in horror. Taylor leaned closer to the girl.

"Susan, he said you told him to, but it was you all along. You went there together, forced her to take the dosed pill, and once she'd taken the drugs and was down, you carved the pentacle into her stomach, just like you did with your brother and Mandy Vanderwood and Brandon Scott and Chelsea Mott and—"

"No! That's not what happened."

Susan's parents were ashen, her mother let out a tiny cry. Taylor ignored them, leaned into Susan's face.

"Then why don't you tell me, Susan. Tell us all what happened."

The girl started to cry, long, racking sobs. "It was Raven," she said finally, hiccupping. "Raven made us do it." At the name, she dissolved into a puddle of incoherent cries, clutching her stomach. Neither one of her parents leaned over to comfort her.

Taylor wasn't inclined to show the girl any leniency,

either. She held the key to this case, tucked deep into her bratty little mind. "Who is Raven, Susan?"

She shook her head, a low moan escaping her lips. "I can't tell you. I'm bound from saying his name aloud. Bound by blood, bound by fire. Bound together, a funeral pyre."

"What are you talking about?" Mrs. Norwood asked. Taylor ignored her.

"Susan. Can you write it? Can you write his name down?"

"No. I can't betray him. He'll kill me." She singsonged the rhyme again.

"I can't believe this," Mrs. Norwood muttered. She reached over, grabbed Susan's hands from her face and slapped her. "Stop being like that this instant and tell the lieutenant who this Raven is. Right now."

Taylor was around the table in a heartbeat, got Mrs. Norwood to her feet. "Ma'am, that's not necessary. Perhaps you and Mr. Norwood would care to step outside while I finish Susan's interrogation." She wasn't giving them a choice, shot Miles Rose a hard stare. He rose and patted Mrs. Norwood on the arm.

"It might be best. I'll stay, I won't let them hurt her." They didn't listen, were staring at their daughter as if she were a stranger.

"She was involved in our boy's death?" Voice soft, Mr. Norwood was still processing, his mouth opening and closing like a guppy seeking water.

Her mother was yelling now. "That's not possible. Susan, tell them right now. Tell them you weren't involved."

The girl straightened in her chair. "I wasn't involved in the murder of my brother, Lieutenant. He wasn't supposed to be a part of this."

"Holy Jesus, you do know something about it. Why, Susan? Why?" Her mother was getting overwrought. Taylor didn't want her hitting the girl again; that simple action shed quite a bit of light on Susan's home life. Taylor slipped a hand under the mother's elbow, touched Mr. Norwood on the shoulder.

"Best let me take it from here. Why don't y'all step out into the hall for a breath of air?"

It took both Miles and Taylor to get them out of the room. Sobbing, Mrs. Norwood allowed her husband to put his arm around her, still staring trancelike at his daughter.

When the door closed, Taylor looked back to the girl. She unfurled the parchment that Ariadne had drawn, put the picture on the table. Susan stared at it, eyes wide.

"Is this Raven?" Taylor asked.

Susan didn't say anything, just nodded.

Taylor rolled the paper back into a tube.

"Tell me everything," she commanded.

Raven drove the Rat back to Fane's house. He turned onto her street and saw the maelstrom—vehicles, uniformed officers walking in and out, even someone with a dog. Oh, no. Oh no, oh no, oh no. Where was Fane? Where was she?

He texted her, desperation making his hands shake so hard that he couldn't get his thumbs on the keys properly.

She didn't answer.

Oh, Azræl, hast thou forsaken me already?

He slammed on the brakes, put the car in Reverse and shot back up onto Hobbs. What to do? What to do?

The light turned red at the intersection of Hobbs and Estes—he was stuck. He took a moment and looked inside, feeling for the tendrils of the souls of his followers. He found none. He was abandoned. All the tenuous threads to his coven had been broken. A heartbreaking sense of loneliness crashed through his body, leaving him breathless with the pain of knowledge. He was alone. Oh, what had he done wrong? The spells were right, the actions just. Why was this happening?

"Why?" he screamed, smashing his hands on the steering wheel.

They wouldn't talk, he was sure of that, but he needed to run, just in case.

He'd been running too much lately.

He turned into the driveway of his house and rushed inside, gathered all of his material goods—his Book of Shadows, his portable altar. His laptop, stuffed into his book bag. A change of clothes and his cloak, his makeup bag. His athamé, slipped into a sheath of soft leather. The tickets to Los Angeles. There was still hope.

He went downstairs, aware that he was breathing fast and hard, like he'd been running for miles. Panic. He closed his eyes and tried to calm his racing heart, then entered the cool, drafty basement.

The smell had dissipated, the freshly poured concrete thin but solid underfoot. He walked over them, blatant dis-respect showering down with each step. The bastards. This was all their fault.

He knew the combination on the lock to the safe. He turned the dial to the right numbers, smiled when he heard the *thunk* that indicated the safe was unlocked. He opened it, reached in, helping himself to the provisions. The metal weapons clanged in his bag. He tossed in as many rounds as he could, then swung the door shut on the empty safe.

Fury, fright, loneliness, all rushed into his mind. He felt the rage begin to build, turned and struck the cinderblock wall. Again, and again, until his knuckles bled, then he turned his hand and pounded his fist against the cement. A red haze covered his eyes as he fought the intractable object. He didn't know how long it lasted, but the release of pent-up anger helped; as the blood dripped from his fist, he could see clearly again.

He glanced at the floor, the new cement dark against the old. He couldn't take the chance of them coming after him.

A canister of gasoline stood quietly in the corner. Raven's eyes fell on it and he smiled. How fitting. That's what he needed to do.

He took his bags upstairs, lugging the heavy one over his

shoulder. He loaded it all into his car, then went back into the house. The gasoline, just enough for a lawn mower date on a given Saturday afternoon, splashed merrily against the walls, the stink welcome in his nose. It was time to shed the chrysalis once and for all.

He took a cigarette from the pack of Camels that had sat on the counter for the past three weeks, the lighter, too. He was careful not to inhale—he would never sully the temple of his body with something so unnatural. A few puffs got the end glowing red, and he threw it down the stairs to the basement. There was nothing.

Frustrated, he took the lighter and a dish towel, walked halfway down the stairs, lit it and tossed it to the floor. A thin blue flame ran from the rag, and the fire caught, chuckling into a roar as it found the edges of the gasoline.

Raven rushed out of the house and jumped into the Rat, his worldly possessions lined up behind him, the stink of fear and regret washing away as he started the car and pulled out of the driveway for the last time. He glanced back, swore he saw a flame waving goodbye to him, and then the house was engulfed.

There was only one place where he would be safe tonight. He drove the car west, to his graveyard, to shelter under the oak. In the morning, he would show them all what it meant to be a God.

Ariadne woke with a start. The image from her dream was vivid against her closed lids. She let it coalesce for a moment, then sat up and began to draw. Bars. A uniform. The pale face of a young man, far from home. Sadness in his eyes.

Then a fire, a raging inferno took him, burning his soul. The boy appeared under an oak tree, in a graveyard, curled into a ball, weeping.

Ariadne knew where he was.

She laid back against the pillows, noted absently that it was deeply dark out. She'd been asleep for several hours.

After a few moments, she threw back the covers and went to her altar, intent. She must meditate on this vision. Find the right path to combat the evil.

If the police wouldn't listen to her, she'd have to do this alone.

Fifty

Baldwin weighed his options for how he wanted to tell this part of the story. He was treading into the most dangerous territory. He wasn't blameless, far from it. But a misstep here could cost him his career. And he was suddenly sure that he wanted to stay at the FBI. He wanted to continue working with the BAU, to help Garrett. All of his early doubts vanished. All he could do was tell the truth, and hope for the best.

"Dr. Baldwin? We're waiting."

Reever gave him a concerned look. "You okay, buddy? You need a minute?"

Baldwin shook his head. "No. No, I'm okay." He took a deep breath, and finished the story.

Quantico
June 19, 2004
Baldwin

The dawn came early. Baldwin had managed a couple of hours of sleep. Charlotte was in the kitchen—he could hear her moving about and smelled fresh coffee. He roused himself from the bed, took a quick shower and dressed.

When he entered the kitchen, Charlotte was at the table, legs drawn up on the chair, her arms wrapped around her knees.

"I know what we need to do," she said.

"What's that?"

"We know it's him, right? We know it's Arlen. It's not just me."

"Right. I have absolutely no doubt in my mind."

"Then it's up to us to stop this."

"Of course it is. We're doing the best we can. The Fairfax Homicide team is excellent. They'll find something."

"Yes, they will. I have an idea, though. I think it's time we circumvent Fairfax and do this ourselves."

"Charlotte, we can't do that. It's their case. We're just consulting, at their pleasure. We push too hard and Goldman will have us off this case in a heartbeat. Don't think he won't, he's getting frustrated."

"Yes, yes, I know. But that's not what I'm talking about."

"Sorry, you lost me."

She sighed, hard and impatient, breath coming out in a huff. "Think about it, Baldwin. We have access to the blood evidence."

He didn't like where this was going. All his warning bells began to ring.

"Yes, we do, but what of it?"

"All we need is a few drops. A few drops on a handkerchief. We conduct another search of the house, and voilà, there's the evidence we need to put this bastard behind bars forever."

Baldwin's breath caught in his throat. "Charlotte. You're talking about—"

She whirled on him, face contorted. He'd never seen her angry, and the sight of it unnerved him.

"I know. I know! But what else can we do? We have to take matters into our own hands. No one would ever know.

And think of all the lives we'd save, of the closure we could give to the families. It's for the greater good."

She was inches from him now, the fire coming off her body in waves. Righteous indignation didn't look good on her. He felt every muscle in his body tense, and realized he wanted to hit her. He'd never felt such a pure, fine rage flowing through his veins.

She grasped his hand and he jerked back as if burned. She ignored that, reached for him again. He froze as her arms went around his body. She began her succubus dance, the moves depending on the siren call in his blood to rise up and meet her. He didn't feel it. She'd killed whatever feeling he'd had for her, all with one stupid thought spoken aloud.

This was not what he wanted. This was wrong, every bit of it. He'd always known that, but this, this open ploy at seduction after suggesting they break every code of ethics he stood for, sickened him. He stepped back and grabbed her arms, holding her away from his body. He couldn't help himself, he gave her a little shake, trying to get her full attention. He stared hard into her eyes, making sure she understood him very clearly.

"You listen to me. I'm going to forget you said this. I'm going to look the other way while you gather your things and get the hell out of my apartment. I'm taking you off this case. You are not to get anywhere near Harold Arlen. Do you understand?"

Charlotte's lips tightened and she wrenched her arms from his grasp. "Fuck you, Baldwin. You can't tell me what to do. You want me just as much as I want you. You can't deny that. And you know in your heart that this is the right path."

"You couldn't be more wrong. Get out, Charlotte. Get out now."

He was yelling, and it took all his effort to ratchet it back down and calm his voice.

She stared at him, the hurt in her amber eyes palpable and deadly.

"Don't you dare try to throw me out of your life, Baldwin. I will make sure you regret it."

"Charlotte, threats? Is that how you keep people in your bed, under your spell?"

"I love you." She started to cry, the tears flowing down her face, dripping off her chin. She didn't try to hide it, stood proudly, back straight, and looked him in the eye.

"I said I love you. You can't tell me you don't feel the same way."

Baldwin just shook his head. He didn't take her threats seriously, really, what could she do? Yes, they'd been having an ill-advised affair, but it wasn't the first at the Bureau, nor would it be the last. He'd get a nasty slap on the wrist, but that was all.

He dropped her arms and walked a few feet away. Charlotte continued to cry, but her eyes were wary now. He could see the realization in them, then the fury began to build.

He turned away and said, "I don't love you."

"Well, we've got quite a problem on our hands. Because I'm pregnant."

He froze, then turned back to her slowly.

"What did you say?"

She set her chin, stared him right in the eyes. "I'm pregnant."

He couldn't identify the emotions running through him. Bullshit. She was bullshitting him. But something in her face told him she wasn't.

"Is it mine?" he asked.

"Fuck you, Baldwin. Fuck. You." Big, sloppy tears coursed down her face. "How could you say that?"

"It's too early to tell. We've only been together a few weeks."

She whirled away and went to her handbag. She dug inside for a moment, then turned and threw something at him. He caught it in midair—a pregnancy test, with two pink lines.

Son of a bitch.

She'd gathered up some of her pride—her face was frozen, all emotions hid away.

"I'll abort it. You obviously don't want it."

"Charlotte, I—"

"Go to hell, John Baldwin. You just go to hell."

In a flurry of invectives and flying red hair, Charlotte decamped from the apartment. He didn't go after her. Too much to absorb. He shut the door behind her and leaned against it with a sigh. God, what had he done? What had he gotten himself into?

Pregnant.

Oh, my God. He'd gotten her pregnant.

And that was only half the problem. For Christ's sake, she'd suggested planting evidence.

He was at an absolute loss.

He slid down the door onto the apartment floor, head in his hands. What to do? He took a few deep breaths. That was better.

The first step would be to go to Garrett Woods and explain that he couldn't have her on the team anymore. He'd gauge whether he needed to tell the whole story once he was in the moment; it was quite possible that Garrett would simply take him at his word and have her moved. If not, he'd have to suck it up and take his punishment like a man. It was his fault, after all. He'd been thinking with the little head.

Should he marry her? Stop her from having the abortion, marry her and have the kid? He never saw himself as a father. Of course, he'd never gotten anyone pregnant before, either.

His cell phone started to ring but he ignored it. He struggled to his feet, gritting his teeth. He felt such heaviness surrounding him, the pressure of the case, the chaos of Charlotte's idiocy, the specter of an unplanned child...

It was too much. He went into the kitchen, splashed cold water on his face, then went to the living room and turned on the television. A breaking news alert flashed red on the screen, and he felt his heart sink. The anchor had tears in her eyes as she delivered the statement.

"The Clockwork Killer has struck again."

"Son of a bitch!" Baldwin hurled the remote across the room. It crashed against the wall in several pieces, the perfect allegory for his life. Broken pieces. Little girls scattered like seed corn in the forest. A suspect with no evidence to tie him to the crimes. And a demented profiler hell-bent on her own personal destruction. His life, turned upside down. How many more disasters could this day bring?

Charlotte

Charlotte sat in her car, white and shaking. She couldn't believe Baldwin had questioned her. *Is it mine?* That bastard. How could he think otherwise? He'd been fucking her every chance he got for over two weeks. How dare he be so callous? How dare he? After all she'd given him. After what she'd said.

She did love him, whether he believed it or not. Her love may not manifest itself in the ways others could interpret, but it was love, nonetheless. She'd never given herself so totally to a man before. Look where it had gotten her. Alone and pregnant, in her car, crying.

She wiped her face angrily. Crying would solve nothing.

He was just scared. That's all. She shouldn't have told him her plan, not until afterward. She should have eased him into this, told him about the baby, let him be happy first. Then he'd understand her plan was flawless, and the right thing to do.

She put the car into gear. She had so many things to do today. She'd prove herself to him, and he would come back. He would. She would make sure of it.

Fifty-One

Taylor was in the conference room at the CJC, getting briefed about a boy named Schuyler Merritt, who Susan Norwood and Juri Edvin called Raven. The pieces were all coming together, fast and furious. They'd sent the Howells home—there was nothing more Theo could help with tonight. The Norwoods had been dismissed, as well. Susan had been escorted to booking after telling Taylor the whole story. About how the four of them had split the crime scenes between them, gone into the homes of their enemies, held guns to their heads, forced them to take the poisoned drugs. About how Raven and Fane had perverted their love and made a movie of their actions. About their practice of witchcraft and vampirism.

Lincoln had worked fast, once he had a name to work with. Schuyler Merritt's history spilled out onto the table with reckless abandon—somewhere, something inside the words might give a clue to where the boy might be.

"I called the reform school he was attending in Virginia. They say he ran away three weeks ago. His parents were notified—by phone and by mail. They sent back a letter saying they were going to homeschool him. The school happily washed their hands of him. Apparently, he'd been quite a handful."

The fax machine in the conference room had been whirring for thirty minutes. The school was faxing Schuyler's records, including his psych reports. The pages fed out of the machine one after another, regimented as any army, detailing incident after incident in the few short months Schuyler had been a resident with them.

Taylor glanced through those pages, wondering how a boy could end up so troubled. Not that she hadn't seen it before, many times. But Schuyler Merritt seemed worse than most.

"Any word on the location of the mother, Jackie Atilio, yet?"

"No, and we can't find Schuyler senior, either."

Taylor turned to McKenzie. "Think he got the parents out of the way?"

"Unfortunately, yes. A cadaver dog is searching the Atilio house and yard, right?"

"Yeah. I haven't heard about a hit."

"Might want to send them over to the father's place, too."

"They've got instructions to go there next. Has anyone been able to place a last-known on either of the parents?"

"Marcus got through to Atilio's husband's commander. He's been on a training mission and out of touch for two weeks, at least. There's no way he could have talked to her."

"Okay. Keep on it."

Taylor flipped over the re-creation of Schuyler's reform school jacket, the faxed pages three-hole punched and put into a binder to keep them from getting lost. The pictures showed a thin boy, vanilla-blond hair cropped short, blue eyes that bristled with anger. His lips were pressed together, the point of his collars resonating with the sharpness of his chin.

The reports from the school were crammed full of incidents, ranging from practicing witchcraft to bullying to homosexual liaisons. The psychologists at the school had no control over him. Regardless of their efforts to reach him he retreated, breaking open now and again to shower them all with righteous sparks of fury. When he'd run away from the facility in the dead of night, there'd been a collective sigh of relief from the schools' administrators. The records also showed that he was grieving the loss of his sister. Separation from her seemed to be the most difficult part of his life.

The girl was the key, according to Susan and Juri. Everything Raven did, he did for his Fane.

Taylor had reinterviewed Susan and Juri, making sure the details about their fourth were as clear and real as possible. They couldn't give her information that was helpful. They didn't know where he was. They didn't know where he'd go. They didn't know squat. Taylor knew they were lying; they held some sort of mythical reverence for the boy they called Raven. But she didn't know how to reach them. She had nothing to dangle, no bait. They were both being charged with murder, and there was no way in hell she was going to let one of them plead.

Fane proved to be of little help, as well. She'd taken up some sort of low chant, was sitting ramrod straight mumbling to herself. It was getting late. Taylor went ahead and had the three of them booked into the jail for the night.

Frustrated, she finally put a call into Ariadne, but there was no answer. She left her a message, asked her to call in. Taylor was wholly unfamiliar with this world, and she had a feeling Ariadne could help. She was sorry she'd sent her away.

She was pacing the conference room when her phone rang.

"Taylor?" a breathless voice, Taylor recognized it as Marcus, though the caller ID wasn't his.

"What is it, man? You sound all out of breath."

"I'm at Schuyler Merritt's house. I think he was here."

"You do? How recently?"

"Very. The Merritt house is on fire."

* * *

The moon was hanging low in the sky, a perfect crescent, the pinprick of light that was the planet Venus sparkling at its tip. The evening was clear, crisp and chilly, the air sharp in Taylor's nose.

She and McKenzie talked a little as they drove into Green Hills, the night streets of Nashville flashing by.

"What do you think he's going to do next, McKenzie?"

"I don't know. He might be on the run, especially when he realizes his compatriots are behind bars. He could stand and fight. I just don't know."

"Is he finished? That's what I want to find out."

He didn't answer, just looked out the window. They were on Twenty-first Avenue, the streets remarkably clear for this time of night. Postholiday letdown; the city was sleepy after their long night on Friday.

"You called Ariadne?" he asked.

"I tried. She didn't answer."

"We need to keep an eye on her. She might take it upon herself to try and track him down. You blew her off earlier, and she probably doesn't trust you anymore."

"Listen, I know you don't put any stock in the occult, McKenzie."

"I don't. But I know enough about it to recognize that some people do. Look at these kids. They've been practicing witchcraft. They believe. They think this boy Raven has put a spell on them so they can't talk. It's not that they don't want to talk, they do. But they honestly believe that they can't. It's fascinating, the phenomenon. Practically Stockholm syndrome."

"You think he has that kind of power over them?"

"I do. Over the girl, Fane, at the very least. They were all in on this plan, all four of them. I think Raven took it upon himself to hurt Ember's brother, and that's where it all went south. He might have thought she wanted him to, but it was a miscalculation anyway. He overstepped his bounds, found the one thing that would break their group apart. You heard what they said about the sex rites. Fane and Raven have been sleeping together. There's going to be a strong link between them. Incestuous relationships like that are sometimes overwhelming for those in them. She loves him because he's her family and she's in love with him as a man. She's not grown-up enough to separate out love from sex. He makes her feel good and makes her feel ashamed of that at the same time. I'll bet money that the dad was abusing her, too. She might have turned to her brother for protection."

"She doesn't seem like much of an innocent to me."

"Innocent, no. But abused, yes. Looking for love any way she can get it? I assume the boy was mistreated too—look at his bisexual tendencies. He equates sex with love. In someone this young, that pathology is oftentimes learned."

Taylor turned on Woodmont, then turned left onto Hilldale Drive. The Merritt house was only a few blocks in, she could already smell the smoke. The usual fall scent of Nashville—burning leaves and rotting grass—was overlaid with the heady stench of gasoline.

The house was unmistakable—black, sooty smears around the front door, a crowd of vehicles, some with lights flashing, others with doors flung wide. The ladder truck was regrouping, the firefighters rolling hoses, the fire hydrant being set back to rights. They'd contained the blaze quickly, gotten it under control and extinguished. Taylor knew how hard their fire department worked, was glad that they'd been so responsive tonight.

She and Simari arrived at the Merritts at the same time, from two different directions. She let Simari pull over, waited for her to secure Max. Marcus was waiting for them, brown eyes haunted.

"What's up?" Taylor asked.

The fire chief was behind Marcus, back to her. When he heard her voice, he turned with a huge smile. He took the few steps over to her, shook her hand. She could feel the small bones in her fingers scrunch together.

"Lieutenant Jackson. Helluva night. You been out here all this time?"

"No, sir. We just got here. Chief Andrew Rove, meet Detective Renn McKenzie, my newest acquisition."

The chief stuck out a meaty hand, grimy with soot. McKenzie shook it, smiled and then surreptitiously wiped his hand on the side of his jeans. Rove looked like a bear in his full fire suit, his hat perched precariously on his round head. His small blueberry-colored eyes were bloodshot and tired, but his smile was sincere.

"Glad to have you, son. We're finished in there. We've been working the place over with a fine-tooth comb. Definitely arson. Your crime-scene techs are in there, gatherin' evidence."

"Great. Any ideas how the fire started?"

"No doubt that gasoline was the accelerant. Ole Sniff found the point of origin where the gasoline had been originally spilled. Started in the basement. Amateur hour. Whoever did this thought the whole house would go up if the fire started low. May have been in a hurry, may have just been lazy."

He turned to McKenzie. "Ole Sniff's our combustible gas detector. Best tracker in the business, can tell any kind of accelerant that's been used. But we did find an empty gas can. If there's more, we'll get it."

"Thanks, Chief. I appreciate you coming out here for this. One of your guys will send the report over?"

"Sure thing." He yawned widely, not bothering to cover his mouth, and ambled off toward his car.

Tim Davis wandered out of the house with several bags in his hands. Taylor jogged over to him. "Hey, Tim. What's in the bags?"

He gave her a tired smile, held up the bag in his left hand. "Soot and ash." He held up the right. "More soot and more ash."

"Great."

"This is just the beginning. There are two bodies in the

basement. The bulk of the fire was down there. The first floor got some damage, but the fire burned out quickly. It's more a smoke problem."

"Whose bodies?"

"Middle-aged male and female. That's about all I could get. ME should be here in a few minutes." He lumbered off toward his vehicle. Poor man, his night was just beginning.

Taylor turned to McKenzie. "Wanna bet it's Schuyler Merritt Senior and his ex-wife, Jackie Atilio?"

"I'm not going to take that bet," he said, eyes grim.

A crowd of people had gathered to watch the fire burn, a few leaking away into the night now that the excitement looked to be past. When the ME's van pulled up, the crowd got thick again. The vehicle stopped. Sam hopped out.

"What's happening, hot stuff?" Sam said, cracking a smile at her.

"Hey," Taylor said, surprised. "I figured you'd be home by now."

"My turn for night shift. I switched with Dr. Fox."

"Well, great. There are two bodies in the basement."

"Burned?" Sam asked, pulling protective gear over her clothes.

Marcus shook his head. "A little singed around the edges. They were buried in the basement in a shallow grave, a layer of thin-set concrete on top of them. The fire burned hot around them, the area looked wrong to the firefighter who was down there. He jabbed it with his pick, it cracked apart easily."

"If they were buried, I'd assume the fire was set after they were dead."

"I think you're right. They're pretty far gone, a couple of weeks at least. Smells pretty nasty down there."

"Okay. Taylor, you want to come?"

"No," she said, but she'd already pulled on booties and purple gloves, secured her hair back. McKenzie waved her on, motioned toward the crowd. He was going to check what people had seen first.

Simari excused herself to go run the perimeter of the scene with Max, just in case there were any more surprises.

Marcus said, "I'll walk you in. They still have a couple of hot spots, but they were able to get here quickly. I do have one witness, said there was a piece-of-crap car that's usually around that's missing. Said the kid who lived here drove it. They can't remember the last time they saw Merritt Senior."

"Be sure you get the registration records for the car so we can put out a BOLO. So Schuyler Merritt was here today. Damn. We were so close."

"We usually are. Watch your step here at the front, it's still a little warm."

The inside of the house was a muck of wet, charred carpet, a distinct line of demarcation where the fire had burned, running its course around the rooms from the basement into the kitchen. The smoke damage was extensive—the house would be hell to get cleaned up. Though if the owner were dead, that wouldn't be an issue, at least not right away.

The air was smoky still, deep with the scent of burned wood and plastic. Taylor covered her mouth with her gloved hand and coughed, followed Marcus down the sooty staircase.

She could quickly see why nothing much had been burned—the only thing in the basement was a large gun cabinet. Stone and metal weren't the best conductors for fire—while the wood in the house had charred significantly, the rest was in decent shape.

The floor had a hole dead center. The two bodies lay side by side, features destroyed by advanced decomposition.

"Jesus. Can we ID them?"

Sam circled the hole, then reached down and touched the wrist of the body closest to her. "Yes, there's plenty left. Teeth might be the quickest and easiest, if you can find their dentist. They're missing a finger each, by the way."

"From the fire? They burned off?"

Sam squatted down for a closer look. "No, a straight-edge, maybe shears? They were forcibly removed."

"Good grief. Marcus, are there personal effects that made it through?"

"Yes. I'll go up and see what I can find. The den wasn't touched by the fire, and it looked like there were some checkbooks and stuff on the desk." He looked relieved as he walked away.

McKenzie came down the stairs a moment later, eyebrow raised at the scene.

"Neighbors say the boy has been coming and going a lot over the past few days. It's all gossip up there—apparently Merritt kept to himself. The woman left, got remarried, took the girl with her, left the boy here. He was gone for a while—that would be the reform school—but he's been back for about three weeks. No one had seen the father for about that time."

"That time frame fits with the level of decomp I'm seeing here," Sam said.

"Any idea how they were killed?"

"Yep. Come here and take a look."

Sam had the head of one of the victims in her hands. Taylor leaned over the grave, she twisted the head to the side. "Gunshot wound. Both of them. Left temporal lobe. Small caliber pistol."

"At least we know what kind of weapon he has," Taylor said. "I can imagine that if a boy with a gun walked into your bedroom and told you to take a pill he was holding, you might be inclined to do it."

"I think you're right," McKenzie said. "That does make sense."

Taylor looked at him. "So where is our boy Raven now?"

Fifty-Two

June 19, 2004
Northern Virginia
Baldwin

Baldwin was sitting in Goldman's office. His personal problems could wait. He was finally focused the way he needed to be on this case. He sent a prayer upward, that the families of the fallen girls would understand. It would be nice to get their absolution, though he'd never forgive himself.

Gretchen Rice had been gone for less than twenty-four hours. There was hope, a chance, that she was still alive. This was it. Their last attempt, a last-ditch effort to nail Arlen to the wall. Despite the shifts watching him, he'd managed to get another little girl.

Baldwin had sifted through the files again and come up with the same answer. All the roads led to Harold Arlen. He knew there was evidence out there, real evidence. The thought made a flash of heat burn in his chest—he was still furious with Charlotte. What was she thinking? They could solve this case, close this case, without cheating. And to do that, they had to search Arlen's house again. Slowly, carefully, methodically. This time, he was going to be in on the search. They'd missed something before, and by God he was going to help them find it.

Goldman finally walked into the office and handed him a sheaf of papers.

"The new warrant just came in. You think we'll find something this time around?"

"I can only hope. This is merely a formality. But I need to be sure. I want to cover every inch of that house, let my people have a chance to see it all firsthand. We missed something. And another girl was taken because of our negligence."

Goldman looked at him, brows knit tightly across his forehead.

"Dr. Baldwin, you know that's not the case. You've been doing this a long time. You know you're not responsible for them. Arlen, if it is Arlen, is responsible. This is his fault, not yours. You didn't kidnap and kill these girls."

"Either way, I want to find Gretchen, and I want to be able to get her home to her parents in one piece."

"That's what we all want."

"Then let's do it."

Baldwin drove up to Great Falls with Goldman. Geroux, Sparrow and Butler were already outside of Arlen's house, waiting for them. Charlotte was off the radar, and that was good. She hadn't called in, and he didn't care. He didn't want to deal with her right now, with the bombshell she'd dropped in his lap. He needed to focus on getting Gretchen Rice back alive.

He'd made an appointment to come in and talk with Garrett Woods late this evening. He'd take Garrett to dinner, expose his secret over steak and whisky, hope for the best. Garrett wanted to know what the meeting was about, knew instinctively there was something wrong, but Baldwin had purposefully been vague, wanting to wait until the search was over today. He had a good feeling about this. He wanted to be able to go in to his boss and lay a victory at his feet before he admitted his actions.

The affair with Charlotte was a huge mistake, and Garrett would help him decide what to do next. Then, he could take whatever steps he needed to rebuild the trust of his team. Because they weren't stupid people. He got the sense they all knew what had been going on with him and Charlotte— there'd been enough sidelong glances and whispered conversations. Sparrow had been especially aloof with him for the past couple of days. Yes, this was the right course of action. He'd fall on his sword, and they could all go back to work without the specter of Charlotte hovering around them like a well-dressed, insistent ghost.

And he could decide what path he wanted to take with his own future.

Goldman and Baldwin exited the vehicle. Goldman did a press check on his weapon—force of habit. The sun beat down on them. It was only about seventy degrees and very clear, a nice change from the past few days. It had been especially muggy for June in D.C. this week, their searches tempered by tendrils of humid oppressiveness. The violent rains had washed away the heaviness in the air.

Geroux was the first to hail them. "We just got here. We don't know where he is."

"What do you mean? Where who is?" Goldman asked.

"Arlen. He's not answering the door. We knocked about five times, and nothing."

"That's impossible. My people have been on him all night. The power was off until early in the morning—there's no way he could have gotten his car out of the garage. Both doors, front and back, are covered."

"Well, I'm telling you, no one's answering the door."

Baldwin rushed up the stairs to the door. "We need to make entry now. I bet the bastard offed himself."

"That's what we're thinking, too."

Baldwin knocked once, hard, then tried the knob. Locked. He drew his weapon, lifted his leg and kicked, hard. Luckily, the dead bolt wasn't thrown. The door swung open with a crash, the wood splintering from the frame. They filtered into the house carefully. Baldwin's heart was pounding so hard he could barely hear the others calling out from the lower floors.

"Clear."

"Clear."

"Garage is clear."

Baldwin was in Arlen's bedroom now. Nothing was missing, nothing out of place. The closet held only clothes. He shouted, "Clear," then went back downstairs.

"We got nothing," Geroux said. "It's like he disappeared into thin air."

Baldwin could hear Goldman in the kitchen giving one of his detectives a major dressing-down. Arlen had obviously slipped out during the power outage. Though there were no open windows and the back door was locked, the front door's bolt hadn't been thrown. It was within the realm of possibility that Arlen had simply waited for the perfect moment and slipped out the door unnoticed.

The detective kept insisting that there was no way that could have happened; he and his partner were on the house all night, the only person who'd been in or out was the FBI chick, yesterday, during the storm. Goldman wasn't hearing any of it.

Baldwin shut his eyes for a minute, both to tune the shouting out and to will his adrenal gland back into submission. He took a deep breath, then another. A thought hit him. Oh, my God. Why hadn't he considered that before?

"The basement. We need to look in the basement again."

Goldman cut off his diatribe. "Why? We've been through it."

"Because there's a tunnel," Baldwin replied.

The basement was quiet as the grave. Baldwin went first, inching slowly down the stairs. If he was right, and he was suddenly sure he was, Arlen could be most anywhere. He couldn't believe he hadn't thought of it before.

He felt the breeze before he saw the opening, smelled the damp, musty air. Old air.

He had a small Maglite in his pocket. He turned it on, splayed the light over the far wall. There. The light spilled into a hole in the wall, a dark entrance to somewhere. The shelving unit was pulled back, the drywall along with it. In the light, it would have looked like seams in the mud, just what you'd expect from an unfinished basement. Baldwin tamped down his anger at the Fairfax crime-scene tech and his own team for missing it. My God, they might have been able to save Kaylie if they had seen this.

He had just turned to signal to Geroux when the shooting started.

He whipped back in a flash, saw Sparrow go down. He trained his weapon on that trajectory, saw Butler fall out of the corner of his eye. He started shooting, moving quickly to the mouth of the tunnel. He butted up against the edge, Geroux took the opposite side. Goldman and his detective had taken cover.

Baldwin started to signal Geroux, but he whipped around into the mouth of the tunnel just as a fresh load of bullets winged through the cool air. Still firing, Geroux took one right in the neck and went down in a heap.

Baldwin squeezed the trigger again and again. The returning shots stopped. There was a gurgling noise coming from about fifteen feet away. He'd hit the shooter. His training took over, he acted to neutralize the threat. Another shot fired, and the gurgling stopped with a strangled sigh.

Quiet. Was that footsteps? No, probably his imagination—his ears were ringing from the shots. Using the flashlight, he scanned the far reaches of the tunnel. Arlen was down, his back to him. He must have been running away when Baldwin or Geroux's shots hit him. Baldwin kicked the gun out of his hand and knelt to feel for a pulse. He was gone.

There was shouting and screaming now, calls to ambulances, the Fairfax County guys making themselves useful. He felt numb, couldn't feel his hand. It took both hands to reholster his weapon. He struggled to get his breathing under control. He finally held his breath to stop the ragged jags of air forcing their way into his lungs, and his heart slowed a bit.

That's when he heard the crying, quiet and faint.

He stumbled past Arlen's body in the dark, used the small beam of the flashlight to guide him, deeper and deeper. He turned a corner and saw Gretchen on the floor, in a nightgown. Her legs were broken, but she was very much alive.

He gathered the girl in his arms, felt her forehead press into his neck. She was sobbing. He realized he didn't know whose tears were landing on the front of his shirt—hers, or his.

Fifty-Three

Nashville
10:00 p.m.

Ariadne had made it her business to know where the various covens met. When she was part of the ruling council, it was her right, and her duty. As wonderful as Wicca was, there were always abusers, those who sought power over their coven members. There was a very specific code of ethics that governed coven work—taking money was forbidden, as was insisting on a physical culmination of the Great Act to be accepted into the coven. In ceremonies, the Great Act was symbolic—athamé plunging into chalice, chalice opening to athamé—instead of actual sex. Priests and priestesses couldn't insist that members worship skyclad—there were any number of rules in place to assure freedom, free will and comfort were always present during ceremonies.

But the ways of man included the sin of power-seeking. Ariadne was the higher authority to whom those abused by the power in their coven appealed. She had a solid working knowledge of where most of the covens in the area practiced, and an even greater antenna for spiritual portals, spots in the wilderness that were especially close to the Goddess.

She'd recognized the place from her dreams as holy ground, both secular and Wicca, a tract of land that had seen the good and the bad, and as such had been imbued with powerful spirits. It was in a private graveyard, on the western edge of Davidson County, down a cow path that led to a clearing off a small two-lane road called McCrory Lane.

Her home was downtown, off Sixteenth Avenue South, just up the street from the area of town known as Music Row. She'd done all the backbreaking restoration herself— tearing out a 1960s avocado-green kitchen, a flimsily paneled den—instead filling the house with white marble and period wainscoting. The walls were painted in rich Easter-egg pastels, edged in white crown molding; the six-paneled doors had crystal doorknobs. The parlor had an original frieze of a chariot race in ancient Rome that she'd restored. She trailed her hand along the chair rail in the hallway as she left, glad that her people didn't see pride as a sin.

The trip to the graveyard took twenty minutes. Through the Village, past the holiday carnage in Green Hills to Old Hickory. To her right, the open expanse of the Steeplechase fields glowed black in the night. She turned left on Highway 100, the shadowy road winding through the surrounding landscape, rolling hills and protected forests and horse farms, breaking open into civilization at Ensworth High School. She drove through the intersection of Highway 100 and Old Harding, dismayed to see stores of modern convenience squatting on newly shriven land, then the road grew dark again.

The turn was up here, just past the Loveless Café and the Shell station. She turned and the friendly lights disappeared, the road plunged into gloom.

There, on the right.

She slowed the car, pulling into the grass on the shoulder. The land was flat here, but joined the woods one hundred yards in. The cow path ran through there, deep into the forest, and exited into a small glade, the headstones of the dead poking up from the forest floor like mushrooms.

She draped her cloak around her shoulders and pulled it tight, warding off the chill. The crescent moon gave a bare light. She could see a few steps in front of her, enough to keep her from tripping. It was quiet tonight, the birds and squirrels were silent as the grave. Someone was near.

Heart beating in her throat, she moved faster, then stumbled into an unseen hole a few feet from the car, twisting her ankle painfully. She bit her lip to stifle her cry. Cursing quietly under her breath, she headed back to the Subaru for a flashlight.

The solid, artificial yellow beam at least allowed her to miss the mole holes. She started off again, slower this time, training the light downward so the boy, if he was here, couldn't see her coming. The trees loomed ahead, black trunks reaching for the sky, limbs raised in supplication.

She was no stranger to the emptiness of the night, the darkened earth breathing around her, summoning, questioning. Alive. All the tiny sighs of brush and grass were heightened in the gloom, and a small bank of fog had gathered in the brush. She could smell rain on the horizon, saw the shadow of a cloud cross under the tip of the moon.

The night was her world, and she its concubine.

Step by step, she inched closer. Forty yards, twenty, ten. She smelled a fire burning, oak and poplar and leaves and twigs being licked by the flames, and slowed to a creep, edging her way closer still. She drew energy from the earth and shielded herself, protecting her fragility with an invisible psychic barrier.

She could see him clearly, lying on his side, a lump under a blanket. His back was to her, she didn't think he could see her. The flickering fire crackled, covering her small sounds. She eased the flashlight off, just in case. The fog curled around him like a lover, keeping him hidden in its dense embrace.

He was asleep. She couldn't read him. Deep breaths mingled with the shurring rush of the wind.

She debated for a few moments, dithering, then moved away from the glade, back toward the car. She shouldn't be afraid of this boy, but she was. Her hands were shaking. She would call the lieutenant, let her come and take him.

She stepped on a twig, the crack of the dry wood a loud retort in the quiet air. She froze.

By the fire, Raven opened his eyes.

Fifty-Four

Taylor tossed her cell phone down into her lap in disgust. "Where is that bloody woman?" she asked for the fifth time.

"I don't know," McKenzie answered, soothing her with his voice. She was damn tired, and wired, and frustrated. How a boy of seventeen could elude them at each step was beyond her. They knew who he was, where he lived, what he drove, yet he was as transparent as a ghost.

"Why don't we go by her house, see if she's just got her phone off?" McKenzie suggested.

Taylor tapped her fingers on the steering wheel, the drumming helping her think. Rush off half-cocked after a woman who claimed to be a witch, or join the search for the teenage killer? Though if she were honest with herself, she had to admit that Ariadne had helped, had cut their investigation time down by days with her prescient perceptions and drawings. That didn't make her a witch, just observant.

"Okay. You have the address?"

"Yes. She's off Music Row."

"Close, at least." Taylor put the car in gear and drove.

It only took five minutes to slip into the quiet streets of

Music Row. Taylor pulled the Lumina to the curb in front of a three-story Victorian—eerily reminiscent of the home of the vampire king, Keith Barent Johnson. This house was fully restored, gaily painted a soft sage-green with sparkling white trim. The walk was cement, two steps up in the middle, then five to the wraparound porch. The porch lights were on, but it was easy to see that the lights inside were off; the front door was stained glass with strong steel bars embedded in the pattern. The soft, glowing red eye of a motion detector alarm system peeked out from behind a coat rack. Smart—an alarm system. This was a safe area, but any intelligent woman living alone would have herself reinforced. Though if Ariadne was a witch, Taylor bet she'd cast all sorts of protective spells around her home.

Not that she believed anything like that could possibly work to prevent a crime.

A white wicker swing with green, yellow and white pinstripe cushions hung from the ceiling of the porch. Taylor could imagine Ariadne sitting in it on warm nights, feet tucked under her like a cat, that glossy black hair streaming in contrast over the white wood.

"She's not here," Taylor said, but rang the bell anyway. A deep chime rang out, no one answered the door.

Taylor turned to McKenzie. "Now what?"

He was staring at the front door, distracted, and didn't answer.

Taylor paced along the porch, glanced around the side of the house. More padded white wicker, a conversational grouping around a large, ceramic chiminea. Exactly squat that would help find Ariadne.

"We have to try something else. We can—"

She stopped, her cell was ringing. The caller ID read unknown name, unknown number. She felt her heart leap into her throat. The last time she'd seen that particular combination on her cell, it was the Pretender, calling to warn her he was coming for her. She signaled to McKenzie, then slowly brought the phone to her ear.

"Jackson."

The scared voice of the witch rang out into the quiet night.

"Oh, thank the Goddess you answered, Lieutenant. This is Ariadne. I found him. I found the warlock."

Taylor was already striding to the car, her keys in her left hand. "We've been calling you all night. Where are you?" she asked.

Ariadne was whispering, the harshness of her voice amplified by the phone's speaker.

"I'm out in western Davidson County. Do you know McCrory Lane?"

"Yes." Understatement, she and Baldwin lived not far from there.

"There's an old deserted graveyard out here—dates back over two hundred years. It's a holy place. I saw him, in a dream."

Taylor stopped short, leaned against the hood of her car. Son of a bitch.

"So you mean you saw him in a dream, is that it, Ariadne? For God's sake—"

"No, no, listen. Don't hang up. I dreamed about it, yes, but I came out here to see, and he's there. He was asleep by the fire. But I think he heard me. I need to get out of here."

Taylor butted the phone against her forehead. *God save me from people who think they can investigate crimes.*

"Yes, you do. Leave immediately. Drive to the Shell station at the intersection of Highway 100 and McCrory Lane, go inside, tell them to lock the doors. I'll get a patrol there as soon as possible. The boy is armed, and he's dangerous. We'll meet you there. It's going to take a little bit— we're at your place now."

"Lieutenant?"

Taylor turned the car over and pulled out onto the street. "Yes?"

"Hurry."

"Don't hang up!" Taylor yelled, but Ariadne was already gone. She cursed, then pulled the flasher out and attached it to the roof. They couldn't waste any time. The revolving light gave her a headache, but she wanted people out of her way.

"Where is she?" McKenzie asked.

"McCrory Lane." She keyed her radio, called Dispatch. "Lieutenant Jackson, E, 10-82, 10-13, 10-54. Suspect located, I need backup, 8 to the Shell station at McCrory Lane and Highway 100."

She heard the affirmatives—she'd called for backup for their suspect, let the troops know he had a weapon and coded him very dangerous—the patrol officers in the area would scramble.

The trick would be to get all the personnel in place and take Schuyler Merritt Junior into custody before the press arrived. The media, local and national, had a vested interest in this case now.

The radio crackled. A patrol was rolling from Highway 70 South, ETA three minutes. Taylor breathed a sigh of relief. Ariadne would be fine.

"What in the name of hell does that woman think she's doing?"

"She thinks she's helping, LT."

"I never asked for help. Like I need Miss Marple for the occult set to solve my case?"

"Well, I never did see Miss Marple in a corset and cloak, but I get your drift."

She smiled at him. "She could give Morticia lessons, that's for sure. Damn stupid, silly woman, running off after a killer like that. I have half a mind to charge her with obstruction. She should have called me. If this goes south…"

He was white-faced beside her, but said, "It's not going to go south."

They were on Old Hickory now, the red light strobing off the fine brick homes, the woods taking on a momentary bloody glow as they flew past. They disturbed a gang of turkeys, feeding too close to the road in the rough off the eighth hole of Harpeth Hills. They fled away from the lights, disappearing off into the brush, tail feathers gleaming white in her peripheral vision.

The radio was crackling—the first patrols had arrived at the Shell station.

Dispatch popped into the fray. "Please advise, Lieutenant Jackson."

"You're looking for a pale woman with black hair named Ariadne. She should be locked inside."

"Negative, LT. No one here like that."

She heard the words, negative, from three different voices. Beads of sweat popped out on her brow, she put her foot to the floor. The Lumina launched itself down Highway 100. She wrestled her gaze from the blacktop just long enough to shoot a searing I-told-you-so look at McKenzie.

Fifty-Five

Raven had felt her, the weight of her presence, long before she stepped on the twig. He didn't know who she was, other than she wasn't a friend. She was strong, this one, but still no match for him. There was strength, and then there was the immutable power of steel and brass, a reality that couldn't be argued with.

She'd fled quickly once she'd known he was awake. He stood, stretched, slipped the pistol from his waistband. A friend at reform school had taught him the right way to handle the weapon; he'd been an eager student. The cold steel warmed to his palm. He held it lightly in his grasp, finger alongside the trigger, gun pointing down the length of his thigh. He wouldn't raise it until he was ready to use it. It was a small caliber weapon, so in order for it to be effective, he'd need to be close.

Like his parents.

Blood flooded his groin at the thought of the two of them, cowering in the living room like rats being sold to a lab. That day, the longest of his life, would never retreat from the recesses of his mind.

His bitch of a mother had walked in on him and Fane and freaked out. They'd known, of course—that's why they'd split them up, sent him away.

"It's not natural," his father had spit at him, the disgust ripe in his throat.

"Natural enough for you," he'd shouted. "You've been fucking Fane since she was four."

"I have never laid a hand on that girl, and you damn well know it."

"Sky, how could you say such a thing?" His mother, her eyes pleading, lost in a world they didn't want to understand.

"Ask, Mom. Ask Fane. She'll tell you. I had to sleep in her room, blocking the door some nights, to keep him off of her. But what we have is different. We were made for each other. We're in love. You can't stop us."

The arguments had gone on and on and on, but in the end, his parents shipped him away. They divorced, his mother silently applying for a dissolution of the marriage for irreconcilable differences; his father signing the paperwork, face pinched white. They'd never spoken after that night, using e-mail to correspond about their family. His mother had always known, he was sure about that. Faced with the undeniable truth, the reality of letting her baby daughter be violated by her loving father for all those years, she just wanted to get away.

It had worked for Jackie Merritt. She quickly found a new man, a good man in her eyes, a soldier, one bred for violence and mayhem who was as gentle as a lamb with her. She remarried. Fane acted out, but Jackie could turn the other cheek, knowing that she was safe from both her Schuylers. Seeing what she wanted to see was Jackie's greatest asset.

Until the night three weeks ago, when Raven had come home. Jackie had entered Fane's room without knocking, the smile fading to horror as she watched her two children bucking together on the bed. Raven, fed up with the constant haranguing about a love that was as natural as it was fulfill-

J.T. Ellison

ing, called a family meeting, insisted that they come. Sat them down in the living room of his father's house, took Fane in his arms and explained that they'd been married. It was handfasting, yes, but that was as legal as a priest and a church in the eyes of their religion.

Their parents hadn't taken it well.

Raven had been standing a few feet away, the gun in his waistband, watching them fight with bemusement. Like it mattered? He caught Fane's eyes and rolled his own. She nodded, it was time. It was amazingly simple—his father first, so he couldn't fight, from behind and to the left, then his mother. They collapsed together, mouths open in remonstration.

The sudden silence was breathtaking.

It only took thirty minutes to dig the pit; the basement was old, the concrete cracked and worn. Dump the bodies, snip off the fingers they needed for their spells, mix up some quick-set, and they were free.

Sweating, tired and jubilant, they had sex in the living room, on the couch, mingling their fluids with the blood of their parents. No one could keep them apart anymore.

That first taste was enough to convince him that it was time to deal with all the rest of the people who'd shunned and abused him. The Immortals would not be stopped.

He came back to himself, realized he was standing in the open, the moonlight glistening on the dew-wet grass. The fog was heavier now; the wisps and tendrils flowed around his feet as he started to move. The woman was in her car, back to him, talking on the phone. He needed to make sure she didn't see him slinking up behind her. He crouched low, below her line of sight in the rearview mirror. He inched forward, closer, closer. She finished her call, dropped the phone in her lap, laid her head back against the headrest.

Now.

He burst around the driver's side of the car. The door was locked—he'd figured it would be. Using the butt of the gun, he shattered the glass, grabbed the woman by her hair, dragged her out the window. She was small, light, fine-boned. The long hair was a perfect handle, he was able to maneuver her entire body out and onto the ground. He perched over her, pinning her down, legs on either side of her. She struggled and bucked, tried to scream, but he punched her with his free hand.

She was pretty. Her skin was very pale, he could see the flush of color the imprint of his knuckles made across her cheek. Encouraged, he punched her a few more times, and she stopped screaming. Blood rushed from her nose, and her lip was split. He reached down on impulse and licked her face, savoring the salty essence of her heart.

He realized he had a throbbing erection. Well, why not? This slut was out here spying on him, she deserved everything she got. He held the gun to her temple, and she stopped fighting. Carefully, he reached back and slid her dress up, over her thighs. His questing fingers found her panties. There was a rending tear and they were off. She started to struggle again, so he hit her with the butt of the gun, slicing open a slit in the soft skin of her forehead. Her head snapped back into the dirt with a dull thud.

He undid his jeans—it was hard to handle the buttons over his erection with one hand, but he managed. He shifted back and down, pushed his body between her legs, using his knee to force hers apart, and thrust, hard, landing home with one shove. She screamed, high in her throat, legs flailing against him, and he jabbed her head with the gun again to shut her up. She was fighting him now, each stroke shifting him back and forth so he didn't have to do any work at all. He leaned over her, took both arms and trapped them against the ground over her head with his left hand while he finished, a blinding white orgasm making him forget who and where he was.

The breath came hard in his throat, his eyes came back into focus. The woman was keening, crying, trying to wriggle away from him. He was heavy enough that she couldn't shift him without work, but she finally managed, pushing him off her, slipping into a ball a few feet away.

It was taking him a minute to catch his breath. He didn't know who she'd called—he needed to leave. Should he kill her? He'd never raped anyone before; he hadn't used a condom, there would be evidence. It wouldn't matter in the long run, he'd seen the hourglass in Fane's room, the small grains of sand slipping inexorably toward their finish, had known it to be a sign. No, he'd leave her here. But he was going to make damn sure she'd never tell anyone.

He fumbled his fly closed and stood, brushing the leaves and grass off the knees of his jeans. She saw him moving, got to all fours and started trying to crawl away. He walked to her—she wasn't going quickly, more like a snail than a crab—and kicked her in the ribs. She landed on her side, the breath going out of her in an audible whoosh.

"Tell anyone, and I'll kill you. Do you understand me, bitch?"

The woman was saying something he couldn't understand. It sounded like an incantation of sorts. He listened closer. She was whispering, hands on her stomach.

"Isis, Astarte, Diana, Hecate, Demeter, Kali, Inana."

The Goddess chant? What the fuck? Who was this person?

He asked her name, she just shook her head, continued the incantation.

Raven felt dread begin to build in his stomach. Fear. He'd never felt such fear. He needed to get away. He needed to get away now. He stumbled backward, falling onto his ass, scraping his hands and elbows. The gun dropped a foot from him; he turned over onto all fours, grabbed it and ran. The Rat was parked on the other side of the road, back in the brush, off the path so no one from the road would see it. He hurried to the vehicle, fumbling the keys and the gun. He had a bad feeling about this. A very bad feeling.

Rattything acquiesced when he put the key in the

ignition, the engine roaring to life. He pulled away from the grove, bumping over the shoulder and onto the road.

He turned right, up McCrory Lane, toward the highway. He had one more place that he knew he could go. One place that had been a refuge, long in the past. He pointed the car east and drove into the night, the echoes of the Goddess chant in his ears. He didn't see the flashing blue lights congregating behind him. He didn't see anything at all.

Fifty-Six

There were three patrol cars at the Shell station when Taylor pulled in. And no sign of Ariadne. McKenzie had been redialing her number on his cell, but there was no answer.

Taylor ran inside and described Ariadne to the man behind the counter, who hadn't seen her. Nor had he seen anyone who looked like the drawing she pulled out. So no Ariadne and no Schuyler Merritt. Shit.

She went back outside, signaled to the officers. "Mount up. Let's drive up McCrory, see if we find her car."

They all piled in their cars and took off, Taylor in the lead. The flashing blue-and-white lights made the road light up like Christmas, and it only took a few minutes until they saw a Subaru Forester parked at the side of the road, just at the rise of the hill. It showed no signs of life, no lights, no engine.

"Her car's there," McKenzie said unnecessarily. Taylor pulled in behind it, the three patrols taking up defensive positions in front and on her flank, effectively blocking the road.

Taylor was out the door in an instant, Glock drawn in a two-handed grip, pointing toward the ground. She eased up to the vehicle. The driver's side window was broken, there was glass everywhere, inside and outside the car. A jagged edge shone dark in the feeble moonlight; Taylor could smell blood.

"What's that?" McKenzie whispered in her ear. She stopped and stood tall, listening. Crying, coming from twenty feet away.

"Ariadne?" she yelled, walking toward the noise. She saw a lump on the ground, yelled, "She's here. Shit. 10-47, 10-67, code 3!" She holstered her gun, knelt down and rolled Ariadne onto her back. She cried out in protest.

"Relax, honey, it's okay. We've got help coming. Where is the boy?"

It didn't take a genius to see what had happened. Ariadne was grimy with dirt and leaves, her skirt twisted, flashing pale thighs smeared with blood. She cried out again as Taylor moved her hands over her in the dark. Broken ribs, probably, maybe a broken jaw. A bloody cut on her forehead.

"When you called, you said he heard you. Was it Schuyler Merritt, Ariadne? Did he rape you?"

A ghost of a nod. She was trying to speak, the words coming out low and jumbled. Taylor leaned her head down, close to Ariadne's mouth.

"Don't know his...name. Pulled me. From the car. Ra...ra...raped me. Drove off, after."

The broken sentences exhausted her, and she let her head drift back down to the ground. Taylor felt for her pulse, reassured when she found it strong and steady. The damage wasn't life threatening.

"Okay, you're okay now. I've got you."

McKenzie was squatting a few feet away. He took Ariadne's hand and whispered, "I'm sorry. We should have listened sooner."

Taylor shot him a look, but didn't stop him. Getting herself and the department sued for letting a witness become a victim was the least of her worries right now.

She heard the comforting sound of sirens. Rescue was on its way.

She held Ariadne's hand tighter. Where was that little bastard going now? They had his woman, his friends in custody. His mother and father were dead, with cops crawling all over the two houses he might retreat to. Where else would he go?

"Ariadne. Do you know where he was going?"

"No," she whispered. Taylor hated this, she hated the fucking hell out of this. Hearing that lively voice so dispirited made her want to hit something.

Rescue pulled up, got briefed and pulled Taylor from Ariadne's side to treat her. The EMTs were females, Taylor was happy to see. Sometimes rape victims balked at being treated by men—the 10-67 had alerted them, but it was still good luck. They had her fastened to a gurney and slipping off into the ambulance quickly.

"Where are you taking her?"

"Baptist," was the brief reply.

Taylor walked with them to the doors, watched while Ariadne was loaded in. The harsh lights reflected the bruise on her jaw and the dislocation of the mandible. Taylor knew that had to hurt, and broken ribs, the sharp ends stabbing into lungs and skin, weren't a picnic, either. Ariadne was being awfully brave, not crying, those luminous blue eyes fixed on Taylor. She shifted under the azure gaze, read the words Ariadne put in her mind and turned away, shoving her hands in her pockets to keep them warm.

"Not your fault," Ariadne said, as clearly as if she'd spoken aloud. "Not your fault."

Fifty-Seven

Baldwin did his damnedest to keep his voice steady. "Geroux and Sparrow died on scene. Butler passed away at the hospital during surgery. Gretchen lived, obviously."

"You took a leave of absence after the firefight, correct?"

"Yes, sir, I did. I felt…responsible. For their deaths. If I'd thought of the tunnel earlier, none of this would have happened."

"And the evidence linking Harold Arlen to the case?"

Baldwin tried very hard not to squirm. Now they were at the meat of the case. What he said at this very moment would determine his future, the future of his team, his life with Taylor. Everything. He swallowed hard.

"Sir, I believe that the blood evidence retrieved from Harold Arlen's dresser was planted by Charlotte Douglas."

There were murmurs from the panel. Reever squeezed his leg under the table.

"And yet her notes are very specific. She was with you the night before the shooting. You made love. You told her that you had a solution to the problem. That you had taken a small vial of blood from the Fairfax County lab, put it on a sock and left it in Harold Arlen's house. Do you deny these allegations?"

"Yes, sir, I most certainly do. I am truly at fault here. My actions got three good agents killed, and for that, I will never forgive myself. But as I stated earlier, Charlotte Douglas brought the idea to me. It was my mistake not to turn her in at that time." He took a breath. "Sir, I never in a million years thought she'd actually go through with it."

"But we have no proof either way. If you had come forward at the time of the shooting, let it be known that the evidence found was somehow in question, perhaps the next girl wouldn't have died. And the woman who you say is responsible is dead, unable to defend herself."

Ah, here we go. The truth of the matter was they had all messed up. There was more to the case than anyone had thought, and Baldwin had been blind. He took a deep breath.

"Sir, I had no way of knowing that Kilmeade was Harold Arlen's partner. I suspected there was something between the two men, a twisted relationship, when Kilmeade allowed Arlen to befriend his daughter. But the odds of two men, two pedophiles, working together? It seemed preposterous at the time. On the surface it looked like Kilmeade was snatching the girls for his friend. But he continued after Arlen was dead. He was obviously the dominant in the situation, and we missed it. That tunnel between their houses was the key. They were shuttling the girls in and out, right into Great Falls Park. If we'd found it earlier… It's beyond the pale, sir. None of us saw it. There were multiple investigators on the case. Unfortunately, I was distracted by the case due to Charlotte's actions, and my own. Couple that with the terrible shock of losing three of my teammates, and I wasn't thinking as clearly as I could have been. It's not an excuse, but it is the truth."

"No, you certainly weren't. Because if you'd been thinking clearly, you would have alerted this body to Charlotte Douglas's illegal actions, and she would have been prosecuted. You would have been prosecuted right alongside her for allowing her to violate the honor and code of the Bureau. I don't know what's worse, Dr. Baldwin. Your lies to cover up Charlotte Douglas's actions, or your lies to cover your own ass."

Reever cleared his throat. "There's no need for that, sir. Dr. Baldwin has been utterly honest and forthright here. He's answered all of your questions as openly and thoroughly as possible. And if I may point out, it's nearly midnight. Perhaps we should break for the day."

"We won't be breaking just yet. We're all in agreement here. Dr. Baldwin's actions were evidence of gross misconduct. There will be serious repercussions. We need to meet privately to discuss what exactly the punishment will be. You may wait outside while we deliberate."

He and Reever had been sitting in somewhat companionable silence for nearly an hour when Baldwin's cell rang. He jumped, startled. It was Garrett. This couldn't be good. He shrugged his shoulders at Reever and answered.

"They're still in there?"

"Yes. Have you heard anything? What did they decide?" Baldwin asked.

"I don't know yet."

"They've been at it an hour. Really, how much more do they want from me? I gave them the truth, just like they asked."

"The whole truth?"

"As much as they needed."

"Well, then. It's going to be okay. You've already been punished enough for this. There's nothing they can do to you that would be worse than the hell you put yourself through."

That was the truth. Baldwin hadn't handled his life very well in the months following Charlotte's revelations, the death of Harold Arlen. And the demise of his team. Instead of facing the music, he'd split town. Taken a leave of absence, run home to Tennessee and spent the next six months practically comatose on his couch. Alcohol had been his friend then, a means to escape the daily torture of the guilt. It had taken a great deal of reassurance from Garrett, then meeting Taylor to drag him out of his depression.

The door to the hearing chamber opened. Reever stood and grabbed his arm.

"Garrett, they're ready for me."

"Okay. Hang in there."

He stowed his phone, squared his shoulders and entered the chamber.

Fifty-Eight

Taylor was only a mile from home, but the succor of the hearth fire wouldn't be hers for a few hours yet. McKenzie yawned in the seat next to her, long and loud.

"Where are we headed?" he asked.

"I thought we could try Subversion, see if he went there. Do you have any other ideas about where he might go?"

"Does he know Juri Edvin's in the hospital?"

"I don't know." She called Marcus. He answered on the first ring. She filled him in on the situation with Ariadne and Schuyler Merritt, then asked him to go over to Vanderbilt. Juri Edvin needed guarding, at the very least. If Schuyler decided to drop in on his friend, they'd be ready for him. He told her the BOLO was out on Schuyler Merritt's car, a silver 2000 Hyundai Elantra. Good, all units were aware to be on the lookout for him, at least.

She was flying down Interstate 40. The only real traffic at this hour was long-haul eighteen-wheelers and a few drunks wheeling their way home from the bars. Cars and trucks alike scattered out of her path, leaving her the far left lane open. She drove fast, the speedometer topping ninety. Running away from Ariadne.

"Damn it, what was that woman thinking, going out there by herself?"

McKenzie shook his head. "She thought she could handle him."

"Yeah, right. The kid's already in the bag for seven murders, plus his parents, and God knows who else. Sure, she could handle him, a lone woman, in the dark, with no back-up. I wish to God people wouldn't be so stupid."

"She thought he was one of her kind. She's very powerful. I'm sure she thought he would bow to her authority. It was misguided, yes. But surely you can see, she was trying to help."

"And nearly got herself killed in the process. She was raped, McKenzie. You know how that affects a woman. She'll never sleep easy again."

"She won't, or you won't?" He said it kindly, but her nerves flared.

"This isn't my fault," she said. They were passing the Hustler store on Church Street. Taylor went up to Broadway and turned left. She wanted to hit Lower Broad, the strip, look through the faces on the streets, see if she could spot her fledgling vampire among the masses.

"Of course it's not. That doesn't mean you aren't blaming yourself. You couldn't have stopped this."

"I could have figured out who Schuyler Merritt was sooner. If I'd listened to Ariadne in the first place…" Her voice drifted off. Instinctively, she knew that wasn't the case. My God, they were only forty-eight hours in and hot on the trail of the final suspect in the case. It was damn fine police work, a group effort, and she knew that. But she still felt like a failure. She was going to carry the image of blood on Ariadne's thighs with her forever.

They drove around for two hours, stopping into Subversion, which only existed once a month, not nightly, as she'd imagined. No one in the building was a part of that particular venue tonight—a dead end. At 2:00 a.m., she turned around at Second and Lindsley, took one last pass up the street, scanning faces and cars. When they hit Hooters, she turned to McKenzie.

"I give up. He isn't here."

"Let's call it a night. We need sleep. Every overnight patrol is on alert, looking for him."

"Do you mind stopping at the hospital before I drop you off?"

"Of course not."

She powered the Lumina up Church Street, turned right at Baptist and pulled into the emergency room entrance parking. They left the car out of the way and went inside.

She flashed her badge at the desk, said they were looking for the rape victim. Ariadne had become a statistic, was forever labeled. Taylor realized what she'd done after the words were out—damn, it was habit. This was why they were trained to distance themselves from the victims, this searing feeling of guilt. She'd never sleep, never eat, never rest if she didn't. But Ariadne felt like a friend, and treating her as a number hurt.

The nurse behind the desk pointed them toward an exam room—at least she'd gotten some privacy, rather than being examined out in the curtains. Under the cacophony of beeping and shouting, Taylor heard the small noises of pain echoing throughout the E.R.—someone was vomiting, a despondent child cried quietly, a woman grunted in the pangs of early labor. Misery, on an epic scale, that's what the emergency room felt like to her.

She knocked on the door to Ariadne's room, entered without waiting for a response.

The witch was in the bed, a soft blue-and-white-checked gown tied at her throat. Her face was a mass of mottled bruises, the cut on her forehead sporting a few stitches, black against the swelling purple bruise. Her eyes were closed, but Taylor could hear the shallow breathing—she wasn't asleep. She went to the bed, resisted the urge to reach out and grab the woman's hand.

"I'm sorry," she said, low and quiet.

Ariadne opened her eyes, the cerulean gaze infinitely sad. "So am I," she managed. Her jaw was swollen and dark with suffused blood. There was an X-ray on the lit radiograph box that showed what looked like a hairline fracture in the lower left mandible.

"They're going to wire me shut for a few weeks," she slurred.

"Don't talk," Taylor said. "I don't want you to hurt yourself."

Ariadne rolled her eyes. "Hey, I might lose a few pounds. Can't be all bad."

Taylor cracked a smile. If she was okay to joke, she'd live. A weight crashed off her shoulders. She stepped closer to the bed to avoid its fall to the floor.

"I will find him," she vowed.

"I know. He will be punished. So will you, if you're not watching. Go careful, Lieutenant." Ariadne was done in. She closed her eyes again. Taylor was certain they'd given her a powerful sedative, something to alleviate both the physical and emotional gashes.

Taylor patted her awkwardly on the hand and walked out of the room. McKenzie stayed behind for a few minutes, then joined her in the hall.

"What did she say?" Taylor asked.

"Nothing. She's asleep. I was just…"

He broke off, and Taylor nodded at him. She knew what he'd been doing, she'd done the same thing. Silently pleaded for forgiveness.

"Let's go."

She'd never felt so wretched as she did at this moment, pulling into her garage, the house lights burning brightly on their new timer, designed to turn on the outside lights at dusk and off at dawn, gaily welcoming her back. The sorrow in her gut wasn't just for Ariadne, but all of the victims—the children who'd been taken, Brittany Carson and her giving rush of life, the boy, Brandon Scott, betrayed by a lover. Nashville wouldn't be the same after this Halloween weekend, would forever be marked by the twisted desires of a teenage boy. The Green Hills massacre would be remembered forever—Ariadne was right; so long as there were living people to remember the dead, they'd reanimate, live on forever.

Would that be her feeling about Fitz, were he never found? Would a memory of the man be enough to suffice?

If she lost it now, there might not be any going back. She opted for being strong, grabbed a Miller Lite from the refrigerator, and went up to the bonus room. Her beloved pool table sat quietly in the dark room, waiting.

She pulled off the cover and drained the beer, grabbed another from the small refrigerator she kept up here for just this purpose.

Racking, breaking, shooting, the rhythm soothed her. She cleared the table in five minutes, playing eight ball against herself, then lined up the balls in a triangle for a game of nine ball. When she sank the seven she had a thought, glimmering in the back of her mind. By the yellow and white striped nine, she felt a peace steal over her limbs. Maybe it was the beer, maybe it was the pool, maybe it was knowing that no matter what, Baldwin would come home and they'd be together. She forgave herself and went to bed.

The phone was ringing. Taylor heard it, some part of her brain recognized the noise. She was so tired, sleep dragging her back into the clutches of darkness. She glanced at the clock—6:40 a.m. Damn.

She answered, forcing her voice to sound alert.

"Lieutenant? Commander Huston here. You need to report to Hillsboro High School. They've gotten a threat against the students. We've put them on lockdown. Looks like your suspect is there, waggling a gun around. He's got a class full of kids hostage, and I've gotten reports that the security officer was disabled, though I don't know details. Get yourself over there. And Lieutenant? Be careful. This boy sounds like he has nothing to lose."

She was already out of the bed. "I'm on my way," she said, breathless, then threw the phone down.

Waning Crescent Moon
Fifteen Percent of Full
Three Days Past Samhain
(Halloween)

Fifty-Nine

"So what do you want to do?" Garrett asked.

They were having breakfast in a little diner they liked. Baldwin hadn't slept. His beard was growing in, itching his cheeks. Reliving the Arlen case was torturous. Having to remember the worst time in his life, his biggest mea culpa, was wearing on him.

And the bastards on the disciplinary committee had suspended him. Possibly permanently.

"Honestly? I want to go to North Carolina and see if I can't help with the Pete Fitzgerald case. I know that the Pretender is behind it. We have no idea how long they're going to play this suspension game."

"Until Tucker is satisfied that you've learned your lesson and won't be going off the reservation ever again. Which is exactly what you're telling me you want to do."

"Garrett, this case is going to explode. I can feel it. And if we're not on top of things, we'll have even more egg on our face. The Bureau doesn't need to have any more bad press."

Garrett raised an eyebrow at him.

"I know, I know. I'm the one generating the bad press right now. Which makes an even better case for me to get out of town and help untarnish my reputation."

"You're suspended, Baldwin. You need to go back to Nashville and quietly play house until they recall you."

He set his fork down, his eggs untouched. "Is that what you would do?"

Garrett gave him a familiar sideways smile. "Of course not. But I'm not you. I can't promise that I can keep you safe if you continue to piss Tucker off. He's got it in for you."

"I know. Thank goodness for Reever. If he hadn't started spouting off they might have actually fired me."

Garrett finished his coffee.

"Go to North Carolina. See what you can dig up. But do it quietly. I'll run interference from here."

"You're the best, Garrett."

"What are you going to tell Taylor?"

He toyed with his coffee cup.

"As little as possible. She's compromised already. She has a serial killer stalking her, her father figure is missing, she's just gotten her command back. The last thing she needs is to hear smut about me and Charlotte."

"I gotta tell you, Baldwin, I think you'd be smart to tell her the truth. All of it."

"She'd never forgive me."

"Baldwin. You've been carrying this load for five years. No one will blame you."

"I don't think so. Not now. The timing isn't right."

"There's never going to be a good time. You know that. Charlotte is dead. The boy isn't. Be careful, man. You don't want to lose her."

"I know. Thanks, Garrett." He stood and tossed a twenty on the table, trying to force the image of his smiling, green-eyed, red-haired son out of his head.

"I'll see you soon."

Sixty

Traffic was at a dead stop. She put the flasher on the roof of her Lumina—she'd kept it overnight, knowing that if something went down in the morning, she wouldn't have the time to go to headquarters and trade her personal vehicle for an official one. And now that she was back at the rank of Lieutenant, that was her right. There weren't enough cars to go around all the plainclothes staff, so they shared. And part of being a good leader, in her mind, was never putting her own comfort above her troops'. They appreciated the gesture, and she didn't feel guilty when she did.

Hillsboro High School was ahead on her right. She eased her way onto the shoulder, scooted around the edge of a black BMW 6 coupe, not even taking the time to covet the magnificent vehicle, and weaved into the parking lot.

The school's parking lot looked like a war zone.

All officers on duty were in attendance, plus the tactical response team. Shit. SWAT, that was never a good sign. The department's hostage negotiator, Joe Keller, was standing next to their mobile command unit in a suit and tie, buffed and polished, gray hair cut in a military flattop that bristled with authority, looking appropriately somber and excited. No one liked a hostage situation, but they did serve to get the blood pumping.

She went directly to Keller, thankful it was him. They'd always gotten along, been in the academy together.

"Keller," she said, coming up on his right. He was staring at the school like it was a bomb ready to go off. "Quite a response you've got here."

"Jackson," he exclaimed, giving her a hug. "Damn good to see you, it's been a while. Yeah, some fool kid's got himself locked in a classroom with thirty kids, a teacher and a teacher's aide. Looks like he broke in last night. Janitor found him, but he's down. The safety officer is down, too."

"What kind of weaponry does he have? I think I know who it is, by the way. His name is Schuyler Merritt, also known as Raven. He's behind the murders Friday night."

"Small-caliber arms. We heard a couple of shots a while back, and an undetermined amount of ammo."

"What were the shots?"

"Dunno. We don't have any more reports of bodies. They might have been warning shots. This boy, you say his name is Merritt? He doesn't seem inclined to talk. Smart kid, though. He took all the cell phones and dropped them out the window, then locked it. We think he's still in that room, but we don't know for sure."

"We gonna make entry?"

"That's your call. Your case, your suspect. I'd certainly like to talk him out first, but I've got a contingency plan in place—the boys and girls know what to do. We can't have him shooting anyone else, either, so we need to plan this out now."

"Agreed. Are any of my boys here?"

"Yeah, I saw Ross and Wade a few minutes ago. Don't know about McKenzie."

"Great, Keller, thanks. I'll be back to you in a minute."

She pulled out her cell and called Lincoln—he directed her to a vehicle ten yards away.

"Sorry, LT, didn't see you come up. We were checking the gun registrations for Merritt Senior. He had a rifle registered, a Browning X-Bolt, and a couple of .22 handguns, a Smith & Wesson and a Bersa Thunder Conceal Carry, and a Smith & Wesson M&P 9-mil."

"That's enough to get the job done."

"Right. The weapons seemed to be for home protection. He wasn't a hunter or else we'd have seen shotguns and semiautos on the list."

"He seem like the type to register everything?"

"Definitely. The paperwork was all in order, he bought them all legally. Four guns listed on the inventory, the rifle, the two .22s and a 9. Got receipts for the ammo too—three boxes of .22 cartridges and a box of 9s."

"So relatively limited shooting abilities, say, one hundred shots between all four guns?"

They looked at her bleakly. "Enough to take out everyone left in that building, that's for sure."

"Okay, I'll let Keller know. Keep tracking stuff down. We don't know what's going to be relevant. Where's McKenzie?"

Marcus rubbed his eyes. "They were transferring Juri Edvin this morning, so he came to take over for me. I was there all night. Not a peep."

"Thanks, man, I appreciate it. Lincoln, anything on the video?"

"The file-sharing sites have it down permanently. They built a block against the video's signature. So we're good there. But *The Tennessean* ran the letter this morning."

"Son of a bitch, you're kidding? I asked Dave Greenleaf not to."

"He gave you more than a day's grace—that's a lot to ask for a reporter."

"It's going to end up as the kid's manifesto at this point." She waved a hand at the grounds of the school, bristling with cops and guns. "We've got Custer's last stand here. Excellent work, guys."

She went back to Keller, filled him in on what they thought the kid had in the way of weapons and ammunition. He told her there was still no word from the suspect, so they were going in. They'd be ready in thirty minutes. She went back to her car to retrieve her vest—damn if she was going to let them have all the fun. She'd make entry with SWAT. Behind them, obviously, but with them nonetheless. Maybe there was a chance of talking this kid off the ledge.

Though as she fastened her Kevlar, she knew that would never be the case. She pulled her hair up high on her head and anchored the mass with a black ponytail holder. She checked her weapons, loaded herself a few extra magazines for the Glock and a speed loader for the pistol she carried around her ankle. It fit perfectly within her boot and was designed for moments of sheer duress. She'd never had to use it, hoped today wouldn't be the first time.

Keller hadn't had any luck breaking through to the boy. He wasn't answering, but at least the shooting had stopped.

She walked up to Keller, loaded for bear. He took one look at her and said, "Whoa. What do you think you're doing?"

"I'm making entry with you."

"Lieutenant, you know I can't let you do that. We've got our assigned roles, our designated fields of fire, all of our contingency plans have been rehearsed over and over. You don't fit into those plans."

"I trained for SWAT, Keller, you know that. I know what to do. I'll stay in the back, but I am going in."

Happily, she outranked him, so she was going to get her way whether he wanted her to go in or not.

"Suit yourself," he said finally. She smiled and walked off to join the column of heavily armed men getting ready to enter the building.

It was time. She felt her focus pinpoint, shuffled into her place behind the initial entry team. Her earwig was itching;

she reached up and adjusted it. The sun broke out, creating a glare on the cement, but that was okay, they were moving now. "Go, go, go!" rang in her ear, and she hustled behind them, weapon drawn in a two-handed grip.

The first body was the safety officer, life's blood glistening on the linoleum. He'd been taken in the throat, a ragged wound, and was dead. The human body carried over five and one half liters of blood in its veins and arteries. Taylor felt sure at least seventy percent of his was spreading across the floor under his inert form.

She felt the pressure building in her chest.

There was chatter in her ear, a sniper was in place, ready to take the shot if necessary. They drew closer to the classroom, listening for sounds. There was nothing. Taylor heard the crashing glass of the windows, the flash grenades were in. The door to the room was open now, there were screams and shouts, the rush of bodies stank with the cold, tangy scent of fear.

There was no shooting, no screaming. She watched as the team cleared the room, saw no one with weapons pointing at them in threatening ways.

Merritt wasn't in the room.

There were a few moments of controlled chaos as the SWAT team took advantage of the situation, brought the hostages out of the room, hustling them down the hall and out into the bright fall morning. She recognized a few faces in the panic, Theo Howell, wild-eyed, and a couple others from his party, all herded together for safety and comfort. Thank God no more were hurt.

The room was clear now. Taylor leaned back against the wall, out of the way. He was here, somewhere. This was his school. He'd know places to hide. She grabbed the two closest SWAT boys that she knew and said, "Follow me."

They stalked along the halls, one foot in front of the other in perfect unison, silent, careful. Each darkened corner held the promise of the afterlife, and Taylor wasn't in the mood to get herself or any of these boys killed. They crept through the school, finding nothing. Taylor started to relax, though how could the boy have gotten away? The school was surrounded.

She heard shouting from the parking lot, panicked screams, and it hit her. She felt the horror well up in her chest.

"He's outside," she yelled, tearing off down the hall, the clanging SWAT members hot on her heels. They flew out the doors and toward the group of evacuated hostages. They had their backs to her, were moving away as quickly as possible.

There. There he was.

She hadn't seen him inside because he was wearing an ill-fitting baseball cap. He must have walked right past her. Goddamn it.

The dyed black hair peeked out from under the edge of the ball cap, she knew this was him. She drew closer, careful not to alert him. The boy had several people cowering in front of him. He had his arms outstretched, a gun in each hand, pointed at the crowd.

She yelled, "Stop right there, Schuyler!"

People scattered, running, crying, but she held her ground, and so did the boy. Sensing this was their moment, the people around him cleared in an instant, and he was alone.

"Turn around! Get on the ground. Put your hands on the top of your head and get down on the fucking ground now!"

He put his hands up and turned, slowly, pirouetting on his right foot. Face to face with him, Taylor was shocked at just how young he really was. She could hear noises in the distance, weapons being readied, knew they were in fact right beside her, but she felt captivated, drawn in by the boy's stare, a mongoose faced with a cobra.

"It's finished, Schuyler," she said. "Drop the weapon and get on the ground."

He continued to look at her, his coal-black eyes flashing.

Their eyes locked together in a battle of wills. He finally blinked.

"My name is Raven!" he screamed at her.

She felt the movement before she saw it. His hand was coming up, the glint of steel, the sunlight flashing off the gun. She didn't think, didn't hesitate, pulled the trigger three times in quick succession. Blood bloomed on the boy's chest and forehead—three kill shots, clean, perfect. Time stopped.

He looked vaguely surprised for a moment, then crumpled in a bloody heap.

"Get the paramedics," she screamed, advancing on him. She kicked the guns out of the way, quickly ran her hands over the rest of his body. He was clean. He looked her right in the eye and she felt a cold slithering down her spine. Blood bubbled over his lip as he died.

Hands were pulling her away now. Her gun was taken from her, standard operating procedure. The blood was roaring in her ears, she felt like she might faint. Cold water was pressed to her lips, Lincoln, rubbing her on the back. She started to come back to herself, realized that the deafening roar of the shots was making everything sound tinny. No ear defenders, she thought to herself, fighting down hysterical laughter.

The boy was lying on the hard ground, eyes vacant, waiting for the ME to declare him. Officer-involved shootings were a nightmare for everyone.

Taylor was segregated, talked to, debriefed, but didn't hear the words leaving her mouth. The roar of the gun, the startled look on the boy's face, the blood blooming in a spurt from the head-shot, replayed itself over and over and over.

Her day was only just beginning. She'd be investigated, cleared of wrongdoing, but saddled with yet another mark on her record.

Dear God, what have I done? He was just a boy. Just a boy. What have I done?

She managed to tear herself away, fumbled open her cell

phone. She needed to talk to Baldwin. He would understand. He would forgive her.

Baldwin answered on the first ring. Her voice sounded foreign, not her own, echoing in her mind as she told him what had happened.

"Taylor, are you all right?"

She wasn't all right. She'd never be all right again. She'd just killed a boy. Not a man, not a leering criminal, but a boy.

It was justified, she knew that. It was what had happened in the brief moment of clarity that she'd experienced before she shot him that was upsetting her.

She'd seen the boy's soul, a dark mass of hatred and fire, at the very moment her finger squeezed the trigger. She'd seen a man before, in her dreams, who glowed with the same sense of righteous hatred, directed exactly at her. She might not have let her finger move otherwise.

When she shot Raven, she'd seen the ghost of the Pretender staring from the boy's black eyes.

Sixty-One

Taylor sat in the Adirondack chair on the back deck. She felt the chill of the breeze, but ignored it, let it bite and chap her. She was beyond feeling at this point, or so she thought. When the phone rang, she saw it was Baldwin, but made no move to answer.

After a few moments it stopped, leaving her in peace. She didn't want to talk to anyone just now.

As instructed, she'd seen the department shrink, and that had helped a bit, but it wasn't enough, not yet. She was on an enforced leave of absence, some vacation time, while they sorted through the mess at Hillsboro High School. She needed to get her head back in the game, figure out what she wanted to do.

Nothing. She just wanted to be.

Erasing the mental image from the shooting was proving to be harder than she'd ever imagined. The memory of those eyes burned into her. The gun snapping again and again. The small splat of blood that flashed from the wounds. The look of sheer surprise on his face as he dropped to the ground. The sunlight glittering off the silver ankh around the boy's neck. No, those images weren't going away anytime soon.

She took a long pull on her beer, eyes closed, basking in the meager sunlight. When she tilted her chin down, she thought she saw a flash of black. A raven? That would be fitting.

"Lieutenant?" a garbled voice asked. The black thing moved closer. Taylor opened one eye fully and saw a face attached.

"Ariadne," she said, shuffling herself a little more upright. "You look like hell, if you'll forgive me saying so."

Ariadne mounted the steps to the deck, sat in the empty chair with a shrug. Her jaw was still wired shut, the bruises still livid, but beginning to fade. A quick healer. Taylor wondered idly how healed she could be, then let it go. Her head drifted back again. She was just so tired.

"I rang the doorbell. You didn't answer."

"How did you find me?"

"Detective McKenzie."

Damn that man.

"I expected..." Ariadne started, her dainty hands shifting in her lap. "I thought you'd be happy. You solved the case."

Taylor looked away, over the woods that backed to their yard. If there was one thing she'd learned in her years in Homicide, there was never such a thing as a closed case. Faces, wounds, last words, the screams of those left behind, images of caskets dropping into cold, hard dirt—these were the things that stayed long after the legal battles ended, the case files sent to storage. She could usually find it in her to celebrate a good solve, but this case didn't fall into that category.

"Oh," Ariadne said. "I had no idea."

Anger flared, giving Taylor a spark of clarity. "You're reading my mind again?"

"It doesn't take a psychic to see you're in pain. Maybe you should put the beer down. Why don't I make you some tea?"

Taylor narrowed her eyes at the witch and polished off the rest of the beer. She tossed the bottle behind her, heard the clink of glass as it met one of its brothers.

"Like that, is it? You're over here feeling sorry for yourself?"

With great effort, Taylor kept her tone civil. "Ariadne, why are you here?"

"I was worried about you. Detective McKenzie told me your man is out of town. You shouldn't be alone right now." There was an admonishment in her tone that fired Taylor up.

"Baldwin didn't have a choice. He would be here if he could."

As she said the words, she realized how upset she was that Baldwin *wasn't* the one cajoling and nursing her back to an optimum mental level. She felt foolish. She'd been avoiding his calls because she'd resented the fact that he wasn't guiding her through this mess. Since when had she become so dependent on him? Was it dependence, or something more?

"Your love for him is your saving grace, you know."

"Damn it, Ariadne. Quit it. That's not fair."

"Oh, Lieutenant. Don't you see? Love is humanity. If you can't feel, you become as empty and drawn as the boy. He had no love, not the right kind, anyway. His path was chosen long before you came across him. But yours? Yours is still being written. You have a choice. Love will save you. If you let it."

"Has love saved you, Ariadne?" The words were cutting, and Taylor felt a moment of sheer remorse when she saw Ariadne flinch.

"I'm sorry. I'm…upset. This has been very difficult for me. I hate taking life, hate it worse than anything. And he was just a child."

"Raven would have killed you and never given it a second thought, Lieutenant. And then he would have turned the gun on the crowd. He'd decided. Couldn't you see that? Couldn't you see he'd given up? His life was forfeit the moment he spilled blood the first time. He knew that. He accepted that. You must, as well."

"My life is forfeit as well, is that what you're saying?"

"No," Ariadne said softly. "You were called upon to be a savior. That is your role, whether you're comfortable with it or not. And saviors have to make sacrifices."

Taylor reached for another beer. "Ariadne, why are you here? Why are you telling me all of this?"

"Because you and I are linked, whether you like it or not." Eyes downcast, she folded her hands gently over her belly.

Taylor caught the gesture, heart in her throat. She set the beer down on the railing untasted, her mind whirling.

"No. It's too soon to tell. Didn't they give you Plan B at the hospital?"

Ariadne smiled, lips thin against her teeth. "I refused. Life is a gift, regardless of its origins."

Taylor put both feet on the deck. "That's a lovely sentiment, but for God's sake, he raped you."

"And you killed him." The words weren't accusatory, but Taylor felt like she'd been struck in the face.

Ariadne scootched closer, took Taylor's hand. She spoke softly. "You had no choice, Taylor. Who knows how many lives you saved? You made a split-second decision. That's what you're trained to do. And it was the right one. That's why I refused the pills. I could feel the stirrings inside me, knew that enough blood had been shed. I made a choice, too."

How simply a life could be ended. A bullet, a flick of a knife. A heart turned to stone in despair.

The phone rang again, long and loud, the pealing bells grating on her nerves. She looked at the caller ID. Baldwin again.

Ariadne smiled. "He won't stop trying, you know. He's bound to you. He will protect you, whether you want it or not. Go to him, Lieutenant. Let him comfort you."

Taylor stared into the witch's blue eyes. Such calm, such purity. So sure of her path, her convictions. Taylor wished she was that certain.

Resistance was futile. She answered the phone.

Baldwin's deep voice came through the line, relief bleeding through each word.

"I didn't think you'd ever answer. Honey, are you okay?"

"Yes," she said, surprised to hear how hollow her voice sounded. That wouldn't do. There was no need to punish Baldwin. She tried again.

"The woman who worked the case with us, Ariadne? She's here. We've been…chatting."

She could hear the smile in his voice. "Good, you need cheering up. And I'm going to help you with that. I have some good news."

"Really?" she asked. "You're coming home?"

"Taylor, better than that. Much better. Honey, we have Fitz. We found Fitz. He's alive. He's hurt pretty bad, but he's alive."

She felt the thaw of disbelief begin.

"What?" she whispered.

"We've got him. He wants to say hello. I'm putting him on the phone right now." She could hear the buoyant joy in Baldwin's voice, and she stood up, focusing on the rustling sounds in the phone's background. A moment later a gruff, familiar voice came through the phone.

"Hey, little girl. How've you been?"

"Fitz? Is that really you?"

The crusty laugh she'd been dying to hear sounded like gold. "It's really me. Who else would it be?"

Goose bumps rippled across her flesh, so intense that Ariadne turned to stare.

"Thank God," Taylor whispered.

For the first time since she'd killed Schuyler Merritt, she started to cry.

* * * * *

ACKNOWLEDGMENTS

There was, as always, a village to help along the way:

Scott Miller—my fabulous agent, without whom I'd be lost.

Linda McFall—my brilliant editor, who has the vision to make these stories sing.

MacKenzie Fraser-Bub—the cheer in every day, and the rest of the Trident Media crew, for all their hard work on my behalf.

Adam Wilson—the rock to our paper.

Megan Lorius—my sister in OCD publicity crime. Thanks for the details!

Deborah Kohan and Christine Khoury of Planned Television Arts, who are just plain wonderful.

Kim Dettwiller of Team Strategies—my Nashville insider and quip manager.

The rest of the MIRA Books team: Donna Hayes, Alex Osuszek, Loriana Sacilotto, Margaret Marbury, Diane Moggy, Heather Foy, Don Lucey, Michelle Renaud, Adrienne Macintosh, Nick Ursino, Tracey Langmuir, Kathy Lodge, Emily Ohanjanians, Karen Queme, Alana Burke, Tara Kelly and Gigi Lau—a girl couldn't ask for a better group to work with. You're the best!

The BMWs (Del Tinsley, JB Thompson, Janet McKeown, Cecelia Tichi, Peggy Pegen, Mary Richards, Rai Lynn Wood) for listening, critiquing and overall encouraging me.

Fellow writers Laura Benedict, Jeff Abbott, Erica Spindler, Allison Brennan, Toni McGee Causey, Zoë Sharp and Alex Kava, for the daily inspirations and sanity breaks.

My buds at Murderati—the very best blog on earth, hands down.

Evanescence, for getting me in the mood.

Keith Barent Johnson, for bidding on a character name

and allowing me to morph him into the Vampyre King. You're a good sport, Keith.

David Achord, who always has an answer.

Andromeda DeArmande, for her blog Spell Works, which helped set me on the path.

Angie and Traci, for tons of great advice on pathwork. No, I won't read the spells aloud anymore. Bad me.

Last, but not least, my darling parents, for loving me through thick and thin, and the rest of my great family, for always being there.

And Randy, my love-struck Romeo. Thank God you fell in love with me. What would I do without you?

This novel was a joy to write—surprisingly, no nightmares! I read a number of blogs and books getting myself into the Goth, Wiccan and Pagan worlds, research I found utterly fascinating. The blogs are easily found through Google searches, but here are a few of the books that kept me on the path during the writing of this novel:

Allen, Sarah Addison. *Garden Spells*. New York: Bantam Dell, 2007.

Belanger, Michelle. *The Psychic Vampire Codex: A Manual of Magick and Energy Work*. Newburyport, MA: Red Wheel/Weiser, 2004.

Buckland, Raymond. *Buckland's Complete Book of Witchcraft*. 2nd ed. St. Paul, MN: Llewellyn Publications, 2007.

Cunningham, Scott. *Earth, Air, Fire & Water: More Techniques of Natural Magic*, rev. ed. St. Paul, MN: Llewellyn Publications, 2006.

Digitalis, Raven. *Goth Craft: The Magical Side of Dark Culture*. Woodbury, MN: Llewellyn Worldwide, 2007.

Grimassi, Raven. *Italian Witchcraft: The Old Religion of*

    Southern Europe (Previously titles *Ways of the Strega*). 2nd ed. Woodbury, MN: Llewellyn Worldwide, 2006.

Hesiod. *Theogony* (Translated by M. L. West). Oxford: Oxford University Press, 1988.

Hesiod. *Works and Days* (Translated by M. L. West). Oxford: Oxford University Press, 1988.

Illes, Judicka. *The Element Encyclopedia of 1,000 Spells: A Concise Reference Book for the Magical Arts*. London: HarperCollins, 2008.

Konstantinos. *Vampires: The Occult Truth*. Woodbury, MN: Llewellyn Worldwide, 2006.

Konstantinos. *Gothic Grimoire*. Woodbury, MN: Llewellyn Worldwide, 2007.

Sabin, Thea. *Wicca for Beginners: Fundamentals of Philosophy and Practice*. Woodbury, MN: Llewellyn Worldwide, 2006.

Theitic, ed. *The Witches' Almanac: Spring 2008 to Spring 2009 (Issue 27)*. Newport, RI: The Witches' Almanac.

Winkowski, Mary Ann. *When Ghosts Speak: Understanding the World of Earthbound Spirits*. New York: Grand Central Publishing, 2007.

J.T. ELLISON

Homicide detective Taylor Jackson thinks she's seen it all in Nashville—but she's never seen anything as perverse as The Conductor. He captures and contains his victim in a glass coffin, slowly starving her to death. Only then does he give in to his attraction.

Once finished, he creatively disposes of the body by reenacting scenes from famous paintings. And similar macabre works are being displayed in Europe. Taylor teams up with her fiancé, FBI profiler Dr. John Baldwin, and New Scotland Yard detective James "Memphis" Highsmythe, a haunted man who only has eyes for Taylor, to put an end to The Conductor's art collection.

the cold room

Available wherever books are sold.

USA TODAY BESTSELLING AUTHOR

TARA TAYLOR QUINN

Continue to follow psychologist Kelly Chapman
in *The Chapman Files* series.

THE SECOND LIE

Kelly's friend, Deputy Samantha Jones, finds herself facing
the case of her career—a case that appears to implicate the
man she loves. (October 2010)

THE THIRD SECRET

This time, a professional acquaintance of Kelly's comes to her
for advice. Erin Morgan is about to defend Rick Thomas on a
murder charge. Rick's apparently been framed. He's also not
exactly who he says he is.... (November 2010)

THE FOURTH VICTIM

Kelly herself is at the center of this next case—she's been
kidnapped. And it's up to FBI agent Clay Thatcher to find
her. Which means he has to figure out who did it...and why.
(December 2010)

Available wherever books are sold!

AWARD-WINNING AUTHOR

JOSEPH TELLER

Harrison J. Walker—Jaywalker, to the world—is a frayed-at-the-edges defense attorney with a ninety-percent acquittal rate, thanks to an obsessive streak a mile wide. But winning this case will take more than just dedication.

Seventeen-year-old Jeremy Estrada killed another boy after a fight over a girl. This kid is jammed up big-time, but almost unable to help himself. He's got the face of an angel but can hardly string together three words to explain what happened that day...yet he's determined to go to trial.

Jaywalker is accustomed to bending the rules—and this case will stretch the law to the breaking point and beyond.

OVERKILL

Available wherever books are sold.

MIRA®

www.MIRABooks.com

MJT2776

REQUEST YOUR
FREE BOOKS!

2 FREE NOVELS
FROM THE SUSPENSE COLLECTION
PLUS 2 FREE GIFTS!

YES! Please send me 2 FREE novels from the Suspense Collection and my 2 FREE gifts (gifts are worth about $10). After receiving them, if I don't wish to receive any more books, I can return the shipping statement marked "cancel." If I don't cancel, I will receive 3 brand-new novels every month and be billed just $5.74 per book in the U.S. or $6.24 per book in Canada. That's a saving of at least 28% off the cover price. It's quite a bargain! Shipping and handling is just 50¢ per book.* I understand that accepting the 2 free books and gifts places me under no obligation to buy anything. I can always return a shipment and cancel at any time. Even if I never buy another book, the two free books and gifts are mine to keep forever.

192/392 MDN E7PD

Name _____ (PLEASE PRINT) _____

Address _____ Apt. # _____

City _____ State/Prov. _____ Zip/Postal Code _____

Signature (if under 18, a parent or guardian must sign)

Mail to **The Reader Service:**
IN U.S.A.: P.O. Box 1867, Buffalo, NY 14240-1867
IN CANADA: P.O. Box 609, Fort Erie, Ontario L2A 5X3

Not valid for current subscribers to the Suspense Collection
or the Romance/Suspense Collection.

Want to try two free books from another line?
Call 1-800-873-8635 or visit www.morefreebooks.com.

* Terms and prices subject to change without notice. Prices do not include applicable taxes. N.Y. residents add applicable sales tax. Canadian residents will be charged applicable provincial taxes and GST. Offer not valid in Quebec. This offer is limited to one order per household. All orders subject to approval. Credit or debit balances in a customer's account(s) may be offset by any other outstanding balance owed by or to the customer. Please allow 4 to 6 weeks for delivery. Offer available while quantities last.

Your Privacy: Harlequin Books is committed to protecting your privacy. Our Privacy Policy is available online at www.eHarlequin.com or upon request from the Reader Service. From time to time we make our lists of customers available to reputable third parties who may have a product or service of interest to you. If you would prefer we not share your name and address, please check here. ☐

Help us get it right—We strive for accurate, respectful and relevant communications. To clarify or modify your communication preferences, visit us at www.ReaderService.com/consumerschoice.

MSUS10R

J.T. ELLISON

32714	THE COLD ROOM	___ $7.99 U.S.	___ $9.99 CAN.
32443	ALL THE PRETTY GIRLS	___ $6.99 U.S.	___ $8.50 CAN.
32909	14	___ $7.99 U.S.	___ $9.99 CAN.
32629	JUDAS KISS	___ $6.99 U.S.	___ $6.99 CAN.

(limited quantities available)

TOTAL AMOUNT	$ _____
POSTAGE & HANDLING	$ _____
($1.00 for 1 book, 50¢ for each additional)	
APPLICABLE TAXES*	$ _____
TOTAL PAYABLE	$ _____

(check or money order—please do not send cash)

To order, complete this form and send it, along with a check or money order for the total above, payable to MIRA Books, to: **In the U.S.:** 3010 Walden Avenue, P.O. Box 9077, Buffalo, NY 14269-9077; **In Canada:** P.O. Box 636, Fort Erie, Ontario, L2A 5X3.

Name: _____
Address: _____ City: _____
State/Prov.: _____ Zip/Postal Code: _____
Account Number (if applicable): _____

075 CSAS

*New York residents remit applicable sales taxes.
*Canadian residents remit applicable GST and provincial taxes.

MIRA®

www.MIRABooks.com

MJTE1010BL